FIREBALL

ROGER STELLJES

Fireball By Roger Stelljes

Published by Roger Stelljes

ISBN 9781947323759 ebook

ISBN 9798614351816 paperback

DEDICATION

It is perhaps something of a parental rite of passage to go on the high school senior year trip with your graduate to be and their friends. And so it was that in March, 2016, my wife and I found ourselves in Playa del Carmen at the massive Barcelo Riviera Maya with a group of parents, some of whom we knew well from soccer and hockey and others, at the time, we barely knew at all. Yet each night we'd all seemingly gather in the Lobby Bar for a late-night drink in the warm ocean air, talking, laughing and becoming fast friends.

One night, late in the week, one of the parents told the others about my books. That naturally led someone to say, "You should write a book about us." And of course, everyone started throwing out plot and character ideas. It's amazing how many view themselves as romantic leads or Jason Bourne.

Now, I always find it flattering that readers would want to be in one of my stories, but for any number of reasons, it rarely goes any further than that. Yet on this occasion it really made me stop and think. Here I was spending the week with some truly wonderful characters who had nicknames like BTG, DeNasty, Heavy G and best of all, Nikki Fireball. And not only are those great nicknames, but there are wonderfully colorful stories behind how each of them came to be.

It dawned on me that it would have been author malpractice not to write a book with characters like that. So, without a real story yet in mind, I said: "I'll do it, you're all in the book." Thus, in the Lobby Bar on a gorgeous spring night along the Riviera Maya, Fireball was born.

Since the trip, we have all continued to get together for dinners and outings. Of course, each time we'd gather, they would all ask, "How's the book coming? What's my role?" "Am I the love interest? When's the launch party?" I'm very pleased to finish this book and share it with those who inspired it.

So, thank you my friends for the great week in Mexico, the story inspiration and your continued friendship. This one is dedicated to you, the Barcelo Book Club!

PROLOGUE

The Eastern 35 cabin cruiser knifed effortlessly through the rolling waves as it moved northwest up the Mississippi River. Jorge was exceedingly skillful in his navigation of the river in the darkness of the night, having often come this way up the river after midnight, sometimes to fish and sometimes to do something else. Tonight was a night for something else.

He slowly edged back on the boat's throttle and let the cabin cruiser's powerful engine ease down to a gentle idle. He scanned the river ahead and behind, searching for but not seeing the small red and green navigation lights of any other boats. As he looked to the west and saw the lightning flashing in the distance, he was confident they were alone on this stretch of the river.

His boss, Felix, emerged from the companionway below, carrying a round thirty-five- pound weight in each hand. "Are we alone?"

"Yes," Jorge replied.

"Very good," Felix replied and then looked down the companionway. "Let's go," he ordered.

Jorge glanced left to see Tito mildly grunting and groaning, holding one end of the canvas body bag as he back-stepped his way up the steps. A moment later T.O. emerged with the other end. The two of them shuffled their feet while they carried the body bag hastily to the back of the boat and then dropped it to the floor with a loud thud.

"Be careful," Felix rebuked mildly. "We don't want the bag to rip."

"Sorry, boss," Tito replied evenly as he leaned down and unzipped the body bag. Even in the enveloping darkness of the night, the beaten and bloodied nature of the body was visible. His interrogation had been exhaustive and thoroughly brutal. By the time it came the man no doubt welcomed his death, mercifully brought about by a bullet to the forehead, the hole from which was now in plain view.

Felix looked to Jorge. "Do you think the two thirty-five-pound weights should be enough?" he asked, seeking confirmation.

"Plenty," Jorge responded. "He can't weigh but one hundred sixty, maybe seventy pounds."

Felix nodded and slipped the weights inside the canvas body bag and tucked them under the body, then zipped the bag back up.

The four of them each picked up a corner of the body bag and moved to the back edge of the boat.

Felix grunted out the countdown as they swayed the body. "One. Two. Three." And in perfect synchronization the body was heaved over the side of the boat. They all watched expectantly as the body bag plunged beneath the choppy surface of the water.

They all looked up to the west to see the rumbling coming from the early June night sky, the constant flashes of lightning painting the clouds in a brilliant kaleidoscope of orange, yellow and blue hues.

"We better get moving," Jorge suggested. "A storm is coming."

1

"IF YOU WANT TO SQUEEZE, YOU MUST HAVE LEVERAGE."

From a quarter mile back, Sam Shead saw the taillights illuminate and the left turn signal start blinking. Now, he thought, was when things would get a little tricky.

He took a left turn of his own and drove up the modest rise in the road. At the top, he made a quick left turn into the developing neighborhood and parked his truck in front of what would eventually be the first house, which was now simply an incomplete concrete foundation. Shead grabbed his backpack, jumped out of his truck and took three long quick strides to the edge of the county road. He took a quick look left and right and then jogged across the road. On the other side he unzipped the backpack and began pulling out his camera and long-range zoom lens while picking his way down the steep, thin ribbon of path to the cover of a grouping of aged oak trees he'd spotted two nights ago and checked out last night. Careful to stay hidden under the canopy, he attached the zoom lens to the camera and then raised it to his right eye while bending down on his left knee and hurriedly focusing.

Click. Click. Click.

Sam pulled the camera with his long-range zoom lens away from his eye and peered across the open field of two hundred yards to the tight circular driveway set in front of the expansive two-story prairie-style house. He'd been worried they would all be in the house before he was able to get the shots, but the men were just loitering around, so he took three more quick pictures and then checked the digital display screen.

"Not bad, not bad at all."

Satisfied with his work, he finally took a breath. Sam reached down to his backpack and pulled out the camera tripod, snapped it open and then secured his camera to the pan head. Next, he pulled out his spiral notebook from his back pocket, flipped it open to the fourth page and noted the date and time – Wednesday, August 8th, 11:48 p.m. He jotted down who was in the SUV he'd followed: Kline and his usual driver, the tiny guy. Then he noticed another flash of light and looked to the east. Another SUV, a black Yukon, arrived and getting out of it was a familiar face; the tall, angular African American that had crossed paths with Kline the last few nights. "And tonight I can see your license plate," Sam murmured as he observed the Yukon through his binoculars.

Sam spent five minutes focusing on his camera and snapping away and had no illusions about the danger of what he was doing. Four of the men he was observing were armed. "And those aren't Tinker Toys," he muttered while briefly glancing down to his backpack and the loaded Glock-17 inside.

Most people would have turned and run from this. But for Sam, it was the most alive he'd felt in years; four years, to be exact. That correlated to when he lost his detective's shield and job, frittered away in bottles of booze, recreational drugs and womanizing that eventually cost him his marriage and then inevitably, his police career.

And the sad thing was that when his mind was right, he was an exceptional cop. That's exactly what St. Paul Police Chief Charlie Flanagan said the last time they spoke those four long years ago. "I'm sorry, Sam. I'm losing a damn good detective but I can't protect you anymore. You're done."

Sam dismissively tossed his badge and service weapon on the chief's desk. "Fuck all of you!" he growled in one last fit of mutiny as he barreled out of the office. His twenty-three-year career was laid to waste.

He wouldn't have, couldn't have admitted it at the time, but Flanagan was, of course, right. In fact, St. Paul Police Chief Charlie Flanagan had gone above and beyond to help him, protect him and give him time and chance after chance *after chance* to get his act together. Sam simply couldn't do it.

He hadn't hit rock bottom. That came a year later.

Sam discovered rock bottom while literally lying wasted, beaten and bloodied in the gutter of a trash-filled alley behind a dingy bar. He'd been mouthing off inside to a burly ironworker who took him out to the back alley and shut him up with several brutal, well-aimed punches to the face and abdomen. Through blurred vision, the taste of fresh blood and cheap whiskey marinating in his mouth, pain searing through his head and chest and sprawled out on his back between two rancid, rusted garbage dumpsters, he *finally* took inventory. He was down to his last four crinkled-up dollars, had no job, no job prospects, was at risk of losing his townhouse, his truck...of losing everything. On nights like tonight he'd often think back to that moment in the alley, lying flat on his back, when he realized what a shit pile he'd made of his life. "I gotta stop," he remembered saying to himself. "I gotta stop."

He needed help. Thankfully, there was still one person who would answer a call from him. A half hour later Richard Lich pulled into the alley, stepped out of his car and took one look at his former partner. "I'm not here to take you home."

"I gotta stop."

"Are you ready? Are you finally ready?"

"Help me, please. I can't do this anymore."

One thing Sam still had as part of his retirement benefits was his health insurance. His old partner drove him to the world-renowned Hazelden Betty Ford Rehabilitation Clinic in Center City, an hour northeast of St. Paul. Dick left him there with a final warning: "Finish this or don't ever, *ever*, call me again."

After twenty-eight days at Hazelden, Sam was clean and he'd stayed that way. He had straightened up his act. But what would the second act of his life look like? Sam burned a lot of bridges on his way to the bottom. He didn't have a lot of favors he could cash in. He did have a decent pension, but he still needed additional income. Finding steady work was a challenge until one night after a Twins game two years ago he and Dick stepped into Fireball, a newly trendy sports bar and nightclub on University Avenue in St. Paul. That night Sam made eyes and openly flirted with the curvy brunette tending bar while drinking nothing but club soda. It turned out the woman tending the bar was also the owner, Nikki, and she batted her eyes and flirted right back at Sam. He was instantly smitten and so was she.

Fireball was a large thriving bar and nightclub and Nikki was always on the lookout for bouncers and security that were smart, savvy and could handle themselves. Sam filled the bill. "You were a cop once—be my cop, my security in here."

Nikki had problems with people dealing drugs inside her large enterprise in its early years, when she was fixing the place up. Now that it was clean and thriving she wanted it to stay that way. Sam watched the club like a hawk and got to know the customers, particularly the regulars. They happily fed him information, often encouraged with a well-placed free cocktail or beer.

A frequent patron and source of info for Sam was Luther Ellis. Luther was in recovery, like Sam. For Luther it had been heroin, and rock bottom for him was a five-year prison stretch. After prison, he'd focused on his home neighborhood on the east side of St. Paul, dedicating his life to helping people get clean, a calling he'd found in prison.

That's what brought Luther into Fireball one night. He met Sam in the men's bathroom. Sam was investigating the report of someone passed out in a stall, the very same person Luther was hunting for. Upon witnessing the spectacle of the man splayed out on the floor of the bathroom stall, Sam's instincts said he should call the police.

"Luther," the man begged from the floor, "help me."

"Let me take him," Luther pleaded with Sam. "He needs help. Sometimes people hit rock bottom and they need a helping hand, you know?"

Looking down at the man pathetically crumpled in the bathroom stall, his head stuck between the toilet and wall, made Sam think back to his moment of clarity in the alley. "Okay, let's get him out of here."

After that night, Sam and Luther became friends and support for one another. Luther came around the nightclub frequently to visit, something Nikki wasn't necessarily pleased about.

"I know you like Luther, that you two have recovery in

common, and I think what he does in trying to help people get clean is quite noble."

"But?" Sam asked, recognizing there was more.

"I can see people who are going to be trouble and Luther is going to be trouble," Nikki answered sternly. "His background, his history, what he does, his constant money trouble—it's all going to be an issue at some point. It's inevitable."

"I think you're overreacting. Luther is harmless."

"It's not Luther that necessarily worries me," Nikki answered. "It's the other people he associates with that do."

Nikki was right about the money. Luther's mother was elderly, poor, and he was her only child and *only* form of support. Turned out voluntarily helping people get clean didn't pay the bills and Luther was in a constant search for more earning opportunities. He'd sought work with local organizations dedicated to helping those with drug and alcohol abuse issues, but his lack of any formal training made him unattractive for any paid position. His tenth-grade education and prison record made it difficult to find other gainful employment. Eventually, things got tight and he went to see Neil Kline, an old friend from prison. Luther asked for a loan and Neil pointed him in the direction of someone who did that sort of thing.

"Don't do it," Sam recalled warning Luther. "Going to a loan shark is a very, *very* bad idea."

"I ain't got no choice," Luther answered. "I need two grand right now or Mom loses the house. If I can get ten grand, I can really give her a cushion."

"Are you delusional?" Sam asked incredulously. "Where in the hell are you going to come up with the ten grand and exorbitant added interest? Tell me where, Luther?"

"I gotta solve this problem I have right now, Sam. As for

the problem that makes? Well"—Luther shrugged in resignation—"I'm a survivor. I'll figure something out. I always do."

Luther took the loan and, as Sam predicted, he couldn't meet the repayment terms. The last time they'd spoken Luther thought he had it under control. "I've got some leverage. The guy who loaned me the money isn't exactly clean, if you know what I mean. I know some things about his business and who he works for. You still have friends with the police, right?"

"Yes."

"Then I can hurt him if he threatens to hurt me."

"What if he does more than threaten?" Sam asked.

A week later Sam got a call from Luther's mother, asking if he'd seen him anywhere. Luther had been gone for two days and she'd received no word from him.

"Is that unusual?"

"Yes," Luther's mom replied nervously. "Normally he's calling me a couple of times a day to check on me."

Sam went out driving around, talking to people in Luther's neighborhood, checking out his usual haunts, his church, the street corners where he looked for people to help, the homeless shelter, the local food banks and the taverns. Days went by and Luther never surfaced.

Deep down, from the moment of the call from Luther's mother, Sam knew that his disappearance had everything to do with that loan. The only thing he had to go on was a name: Neil Kline, the old prison friend of Luther's whose name came up when they were talking about the loan shark. Sam went to Dick with what he suspected. His old partner was sympathetic and investigated Luther's disappearance but came up empty.

"I'm sorry, buddy," Dick reported two months ago while

eating lunch at Fireball. "I've come up with nothing. No Luther, nobody who knows where he is or what might have happened to him. I went through his mom's house, his old beat-up car and anything else I could tie to him and there's just nothing to go on."

"What about Kline?"

"He says he's concerned about Luther as well. Kline said his old cellmate checked in with him every few days and he hadn't heard from him in some time."

"I'm sure he was devastated."

"Actually, I kind of thought he was. If it was an act, it wasn't awful."

"And what did Kline say about the loan shark? Anything?"

"Kline said he knew that Luther had some money issues and pointed him in the direction of a couple of names he'd heard of, but he didn't know if Luther actually took a loan. He said he, like you, counseled him *not* to go down that path."

"He took a loan. He told me he did. Did you check out these names Kline gave you?"

"I did."

"And?"

"None of them said they loaned Luther the money. They didn't know Luther, nobody named Luther had presented themselves to them, but all admitted they knew Kline and that if Neil sent someone their way, they'd have considered making a loan."

"This is all bullshit, Dick!" Sam railed in anger. "Kline knows what happened to Luther. Maybe *you* need to press him harder."

"With *what* exactly?" Dick asked, turning in his barstool to face his old partner. He was a little ticked at suddenly being slammed for having performed what was, in the first place, a solid favor. "What should I push with? If you have anything, hot shot, I'm all ears. But I'm not going to go busting my hump for this convict friend of yours with nothing but my dick in my hand."

Sam simply stared down at his club soda, rightly chastised.

"Yeah, that's what I thought," Dick replied edgily. "I still know how to do this job, even without you. You know the game as well as I do. If you want to squeeze, you must have leverage. You think Kline is dirty, and perhaps you're right. But if he is, I don't have any leverage with him—nothing. And he knows it, which is probably why he was more than happy to talk to me to begin with. He wasn't the least bit worried...and you know why? Because he either had nothing to do with it, or if he did, he knew I had jack shit on him. If Kline is an operator as you say, then he is not unfamiliar with how this all works, Sammy Boy. Smart, successful career criminals make a career out of it for a reason, you know."

"He can't be that smart if he ended up in the joint."

"Not necessarily," Dick answered. "It's like my buddy Mac McRyan says..."

"What," Sam interrupted sarcastically, "more pearls of wisdom from Boy Wonder?"

"Yup. If I may continue."

"Oh, please do."

"Thank you. Mac says a guy goes to prison as a criminal and one of three things will happen to him. One, he realizes the errors of his ways, straightens his shit out, becomes a decent citizen who paid his debt and that's the end of it. Two, he learns nothing, goes back to his old ways and ends right back up in the can and will be stuck in the cycle for life."

"And what's three?"

"He becomes a smarter criminal."

"You think that's Kline?" Sam asked derisively.

"I think it is entirely possible that he is number three. The only thing I have proof of is number one. Look, I appreciate that this Luther was a friend, but if you want my advice, drop it. He had some bad history and circumstances that probably just caught up with him. As unfortunate as that all is, it is not your concern. Your life is good now. You have Nikki, the job...it's all good. Don't get mixed up in this. You owe this guy nothing...*nothing*. Just let it go."

Sam heard what Dick was saying, but in the end, he didn't listen. Luther's disappearance kept gnawing at him. He needed an answer.

Based upon everything Luther had told Sam about Neil Kline, about what an operator he was, Sam was certain that Kline knew something about Luther's disappearance. Finally, a week ago he decided to try and find something for Dick to work with. That's why he was out sneaking around. He could never close the case by himself. But if he could give his old partner something *real* to work with, if he could give him some leverage, that would be just as good.

He was on his fourth night now of following Kline around and almost like clockwork, his path seemed to cross with the other guy in the binoculars. The tall, wiry African American known as T.O. that arrived in the Yukon. The body language, the conversations between the two of them told him they were simpatico, that they were doing business together. What business he wasn't sure, but late-night meetings such as this screamed that it was illegal and it smelled to Sam of drugs, though he'd yet to see any.

Sam had tried to follow T.O. after he and Kline's last little late-night meet, but lost him quickly once they got back into St. Paul and the tangled web of streets on the east side.

Kline was easier to follow because Sam always knew where to find him. He was either at the repair shop he owned or was being driven around town in the Tahoe by his driver. As Sam took additional pictures of Kline talking to his cohort, another set of headlights illuminated the drive up to the front of the house.

"Who's this pulling up, I wonder?" Sam mused to himself as Kline and his friend turned to the Cadillac Escalade easing in and parking perpendicular to the house.

Sam reached again for his binoculars. As he peered down from his heightened perch he could tell that there was a distinct look of surprise replaced by instant respect on the faces of Kline and T.O. when three people climbed out of the Escalade. The arrivals consisted of two men and a woman. The first man was decent height, maybe six feet or a little more with burly shoulders. The other man was attired in a dark business suit. He had a goatee around his mouth and appeared tanned. The woman was perhaps five-five or six, wearing heels and a black dress that hugged tight to her body. She turned in Sam's direction and he immediately recognized her.

"Holy cow, what in the world is *she* doing here?" Sam exclaimed, gripping his binoculars tight in excitement.

He made a quick notation in his notepad about the arrivals and the Escalade. Reaching back for his camera he pulled it up to his eyes, focused the long-distance telephoto lens and began snapping in quick succession. "Dicky Boy, I think I've got something for you to work with now!" Sam murmured happily as he snapped away. "This is what I'd call a break in the case."

Sam observed as the five of them talked in a group on the expansive cobblestone sidewalk laid out between the circular driveway and the front portico of the house. The man in the business suit appeared to be doing most of the talking, occasionally gesturing at the group before they all walked inside.

He tried with both the binoculars as well as his camera, but he couldn't get the license plate on the Escalade. His view was of the driver's side and he needed a better angle to see the front plate. "Dammit. I gotta get that plate number," he muttered as he moved to his left from under the cover of the trees, carefully picking his way down the steep pitch of the hill to a flatter landing. His angle improved, he could make out the front of the Escalade and quickly snapped several photos. "Got it."

But now he was exposed in the openness of the hill and the illumination of a nearby street light. He'd drawn attention, as a man exited the house and urgently pointed, gestured and yelled in his direction. The men left outside to no doubt provide security turned and looked toward the hill. Two men jumped into an SUV and peeled around the circular driveway, obviously coming for him.

"*Shit!* I think I've worn out my welcome."

Sam scrambled back up the hill and grabbed his backpack, quickly stuffing his camera, the tripod and binoculars inside as he ran. He sprinted across the road, pulled out the key fob for his truck and had the engine started before he opened the door and jumped inside, peeling rapidly away, driving ahead and deeper into the housing development and away from the hill he'd just abandoned. A minute later he was navigating his way through an office park back toward Interstate 94.

"I got myself The Avocado on film and his license plate. What say you now, Dicky Boy?"

Forty minutes later, Sam slipped his key into the back door and opened his way into the back office of Fireball. It was nearing 12:45 a.m. and last call had no doubt been announced, although music was still playing and he could still feel the hum of activity. As always there was a line-up of taxis and Ubers outside the front door waiting to take many of the remaining patrons safely home.

Sam reached into the private refrigerator behind Nikki's desk and pulled out a can of soda water. He had plopped himself down onto the old black leather couch when the door opened and Nikki came storming into the office, then instantly smiled. "Hey there, handsome," Nikki greeted as she approached and leaned down for a kiss.

Sam kissed her back and pulled her down onto the couch. Rolling on top of her he continued kissing her, which Nikki began to eagerly return. Not exactly sure what had gotten into him, he then reached behind her and worked his way up under her black Fireball tank-top, reaching for the clasp to her bra.

"My gosh, Samuel Shead, what do you think you're doing?" Nikki exclaimed, looking up into his eyes, not necessarily stopping him but curious where this sudden passion came from.

"What do you think I'm doing?" he replied as he leaned down again and kissed her neck. He kept his hands moving back up under her tank and expertly popped open the clasp of her bra with his left thumb and index finger. "I haven't seen you in four nights."

"Are you crazy? We're closing things down," Nikki replied as she squirmed away with a smile and a laugh. "Whoa! Just whoa!" She held her hands up. "Stop for a second."

"Okay, okay," Sam replied, holding his hands up with a hungry leer on his face.

"What's gotten into you?"

"I don't know. I guess I've had a good night. A *great night,* actually."

"Doing what, exactly? As I recall, I gave you the night off. In fact, you've had the last four nights off."

"I found something that will help Dick reopen his investigation of Luther," he said as he moved to kiss her again. Nikki resisted briefly but then gave in and kissed him back until Sam once again started getting handsy.

"Hold on! Hold on!" Nikki exclaimed, pulling her mouth back from his and pushing away. "Sam, let me go. Let. Me. Go!" she admonished as she reached back and refastened her bra.

Sam, slightly disappointed, nevertheless did as he was told and slowly released her from his embrace. It was closing time. The entrepreneur had work to do.

"This is to be continued tomorrow night," Nikki said with a big smile before leaning in to kiss him again quickly while escaping his reach. "We'll go out after work and then go back to my place, okay?"

"Okay."

"So, are you done with your late-night prowling around?"

Sam smiled. "Yes. I just need to meet with Dick and then I'm sure he can take it from there."

"Good," Nikki answered as she came over and pecked him on the lips one more time, lingering for just a moment while cupping his chin in her right hand. "I kind of like having you around, and I don't like the idea of you out prowling around looking for whomever made Luther disappear."

"Then I'll see you tomorrow night," Sam answered. "I'll be back to work."

He'd have loved nothing more than to go home with her tonight and cuddle up in bed, but Nikki was a divorcee, and she and her ex-husband shared joint custody of their sixteen-year-old daughter. Nikki didn't think it was proper for Sam to be spending the night when her daughter stayed with her. So tonight Sam was going home alone.

Fifteen minutes later and hungry, Sam wanted food. It was Taco Bell to the rescue, just a few blocks from his townhouse and available for him at 2:30 a.m. He handed the cash to the window attendant and grabbed his little bag of late night heaven: two grease-dripping Burrito Supremes, along with two soft tortilla chicken tacos with packets of medium hot sauce tossed in.

As he turned left out of the drive-thru lane, he reached down into the plastic bag and grabbed one of the soft tacos. He was unwrapping it with his hands while also turning the wheel to the right, merging his truck onto Burns Avenue.

"What the..."

The truck came out of nowhere. It rammed into the front left of his truck, careening him into the curb to the right. The impact snapped his head left, slamming it hard into the truck's frame, concussing him and causing him to blackout for just a moment.

Sam slowly opened his eyes, dazed. The right side of his head was lying against the steering wheel. Pain was radiating through his body. He glanced to his right, seeing his gun on the passenger side floor mat. *I need to move*, he thought, moving his right arm to reach, but his body was responding slowly, too slowly.

The driver's side door was yanked open. Sam tried to raise his left arm in defense, but the large thick man batted it away before punching him in the face and then grabbing the back of his head and smashing it into the steering wheel twice.

The man unfastened the seatbelt, threw his big right arm around Sam's neck, tightened it like a vise and dragged him by his neck out of the cab of the truck, then threw him hard down to the pavement.

"*Ohhh. Ohhh*," Sam groaned as he was kicked in the ribs twice and then tried to push himself up to try and fight back. He gutted out a, "You motherfuckers," as he coughed, spitting up blood as he pushed up with his arms, still thinking that if he could just get to the truck and his gun he could get away. Then, even as he was up on all fours spitting and coughing, he was kicked in the ribs again.

"*Oooff*."

And then Sam felt it coming.

He glanced left just as the crowbar came swinging down into the back of his neck, sending him back facedown into the pavement, pain coursing through every part of his beaten body. He saw the crowbar rise swiftly again and Sam's last sinking thought as it came crashing down was that his fate would be the same as Luther's.

2

"YOU DON'T HOLD ANYTHING, ANYTHING OVER ON THESE PEOPLE."

Michael McKenzie "Mac" McRyan gazed out the window of his first-class seat as the plane approached the Twin Cities from the west. The modern downtown Minneapolis skyline, impressively alight on a crystal-clear August night, was visible to the north out of the left windows of the plane.

This was his first trip home since March, but he suspected it might become a more common occurrence. The political mid-terms were coming in a few months and his wife Sally had been recently promoted to senior political advisor to the President of the United States. It was the intention of the Thomson Administration to buck the historical trend that the party in the White House lost, and at times, lost big in the mid-term elections. The President and his right-hand man, Judge Dixon, were bound and determined to do everything they could to avoid history repeating itself. The Judge and Sally, as his number one lieutenant, were tasked with seeing that didn't happen. The two of them were to work with the national party, be available for consultation with local party figures and, when need be, provide access to the President. And the President intended to fire up Air Force One and be out campaigning from Labor Day through election day as much as possible with Sally and the Judge along for the ride. "I'm just warning you, I'm not going to be around all that much for the next three months or so," Sally cautioned. "Wherever the President goes, I go. I'm going to be on the road *a lot*."

Indeed, two days ago Sally left with the President on a tour of European allies. Upon their return Sally would be in town for a few days and then, "We'll be going to Asia for eight days. Then after that, politicking right up to the elections."

"I'll see you on Wednesday, November seventh then," Mac replied across the dinner table at their new favorite Italian restaurant.

"The good news is, once it's all over I'll probably be able to slip away for a short three or four-day vacation, so think of where you'd like to go," Sally answered and then took a sip of her wine. "In the meantime, it'll give you some chances to go home and see your mom and your friends."

"I was thinking the same thing."

"And while you're doing that, maybe you should do one other thing."

"What's that?"

"Contemplate what you'll want to do with your life in two years when we head home."

Not long after they'd moved to D.C. and she went to work at the White House, Sally said she wanted four years. She wanted to help get the President re-elected and then she'd be done. That was their deal, although Mac was always somewhat skeptical about it. "And you're sure we'll be moving back? Just like that, huh?"

"Yes, of course. Do you question that?"

"Shouldn't I?"

"Why would you say that?" Sally protested.

"Because you've had this meteoric rise and moved into the inner circle, Sal. You're now a senior advisor to the President of the United States. They've invested a lot of time and effort in you, developing you, turning you into someone very valuable. You think they're going to just let you up and walk out if there is a second term? Color me skeptical."

"That's not their call."

"Oh, that's a good one!" Mac guffawed loudly. "Honey, President James Thomson and Judge Dixon didn't get where they are without being awfully persuasive. If the President wins in two years, you're a little naïve to think you're not going to get the hard sell and an offer you can't refuse. He'll dangle something tantalizing in front of you that will be just too good to pass up and you'll be coming to me saying, Mac, about that four years...how about we make it eight?"

He could tell he was hitting her with something perhaps *she* hadn't given much thought. Whether she honestly believed it or simply realized it was the best thing to say at this point, she held firm. "I made a promise and I plan to live up to my end of the bargain." She said it with conviction, but Mac detected some doubt in there as well.

"We'll see," was Mac's tinged, unconvinced reply. "We'll see."

"Look," Sally stated, "I'm going to see this through. I have four years of around-the-clock work in me. I've got almost two years in and I know the two ahead are going to just be killers. I just don't think I could work *another* four years in the White House. I don't think ... I could take it. I don't have that much bandwidth."

And there it was, for the first time, uttered out loud. Mac had long wondered when the toll of working in the pressure cooker of the White House would start to take its effect on her. In his time in Washington, he'd met people who'd done their time at 1600 Pennsylvania Avenue. They all said the same thing to varying degrees. Working in the White House was an amazing and special experience. It was also a meat grinder that chews people up and spits them out.

"It's a heck of a ride, but you can only do it for so long," the HUD Secretary said to Mac one night at a White House state dinner. "I loved it, but at a certain point you no longer can keep up with the pace of it. The President gets to sleep at night. The staff"—he shook his head—"not necessarily. Your body and mind can only take so much and then you have to get out."

Mac had been watching for those signs in Sally.

Back in the spring, their honeymoon was eight of the best days of their lives. Just the two of them on a private Caribbean island. On their flight down Mac made a rule. They could only check their phones once a day. That was it. Otherwise, their sole focus was to be on each other. The sun, beach, boat and water, as well as no phones, no calls, no e-mails, no texts and even no television news had been a great and revitalizing escape.

But having slowed down and taken that long break, it was hard for Sally to get back in the nonstop grind with the same unabashed enthusiasm. Ever since her return, she'd shown subtle and growing signs that the grind of the job was starting to wear on her. There wasn't quite as much enthusiasm in the morning; that constant bounce in her step she used to have at the start of a new day had faded. And at night she'd seemed wearier and it wasn't unusual for her to fall asleep with her work papers lying around her, with her reading glasses which she now needed askew on her nose. In one sense, it was adorable. In another, Mac wondered if she was starting to hit the proverbial wall. Now she'd kind of admitted it.

"Don't get me wrong. I love what I'm doing," Sally answered. "But the hours..." Her voice drifted off. "I know I won't want to do this beyond what I've committed to. I might stay in politics because you're right, I've made something of a name for myself. There will be other doors open to me, but whatever it is I do, it isn't going to involve one-hundred-hour, seven-day work weeks, I can tell you that."

"Well, that's good to know," Mac answered. "I mean, your hours have been crazy, especially lately."

"There's a lot of work to be done," she replied. "But look, *this* conversation is not about me. It's about *you*."

"Let's worry about this more when we actually have something to worry about," Mac suggested. "Why make decisions before you have to? Two years is an eternity in politics and in life. Let's assess things when the time is right. The reality is, neither of us will lack for options."

"It'll be here before you know it."

"And when it gets here we'll deal with it."

"Still, just give it some thought. I mean, these four years will have really been about me. Our next move is going to be about you."

For the first time in a couple of years, Mac started to think about what might be next. He was thirty-five, going on thirty-six in December. What did he want to do? Did he want to be a police detective again? A businessman? An investor? A hockey coach? Did he want to rehabilitate houses and then rent them out or flip them? Money wouldn't dictate what he did; he was secure in that regard. He didn't need to work another day in his life if he didn't want to. But that wouldn't work. He would need a purpose. He just wasn't sure what his purpose was.

As he grabbed his suitcase off the baggage carousel his phone rang, displaying a 612 area code number he didn't recognize. Then, for whatever reason, it got a little tingle of excitement.

"McRyan."

"Please hold for Charlie."

~

"Do you want me to drop anchor?"

"No," Felix replied to his man Jorge, "it's calm. Just keep floating along here."

He scanned the dark night, the only light provided by the half-moon pushing illumination through the partly cloudy sky and the small red and green night navigation lights of the boat. Grey Cloud Island was to their east. It was largely uninhabited other than the casting yards on the northwest end of the island, visible only because of the three or four flood lights dimly lighting and framing the outer perimeter of the yard. This area of the Mississippi River was not popular with recreational boaters, but on a clear night such as this, they'd occasionally run into a small boat or two engaging in some night fishing. The little islands and inlets around Grey Cloud Island to the east and the other small islands to the west were good for bass fishing and this area of the river was known to contain large catfish.

"Bring the body up," Felix ordered.

Terrence Orr and Felix's other man, Tito, grunted and huffed as they hauled the sagging body bag containing the dead body of Shead up from the under compartment and then dropped it with a heavy thud on the boat's deck.

"What did this motherfucker weigh?" Tito groaned, reaching around with his hands to rub his lower back.

"Put in the weights," Felix ordered.

"You really think we need more weight?" Terrence Orr asked incredulously, wiping sweat from his brow.

"If the body is going to sink in the colder water down below the surface, we need more weight," Felix commanded.

"Okay," Tito replied skeptically as he leaned down and rested on his right knee. He unzipped the body bag to reveal Shead inside. The man was almost unrecognizable now, such had been the extensive totality of his interrogation.

"I have to say I kind of respect the guy. He was one tough motherfucker," Jorge remarked.

Sam Shead had not bowed down. He'd absorbed an absolute pounding from Felix, at one point defiantly screaming, "*Is that all you got, you motherfucker? Is that all? Come on! Again! Hit me again, you fucking pussy! Again! Come on, you...*"

Felix had swung, connected and knocked Shead's head hard, sending two teeth flying from his mouth. Shead snapped his head forward again, snorted, spit out blood and then just smiled, a bloody smile, as if to say bring it on. He knew he was never going to leave the room alive, but it was a test of his will as to whether he'd give in. "I'm going to make you beg me like a dog to kill you!" Felix screamed as he smashed his fist into the ex-cop's face again.

Shead just smiled back at him and replied quietly, "Fuck you! Fuck all of you! You're all fucking cowards!"

Felix had walloped him with another left. "Tell me what I want to know!" He hit the former cop again in the face. "*Tell me!*"

"Cut me loose. I'll take all you fucking pussies!" Shead had railed in reply, fighting against his restraints, pushing the chair forward, spitting blood at Felix and at anyone else within reach. *"I'll beat every last one of you, you fucking pieces of shit!"*

Felix punched him twice in the face and then two more times in the abdomen. "Who did you tell about what you saw tonight? Tell me! *TELL ME!"*

Shead simply laughed and mumbled quietly, "I didn't tell anyone about anything. And, my dead mother punches harder than you, you fuckstick."

"Okay then," Felix replied as he walked to the corner and reached for a sledge hammer. "*Let's see how you like this, tough guy!*" Felix swung the sledge hammer down into Shead's right leg.

"*Ahhhrg! You fucker! You fucker!*" Shead screamed, his body shaking in agonizing pain.

"*Tell me what I want to know!*" Felix screamed, swinging the sledge hammer again.

They went around and around like that for hours. In the end Felix, incensed, beat on the man long after he'd lost consciousness. His face, hands, arms, legs...Shead's whole body was a beaten mass of hamburger.

Tito grabbed the blood-soaked white t-shirt with his left hand, with his right hooked two fingers through a belt loop on the dead man's blue jeans and pulled the mutilated body toward him. Orr then slipped the four thirty-five-pound weights under the body. Tito dropped the body on top and zipped the bag back up.

"Let's get this piece of shit in the river," Felix ordered.

All four men groaned and struggled as they began to drag the dead weight of the body.

"Geezus, he is fucking heavy," Jorge grumbled as the four of them slowly shuffled with the three hundred seventy-five pounds of combined weight, the dead body and the steel weights inside the bag, dragging it over to the left corner of the stern.

"We have to pick him up," Felix stated. "On three. One. Two. *Three!*"

Grunting, they lifted the body up and rested it on the gunwale of the boat. He was simply too heavy to heave into the water. Instead, the four of them lined up and then shoved the body over the edge.

"Shit," Felix shouted as his end of the body bag got caught and hung briefly on one of the boat's metal cleats before it went full over into the water.

"Did the bag rip?" Orr asked worriedly as the body quickly disappeared below the surface. "I thought I heard a rip. Did you hear a rip? I swear I heard it."

"I think we're fine," Felix replied, scanning the dark water, "it went right under."

"How could it not?" Tito moaned, wiping the sweat off his brow.

Just then a small fishing boat came out of a cove to the northwest of their position.

"We better get out of here," Jorge urged.

Felix nodded and Jorge fired up the boat's engines and slowly turned the Eastern 35 cabin cruiser around and cruised away south.

Felix and Orr watched out the back of the boat.

"I'm glad that's over," Orr said quietly.

"Don't ever bring someone like Luther Ellis around again!" Felix growled, poking Orr hard in the chest. "I don't want to have to clean up any more of your messes."

"Who are you?" the tall and angular Marcus Swinton asked as he was led into the interrogation room.

Mac looked to the sergeant who sat Marcus down into the metal chair. "Thanks, Jay."

"No problem, Mac. Give my best to Sally."

"Will do."

"I asked you who are you?" the young man barked angrily, sitting in the chair, arms folded, a petulant look on his face.

"I'd watch the tone there, Marcus," Mac replied, not yet looking up from the police report. "My name is Mac McRyan. I'm here as a favor to Charlie."

Fat Charlie Boone was, at one time, a notorious and flamboyant crime figure on Minneapolis' north side. Charlie ran the drug and related trades up in that end of town for nearly twenty years. About ten years ago, he'd dropped out of sight and drifted away from the drug game. In the intervening years he slowly re-emerged as a businessman with significant interests around the Twin Cities. While not exactly considered legitimate, people generally recognized that Charlie was no longer touchable on the criminal front and that he instead was actively trying to make a positive difference in his home neighborhood. His base of operations remained a one-story brown brick office building he owned on the corners of Lowry and Penn Avenues in the heart of north Minneapolis. In the last several years Charlie purchased much of the commercial property in a two-block radius of his office, both starting and bringing in businesses and restaurants, revitalizing the long-neglected north side into a thriving neighborhood community. It would be his legacy.

However, despite his withdrawal from his criminal enterprises, Charlie was nevertheless a man who kept himself informed of the workings of the criminal underground of the Twin Cities. He was networked like few others and, when it suited his business or personal interests, was willing to communicate with certain people in law enforcement he trusted. Mac was one of those few people.

Some years ago, Charlie provided a valuable lead on a kidnapping case that involved the daughter of St. Paul Police Chief Charlie Flanagan. The tip proved vital to the saving of the girl. However, a guy like Charlie Boone didn't provide information for free. He believed in quid pro quo. So from time to time Charlie called Mac, seeking his assistance. Occasionally a member of Charlie's vast network of family and friends would find himself on the wrong side of the law and he would call Mac and ask if anything could be done. That was the nature of Charlie's call three hours ago. Mac was now in an interrogation room with Marcus Swinton.

Marcus was the son of Tony Swinton, an old friend of Charlie's from back in his criminal days. Back then Tony provided muscle for Charlie. When Charlie ended his drug operations, Tony wisely took the money he'd earned and went back home to rural Kentucky and opened a small horse farm, where he now stabled racing horses. His son Marcus was in the Twin Cities, but not following in his father's former criminal footsteps. Instead, Marcus was an excellent basketball player, a sophomore and the starting off-guard for the Minnesota Golden Gophers.

"Your godfather asked me to come here and see if there was anything I could do," Mac stated.

"I assume he told you to get me out of this."

Mac snorted and let some attitude of his own flow. "I don't work for Charlie, you arrogant little prick. I'm not one of his boys, Marcus. Charlie doesn't tell me to do shit. I'm here as a favor to him, but it doesn't mean I have to do a damn thing for you. I'm just as happy to call Charlie back and tell him not this time, the punk's not worth it."

The look on Swinton's face told Mac he now had his attention.

"I need to see something that makes this all worth *my time* and *my reputation*. And to be perfectly honest, your attitude, your sense of entitlement, the way you're slouched in that chair, your lack of respect or even understanding of your predicament all say to me that I should just walk back out this door and say the hell with it. And you know what, Marcus? If I do just that, Charlie will believe me and you'll be hosed."

Marcus already had a history of trouble at the U for theft from a dorm room and was on probation. Another legal issue and he'd likely be cut loose from the team and his promising college hoops career would be in grave jeopardy. And at this very moment, Marcus's career was at risk for one of the dumbest reasons Mac could have ever imagined. He'd been arrested for using a fake ID while trying to buy beer at a liquor store in St. Paul and then, rather than accepting a simple citation, he gave the police officers so much grief they cuffed him and dragged him downtown. Now he was sitting in a police interrogation room and giving attitude to someone who could get him out of the jackpot he found himself in.

The young man got the message. He sat up straight in his chair and pulled it up to the table, clasped his hands in front of him and said humbly, "All I was trying to do is buy some beer."

Mac remained standing, leaning against the wall. "What's the legal drinking age?"

"Twenty-one."

"Which is stupid, I think," Mac replied, folding his arms.

"But the law is the law and you, as a high-profile scholarship athlete who is not yet twenty years old, nevertheless thought it was a really good idea to use a fake Tennessee ID to buy beer?"

"I did it all summer in Kentucky."

"I got news for you. This isn't small town, backwater, do whatever the hell you want Kentucky."

"But it was my turn to buy."

"No, Marcus, this much I know. In your position, a college athlete with profile, it's never your turn to buy. It can be your turn to *pay*, but never to *buy*. You know, back in the day I played hockey at the U."

"You did?"

"Yes," Mac answered, nodding. "And you understand how big a deal that is over there, don't you?"

"Yeah." Marcus nodded respectfully. "Hockey players are tough dudes. I've hung out with a few of them."

"And in this state, hockey's a bigger thing than basketball."

Marcus shook his head in disbelief. "I'm from Kentucky, man, we don't have much hockey down there."

"The point is I, like you, needed to be careful. People knew who I and my teammates were. We had a target on us because there are plenty of people envious of the positions we held, so we had to be careful. You want to drink, go ahead and drink. I did when I was in school. But in your position, what you don't do is buy at a store with a fake ID, particularly a store owned by a guy whose kid played football at Wisconsin."

Marcus's shoulders slumped. "Are you kidding me?"

Mac smirked. "Yeah, that guy would think nothing of screwing with the U if given the chance, which is exactly what he saw when all six-foot-five of you strolled into his store."

"Shit." Marcus sighed in exasperation. "I walked right into it, didn't I?"

"I'll say," Mac replied. "And then you give the cops shit? So much shit that they feel compelled to drag your arrogant ass in here. Really? Are you stupid or something?"

"No... I'm not."

"Well, it sure as hell looks like it."

Marcus couldn't really offer a reply. He did look stupid. After a moment he asked, "Is there any way I can get out of this?"

"Why should I help you, Marcus?" Mac asked, making a point of dramatically flipping through the file. "I read your record here and I see plenty of evidence of someone who doesn't think he has to follow the rules. I have theft from a dorm room in here. I also recall reading an article in the paper where you were suspended for two games last year for violation of team rules."

"Look, I wasn't trying to get into trouble here."

"Nobody ever *tries* to get into trouble, but some people, such as yourself, have a real talent for it. I mean come on, Marcus, you had to know there was risk, right?"

Marcus nodded.

"Dude, I watched a few games last year and you're a good player. But I question the intellect of someone who'd risk throwing away his college career for a case of Coors Light. I could help you here, but what's to say a month from now you won't be in this same jackpot for doing something else just as stupid?"

"I won't."

"How can I know that?"

Marcus looked up and said quietly, "I just...I won't. I promise, I'll never do something this dumb ever again."

Mac wasn't convinced and asked, "What kind of student are you? I'm sure you know your scoring average and shooting percentage, but what's your GPA?"

"3.55."

It was Mac's turn to be surprised. 3.55 as an athlete at the U was very respectable. Quite good. "What are you looking to study?"

"I want to get a business degree."

"Any particular area?"

"I actually kind of like finance. I'm hoping to get into the Carlson School of Management. My advisor says that if I have a good semester and being an athlete and all, he thinks I can get in."

Mac nodded but remained perplexed by how Marcus got himself into such a jackpot. "With grades like that how the hell are you here? How the hell do you get into a theft issue in your dorm?"

Marcus looked Mac in the eye. "I screwed up. I know I've screwed up."

"But why?" Mac wanted to know why the kid put himself in this situation. "Why risk this? That's what I want to know."

"The theft was kind of a revenge thing, but I shouldn't have done it," Marcus answered. "Tonight, I knew I shouldn't do it but...man, I screwed up." He sat back in his chair and looked to the ceiling, shaking his head in disgust at himself.

"Why'd you screw up?" Mac pressed. He wanted an answer. "Why risk what you have? *Why?*"

Marcus exhaled, met Mac's gaze again and made an admission. "I guess sometimes, Mr. McRyan, I like to be the star. I like to be the man. I like to be the one people are talking about."

Ego. *That* Mac could understand. It didn't make what Marcus did any less dumb, but this Mac could at least relate to. It was ego. Mac had plenty of it himself now, and far more back in the day. When he was Marcus's age he and his buddies were locked out of their off-campus apartment. They made it up to the roof and Mac tied a garden hose around the chimney stack and rappelled down two floors to their balcony so he could go in through the unlocked sliding glass door and let everyone in. The hose could have untied from the chimney at any moment. The hose could have slipped through his hands or ripped apart and he would have dropped forty feet to the ground. It was beyond stupid. Yet he'd had a few beers, there were cute girls with them and he knew that if he did it his friends would talk about it for years and when they did, they'd remember him.

"That much I think I can understand, Marcus. But basketball will just have to be enough. Stand out all you want there, but otherwise, you need to keep your head down. Way down, because I can guarantee you, this *is* your last chance."

"Can you help me?"

"Are you going to keep your shit clean from now on?"

The young man nodded, looked Mac in the eye and said sharply and respectfully, "Yes, sir. I promise you I will."

"Alright," Mac answered. "Sit tight and let me see what I can do."

~

Neil Kline reviewed the day's receipts for the repair shop. There were two kinds of receipts he needed to evaluate: the ones for auto repair and then the day's take that had been delivered over the last two hours. The auto repair books were already reviewed and reconciled. Now those receipts needed to be amended to filter through some of the cash sitting in the safe behind him.

"Was it a good day?"

Neil looked up to see Mr. White standing in the doorway. For a lawyer, the man had the uncanny ability to sneak up on people.

"The usual," Kline answered. "I feel comfortable moving about thirty-six percent of today's take through the receipts. The rest"—he pointed to the satchel on the floor—"can go up to the cash house."

Mr. White seemed to be reviewing Neil's answer, running the calculation through his head, and then nodded his agreement. "Felix's men will be by to pick it up shortly."

"Jockey Mike and I could take it up there ourselves," Neil replied. "It's not a problem."

Mr. White smiled. "I know, and you will once again once things settle down and you seem to be of a little less interest to certain people. And on that front, I can assure you that a certain someone will no longer be watching from that hill up at the house."

"So they..." Neil left the question hanging.

"They did," Mr. White affirmed. "He will not be back, ever."

"That's good to know, but..." Neil's voice trailed off.

"But what?"

"He was an ex-cop, right?"

"Yes, so?"

"Don't you think taking out a cop brings unnecessary heat? Even if he's an ex-cop?"

"Who knows he's gone, Neil?" White asked, slipping his

hands into his dress pant pockets. "Who? Nobody knows where Luther is. Nobody will know where this man is. And it had to be done. You were there yourself. The man saw too much. That had to be contained."

This was a discussion Neil thought he probably shouldn't be a part of. But at the same time he questioned the wisdom of what had been done. Taking out a nobody like Luther was one thing. People like that vanished all the time. But disappearing an ex-cop was an escalatory step. "I'm just saying, it's the kind of decision that might raise the ire of some others."

"What others?" White replied. "Like the police?"

"Yes," Neil mused, sitting back in his chair. "Shead was a cop. He probably had friends."

"I'm sure he did, but without a body and without any other evidence left behind, what will they find?" White answered calmly, sensing Neil's real worry. "Listen, Shead is gone, will not be found and we shouldn't have any more visitors or people following you or T.O. around. But all the same, we're going to be careful for a bit and keep you in the shop. If you do notice anyone paying some special attention to you, you best let us know so that we can deal with it."

"I'll keep an eye out."

"You do that." And with that, White quietly departed. Neil returned his attention to the computer monitor, trying to finish his analysis of the actual inventory for the shop. He didn't get very far.

"So they got rid of that ex-cop who was snooping around, eh?"

Neil looked up to see Jockey Mike, his driver, in the doorway. "You overheard all of that?"

Mike nodded, his diminutive five-foot frame leaning

against the door frame. "Isn't that what you pay me for? Isn't that what you should pay me *more* for?"

"Dammit, not when Mr. White or any of the others are around. You should not be listening in on any of that business. Have you been?"

Mike didn't respond. He was guilty as charged.

"You shouldn't know that shit. You don't want to know that shit. That shit can get you killed."

"Maybe if I were paid more, I wouldn't care."

"I'd think twice if I were you about what you just said," Neil warned. "You don't hold anything, *anything*, over on these people."

"What? It worked in prison."

"That was different, little man. That was fucking with prison guards or regular old cons. These guys?" Kline shook his head wearily. "You should know by now that these guys are something *entirely* different."

"I'm just saying I could use a little more, you know."

"Yeah, yeah," Neil replied dismissively, having heard the complaint many times before. Neil would have liked more in his pocket too, who wouldn't? But there wasn't a lot of legitimate work out there for someone with his background. So, ruthless as the bastards were, it was currently the only game in town. "Be glad you have what you have. There isn't a lot of call out there for broken-down, drug-addicted ex-jockeys with no other discernible skills, other than exceptionally good hearing and a valid driver's license. Now for the last time, stop listening in on conversations unless I instruct you to."

Mike held up his hands. "Look, Neil—"

"No, you look," Neil replied angrily. "These guys we're working for will not hesitate to get rid of me, *or you* for that matter, if we become even the most remote of a liability.

Right now, I'm valuable to them and as such, they let me let you hang around and drive. You look harmless, but if they think you're listening in on shit"—Neil raised his right hand—"you'll disappear like *that*." He added a loud finger snap. "Keep your mouth shut and mind your own damn business. If you don't, I'll put your drug-addled ass back on the street. See how long you last out there without the means to pay for your painkillers."

"Neil, please don't do that," Mike pleaded.

"Then knock it the fuck off before you get us both killed."

3

"CLOSE CASES."

After helping Marcus Swinton with his issues, Mac went home. Home was the house he and Sally owned on Berkeley Avenue in the Macalester-Groveland neighborhood of St. Paul.

The house was Sally's as she'd kept it as part of her divorce from her first husband. When she asked Mac to move in, it became *their* home and Mac proceeded to completely remodel and modernize it. When Sally took the job in Washington they had a decision to make; keep the house or sell it. Given all the work Mac had done to rehabilitate it, they decided to keep it. If and when they came back, they'd need a place to live and the house was fully and completely remodeled to their liking and located in a neighborhood and city they both loved.

While his old bed felt comfortable and familiar, he nevertheless slept fitfully for a few hours until he was snapped awake by an ambulance siren roaring along Cleveland Avenue a few blocks away. Stirred awake, he laid in bed for a few minutes and his stomach felt empty. It was 5:30 a.m. and there was a perfect solution to this problem.

There were many things he missed about St. Paul, but one of the biggest was simply having breakfast at the Cleveland Grille with Dick and Dot. So, before he made his 8:30 a.m. tee time at Town and Country Club, he decided to surprise his old partner and his lady friend.

The Cleveland Grille was a St. Paul institution. It was old, a little dingy, with a well past its prime interior and décor. Nonetheless, it was the most popular breakfast spot in the city. Dot had worked there for over twenty years and when it came on the market, she managed to scrape enough together to buy the place. Mac helped her with the purchase, having a lawyer from Lyman Hisle's office review the papers and made her an essentially interest-free loan to cover her last little bit on the down payment. Essentially interest-free meant occasionally he could eat breakfast on the house. That was the interest. Dot was now in her middle fifties, yet still wore her same yellow and white Cleveland waitressing uniform, which was far too tight on the top. That was especially for Dicky Boy who loved to do nothing more than sit in his regular back-corner booth, read the paper, eat breakfast and watch Dot bounce around and sway her hips while she bustled around the restaurant waiting on him and her other favorite customers.

It was 6:10 a.m. as Mac strolled along the front sidewalk on Cleveland Avenue and looked to his left to see Dick sitting in his customary booth, a pot of coffee in front of him and three newspapers, one of which he was reading. Now usually when Mac arrived he'd just walk right in the front door and head right back to Dick's table. Not today.

He stood at the hostess stand, waiting to be seated by Dot, who was working the cash register. Dot looked up and asked, "Just a single, honey?"

"Just a single, honey?" Mac repeated mockingly and then watched as his voice registered with her.

"Mac?" Dot asked, looking closer. "Oh my God, Mac. What the hell?"

"I was getting a little worried there."

"Well, you look *so* different," she replied, coming out from behind the counter to give him a big warm hug and a kiss on the cheek. "You're so scruffy," she said as she rubbed her hand playfully along his cheek. "And my goodness, your hair, it's sooo...long for you. Has Dick seen you?"

"No."

"Oh good," she replied giddily. "Let's go surprise him."

As Dot walked him back toward the corner table Dick looked up briefly, then back down at his paper and then snapped his head back up. "Jesus Christ, it's Grizzly Adams," Dick howled, getting up to take Mac's hand.

"Hardly," Mac answered. "Can I join ya?"

"Absolutely," Dick answered happily. "When you show up, I seem to get to eat for free."

"Are you still charging him?" Mac asked Dot with a big smile.

"The bills need to be paid. He pays." Then Dot whispered in his ear, "Well, maybe not all the time."

Mac just laughed.

"The usual, honey?" Dot asked.

"Of course," Mac replied. "Plus a cup for coffee and a really big ice water, too."

"On its way."

"What's with the beard?" Dick asked. "I didn't even recognize you walking over here."

"Good, I like flying below the radar." Mac was sporting a not quite full beard, but a thick dose of darker stubble. "I've been going stubble heavy for a month or two."

"Sally must approve."

"She says it makes me look ruggedly handsome. So naturally I've let it grow out even more."

"Hell, I can't even really see that canyon of a dimple in your chin, which is probably why you didn't register with me at first. And the hair. What's with the hair? I mean it's not quite down to the shoulders, but for you, that's long."

"I decided to make a change is all." It wasn't that conscious a choice.

A few months ago, when it was time to get his usual haircut he had to cancel at the last minute and he didn't immediately reschedule. Then he looked in the mirror one morning, liked the slightly longer look and so did Sally.

"I like to run my fingers through it," she said one night in bed.

That was good enough for him. He decided to let it grow out some, comb it back and let it flow. It wasn't long hockey flow-like, at least yet. There was no need for a ponytail nor would there ever be; he would never let it get to that. But it was longer and he had a little natural waviness in the back.

"You're not having a mid-life crisis, are you?"

Mac cackled. "No. No, I'm not. Cripes, I'm not at mid-life yet. I should be at least forty, shouldn't I? I haven't bought a motorcycle or a sports car. I'm not trying to compensate for anything, I'm just trying something new is all, changing up the look. And Sally approves so if she likes it, I'll go with it for a while."

"Does the longer hair fit in at the golf course?" Dick asked, noting Mac's attire of a black golf shirt and gray golf shorts.

Mac shrugged. "It's not *that* long. Besides, country clubs like Town and Country can always use a little mild nonconformity."

"What's the handicap these days anyway?"

"I'm a little under a three right now. I think my index is 2.8."

"Somebody's been playing *a lot* of golf."

"I have to fill my time with something. It's golf, a little scuba diving, some day-trading."

"Ah, the life of the idle rich."

"Jealous?"

"You're such a dick," Dick replied with mock bitterness. "But the last time I talked to you, you said you were going to buy another investment property to remodel."

"I was. I thought I had a nice little brownstone three blocks away from ours in Georgetown all teed up a couple of weeks ago. That would have kept me busy for a good four or five months. But then the seller decided I wasn't offering enough and wanted another fifty thousand. Based on what I wanted to do to the place, and what I thought I could sell it for once I was finished, I wasn't sure I'd make enough profit to make it worth my time so I walked away."

"You think he might call back?"

Mac shook his head. "No. His read on the market was better than mine. Someone paid him what he wanted last week."

"And what's up with your bride? Is she still hot or is she letting herself go now that she married your sorry ass?"

"My wife is still exceptionally hot," Mac replied with a grin. "She got promoted to Senior Advisor to the President. She and the Judge are running the White House operation for the mid-terms. I may not see her until November."

"She's really moved up in the world," Dick remarked. "Amazing, really," he added while looking at his ringing phone.

"Do you need to take the call?"

"It can wait. So, how do you feel about the promotion? I assume that's a lot of responsibility for her."

"Great, I'm happy for her. She's making the most of her four years in D.C."

"Four years?"

"Yeah," Mac answered. "She said she wanted four years in Washington and then she wanted to come home. She made that deal with me."

"You think she'll walk away if the President wins again? You think she'll want to?" Dick asked skeptically. "You think they'll let her?"

"She says she will, but I share some of your skepticism, so we shall see," Mac replied, thinking back to his conversation with Sally from yesterday. "I take it as a good sign that she's been pushing me to think about what I'm going to do when we come back."

"Really?" Dick asked, suddenly interested. "You know the chief will take you back in a heartbeat. Hell, your badge is still sitting in his desk drawer."

"I don't know."

"I see. Maybe a better question is what does Sally want you to do?"

"She didn't say," Mac answered with a slight grin, "it's up to me."

"*Sure* it is, pal," Dick replied sarcastically. "I bet she doesn't want you to be a cop."

"I don't think that's true," Mac answered, shaking his head and pouring some coffee. "I think she just wants me to be happy."

Dick shook his head. "That girl loves you, so of course she wants you happy. But she also wants your ruggedly handsome rich ass safe and secure. You've got money, brains and contacts so you don't need to put yourself in the line of fire anymore. If I had to guess, that's what that pretty thing of yours is thinking. One could hardly blame her if she is."

Mac sat back, smiled and shook his head. "Buddy, I don't think she's pulling the classic Minnesota passive aggressive 'maybe you'd like something else if you'd just give it a try' bit. I don't think she's being devious in that way at all. Trust me, buddy, we have a clear line of communication. If the fiery redhead disapproves of something I'm doing, she tells me in no uncertain terms."

Dot delivered their breakfasts. As always, Mac had the breakfast burrito and ate in delight the mixture of egg, sausage, ham, cheese, peppers, sour cream, tomatoes and salsa. They talked about the surprise of the Twins season, the optimism of the Vikings and the new center acquisition for the Minnesota Wild.

"Do you think the Wild will ever win the Stanley Cup?"

Mac shook his head. "If they do, I think I will then be able to die a happy man. Just once, *just once*, the Stanley Cup should live for a year here in the State of Hockey. Chicago and Pittsburgh have had it enough."

As Dot swung by to clear away their plates and drop off another pot of coffee, they returned to the subject of Mac's future.

"Really, Mac. What are you going to do?"

"I don't know," Mac answered, wiping his hands with a napkin. "It's two years away, I don't have to decide right now. Who knows, maybe events or fate decides what I end up doing. I'm not stressing over it."

"But you'll want to do something," Dick pressed. "What?"

Mac suspected his good friend wanted his old partner

back, but was that what he wanted? He missed some elements of police work, particularly the hunt and a good complex case with layers to peel back. That was the kind of challenge he relished. However, the administrative and political bullshit that went with the job was something he did not miss and there was often more of the latter than the former.

"I know this much, Dicky Boy, I'm not going to be some guy who sits around. I can't keep doing that. I'm too young and I'm not going to like, retire. Heck, I feel like I've been partially retired the last two years."

"A lot of people would love to have your life."

"I get it, but to be honest, I'm getting a little bored." Mac poured himself a new cup of coffee and added some cream. "So if and when we do get back here, I'll have to get a job of some kind. I need to be active and doing something meaningful."

Dick nodded as he poured a new cup of coffee for himself. He then added in some sugar and cream and made a show of slowly stirring it all together. Mac had seen the act before. It was what Dick did when he was contemplating whether to offer his thoughts on a topic.

"Spit it out."

"What?"

"You have something you want to say. Say it."

Dick took a sip of his coffee and sat back and looked Mac square in the eye. "My view is that you should do what you were put on this earth to do, Mac. Do what you do better than anyone I've ever come across, including your father. Close cases. You're nearly twenty years my junior and you can investigate circles around me."

"Knock it off."

"It's true, and it doesn't bother me a bit," Dick replied in complete candor. "In my opinion, you sitting there in Washington not working cases, is a complete and total waste of elite investigative talent. FBI Director Mitchell knows this as well, which is why he's always trying to recruit you. If you come back here to St. Paul, talk the chief into some sort of special case unit. I'd work with or even *for* you in a heartbeat."

"Well, to answer what is obviously your *real* question, partner—yes, I could see me coming back to some kind of police work, but it has to be the right kind of job. What you just mentioned *might* be the right kind of gig. I do know this, I kind of miss the action."

Dick held up the front page of the *Pioneer Press,* St. Paul's daily newspaper. "Sometimes the action isn't so great."

On the front page was an article about a trial of Minneapolis and St. Paul police officers involved in the shooting of a motorist a year ago along Highway 280, a short four-lane highway that divides Minneapolis and St. Paul. The motorist had led the police on a brief high-speed chase that started in Minneapolis and ended just inside western St. Paul, thus involving both jurisdictions. When the vehicle stopped the officers got out and approached the vehicle, weapons drawn. Video footage of the incident taken by a bystander showed two Minneapolis officers, one at the driver's side door and the other at the passenger's. Two St. Paul officers who'd joined the pursuit were stationed behind the vehicle, also with weapons drawn. On the footage, you could hear the Minneapolis officers calmly ordering the driver to keep his hands up and then suddenly, there was an urgency to the officer's commands and then both Minneapolis officers fired, killing the driver. They both later claimed that they thought the driver was reaching for a gun. The problem was, the driver was unarmed, a fact confirmed a mere minute after the shooting when St. Paul Patrol Officer Jack Morgan was heard on the video taken by the bystander saying, "There is no gun in the car."

"I've followed that case a little bit from afar," Mac stated. "It starts today?"

"Yeah, they finished jury selection yesterday," Dick answered. "It's been getting a fair amount of coverage. That bystander video will be Exhibit A, I'm sure."

"Has there been any impact for you guys? Any trouble or blowback on the streets?"

Dick shrugged. "Some, although I think it's much worse over in Minneapolis. Their guys shot the driver, ours didn't." He changed subjects. "Speaking of old cases, anything new on April Greene from that Rubens case?"

Mac shook his head. "Silence. Wire and I check in with Galloway and Delmonico over at the FBI every week at this point, but as of now the trail is ice cold. No sign of her and no word from her. Nevertheless, I half expect a phone call from her any minute."

"So you think she'll come back eventually?"

"She as much told us so. I have no doubt she wants another crack at Wire and I because we won the first fight but we didn't completely knock her out. At some point, I think she'll re-emerge to play her ... sick game. She'll either call or, more likely we'll find a pink carnation lying by a dead body and we'll know the action is starting again."

"Speaking of action, what time are you on the tee?"

"8:30 and then lunch after. I'm playing with a couple of college buddies, the ones who built the coffee shops."

"Is this round of golf their way of saying thanks?"

"That," Mac answered, "and they have a new business

opportunity they want to talk about. What's your day look like?"

Dick looked at his ringing phone. "I don't know, but right now I better take this call. It's the third time she's tried to reach me."

4

"WELL, AREN'T YOU THE POLICE?"

Dick pulled into an open parking space, emerged from his car and looked up at the new large neon red Fireball sign ablaze on the roof of the building.

Fireball was located on the southeast corner of University and Snelling Avenues in St. Paul, and to say it was thriving would be an understatement. In one half of the bar there were tall black vinyl booths and pub tables organized to allow for viewing of the twenty-five massive televisions mounted high on the walls or hanging from the ceiling, allowing sports fans to take in any event. The other half of the bar was an expansive nightclub, with a dance floor and small concert stage. Fireball offered live music Thursday, Friday and Saturday nights and a DJ on other nights. The two sections of the building were separated by the massive long rectangular bar from which the bartenders served both halves of the huge club.

With a large expansive parking lot situated to its east and behind it, the nightclub was ideally situated on the Green Line of the Twin Cities light rail system. It was just a ten-minute train ride to the east to Wild games at Xcel

Energy Center in downtown St. Paul, a ten-minute ride west to Golden Gopher games on the campus of the University of Minnesota, or in another ten minutes you could be in downtown Minneapolis and watch the Twins, Vikings or Timberwolves or catch a show at the Guthrie or one of the many theatres along Hennepin Avenue. And in a couple of years, a new MLS soccer stadium for the Minnesota United FC would open one block to the south, bringing with it the enthusiastically diverse millennials who loved soccer and the festive parties that went with it.

And to think eight years ago the bar was emblematic of the decay of the neighborhood. The area was gentrified, with flailing businesses, past their prime retailers and an undercurrent of danger and criminality all creating an aesthetic of decline. Shady's, Fireball's predecessor, was a nightly blight on the area, drawing police calls for fights, lewd behavior and drunken patrons.

Only one person seemed to have the vision of what the area and Shady's could become. That was Nikki, or as everyone now called her, Nikki Fireball. That wasn't her real name, of course. But for Lisa Nicole Franco, being known as Nikki Fireball was a far more exciting and marketable moniker.

Nikki was quite the visionary and entrepreneur, the only person who thought the dilapidated Shady's could become something special. Dick was with Sam the night he met Nikki and there had been many good nights over the last few years; good nights for his old buddy and former partner who finally had his life back together. A friend who was now not answering his phone and apparently hadn't been for over a day. As he opened the back door and stepped inside, he was left with a distinct feeling of unease.

"Dicky," Nikki greeted him when he came in the door.

"Thanks for coming." Nikki hooked her arm around his and led Dick over to a table with three other people. "These are two of my boys. This is BTG." Nikki pointed to a man who must have been six-foot-six.

"BTG?" Dick asked.

"Big Tall Guy," BTG answered.

"Right."

"This is Heavy G," Nikki introduced a slender man a good four inches shorter and significantly thinner than BTG.

"Heavy G?"

"It's actually Steve Gustafson but I used to carry some more weight, hence—"

"Heavy G."

"And, of course, you know Denise."

"Ahh yes," Dick replied, shaking hands with the legendary Denise, who because of her tart treatment of rude customers was known as DeNasty. "So what's up with Sam?"

"I'm worried," Nikki started. "He hasn't returned any of my phone calls, he's not at his townhouse and he missed his shift last night."

"When did you last see him?"

"Wednesday night, or I suppose early Thursday morning, he stopped in just before closing time—12:30, 12:45—something like that. It was his night off but he stopped in and we talked. It was the first time I'd seen him in several nights, in fact. But when I saw him, he was in a really good and amorous mood."

"You two didn't, did you?" DeNasty asked.

"Boss, are you getting a little busy in there?" BTG added with a big smile.

"All of you stop it," Nikki replied with a dismissive wave.

"Although, I will say Sam was certainly in the mood to do just that."

"Was there anything in particular that had him in such a good mood?" Dick queried.

"He said it was something he'd been working on, something related to that Luther Ellis guy. He said he got a big break, was excited and that all he needed to do was call you. I could tell he was all pumped up about it and I guess one thing apparently led to another for him."

"What happened after that?" Dick asked.

"Well, he went home. My daughter was staying at my place that night so when she does, Sam would go home to his townhouse. When he left Wednesday night, I assumed that's where he was going. He said he'd see me the next night when he came to work."

"And he didn't show?"

"No, and I tried to call him a few times during the day and he never picked up or called me back and then he didn't show last night."

"And he still isn't answering his phone," BTG added. "I've tried, G has tried."

"Even I've tried, and he knows how angry I get if he doesn't answer," DeNasty added.

Dick didn't add that he had tried as well on his way over. Despite the light banter and attitudinal posturing, all four of the people sitting across from him were extremely concerned.

"I didn't know what else to do," Nikki stated.

"Have you called the police?"

"Well, aren't you the police?"

"Of course. I just meant have you filed a missing person report?"

"No, I just called you."

"Have you been to his townhouse?"

"Yes. I went in quick, looked around and he wasn't there, nor was his truck."

"And you haven't seen or heard from him since Wednesday night, just after closing?"

"No."

"And it's unlike him to not respond to calls or texts?"

"*Extremely*," Nikki replied. "He's more of a phone junkie than my sixteen-year-old. He's always on it and usually if I call, he calls right back or texts back with a bunch of emojis or gifs and I've heard nothing."

"And when he left on Wednesday, what did he say?"

"Other than he would be in the next night?"

"Yeah."

"The only other thing I remember him saying is that he needed to call you. Did he?"

"No," Dick replied, shaking his head. "Nikki, what was he supposed to call me about?"

"All I know is it had something to do with Luther."

"He was still hung up on that?" Dick asked as a sense of dread swept through him.

"Yes," Nikki answered. "I told him he needed to let that go. What Luther did, trying to help people beat drugs, was an honorable thing, but some of the people he had to deal with—" Nikki shook her head worriedly, her eyes moistening. "They were people who hung around dangerous people."

"But that wouldn't stop Sam," Dick answered. His old partner was not one to ever back down from anything.

"No, it didn't. He'd taken the last four nights off to investigate something involving Luther. After Wednesday night, he said he had something for you to work with. I was relieved."

"What? What did he have for me to work with?"

"He didn't say. He just said he needed to call you. You're sure he didn't call? Maybe you missed the call."

"He never called me, Nikki," Dick answered. "I've checked my cell phone, at the office and at home. He has not called me."

"Oh Dick, something happened to him," Nikki cried. "I just know it."

"Now, Nikki, we don't know that," Dick answered quietly, reaching for her hand. "That's not what has me worried."

"What does?"

"Look, before you get all freaked out about doomsday scenarios here, there is one other less drastic thing that could have happened," Dick suggested.

"Which is?"

"Sam fell off the wagon and he's embarrassed and not responding." At this point, that was Dick's hope.

The four of them looked to one another and nodded. "You know that's possible," BTG said, looking to Nikki. "My dad's a recovering alcoholic. Every day is a challenge for him."

"He ever fall off the wagon?" Heavy G asked.

BTG nodded. "Oh yeah, more than once and when he went off, he went *off*. The last time was about eight years ago and I had to pick him up from detox. I think me having to be the one to get him out finally got him to stay straight, but like I said—every day is a battle."

"So that could have happened," DeNasty offered, reaching her arm around Nikki's shoulders.

Nikki grabbed onto that hope for a moment, but only briefly. "If that happened, he'd have called. He would have responded and he hasn't. I'm still worried something happened to him."

"I'm on this," Dick answered reassuringly, far more than he felt. "I'll find him."

~

Mike McHugh and Kent Forbord made Mac a wealthy man.

The two started the Grand Brew coffee franchise ten years ago. As they were trying to start their first coffee shop they were struggling to come up with the last ten thousand dollars in financing. Mac, then in his first year as a uniform cop, would have seemed like an unlikely source for the needed money. However, his parents had established a college fund for him that he'd hardly used. He'd received an athletic scholarship at the University of Minnesota for hockey and, based upon his college grades and accomplishments, a partial scholarship from William Mitchell College of Law. There was money left in the college fund and Mac was looking to move it into an investment that would provide greater return.

Mac met both McHugh and Forbord while drinking coffee in the Coffman Student Union at the U. He'd lamented with them back then about the lack of good coffee options on campus. His friends thought there was an opening for a more unique coffee experience than what you found at the corporate Starbucks and Caribou. One night over beers, the two of them explained they were ten grand short of starting their dream.

"You need ten grand?" Mac asked at the time. "That's all you're short?"

"Yeah," McHugh had responded. "The banks have been tight so we've had to scrape up our last dollars to do this and we're still short. Do you know someone who'd like a little piece of the business?"

"Sure," Mac answered. "*Me.* What's your business plan?"

Mac's two buddies explained their vision for a coffee shop that was more comfortable, local and affordable. They had identified a small building on Grand Avenue near Macalester College that they could renovate if they could get over the financial hump. Mac liked their vision and the idea of getting in on the ground floor of something. At worst, he'd blow ten thousand dollars on his two friends' dream. If they made a go of it, he'd share a little in the profits. Mac could have never dreamed what the Grand Brew would become.

Nearly three years ago his two buddies sold their business, which at the time had over one hundred coffee shops throughout the Upper Midwest, to a large grocery conglomerate that had now taken the Grand Brew chain national. His two friends made out like bandits, as did their small minority investor. Now, his two friends were back in front of him with an opportunity.

"You don't need my money, guys," Mac stated as he eyed a slippery fifteen-foot downhill putt on the eighth green. "I mean, thanks to you two I'm quite comfortable. But I can't swim in your end of the money pool when it comes to investing." Mac took two quick practice strokes and then lightly struck the putt, watching his golf ball slowly roll down the hill, breaking to the right and gliding just around and behind the cup, missing on the pro side at least.

"Never up, never in, Mac. Nice par," McHugh complimented as he hit the ball back to Mac.

"Mac, no, we don't need your money, not at all," Kent continued as he put his own golf ball down and removed his ball marker and started eyeing up his five-foot bogey putt. "The reason we don't need your money is because you had a little faith in us many years ago. It's time for us to pay it forward." Kent struck his putt and made it.

"Yeah, Mac," McHugh added with a big grin. "This start-up company we're investing in could do really well. It's a great opportunity. We're here to pay you back."

"Guys, you don't owe me," Mac stated as he slipped his putter into his golf bag and then jumped into the golf cart with McHugh. "I made out pretty well. If anything, I owe you guys."

"No, Mac, we owe you. This is a good opportunity that we are extremely optimistic about," McHugh replied and then he started ticking off the investors. "There are some pretty big names getting in on this, the usual blue blood types. The Bartletts, Carltons, Sterns..." He looked over to Kent. "Who else?"

"Jason Booth, Denny Claridge, the Moran family that own the furniture stores, Rosie and Alberto Santiago who have the De La Cabo Mexican joints you see all over town. Bart Whitecraft, the local corporate raider guy," Forbord added. "Heck, even the woman who sells the guacamole you see on television all the time."

"Peterson. Laura Peterson, right?" Mac asked. "I saw a *Star Tribune* article on her recently."

"Yup, that's her," McHugh answered. "She's actually coming in as one of the biggest investors on this thing, and Booth and Claridge—those guys are no joke. They were part of the group that bought out the coffee shops. They're big time and only get involved when they think something is going to take off."

The three of them moved to the ninth tee. McHugh, who had the honor, teed his ball up. While he did, Kent kept talking. "So Mac. We think we're going to do really well with this and we wanted you to get in on it as a way of saying thank you."

McHugh drilled his drive down the middle.

"Nice one, Mikey," Mac remarked and then lined up his drive. He took one practice swing and then stepped up to the ball and swung his three-wood, watching as the ball drew from right to left and landed on the left side of the fairway, leaving him in a good position.

"Silky smooth," Kent admired as he stepped onto the tee. "Someone is playing a lot of golf."

"He has the time to do it," McHugh needled. "And the money."

"Yeah, yeah," Mac replied as they jumped into the golf cart and drove down the fairway. The ninth hole at Town and Country Club was a par four that ran due west. Mac's drive had come to rest ten yards short of the end of the fairway before a steep hill that ran down to the green. From the edge of the fairway you could look out over the Mississippi River, and farther to the west you took in perhaps the best view of the downtown Minneapolis skyline that you could possibly find.

"It's a hell of a view," McHugh remarked as they took in the scenery before them. "I've taken a picture of it many times with my phone." There was a foursome down below them butchering their way around the green. They would have to wait to hit their approach shots.

"Okay, you two," Mac said with a smile, interested in the opportunity but a little wary of the commitment. "I'm interested in this and I'm also interested in finishing my round and taking your money without distraction. So if I were to get in on this, how much do you suggest?"

"Nothing that would at all imperil your financial status," Kent answered. "But there is a minimum to get in."

"Which is?"

"Quarter million."

"Hmm," Mac murmured as the group below had cleared the green. Mac grabbed his gap wedge, which was typically his one-hundred-twenty-five-yard club, but with the severe downhill making the one-hundred-fifty-yard approach play significantly shorter, thought it was the right choice. Mac swung nice and easy and watched as the ball seemed to hang in the air forever before it finally came down just on the front left of the green, still some thirty feet from the hole, which was in the back left corner of the green. "Should have given that a little more."

The three made their way down to the green. McHugh and Forbord also had long putts. All three managed to two-putt for their pars.

As they reached their golf carts McHugh piped up, "So Mac, what do you think? You want to come in with us?"

"Two hundred fifty grand?" Mac asked, confirming the amount.

"Two-fifty," Forbord confirmed.

"Well boys, I think I could swing that," Mac answered as he reviewed the front side totals on the golf card, charting the progress of their match. Mac was winning the match thus far with his two buddies, up a robust thirty bucks at this point. "Besides, it'll be less than two hundred fifty thousand after I polish you two clowns off on the back side. You're both just a little behind."

"Big talker."

"I'm just saying the press is available if you want to double the bet."

"*Press!*" McHugh and Forbord replied in unison.

5

"I DON'T THINK THEY FORGAVE THE LOAN."

Dick pulled on white latex gloves and then slid the key Nikki had given him into the deadbolt for the front door of Sam's townhouse. The townhouse was one in a line of eight. It had a narrow two-car tuck-under garage with two stories resting over the top.

Once inside, Dick soaked in the atmosphere of the townhouse. It gave him a feeling of vacancy, of an eerie, cold quiet that overtakes a place when it hasn't been lived in for a while.

Dick walked into the kitchen and noticed that there were no dishes in the sink. He opened the dishwasher and counted two dishes, three glasses, a spatula, serving spoon and set of tongs, all dirty. "That's unusual," Dick muttered.

One would assume that with his wild past, proclivities with the ladies, with the bottle and a wide range of recreational drugs, Sam Shead would have been something of a slob. Nothing could be further from the truth. Sam was always meticulous about his home, vehicle, locker and his desk. Dick thought it would have been unusual, extremely unusual for Sam to let dishes sit that long, even clean, in the dishwasher. He opened the door under the sink to check the garbage and there was an immediate foul odor. Again, something Sam would not have tolerated. If he was planning on being gone for even a day, Sam would have put the trash in the garbage can outside.

He stepped out of the kitchen and quickly evaluated the living room and dining area. The small, four-person tabletop was empty, the chairs pushed in. The couch and two chairs arranged around a small coffee table seemed all in order. The remote controls for the television and audio equipment were sitting side by side one another on the table.

Dick made his way up the steps to the second level. The master bedroom was to the right and the bed was made and a little cold to the touch. In the closet, Sam's clothes were neatly arranged. The dirty clothes hamper was half-full. In the bathroom, his toothbrush was sitting in a small glass. It was dry to the touch. Dick opened the shower door and reached inside for Sam's razor which was dry, as was the shower floor and area around the drain.

Across the hall was the tiny spare bedroom, which Sam used as an office. Inside there was an old metal desk pushed against the wall. Sam was a freak about his desk as a cop and he was in his own private life, so it seemed. There were always ten pens and ten pencils in his cups on his desk. He always kept miniature Minnesota and American flags on his desk, as he did here. Any documents were always perfectly stacked, not a paper askew. Rarely would he leave his desk in any state of disorganization. Even in a hurry, on a rush to get out, he would make sure the pencils and pens were in the cup and the papers were orderly and organized.

"This seems off."

Sam's desk had ten pens and ten pencils and they were

in their cups. There were the Minnesota and American flags centered. And there were documents, and they were stacked, but far from neatly.

The desktop itself held two stacks of papers. When Sam was Dick's partner, those papers would have been neatly, perfectly stacked. In fact, Sam would constantly hold a stack of papers up so that he could smooth the stack and set it down so it was perfect, a mild OCD-like tendency. In this case, the stacks were not organized in that fashion. They were stacked with ends of pages sticking out in various directions.

The Sam he knew would not have left his desk like that. Such a state of affairs would have offended him.

The two filing cabinet drawers were just slightly ajar. Sam was compulsive enough that he wouldn't have left the drawers that way. In the left file drawer he found a gap. It was in the N section of files and he immediately thought *notebook*. If Sam was working something, he would keep a notebook and he always filed his notebooks in his N file. The slot for N was empty; even the hanging folder was gone.

Dick moved over to the closet and opened the folding doors. Hanging inside was Sam's leather gun case, but his Glock-17 was missing. "So whatever you're up to, you felt like you needed your gun."

Sam liked photography and owned a high-end Canon camera with a telephoto lens. There was a Canon case for it resting on the overhead shelf, but there was no camera or telephoto lens inside. Mac looked back to the desk and noticed there was no computer. He looked down underneath the desk and he saw a power strip plugged into the wall, but there was nothing plugged into it. Yet there was a deep rectangular impression in the carpet that could have potentially been formed by a computer tower.

With his concern only increasing, Dick left the spare bedroom and went all the way down to the basement and peered into the garage. As Nikki said, Sam's Chevy Silverado was not inside, although his Harley was on the far side, covered with a tarp. Thinking back to the garbage in the kitchen, he quickly checked the wheeled garbage can and it was three quarters full.

Dick closed the door and went outside and started knocking on neighbor's doors. The townhome development was of an older vintage, as were many of its residents. The owners of the two townhouses to the left and the one to the immediate right of Sam's were all home. Each neighbor knew Sam but hadn't seen him in at least a couple of days.

"I usually am out walking the dog in the late afternoon when Sam would leave for work," his neighbor to the right said. "But I haven't seen him the last two days. It's been pretty quiet at his place."

"How about his pickup truck? Have you seen that?"

The neighbor scratched his chin for a moment then shook his head. "I can't say that I have. I'd notice it too—it was a big one, dual cab kind, and you kind of know when he pulls in because it's a little loud with that big engine in it."

"Has there been anyone else looking around, perhaps looking for Sam?" Dick pressed.

The neighbor shook his head. "No, sir. Not that I've noticed, anyway."

"Tell me," Dick asked, "are most of the residents around here like...you know..."

"Retired," the neighbor replied with an amused crease of a grin.

"Yes, sir."

"Pretty much," the neighbor replied with a nod.

"So not a lot of late-night parties?"

The neighbor chuckled. "No. I'd guess this time of year most of us are in bed or close to it when the sun is setting." That would mean a late-night foray into Sam's townhouse by someone would be less likely to be noticed, Dick thought.

Dick was about to walk away when he turned to ask one last question. "When do you have garbage pickup?"

"Thursday, so yesterday."

"Okay, thanks."

For someone as much a neat freak as Sam, it would have been very unusual for him to have missed that. Dick went back inside Sam's place and took one last look around and a feeling of anxiety slowly washed over him. Sam's gun was gone along with his camera. "Items you'd want if you were tailing or investigating someone," he muttered to himself.

The askew papers and the unclosed drawers were more of a reach. Perhaps he was reading *too* much into that, except that he knew Sam like few others and the condition of his desk was truly uncharacteristic. That, and the carpet indentation for the computer said to him someone had been through.

His pickup truck was gone and hadn't been seen in days based upon his quick canvas of neighbors. The shower and toothbrush were bone dry, again hardly definitive, but indicative of the fact Sam hadn't been home for a few days. And if he wasn't here, he would be at work or with Nikki, yet he wasn't showing up there either. And as far as the going on a bender idea went, an idea he'd used to try to calm Nikki, Sam clearly hadn't gone off the wagon at home.

Something was very wrong here, a point he made to his captain.

"You really think he's in trouble?" Captain Marion Peters asked Dick.

"I think so, boss. He's not responding to any calls to his phone. He hasn't been home for a couple of days at least and if I didn't know better, I'd say somebody went through his townhouse. Things were not the way I'd expect them to be and some things seem to be missing."

"Well, I've got the missing persons bulletin out so we'll see what that turns up," Peters stated. "But you know, there is one other possibility."

"I know, that he started drinking again," Dick nodded. "At this point I hope that's the case, but there was no indication a breakdown like that was coming. But if he doesn't show up soon, I'd like to see if we could send a forensic team to his townhouse to see if they can find anything that the naked eye can't."

Peters wrinkled his nose. "Not yet. Dick, we don't have any evidence of a crime."

Dick didn't like that answer but also had little to argue back with, at least yet. Instead, he asked for something that wouldn't cost anything. "I know I owe you some paperwork. But if it's all the same, I'd like to spend some time on this and see if I can track him down."

Peters nodded his approval. "Do that. If you find me something concrete, we can start applying some resources."

Dick spent the afternoon hunting for just that something. First, he was on the telephone, calling anyone he could think of that would still be in Sam's network. There was a call to his ex-wife, who was pleasant, but she hadn't spoken to Sam in months. She had remarried two years ago and had moved on. "We don't speak to one another often. The last time we did, we had a good talk, Dick," his ex-wife Amy said. "He seemed like he was in a better place."

He called other cops that Sam ran with back in the day, some still on the job, others retired. Nobody had heard from

Sam, but all promised to keep their eyes and ears open. Not wanting to alarm Nikki any more than she already was, he called DeNasty at Fireball for an update. There was still no sign of or word from Sam.

Dick opened his lower left file drawer, found the letter E on the green hanging files and pulled out a manila file folder labeled Luther Ellis. Nikki said Sam found something and all he had left to do was call Dick.

"With what? What did you find, Sam?" Dick muttered as he started flipping through the thin contents of the folder: the background on Ellis, his address, prison record and his own sparse investigation notes. Luther needed money. Sam said he thought Luther had gone to some people in his old life who had access to money, people he'd done time with out at Stillwater. In the folder Dick flipped to the picture of Neil Kline, the one name Sam had from Luther.

Kline went to prison for drug possession and intent to distribute. Both on the street and in prison, Kline had the reputation as an operator. Not necessarily a boss kind of operator, but more the profile of someone who was very useful, an excellent middleman who knew people and formed relationships. The prison record indicated that Kline was suspected of running contraband in the prison, but an investigation came up empty. He was released five years ago and completed his parole without incident and was running an auto repair shop on Rice Street.

The story Sam had told Dick was that Luther, in need of the money, went to Kline who referred him to some people who could extend him a loan. Sam said Luther got a loan and was in the hole, but then claimed he had something to hold over on the loan shark. "Hell, they might just forgive the loan," Luther reported to Sam.

It was now mid-August. It was early June the last time anyone saw Luther.

"I don't think they forgave the loan," Dick mused as he flipped through the file.

Sam had asked Dick to investigate Luther's disappearance, but the dead-end arrived quickly. With no body, no evidence, no witnesses and no timeline to work with, Dick had nothing to go on and other cases required attention. He moved on. As it turned out, Sam just couldn't let it go.

"What the hell did you get into?" Dick murmured to himself.

The picture of Kline stared at him as footsteps approached his desk. He looked up to see Peters, who had a small white slip of paper in his hand and a forlorn look on his face. "This is the address to a casting yard down on the Mississippi River in Cottage Grove. You best get down there."

"Why?"

"They just fished a dead body out of the river."

"And?"

"You just better get down there."

6

"LEOPARDS DON'T CHANGE THEIR SPOTS."

Dick held up his shield to the Cottage Grove officer manning the rolling chain link fence gate. The officer quickly checked the badge and then waved to another officer who pulled the gate open. Dick motored through and drove toward the collection of flashing lights. As he put his car in park he peered to his left at the group of people milling around the medical examiner's wagon. When he reached the gathering he found Cottage Grove police officers, Washington County sheriff's deputies and then his good friends, St. Paul Detectives Pat Riley and Bobby Rockford. When he saw Riles and Rock, his heart sank. The news was bad and his captain knew he would need friends at the scene.

Seeing Dick arrive, Riles and Rock approached his car. "It's Sam, isn't it?" Dick asked Riley.

"I'm afraid so," Riles answered sadly. "Dick, Sam was—"

Dick pushed past Pat before he could finish and walked toward the body, zipped up into a black nylon body bag lying on a stretcher, ready to be lifted into the coroner's van. He approached the county medical examiner. "He was my old partner and a good friend. He was a friend to all of us," Dick added, gesturing to Riley and Rockford. "May I see him?"

As Riles and Rock gathered around him, the medical examiner solemnly nodded and slowly unzipped the body bag to the halfway point and pulled the sides open. Sam's face was almost unrecognizable and farther down, there were three gunshot wounds on the left side of his chest. Dick looked up to the medical examiner. "Tell me."

The examiner took a breath and folded his arms. "It looks to me like before he was shot, he was beaten and beaten badly. The trauma, the bruising and cuts around the face in total and the mouth in particular, is extensive. I just briefly examined the inside of his mouth and he is missing several teeth." The doctor unzipped the bag a little farther and pointed to Sam's swollen hands. "Look at the bruising and swelling here."

Shead's hands were mangled; no two fingers pointed in the same direction.

"Tortured?" Dick asked.

The medical examiner nodded. "That's a possibility. Looks to me like all his fingers are broken and who knows what else. You'll also notice what appear to be ligature marks around the wrists. There are similar marks around the ankles."

"Restrained?"

The medical examiner nodded. "It would seem so, Detective."

"How long has he been dead?" Riley asked.

"I'm not sure on time of death yet, but based on the overall condition of his body, he hasn't been in the water *that* long," the medical examiner answered.

"He was last seen Thursday morning around 1:30 a.m., so

that gives you your time window," Dick replied and then nodded to the doctor, who re-zipped the bag.

"I'll start right away, Detective," the medical examiner stated. "I'll call you as soon as I have something."

With that the medical examiner pushed the body into the back of his truck and was ready to leave for the lab.

"Where was the body found?" Dick asked.

Riles and Rock led Dick to the shore of the lake. "Straight out in front here is what is known as Baldwin Lake. It stretches across to that long run of shoreline over west, which is actually an island. If you look south, you can see all those boats. They're floating in what is the wide opening out to the Mississippi River, which traverses north on the other side of the island. If you look up to the right here to the north, in those thick trees you can just see the start of a narrow channel that also leads back to the Mississippi."

"This is really all part of the river then?" Dick asked.

"Yes," Rock answered. "This area here is designated as a lake but it's really just all Mississippi."

"And where was the body found?"

"In the water near the shore of the island across the lake. A couple of guys out fishing were casting for bass in the little coves of the island and saw the right arm of Sam's body caught up in the branches of a tree that were hanging down into the water."

Dick nodded. "So he was abducted somewhere, interrogated, beaten, shot and then dumped in the river."

"Weird, though," Riles replied, offering some analysis. "If you go to all that trouble, why not weigh the body down enough so that it isn't found?"

"Maybe whoever did this tried that," Rock answered. "And failed."

They both looked to Dick. "Do you have any idea who might have done this?" Riles asked.

"I might," Dick answered tersely, "But first I have to go see someone."

Felix always made a point of having a man monitor the police scanner. When his man heard about a body reported in the Mississippi down in Cottage Grove, he immediately reported it. Forty-five minutes later Jorge, Tito, Felix and Mr. White were back on the boat.

"Dammit," Felix bitched quietly as he watched the recovery efforts to the north through his binoculars.

"You said the body bag caught on the side of the boat?" Mr. White queried as he observed the body being pulled out of the Washington County Sheriff's rescue boat and placed onto a stretcher.

"On the cleat and...I don't know, maybe it ripped a hole in the bag. It was a big body and we had to place extra weights in the bag so he'd sink to the bottom. With the weights and his body, it was damn near three-hundred-fifty pounds of dead weight."

"But you saw the body go under?"

Felix nodded. "Yes, right under so I didn't really give it another thought."

They gently drifted with the light river current a comfortable distance away amongst some other pleasure boats out enjoying a beautiful August Friday afternoon.

Felix dropped the binoculars from his eyes, went to a cooler and grabbed two beers. He set one in the cup holder near White and opened the other for himself. It was warm out and the cold beer tasted good going down, contrasting with his dour mood.

"My friend, this may be somewhat problematic," White mused an hour later as he continued to observe the festivities through his own set of binoculars.

"How so?" Felix asked, sitting up in his chair with his beer in his right hand and putting the binoculars back up to his eyes with his left.

"Look to the shore there by the casting yard and the group of men."

"I see them."

"Do you see the shorter round man in the brown suit with the bald head?"

"Yeah," Felix answered. White watched as the identity registered with Felix. "Is that Lich?"

"Yes, I think so. Shead was his friend."

"So?"

"*Soooo*," White replied with calm annoyance, "I think he will investigate the death of Shead quite vigorously."

Felix, while visibly irritated the body had been found, was not at the same time overly concerned with the possible ramifications. "Let him investigate, there is nothing to find. Whatever Shead saw he's taking to the grave with him."

"He gave you nothing despite the harshness of your methods?"

Felix nodded. "Nobody could withstand that punishment and not give up what he'd seen or who he'd told about it. I've never beaten someone like that before. He told us everything he knew, *everything*."

"And he told nobody of what he witnessed?" White asked.

"No," Felix answered, shaking his head confidently. "He told nobody. He repeatedly said he had this Lich guy investigating the disappearance of Ellis. But other than that, he hadn't told nobody anything."

"Ellis," Mr. White mumbled tersely. "That should not have happened, him seeing the operation at the house."

"That's why I made Orr part of handling it," Felix answered. "It was his mistake that brought this attention to begin with."

"And Shead told nobody else of what he saw at the house?" White persisted in asking, still skeptical.

"He didn't have time. He saw what he saw a little before midnight and we had him in our hands by 2:00 a.m. The only place he went after watching our house was to Fireball."

"The bar?"

"Yes. He works there and he and the owner had a thing going."

"Sexual?"

"Yes. Fireball was the only place he went and he was there for a very short time."

"And you interrogated him on that point? He said nothing to the people at that club?"

"I spent a lot of time on that very subject, *a lot of time*. I'm telling you, he said nothing. Said he spent twenty minutes making plans with his girlfriend for the next day and that was it. We took him down fifteen, maybe twenty minutes after he left there. He spoke to nobody else. We examined his phone. He made no calls after we saw him up on that hill. We recovered his camera and therefore the pictures he took. None of the pictures were downloaded to any other device. His truck is at the bottom of the Mississippi another fifteen miles downstream. We have his computer from home and have searched it, including his e-mail and there is no mention of anything relating to us, our operation, Neil or Terrence."

"Still," White stated with concern, "this Lich, as you may recall, did at one point pay a visit to Neil after Ellis went missing."

"He did," Felix replied flatly. "Neil gave that detective nothing and he never came around again." He dropped the binoculars from his eyes. "And you know why? Because there is nothing to be found. Luther Ellis is gone and he will not be found. The police have nothing on Neil. Now that Ellis and Shead are gone, they also have nothing on Orr."

"They have Shead's body, though."

"Which is a complication I'd have obviously rather avoided, but they'll find nothing on him. There will be no trace evidence on his body. We were very careful. Anything on him that was not washed away by the water will tell them nothing of where he was or who did it to him."

"Still," White responded, pulling the glasses down from his eyes, "we have much invested here after all these years."

"What's your point?"

"Nothing can be found."

"Nothing will."

"And if it is?"

"Then," Felix replied quietly, "I'll deal with it like I always do."

Dick pulled up to Fireball to find Mac waiting for him. "Thanks for coming."

"I'm sorry about Sam."

"Me too," Dick replied sadly, looking down to the ground and gathering himself before he went inside. "Me too. Look Mac, I had a thought about something on the way over here." Dick explained his concern.

"Given what you told me over the phone, a similar thought had occurred to me," Mac replied. "Do you want me to handle that part?"

"Would you?"

"Not a problem."

Dick had called ahead to BTG to let him know he was coming with bad news. As such, Nikki and her friends were waiting for them inside her office. Mac distanced himself from the group, leaning back against the wall, his hands in his pockets, while his partner delivered the news. In a case like this, the go to phrase *I'm sorry for your loss*, didn't quite seem to cut it when you were breaking the news of the death of your good friend and old partner to the woman he loved. It was all Dick could do to keep *himself* together. Mac watched Nikki as Dick gently described what happened. Her expression said she knew what the outcome was going to be, but knowing it was coming didn't make it any less devastating.

"I knew it, Dick!" Nikki cried as she stepped up and into Dick's arms. "I knew it! I knew it! *I knew it!*"

"I'm so sorry, Nikki. I'm so sorry," Dick whispered quietly as he hugged her tightly. Her friends gathered around as well, offering support, gently rubbing her back as she sobbed.

After a few minutes, Nikki pulled away from Dick and wiped the tears away from her face. Denise led Nikki over to the couch. Her oldest and best friend put her arm around Nikki's shoulder while Nikki leaned her head in. The room remained quiet for what seemed like several minutes, everyone deep in their own thoughts.

"What happened to him?" Nikki finally asked. "Dick,

what happened? How did he end up in the Mississippi River?"

"I don't know yet," Dick replied quietly and then looked up, "But I'm thinking it had something to do with Luther Ellis. You said Sam was going to call me. That had to be because he saw something that he thought related to Luther's disappearance. However, he must have been spotted and drew the attention of someone and ..." His voice drifted off. "He obviously didn't see them coming."

"Dammit," Nikki replied shaking her head, dabbing her eyes with Kleenex. "I should have ... I should have told him no, not to do it. That damn Luther was no special friend," she wailed bitterly. "He was trouble. I knew he was trouble. I should have put my foot down. I should have told him to keep his ass here at work."

"Nikki, Nikki, how could you know?" DeNasty murmured, putting her arm around her boss. "How could you know all of that?"

"I just...should have. Because it was Sam. I knew it was trouble. People don't just vanish and if they can make one person disappear, they can make another person disappear. But I thought—"

"He knew what he was doing," Mac finished the thought for her.

"Yes," Nikki replied, starting to cry again. "I knew he was still bothered by that damn thing, by Luther just up and disappearing. He would bring it up from time to time. He was just bitter about it, that these people just made him vanish like it was no big thing." She looked to Dick. "He even said he'd talked to you about it."

Dick bowed his head as if in shame. "Nikki, we did talk about it and I did investigate Luther's disappearance, but I had nothing to go on. I tried to explain that to Sam and it got heated. In fact, we hadn't really..." Dick started to choke up. "We hadn't spoken since," he said in a hoarse whisper, trying to keep his emotions together.

"No, no, no," Nikki replied sternly, "Do not take any blame for this, do you understand? He understood, Dick. He wasn't mad at you. He knew the limits of what you could do."

"But Sam wasn't a cop," Mac suggested. "So he figured he could explore it himself without the constraints of the law."

"I think so," Nikki replied, her eyes closed, trying to breathe in some air. "And it got him killed."

"Yeah," Dick added, "I think it did."

"What are you going to do about it?" DeNasty asked sharply.

"I'm going to do my job," Dick answered. "And do it better."

"Nikki," Mac asked, doing the favor Dick asked for. "That last night you saw Sam, what was it he said again?"

"Nothing really, other than he needed to call Dick."

"Did he give you any names?"

"No."

"Any locations?" Mac pressed. "Did he tell you where he'd been? Towns, roads, anything?"

"No."

"No details whatsoever?"

"No, none," Nikki answered.

"Has there been anyone unusual hanging around since you last saw Sam? Whether here at Fireball, at home or anywhere else?"

"No."

"You're sure," Mac pressed. "You're absolutely sure?"

"Yes. Why?"

Mac looked to BTG, Heavy G and then Denise before returning his gaze to Nikki, "Listen, all I can say is that Sam must have witnessed something he wasn't supposed to see. Something significant enough that caused them to grab him not long after he left *here* that night. And after he was taken, he was interrogated. *Harshly*." Mac let that hang in the air for a moment. "Nikki, that's why I was asking if he said anything beyond that he needed to call Dick."

"No," she replied shaking her head vigorously. "He didn't say a thing other than that. I swear."

"You're sure?"

"Yes. Now why are you so insistent?"

"Because whoever this is took out a cop. He was an ex-cop to be sure, but he was one of us. Taking out a cop takes a certain kind of ruthlessness and if they weren't concerned about the ramifications of that and are worried about what Sam saw, heard or witnessed, they wouldn't hesitate to take out anyone else who he might have told about it."

"Oh my gosh," Nikki murmured, putting her hands to her chest. "You think we're—"

"In danger?" Mac answered. "Possibly. The most obvious people Sam would have talked to were the people in his life he was close to. The four of you in particular were the most important people in his life in recent times."

"What do you suggest we do?" BTG asked, sharing a wary look with Heavy G.

"Look, I've been working this through my head and I think if they were going to come after any of you they would have done it already, but we just can't be sure of that," Mac answered coolly. "So for the time being, nobody goes anywhere alone. You hang together. If you see anyone that doesn't look right, you call Dick or 911. If you see anyone paying unusual attention to the bar, where you live, or if you sense you are being followed, you call Dick or 911. If after you close for the night, anything seems amiss in the morning, you call." Mac looked to the bouncers. They were good-sized and knew how to handle themselves physically he suspected, but in this case that didn't matter. "Listen, you two big guys, if anyone is inside the bar and you're getting the vibe they're trouble or paying too much attention to Nikki, you two keep an eye on them but you call for help. Don't take these guys on. Do you two understand?"

BTG and Heavy G nodded.

"And you all stick together," Dick added again. "Watch each other's backs. Keep your guard up."

"We will," BTG answered. "I'll make sure of it."

"Nikki, in addition to your guys I would strongly suggest you hire some extra security, at least for a little while," Mac suggested. "I know an ex-cop who owns a security company that employs all retired police or military officers. They're discreet and professional, they won't interfere with your nightclub operation, but they'll also provide a couple extra sets of trained eyes and they know how to handle themselves."

"Do you think that's really necessary?"

"Yes." Mac took out his cellphone. "I think it would be wise for you to hire them for a week and have them watch your back and those of your good friends here."

"Okay, I'll do it."

While Dick and Nikki's friends consoled her, Mac made the initial call and arrangements. Coleman Private Security was owned by Fred Coleman, a former St. Paul cop. Coleman knew Sam Shead, was on the force with him and was more than happy to watch over Nikki for a week. "At whatever price she can afford, we'll make it work." Coleman arrived within an hour with another man and went to work.

Between Coleman running security, BTG, Heavy G and the rest of Nikki's crew looking after her, Mac and Dick decided it was time for them to leave. It was 9:40 p.m., the sun having long since set when they walked out the back of Fireball. As they walked into the parking lot, Mac appraised the mental state of his friend.

Mac knew Sam Shead professionally and by reputation, but not personally. While saddened by the death of a former police officer, it was not a shock to his system like it would be if something had happened to Dick, Riles or Rock. However, for Dick, it *was* that kind of a shock.

"Listen, why don't you go home and be with Dot?" Mac suggested. "Riles and Rock are monitoring things down in Washington County. You can regroup with them in the morning."

"No," Dick answered, shaking his head. "I love her, but Dot is not what or who I need right now."

"Okay. What is?"

"What I need right now is to have a drink to Sam and figure out what I'm going to do next. I have to nail these bastards, whoever they are."

"Then let's go to my house," Mac suggested. "Because I can tell a bar with people is not going to be the place for you."

Upon arrival, the two made their way immediately down to the basement and Mac's bar. Off the back shelf Mac grabbed two thick, substantial tumblers, broke open a bottle of Hudson Bay Bourbon Whiskey and poured them each a drink.

"To Sam," Mac said, offering his glass.

"To Sam." Dick replied and then took a long drink, exhaled and sighed, "Ohh, that is so smooth." He took another sip. "That is so, so smooth. Back in his drinking days Sam would have loved this."

"My motto is if you're going to drink booze, drink good booze," Mac replied, savoring the whiskey. "Hudson is good bourbon."

"I love the motto, I just don't have your kind of money to live it," Dick answered.

"I know you don't, nor do Rock or Riles," Mac answered. "So when I get you guys down here, I make sure I have liquor like this for you."

"That's what friends do," Dick replied, extending his glass.

"Damn straight," Mac answered, clinking glasses with Dick before downing the rest of the glass.

While Mac poured another, Dick said, "You were my partner, but before you, Sam was. He was my partner for a long time."

"I know," Mac answered. Dick was in a personal funk when Mac was assigned to him. Over time Mac realized the funk was due, at least in part, to Dick having lost his long-time other half. Dick eventually worked his way out of it, particularly as he and Mac got to know one another and became close friends.

"They tortured him, Mac," Dick muttered, staring down into his glass and its light brown liquid. "They *tortured* him. They beat him until he couldn't respond. He experienced a lot of pain, *agony* before they shot him, three to the chest, right to the heart, and I'll bet at very close range." Dick closed his eyes and slowly shook his head. "I should have worked it harder."

"You should have worked *what* harder?" Mac asked, only knowing bits and pieces. "What is this really all about?"

Dick gave Mac the background on Sam and Luther Ellis.

"Luther just up and disappeared, Mac. He was just gone. There one day and gone the next."

"No trace? Nobody saw Luther get taken, abducted, shot, anything?"

"No. He just vanished without a trace." Dick explained where Luther lived, which was on the blue-collar rough and tumble east side of St. Paul just northeast of downtown and what he was doing to help people beat drugs. "I mean, he was probably going around to street corners where the dealers work. I talked to some of those guys. I wasn't sweating them, I just talked, asked if they'd seen Luther."

"And what did they say?"

"By the time I went around to the corners and typical drug locales, he'd been gone something like ten days. Nobody had seen him, heard from him or heard anything about him."

"Nobody disappears without someone knowing something," Mac argued. "Someone knows the explanation, the why, the where, the what of it all."

Dick shook his head. "One guy I talked to, I remember his street name was JuJu. A little guy, but chatty. You could tell he'd been in the drug game for a long time, understood the rules, the hierarchy and his little place in it. He said Luther was a good guy who knew the game, but had seemed to say *fuck it* to the rules and didn't seem afraid to stir up some trouble. To get in someone's face about drugs, buying, dealing, addiction, all of that. Luther claimed he knew what was going on and who was responsible. He was becoming *too* disruptive."

Mac shrugged. "Same old story. Someone does that and they end up dead. News at eleven."

"I'd typically agree. They kill you and make an example

of you. But then JuJu said something that indicated the game was being played a little different."

"Which was what?"

"This JuJu said there wouldn't be a dead body. He said that was old school, drop a body somewhere where everyone could see and it made a point. Don't cause trouble, don't rock the boat and keep your mouth shut or end up like Luther. But JuJu said that doesn't happen anymore. He said instead now people just up and disappear."

"Disappear?" Mac asked and then instantly got it. "If you drop a body, that brings attention."

"That's right," Dick replied. "It used to be the case in the drug scene that there would be beefing about territory and you ended up with gun play and bodies. Now that will still happen from time to time, but not like it did say, five or ten years ago."

"Dead bodies are bad for business," Mac suggested. "So you just make the body—"

"Vanish," Dick finished. "No body, no evidence of murder, the problem just quietly goes away and the same message is sent, just a little more subtly and quietly."

"How long has that been the case?" Mac asked. "Where guys are here one day and gone the next?"

"I asked JuJu that question and he wouldn't answer it directly. He just said it seems like guys you get used to seeing are suddenly gone. That's all he'd say."

"So maybe that explains Sam," Mac suggested. "He was doing something in probing Luther's disappearance that made someone uncomfortable and they decided to make Sam gone by first interrogating him, then killing him and finishing the job by dumping his body in the river." But then he had a question. "I wonder why his body just didn't end up at the bottom of the river?"

"I don't know," Dick replied, slamming the rest of his drink and holding his glass out. "I wish that dumbass would have let this Luther thing go. I don't know what the hell he was thinking."

"You've mentioned this name of Neil Kline. What's his story?"

"Neil Kline and Luther were in prison together. They both got clean together in prison and they became friends."

"When you poked around Luther's disappearance, I presume you questioned Kline?"

"I did," Dick replied, leaning back on his barstool. "But I did that really as a favor for Sam. I had nothing on Kline."

"What did Kline say about Luther's disappearance?"

"That he was worried about his old friend. That he hadn't seen him, that he hadn't been around and that he couldn't think of anyone who would want to hurt Luther."

"Luther had money trouble, right?"

Dick nodded. "And I asked whether Kline pointed Luther toward any guys who were in the business of loaning money. He pointed me toward three guys and before you ask, yes, I tracked them down and none of them claimed to have loaned money to Luther."

"You didn't have any leverage on them, did you?" Mac asked.

"No."

"Do you think those guys were telling you the truth, the loan sharks?"

Dick leaned forward and put his face in his hands and rubbed his eyes. "My gut says yes, but how would I really know? Kline, on the other hand, I think was genuinely remorseful about Luther. My radar says he's dirty, but I don't think he cares if I think that because I have nothing on him." Dick was so remorseful and buried in guilt, he couldn't see what he had.

"I disagree. You have more than you know. You're too close to it so you're not necessarily seeing what I'm seeing here."

"Enlighten me."

"Okay," Mac responded as he poured them both another drink. He then reached inside a drawer behind the bar and found a small notepad and pen. He started jotting down notes.

"We have Neil Kline, that's number one. It's time to start going deep on him. Number two, while nobody would have given two shits about an ex-con named Luther Ellis, now we have a dead ex-cop. Not only that, unlike Luther, in this case we have a dead body. It was found in the river. He was beaten. He was shot three times. All of that tells us something. It gives us a rough beginning and ending timeline. What happened in between? And can Neil Kline and the people that he runs with account for all of their time in that time window?"

Dick's mood didn't exactly brighten, but Mac had him sitting up and nodding now. "On Kline, my take is he's pretty smart. Don't you think he'll be expecting me?"

"I should certainly hope so."

"Yet you want me to go back at him? I still have no evidence."

"No, not yet you don't and I'm not saying tomorrow morning you go get in his face. But let me ask you a question. Do you believe in coincidence?"

Dick shook his head.

"Neil Kline is a player in this little story that's unfolding here, so he is someone you need to once again start paying attention to. You feel he's dirty, so he probably is."

Dick nodded. "I suppose you're right."

"And more importantly, if Kline was involved in this, it probably wasn't alone," Mac continued. "I mean, you looked at him. Is he the kind of guy who on his own takes down someone like Sam?"

"No way," Dick replied, head shaking assertively. "No way, no how. He's a facilitator—he's no killer."

"Who is he facilitating for then?" Mac prodded. "Leopards can't change their spots. Chances are he's working for someone doing something illegal. He must communicate with those people. You start watching, you start finding those people and once you know who they are, then you see who they talk to and run with. And all the while you start thinking of ways to leverage Kline and get him to talk."

"Put us between him and his bosses."

"Exactly," Mac answered. "It'll take you some time, but I think they're probably nervous right now. I guarantee you they did not intend for that body to be found in Baldwin Lake. They were trying to put Sam's body on the bottom and someone screwed up."

"And if we're watching—"

"Maybe you find out who the screw-up is."

Dick sat back in his chair and while a smile didn't cross his face, a look of hope did. And then he had a question. "Will you help me? I need you on this one."

Mac took a moment and then a long drink from his glass. "I can't promise you if this thing takes weeks I can see it through. *Buuuuut*"—Mac offered a small crease of a smile—"while I'm here, you know I'm in."

7

"HE SAW SOMETHING SO VITAL, SO SIGNIFICANT, THAT THEY HAD NO CHOICE."

They drank until Dick was slurring his words and resting his head sideways on the bar, drooling on the coaster for his glass. Mac muscled him from the bar over to the sectional couch, shoved a couch pillow under his head and tossed a fuzzy blanket on him and went up to his own bed. While it was still dark thirty Dick got himself up, made a terrible racket stumbling around the dark kitchen and then was out the door. The disturbance awoke Mac and when it did, he realized he had a massive throbbing headache. Beer often left him full, but rarely hungover. Drinking nothing but bourbon—hangover. This time, it felt like someone hit him in the head repeatedly with a sledgehammer. He laid in bed for five minutes contemplating his options and then decided to get up.

He had a proven game plan for getting rid of the hangover. First, he went down to the kitchen and consecutively drank three large glasses of ice water. It helped hydrate him and wake him up. Second, between the second and third glass of water, he added two Ibuprofen. Finally, nothing helped purge his system of the alcohol like a morning run.

He dug out his old running gear, slipped on his running shoes and inserted his earbuds. Then he selected some lighter rock and took a long run to sweat the booze out of his system. And it was a good hour-long jog in the early morning August humidity, getting him out onto the St. Paul streets.

He enjoyed Washington and all there was to see and take in. He often took his morning runs along the National Mall and amidst the monuments, but for Mac, he'd take St. Paul any day of the week and twice on Sunday. As he ran along stately Summit Avenue, took in the bluff views while running south along Mississippi River Boulevard and then turned back east along Ford Parkway, he at once felt home and comfortable.

After a quick shower he dressed in a pair of new blue jeans, a cream-colored button-down shirt and a light brown Houndstooth sport coat. For now, he ignored the gun safe in the basement; he wasn't going on full duty, he was just lending a helping hand. Nevertheless, he was in early, entering the homicide offices by 6:30 a.m. as it was just starting to stir. Dick was in by 6:45, a massive gas station coffee in his hand, bloodshot eyes and a sour look on his face.

Dick opened his desk drawer, took out a bottle of aspirin and filled his hand. "My head. Why the hell didn't you stop me?"

"Like you were going to be stopped," Mac quipped in reply.

Rock and Riley arrived soon after and the whole group, along with Captain Peters, made their way up to Chief Flanagan's office by 7:00 a.m.

"Mac boy, how are you?" the chief greeted as they all came in.

"I'm well, Chief. It's good to see you, although obviously I wish under different circumstances."

"Agreed," Flanagan replied and then waved for everyone to take a seat. As he sat down behind his desk the chief did very briefly grin, happy to have all of his boys once again in the same room. "Mac, do you want your badge back yet?"

Every time he saw the chief there was the offer to come back.

Mac shook his head "Chief, I'd just like to give a hand if I can. I didn't know Shead well, but you all did and he was one of us, so I think that counts for something."

Flanagan nodded. "If you change your mind, or if the case dictates, you let me know."

"Yes, sir."

"What do we have?" the chief asked, first pointing to Riley.

"The autopsy is not yet complete," Riles reported, flipping through his notes. "We should have something later today from the medical examiner on that. Rock interviewed the two guys who initially found the body."

"They were slowly trolling the shoreline, north to south," Rock added. "They saw an arm caught in some branches hanging down into the water. They're the only witnesses thus far and beyond finding the body, know nothing else of use."

"Any idea what time or from where his body was dumped into the river?" Captain Peters asked.

"No, not yet," Rock answered.

"When was the last time someone saw Sam?" the chief asked.

"Around 1:30 a.m., give or take, Thursday morning when he left Fireball," Dick answered. "I've been to his townhouse and I don't think he ever made it back there." He related his visit to the townhouse and his findings. "We need to get a forensics team over there to see what they can turn up."

"Hold on for one second," the chief asked. "Do we know that Shead was taken here in the city? Is this our case? Should we even be investigating?"

"I think it is, Chief," Mac jumped in. "Sam told Nikki he was going home. If that's the case, I think it is safe to presume that Sam was taken somewhere between Fireball and his townhouse. Fireball is on the corner of Snelling and University. As I understand it, Shead's townhouse is just off White Bear Avenue in the Battle Creek area. Both are within the city limits. It seems wholly appropriate to at least begin an investigation to see what we can learn."

"So we think he was taken. Taken by whom?" Flanagan asked.

"We don't know," Dick answered. "But we have a person to at least start with and his name is Neil Kline." Dick explained what he knew about Kline, about Luther Ellis and Sam's interest in the two of them. "Luther Ellis went to Kline and not long after, he disappeared without a trace. It's as if he just vanished. Sam was poking around that disappearance and now he's dead."

"And it seems rather clear that whoever killed Sam and then dumped his body in the river was interested in seeing him vanish as well," Mac added.

"This Neil Kline...who is he working for and what illegal activity are they engaged in?" Peters asked.

"I think that's what we need to start trying to find out," Riles answered.

"Then get to it," the chief ordered.

Dick, Rock and Pat went back to their desks to start organizing the case. While they did, Mac took a quick moment to stroll around the homicide unit and say hello. Double

Frank and his partner Kurt Fisher were in and offering to help Dick with his case. Mac's cousin Paddy, who on occasion worked with Dick, was in and offered his assistance as well. Others were milling around murmuring and shaking their heads.

Then an old friend came into the homicide offices.

"Hoooollyyyy shit! Tommy Ortega, as I live and breathe," Mac exclaimed, sticking out his right hand. "What are *you* doing here?"

"I should ask you the same thing," Tommy replied in return with a big grin, dropping Mac's hand and giving him a big bear hug. "Good to see you, bro. What are *you* doing here?"

"Helping Lich with this Sam Shead homicide. But seriously, you're here in St. Paul? Why don't I know this? Last I heard, you were working for the police in Denver."

"I was, but my wife got transferred back here for her job three months ago. I was a homicide detective out in Denver so when I returned, St. Paul had a need that I could fill. It's good to be back."

"You know this guy?" Dick asked with a wry smile, tossing a thumb at Ortega.

"Do I know this guy? Only since I was ten years old. He's a high school buddy and football teammate, man," Mac replied. "He's a Cretin Derham-Hall Raider and a hell of a speedy wide receiver who, as I fondly recall, also knew how to work his way around a keg tap and fed me my first beer."

"Well, you gotta celebrate after victories don't ya? I mean, we were state champs, baby!" Tommy added with a big laugh. "This dude threw the tightest soft little spiral. Could drop it right in my hands. McRyan to Ortega for six. You could find that in the high school box scores in the paper most Saturday mornings. We couldn't be stopped."

A crowd gathered while Mac and Tommy reconnected, falling into old routines, jokes and stories. "My gosh, what's it been, man?" Mac asked in happy disbelief at seeing his old friend. "Five, six years?"

"At least," Tommy answered. "I missed the last class reunion, being out in Colorado and all, but like I said, I'm glad to be back."

"You want in on this Shead thing?" Mac asked, looking over to Dick for approval, eager to work with his old partner *and* his old friend.

"Yeah, it would be good to work with the *famous* Mac McRyan."

"Whatever."

"Nah, man," Tommy answered with a big grin, "I've heard the stories. You're a legend around here, bro."

"Legend?" Riles asked in mock disbelief.

"I think I'm going to be sick," Rock added with a groan.

"Enough of all that," Dick interjected impatiently, "Ortega, if you want in you're in, but I don't want to hear any more of this legend shit. His ego is big enough already."

Dick gathered everyone directly involved in the investigation. The case and evidence, which was far from overwhelming, was laid out on a long table. "First impressions?" Dick asked as everyone stood around the table evaluating.

"There is a lot of unaccounted for time between when he was last seen and when he was found," Double Frank stated as he unwrapped a piece of gum and slid it into his mouth. "It would help to narrow that window."

"He never made it home?" Fisher asked.

"No," Dick answered. "I checked his place out yesterday afternoon after his lady friend called me. He hadn't been home. His truck was not in the garage and I think his computer was taken. I did confirm with Nikki that he had a computer, so I think whoever took him got into the house and took it. Also, they may have taken a file or two out of his desk drawer and went through the papers on his desk. The bare essentials of a quick get in and get out search."

"But nobody remembers hearing or seeing anything at the townhouse?" Fisher asked, taking a sip of coffee out of his St. Paul Police coffee mug.

Dick shook his head. "His neighbors are retired types—in bed early, asleep late at night, hard of hearing—you know the drill."

"Shead didn't have a security system?" Ortega asked.

"Nah," Dick replied with a head shake. "He lived alone, didn't have a lot of valuables and I doubt he felt the need for the added security. That, and he had a Glock-17 and some knowhow in using it."

"Is the gun missing?" Riles asked.

"It wasn't in its holster that was hanging in the closet."

"No signs they took him at his townhouse?" Rock asked.

"None," Dick answered, "But a forensics team is being sent over to his place to see what, if anything, they can find."

"I'd get his financials," Mac suggested.

"What for?" Dick asked.

"See if he spent any money *after* he left Fireball. See if his credit card is still being used. What can it hurt?"

Dick nodded and looked to Paddy.

"I'm on it."

"We need to trace his steps after he left Fireball," Riles yelled from the coffee pot stand, filling his cup. "If he was heading home, how many likely routes are there to his townhouse? Maybe we can find his truck."

Rock went over to a file cabinet and pulled out a city of St. Paul map and put it up on a rolling cork board in the corner that he then moved over near the group. He put a pin on the corner of Snelling and University to mark Fireball's location. He put a pin on the board representing Sam's townhouse on the eastern edge of St. Paul in the Battle Creek neighborhood, a distance of six to seven miles. There were many ways he could have gone home with the only certainty being that he would have taken Interstate 94 east for much of the journey.

Double Frank exhaled and spoke for the group. "Lots of possibilities."

"Did you find Sam's phone?" Mac asked Dick, Riles and Rock. "Was it on his body?"

"No," Riles answered. "Medical examiner didn't find it on his body or in his clothing."

"I'm sure whoever took him took the phone," Rock added. "He was interrogated. Undoubtedly the people who did that checked his calls and texts as well."

"We should get someone over to his cell phone provider," Mac suggested. "Did Sam have the GPS turned on for his phone? If he did, that could give us some answers on the route he took home as well."

"Paddy," Dick ordered, "let's get on that too."

"Consider it done," Paddy answered, grabbing his notebook, now on the search for Sam's financial and cell phone records.

"Paddy, if you need to call either Kathleen Foote or Carol Johnson over at the county attorney's office. They know the drill and procedure on cellphone subpoenas," Riles suggested.

"If the GPS was on, that might give us an idea of where he was taken," Ortega observed.

"It could do more than that," Mac added and then looked to Dick. "He was tortured or at least we think so, right?"

"What's your point?" Dick asked.

"My point is this. He saw something so vital, so significant, that they felt like they had no choice. I'm hoping that if we get GPS, we may not only get the route he took home and perhaps the location of his abduction, but we may also get an idea of where he'd been spending his nights *before* the abduction and maybe get an idea of what the heck he saw. I mean, from what you guys described whoever did this to Sam beat the shit out of him to find out what he knew or saw, but I suspect also who he might have told about it."

"Is Nikki safe?" Rock asked. "I mean, if these guys..."

"Got that covered," Mac answered. "We have Coleman's guys guarding her. Although to your point, I think if they'd gotten Sam to give them a name or names, these guys would have acted by now. Nikki, based on what we know right now, may be the only person he talked to before he was taken. From what she's told us, Sam told her nothing other than he found something that he needed to talk to Dick about."

"Which was what?" Riles asked.

"Don't know," Dick answered. "He never got to make that call."

The group stood around the table for a few minutes having side discussions, all except Mac who just stood with his arms folded, deep in thought. After a few minutes Rock sidled over. "You're awfully quiet. What's going on in that brain of yours?"

Mac shook his head. "I don't have anything to hang my hat on, Rock, but I think you guys have some threads to pull on here. Kline, for starters."

"We should go drag that asshole in here right now," Rock growled.

Mac shook his head and playfully wagged his finger. "No, not yet."

"Why not? He's mixed up in this," Rock argued. Bobby Rockford was a blunt instrument. The big man believed in his ability to intimidate and was in the mood to exercise it.

"True," Mac answered, dropping himself down into and then leaning back in his chair, arms behind his head, "but you can do that anytime. Kline is not the target here—who he reports to is and if you watch him, he will eventually lead you there. And you know what? If he had some role in what happened to Sam, he's probably a little nervous that the body surfaced, so—"

"Maybe they're nervous," Rock finished the thought.

"Right," Mac answered. "You guys can drag Kline in here anytime you want, but in my opinion, it would be more useful to develop a little more intel before you do." Mac looked around the homicide unit. "A lot of folks are itching to help out on this. I say put them to work with some loose surveillance on Kline, start taking pictures, plate numbers, the usual and see what the computers belch out."

"What else are you thinking?" Riles asked Mac, suspecting there was more.

"What was it Nikki said? She said that Sam had to call you," Mac said, pointing to Dick. "That he found something that would help you with Luther's disappearance. Whatever that was, he saw it Wednesday night. Where was he and what the heck did he see? We need *that* location. Find that and maybe we figure out what he saw."

The group was working together, but since Shead was Dick's good friend, the guys were deferring to him.

"What are you thinking, Dick?" Mac asked.

"You're right about Kline. I've already talked to him so I'm a familiar face that he's apt to remember. Rock and Riles, you guys along with Double Frank and Fisher, team up and check him out. Maybe grab two more guys so you have numbers. If he is involved, he's likely to be looking around for the po-po, so rotate people through. I think you can pick him up at this address, which is an auto repair shop on Rice Street. It's where he works. It's a Saturday, so they'll be open."

"What are you up to?" Rock asked.

"I just got a text message that the initial autopsy is complete. Mac, Ortega and I are going to go see the medical examiner."

8

"AND WHO THE HELL IS THE AVOCADO?"

The medical examiner's office was a short five-minute drive to University Avenue, just north of downtown. Dick, Ortega and Mac were led back to the examination room. The doctor looked tired, having worked through the night, but he'd also known Shead back in the day and wanted to move quickly on the examination.

When they entered the room Sam's body was lying on the gurney, zipped up into a white plastic body bag. Dick froze in place and took a deep breath.

"You need a minute?" Mac asked quietly.

Dick shook his head, muttered, "No," and looked to the doctor. "Doc, what have you figured out?"

The medical examiner hesitated for a moment and then exhaled. "I found a few things and confirmed a few others."

"Don't hold us in suspense," Dick replied.

"It took some calculation, but based upon the water temperature of the Mississippi River and the body temperature, I think Sam Shead was killed sometime between 10:00 a.m. and 4:00 p.m. on Thursday."

"That's a sizable time range," Ortega remarked.

The medical examiner nodded. "It's difficult because he was in the water for some time so with the body and water temperature, it's a little difficult to pin it down more exactly."

"And we can assume they dumped him in the river then sometime after dark Thursday night," Mac deduced, taking notes of his own.

"What else, Doc?" Dick asked.

The doctor reached for a small plastic bag. "As I was conducting my exam and removing his pants and underwear, I found this small patch of fibers in the waistline."

Dick took the small plastic evidence bag and held it up to the light. He looked to Mac and Ortega, who were also peering. "What do you think?"

"Fibers. Light in color," Ortega observed, putting on his glasses for a closer look. "It looks like fabric."

"It does, indeed," Mac replied and then looked over to the doctor. "Is that...cloth...or canvas, maybe?"

"I was thinking canvas, or at least that was my first thought. I'm going to have the fibers analyzed. They're manmade, no doubt. They're not from the river."

Mac snorted. "I was going to ask in a minute, but I presume there is evidence he was restrained?"

"Yes, there are ligature marks around his wrists and ankles. He was tied up."

"Right, so these fibers could also be rope, perhaps?"

"Maybe," the doctor answered. "Lab should be able to identify it."

"On the rope thought," Mac pressed, "if it was still on the body and at his waistline, that would possibly suggest that when they dumped him in the water they had some sort of weight tied around him to get him to the bottom. Could they have tied the rope around his waist?"

The doctor thought for a moment and then shook his head, waving for them to follow him to Sam's body. The medical examiner opened the bag and reached for the hands. "He was restrained, but I think it was with a restraint of some kind, *not rope*. Look at the swelling around his wrists," The doctor unzipped the bag farther, "and around the ankles. If a rope was used there would be some gaps in the bruising. What do you see?"

"No gaps," Ortega answered first. "So a belt or a leather cuff, something like that?"

"That would be my thought," the doctor answered. "Whatever it was, it was *tight* to the skin."

"But whoever dumped the body in the river would have had to weigh the body down somehow," Mac speculated. "If not by using a rope and a weight, maybe a... body bag of some kind?"

"Put the weights inside the bag, zip it up and down it goes," Dick added.

"He was a big guy. It would require an extra hundred fifty pounds, maybe. I have him zipped up in a fairly heavy plastic bag here, but would it hold all that weight, floating down to the bottom of the river?" The doctor shrugged. "I don't know—maybe, maybe not."

"How about a heavy canvas bag, though?" Mac posited. "You use the plastic bags here, Doc. These guys could use whatever. They put the weight in the bag and down it goes, except the bag somehow fails and the body comes back to the surface."

"And these fibers are from whatever they used," Dick finished and looked to the doctor.

"Only one way to find out," the medical examiner replied. "We'll have them analyzed and I should end up with some sort of answer on that."

Mac had moved on and was looking at Sam's body. "Doc, what did they do to him?"

"Sam Shead was beaten repeatedly about the head," the doctor reported matter-of-factly. "To be honest, I think someone stood in front of him and bludgeoned him. They just beat him and beat him and beat him. And there wasn't a damn thing he could do to stop them. There are no defensive wounds whatsoever." The doctor walked back to his desk. "I do think that whoever hit him was left-handed, for what that's worth. The bruising is far more pronounced on the right side of Sam's face. The bruising is lighter on the left side."

"So," Mac suggested, having moved to the coroner's desk chair. "Punched him left-handed and then what? Slapped him with the back of his left hand?"

"Right. I think it's quite likely the puncher was left-handed. His right jaw and orbital bones are broken. He had eight teeth knocked out, all front and right side."

"What about his legs, Doc?" Ortega asked, leaning down, examining Shead's lower extremities. "Those look all mangled to hell."

"Both lower legs were shattered," the doctor nodded in reply. "To do that they hit him with something. A bat, a hammer, a crowbar, or something."

"They just beat the shit out of him," Dick stated angrily.

"They sure did," the medical examiner replied with a sad head shake. "After a while I think they did it just because they could."

"It wasn't just the head, either," Dick said, flipping through the report, "I noted bruising in the midsection as well."

"That's correct, Detective," the doctor responded. "He was hit and punched repeatedly in the abdomen. Detectives

—" He took his glasses off and shook his head somberly. "Sam was beaten to a pulp. His death was a very painful and unmerciful one."

"I'll say," Ortega muttered, shaking his head.

"Anything else?" Dick asked as he looked at his phone and furrowed his brow. "Excuse me, I need to take this call."

"You were saying?" Mac continued as Dick stepped away.

"When they were finally done they put him out of his misery. Three to the upper chest."

"And the slugs?" Ortega asked, jotting down notes.

The coroner reached for a folder on his desk. "Ballistics report says the gun was a Beretta. Parabellum slugs suitable for comparison if you find the gun."

"Thanks, Doc," Mac said and then looked to Dick. "What's up?"

"We need to go see Nikki."

A little after noon Nikki arrived at her bar. Coleman quickly inspected not only her office but took a quick look around the entirety of the bar. Given the all clear, Nikki went into her office and once by herself sat down behind her desk and turned on the computer. It wasn't but a minute later that she looked over to the couch. The old leather couch was one of her first furniture purchases after she'd made a dollar or two post-college. It was in her first house during her marriage. She'd kept the couch after the split from her ex-husband and moved it into her office.

She pushed herself up from the desk and sat down on the couch, leaned back against the cushions and closed her eyes, thinking back to Wednesday night and wishing she'd indulged Sam's desires.

The door creaked open and Denise poked her head in. "Hey."

"Hey," Nikki replied, not moving, closing her eyes once more.

It wasn't just Denise but also Leslie, Roux and Trish, waitresses and friends who'd been with her for years.

"Have you heard anything new?" Denise asked.

"No," Nikki replied quietly, lightly shaking her head.

"You sure you want to be here?" Leslie asked. "We've got this covered, boss."

Nikki opened her eyes and smiled. "No, honey—the townhouse is empty, quiet and feels cold. I can't take it. You guys are *here.* Here there at least might be a distraction. Here I can work on something and maybe...forget a little, you know?"

"Yeah," Roux replied, coming to sit down next to Nikki, taking her hand. "You know, we just wanted to say whatever you need, anything, you let us know. If it's watching your daughter, covering something here at the bar or running an errand. We'll take care of it."

"And boss, I have a bunch of food in the car for you to take home," Trish added. "Easy stuff you can pop in the oven or microwave."

Nikki leaned into Roux's shoulder. "Thanks, you guys."

"No sweat, boss," Denise added, coming to sit down on the other side of her. As she did, the cushions sunk a little deeper and from between them something popped up. "What's this?" she asked as she pulled up a small steno notebook.

"Let me see," Nikki replied as she flipped the notebook cover over and immediately recognized Sam's writing. His unique block styled penmanship with the soft felt tip pens that he preferred marched across the blue lines. There were just a few pages with notations, but the last page was dated August 8th, the last night she saw him.

"How did that get there?" Roux asked.

"I know exactly how," Nikki replied. "I need to call Dick."

Twenty minutes later, Dick, Mac and Ortega entered Fireball via the backdoor to Nikki's office. Nikki was waiting for them with Denise.

"What do we have?" Dick asked.

Nikki handed him the steno notebook, explaining how it was found. "It looks like his notebook, Dick. That's his handwriting."

"There's no doubt about that," Dick answered as he reviewed and flipped through the pages of the steno book and then handed it over to Mac, who along with Ortega, quickly did the same.

"I see one familiar name," Mac stated with a smirk.

"Neil Kline," Dick answered.

"Who's Neil Kline?" Nikki asked.

"It's a name Sam gave me few months ago," Dick sighed. "I suspected that when you told me Sam was still chasing after what happened to Luther. He'd been looking up Neil Kline again."

"Are you going to go after this Kline guy?"

"Nikki, honey, we're already on it."

"There are a few other cryptic references in here as well," Mac replied, nodding and then looking to Dick. "We should get going on this."

Once outside Mac was flipping through the pages again. "Sam wasn't exactly thorough in his note-taking, was he?"

"Oh, hell no," Dick answered with a chortle as he used the key fob to unlock the car. "I often wondered why he bothered to even carry a notebook."

"Well," Mac replied as he dropped down into the passenger seat, "he certainly didn't write them assuming someone else might have to use them. When you're on surveillance, if that's what he was doing, and you're watching from a distance you only have so much time to jot stuff down. How good was his memory?"

"It wasn't...what do you call it, like what that guy on the TV show *Suits* has—"

"An eidetic memory," Ortega finished.

"Right," Dick answered as he turned right onto University Avenue. "He didn't have that but, my gosh, he had amazing recall and always seemed to know exactly what to write down. He could interview a suspect for hours, end up with one page of chicken scratch cryptic notes and he could then type out everything the interviewee said, word for word. All he needed was a word or two and he could recall the whole interview he'd had with someone. But, as you said, the notes mean absolutely nothing to us."

"Well, it's just one or two-word phrases," Mac answered. "But there is more than nothing here, particularly on the last night. He has a notation for N.K., which I presume is Neil Kline. There is also a notation for a T.O. A license plate number for a Yukon and then a reference to 'The Avocado,' whatever or whoever that is."

"I agree, N.K. is Neil Kline," Dick replied. "I don't know who T.O. is."

"Well he has a notation for him. In fact, on the 8th, there are notations for Rogers, N.K. (2), T.O. (3), Black Yukon/dark rims and the plate number. Escalade/black (4) and 'The Avocado'."

"What do the parentheticals mean?"

"Number of people in the vehicle maybe," Ortega speculated. "You know, Kline arrives, he has two in the car with him, something like that."

"What do you think he was watching?" Dick asked.

Mac pursed his lips for a moment. "Some sort of meeting, maybe. I mean, otherwise why write down the attendees and number of attendees?"

"Who is Roger?"

"It's not an apostrophe for possessive, Dick. It's not Roger's. It could be Rogers, the city, maybe."

"That's northwest of Minneapolis, right? It's on 94 going toward St. Cloud?"

"Correct."

"That's just a little town, isn't it?" Ortega asked.

Mac shook his head. "Not anymore. It's a full-blown bedroom community now with all the bells and whistles. Lots of people living and lots of business being conducted up there these days. One of Sally's little nephews had a hockey game up in Rogers last year and I was home at the time so I went up and watched. I drove by chain restaurants, big box retailers, not to mention a boatload of monstrous warehouses to get to the very nice hockey rink. But ..."

"But what?"

"We have no idea if that's where he really was. I'm guessing based on one word that could be misspelled," Mac answered, holding up the notebook. "However, that said, we do have this T.O. and a license plate to go with it. That gives us another piece to focus on. Now, if we could just find his phone and if the GPS was on, we'd have an idea of where it was he was watching."

Dick's phone rang. "It's Paddy," he said to Mac and then answered. "Whatdya got? Uh-huh, okay." To Mac he grinned. "You're prophetic. Paddy's got Sam's phone records."

"And the GPS?"

"Turned on."

"Let me talk to him," Mac replied. Dick handed him the phone. "Paddy, run this plate number before we get back."

9

"AND THUS, A CRIMINAL CONSPIRACY WAS BORN."

The White Law Offices could not be found on the Internet, nor would there be a listing in the Yellow Pages. The firm nor White's name would appear in Martindale Hubbell, Avvo, FindLaw or any other type of legal listing, or even on the plain white modest clapboard house that served as his office. He operated a very private and extremely low-profile law firm as a solo practitioner with a legal practice focused entirely on the needs of a single client. There was no associate attorney, paralegal or secretary. Were legal services involved requiring public exposure, such services were discreetly referred to a select few local law firms which were comfortable with White's oversight and opaqueness.

The arrangement had worked well for the past number of years as the organization methodically expanded its operations. Sipping an espresso, Mr. White peered out the front window through a slit in the curtains and watched as the black Lincoln Navigator turned right into the narrow drive and pulled around to the widening of the driveway nestled between the back of the house and two-car garage. It was a different SUV each day. They controlled a fleet of SUVs that would make Hertz jealous.

A few moments later Felix came in the back of the house, a black duffel bag slung low over his left shoulder. He nodded to White and immediately dropped the bag on the desk. White unzipped the bag and silently marveled at the mass of cash inside. It seemed like more came through the office every day. Of course, it seemed like they were adding new revenue streams by the day; not only in the Twin Cities but in other places as well. More money to launder through the law practice, not to mention their other miscellaneous entities, and what wasn't laundered would be shipped back to Mexico.

White opened the double closet doors. To the left was the safe and to the right the long table with the money counter, similar to what they had out at the Rogers house as well. Felix took out each bundle and ran it through the machine. White would log the total on his computer spreadsheet. Once all the money was counted, the safe was opened and the money was stored inside, less what was needed for payroll. The men running the crews were paid a base salary in cash and then given cash to pay their crew. If certain thresholds were exceeded, cash bonuses were paid.

Felix was a generous boss if you were an earner. If you operated your area quietly and profitably, he took good care of you. If you didn't, he could be the harshest and most impatient of bosses, quite willing to send clear messages for others to hear. The two of them spent an hour counting out basic salaries and then bonuses for crew leaders getting it done.

Even though it was still early in the day, Felix went to the small credenza behind the desk, opened a drawer and pulled out the small bottle of Tequila that White kept for him. Felix poured a small amount into one of the glasses sitting by the ice bucket and knocked it back before pouring himself another glass for sipping. Their boss, Javier, wanted to talk and Felix was bracing himself for it.

White reached inside his desk drawer and pulled out a satellite phone case. Felix didn't waste any time taking the blame when the call started. "That damn body, it should have just stayed down in the water and we'd be fine," Felix moaned. "I'm sorry, cousin."

Javier took the news calmly. "There is nothing we can do about that now, it is done. My concern is what comes next? What's our containment strategy?"

"We monitor and we adjust," White replied evenly.

"What have you in mind?" Javier tested.

"We've made changes to our procedures."

"Such as?"

"We are walling ourselves off from our retail locations for the time being," White answered as he took a drink of his coffee. "Money is neither coming into them nor is product going out. We have made adjustments."

"We'll take a hit, though," Felix warned.

"Not much of one," White answered confidently to Javier. "We will not lose money doing things this way. However, our use of it in the specific ways that you and Helena want will be delayed is all."

"You think we need to do this?" their boss questioned.

White signaled Felix to reply. "Yes, cousin. This former cop had a friend on the force, a detective. He paid one of our people, Neil Kline, a visit some time back on that Luther Ellis business. Ellis was a friend of Shead. Now, you know

Neil and how valuable he has been to us in setting up and running our operation. To protect him we think it important to wall him off for now."

White picked up the thread. "What that means is neither of us will be paying any visits to Neil at the repair shop or, for that matter, to any of our other locations for the time being. If the police are watching we will give them nothing to see."

"And Neil will not be going to make pickups. For now, he's running his shop and that's it," Felix finished.

"You're going to make him a saint!" Javier observed with a chortle.

"No, Javier, just a bland citizen not worth a second look."

"Well, let us hope the police come to that conclusion. What if they don't?"

"Then I'll handle it," Felix answered darkly. "I will clean this up, cousin. That is how I will contain it."

~

Mac, Ortega and Dick made their way back into the Homicide Offices to find Rock and Riley looking over the shoulder of Paddy, who was stationed at his desk working his computer.

"What do we have?" Dick asked excitedly, throwing his suit coat over his desk chair.

"The license plate you called in from the notebook was for a black GMC Yukon registered to a Terrence Orr," Paddy answered, holding up a manila folder for Dick.

"That would be T.O. then," Mac noted.

"And is Mr. Orr a fine upstanding citizen?" Dick asked as he opened the folder.

"Ahh, that would be a no," Rock replied sarcastically.

"He did himself six years in Stillwater for aggravated assault," Riles added. "And take a big guess who was serving at the same time?"

"Neil Kline," Mac and Ortega answered in unison.

"*And*?" Paddy asked teasingly, looking up.

"Luther Ellis," Dick finished and then snorted, shaking his head as he flipped pages in the folder for Orr.

"Correct," Paddy answered. "Their time overlapped for nearly four years. Kline was in for about a year already when Orr showed up and was out about eighteen months before Orr."

"And thus a criminal conspiracy was born," Mac declared. "Sam Shead was following this Neil Kline character. Orr, or at least his Yukon, appears to be in the same place as Neil Kline that night. The question is, do we have any idea where that might have been?"

"Maybe," Paddy answered and everyone gathered around his computer. "I've been figuring out how to use this GPS tracking data from the cellular provider." Paddy began maneuvering his mouse, pulling up the data for August 8th. "I think I've kind of figured out how to do it," he added, making another mouse click.

"It's a little scary the phone companies have this data," Dick reflected. "It feels very Big Brother-like."

"Okay, I think I'm set here. Should we look at Wednesday night?" Paddy asked.

"Yes," Dick replied, "Where was he at seven?"

Paddy worked his way through the data and put in 7:00 p.m. as the time parameter. At that point in time Sam was stationary on Rice Street north of the Capitol building.

"Sitting in one place for that long, that's got to be surveillance," Rock noted.

"Neil Kline manages the auto repair shop one block to the north."

"He starts moving at 9:35," Paddy reported. The group watched as the data from Sam's phone showed him making his way in a loop around St. Paul. It started from Kline's shop on Rice Street just north of the state capitol building and downtown St. Paul, over to the east side with three different stops along Payne Avenue. Then he made his way south of downtown through the working-class enclaves along the Robert Street corridor. After that, he looped back northwest to the neighborhoods along West Seventh Street that rested southwest of downtown St. Paul before making his way onto the Crosstown Freeway into south Minneapolis.

"What was that, six stops?" Ortega asked. "All short, five to ten minutes."

"Pick-ups, possibly," Dick suggested. "Or drop-offs."

"Kline has a history in the drug trade, but let's face it, we're just *guessing*," Mac cautioned. "We don't even know for sure that Sam was even following Kline—we're just *assuming* based on his notes. It could be Orr he's following. And if it is Kline or Orr, another problem is that all these stops are in commercial areas with multiple businesses, so we don't know exactly *where* he's stopping. He could be dropping off dry cleaning, buying groceries and picking up takeout for all we know." Mac looked over to his cousin. "Paddy, in putting together your brief history on Orr did you get any idea as to how he operates? All I've seen is assault and some gunplay."

Paddy nodded slightly while maneuvering the mouse. "It's interesting you mentioned drugs. I contacted a buddy in the narcotics unit. Orr is a name they know, but more as muscle, not necessarily drugs. A friend in Vice checked, and

Orr is in their database. He's known to make loans and maybe run some girls."

"He's another operator then," Riles declared.

"Yes," Paddy answered. "But low profile."

"Criminals can learn," Mac suggested. "They can get smarter and when they do, they get much harder to pin."

"Loans. That might fit with the Luther Ellis angle," Dick ruminated. "Although Orr was not a name that Kline mentioned to me."

"Of course not," Riles replied. "Kline wasn't going to point the finger at his buddy, so he gives you names he knows are dead ends. I mean with Luther gone, who could possibly know otherwise?"

"Let's not get ahead of ourselves here," Mac cautioned. "However, given both Kline and Orr show up in Sam's notebook on the eighth, the possible connection between them is certainly worth a deeper dive," Mac added.

Paddy moved the mouse to restart the GPS track again. Shead now made his way out of St. Paul on Interstate 94 into Minneapolis, around the southern edge of downtown and then north on Interstate 94, exiting onto West Broadway and proceeding to make a loop through north Minneapolis with three stops that combined took a little over thirty minutes. By 11:30 p.m. Shead was back on 94 and his next stop was twenty-five minutes later.

"Rogers," Dick stated, looking to Mac. "You were right."

"Kline, Orr and then The Avocado," Mac answered.

"Do we have any idea what The Avocado is?" Rock asked, taking his turn at flipping through Shead's notebook.

"Nada," Dick replied.

"The infamous Sam Shead shorthand, huh?" Riles asked knowingly. "One word tells a three-page story."

"You know it," Dick answered, shaking his head.

"Again, we're assuming The Avocado, whoever or whatever that is, was identified in Rogers," Mac warned. "It's Sam's shorthand. He could have viewed this Avocado anywhere along the way."

"But Sam saw something significant *that* night," Dick countered. "Nikki told us that he finally had something for me, so whether it was in Rogers or somewhere along the way up there, Sam saw something that got him killed."

Paddy flipped computer screens and pulled up Google Maps for Rogers and the streets and roads used by Shead. "He drives through this area of warehouses and business parks. Once he's through all of that he comes to this intersection and takes a left turn, drives ahead for maybe a quarter mile and then he stops right in this area here."

"Which is where exactly?" Dick asked.

"It's just on this county road, or maybe just off it. The last dot puts him here just below the road. Maybe there is a street there not yet in the maps program," Paddy answered. "He stops right here. He goes no farther. To the south of his position is what looks like a new housing development. Then to the south of that development is a grove of trees and then the warehouses and office parks. To the west on that road is another housing development and then Rogers High School. To the north is a large plot of land with this house sitting in the middle of it. To the east it's pretty open, with some scattered houses and then this body of water is Diamond Lake."

"How long does he stop there?"

"A good hour," Paddy answered. "The GPS shows no movement for sixty-four minutes."

"More surveillance," Dick stated.

"I suspect so but hard to say. And what is he looking at if he is?" Paddy continued.

"We'll have to go and see," Mac stated. "Sixty-four minutes. Something there had his attention."

"What did he do next?" Riles inquired.

"After that hour he leaves this location, drives back the way he came through Rogers and makes his way back to I-94. His next stop is—"

"Fireball," Dick finished. "He went to Fireball."

"Correct," Paddy noted. "He arrives at 12:45 a.m."

Shead stayed at Fireball for forty minutes. The GPS data confirmed what Nikki and the others at Fireball reported. He was on the move again by 1:30 a.m. He departed the bar and drove south on Snelling Avenue and then turned left and took the ramp to east Interstate 94. He proceeded through what the locals called Spaghetti Junction where Interstates 35 and 94 converged and weaved through a tight canyon-like corridor on the northern edge of downtown St. Paul and remained on I-94 traveling east another five miles until he reached White Bear Avenue.

"It's 2:00 a.m. He's heading home," Dick noted. "You exit south on White Bear Avenue to get to his townhouse."

Once he exited White Bear Avenue, he motored two blocks south and then turned left onto Suburban Avenue, went a half-block and then stopped.

"He's making a run for the border. There is a Taco Bell right there," Paddy offered, pointing at the screen.

"How would you know that?" Dick asked.

"Seriously?" Paddy the carousing night owl replied in astonishment. "I know every fast food joint that is open at that time of night in St. Paul. Every. Single. One."

"He did always like his fast food," Dick muttered with a headshake. "I must have put on twenty-five pounds working with him. I still have those pounds."

"It certainly looks like an exponential return on investment then," Mac smirked.

"Wow!" Ortega roared in laughter at the cheap shot.

"Shut up, you little flat belly bitch," Dick retorted.

"Mac's just jealous he doesn't have the fine thick layer of protective coating we all have protecting our abs," Riles mused.

"Yeah, his abs are *dangerously* exposed," Rock added with a sneer.

"*Ahhh*, I see. So a constant diet of beer and chicken wings creates a thick coating of Kevlar," Mac retorted. "Who knew?"

"You're frickin' ruthless," Ortega remarked to Mac.

"They give as good as they get."

After the stop Shead proceeded east again on Suburban and then veered right onto Burns Avenue and then his movement stopped.

"That's it?" Dick asked, confused.

"That's it," Paddy answered.

"What's there?"

"Nothing," Paddy answered with a shrug of his shoulders, sitting back in his office chair. "It's a street, a wetland on the west side and a few daytime businesses to the east." Paddy sat back up and pointed to the screen and a small building. "That building on the east side is a dental office."

"And that's the end of the GPS tracking? It ends right there?" Mac asked.

"Yes," Paddy replied. "This is the last hit we get. There's no more data after that."

"That's where he's taken," Riles stated, pointing to the screen. "Right there."

"Let's go," Dick ordered.

Twenty minutes later they were all at the intersection of

Suburban and Burns Avenues. While the others scanned around the area, Mac and Ortega slow walked south on Burns Avenue. A half block ahead, Mac saw debris lying in the road and jogged toward it with Tommy close behind. Reaching the small field of debris, Mac crouched down, pulling out some rubber gloves out of his right suit coat pocket. The debris was a combination of broken white, yellow and black plastic.

"With all this debris, there had to be a collision here, right?" Mac asked, looking up to Paddy.

"I agree. That white piece of plastic looks to be for a headlight and that yellow piece sure looks like the plastic light casing for a turn signal." Ortega picked through the pieces with the tip of his shoe. "The black plastic pieces with that matte finish, those could be from a bumper. The pieces have been driven over for a couple of days here so they're crushed down pretty good."

Mac took a pen from his jacket pocket and picked through the pieces of debris. "There are a couple of sizable headlight pieces left here, though. These pieces that drifted closer to the curb over here."

Everyone else saw what Mac and Ortega were doing and drove over to them. "What do you have?" Dick asked.

"Something definitely happened right here," Mac answered, standing up and gesturing to the debris. "A crash of some kind."

"Let's see if we have any accident reports for here," Dick stated and went to his police radio. He was back a minute later. "Nothing on this street recently. Certainly nothing since Wednesday night."

"Guys, this is two different kinds of glass," Ortega added, still crouched down. "The yellow pieces of plastic glass have slightly different tints."

"Or one is dirtier than the other," Lich mentioned.

"Or older," Riles offered as another alternative. "Sam's Silverado was what, five or six years old?"

"At least," Dick answered.

"We've got some tire skid marks as well," Rock noted, stepping back from the group. "The vehicle, probably Sam's, was going southeast here and all of the sudden hits the brakes."

"And the collision is right here," Mac replied and stood up. He looked back to the northwest, traced the track that Sam's truck was taking, veering to the right onto Burns. He looked across the street from the collision site and into the parking lot for a dental clinic with a driveway to the right of the building that led to the parking lot in back and he instantly could see the set-up.

"Sam was being followed, probably by at least two, maybe three vehicles," Mac stated, walking across the street to the short driveway and then stopping and pointing back north toward Suburban Avenue. "He stops at the Taco Bell and at that point, they knew what we knew when reviewing the GPS data—that after he left Fireball he was heading home. So one vehicle is behind him, following when he pulls into the drive-thru at Taco Bell. Assuming they know his address, they know that once he pulls out of the drive-thru lane he'll turn left on Suburban and then veer right onto Burns here." Mac pivoted to his right and pointed to the dental office. "The second vehicle, probably a truck of some kind, rolls ahead and pulls into the driveway here for the dental office. The driver turns around, shuts off his headlights, and lays in wait behind the corner of the building here. You see the glass windows wrapping the entire corner of the building? The driver can look through the window and see the headlights coming. And when the time is right..."

"He accelerates down the short driveway and rams Sam right there," Riles nodded, pointing to the collision site straight out from the driveway to the dental office. "Sam didn't see it coming until it was too late."

"The trailing vehicle comes up and pins him from behind. Shead can't move," Ortega added.

"And the driver rammed him hard. He had to stop him," Mac continued. "And since Sam was rammed hard he's dazed, perhaps injured, so the men in the vehicles drag him out of his truck."

"And Sam's truck is damaged but probably good enough to drive away from the scene," Rock speculated. "At least good enough to drive away from here. They dumped it somewhere or its been turned to scrap metal by now."

"And they throw him into another vehicle," Dick said, picking up the thread. "And as they're pulling away from the crash site here, they get into his phone and shut off the GPS tracking." He took another look around the scene. "Okay, let's secure this area. We need to get a forensics team down here. Maybe they can make something of all of this debris."

"We should see if any of these businesses had security cameras operating," Paddy suggested and made a beeline for the dental office for starters.

Dick stood with Mac and Ortega at the end of the driveway and looked back north on Burns toward Suburban, then back to the side of the building and then farther to the south and shook his head.

Mac voiced what Dick was thinking. "For doing this on the fly, this was a really good spot. It's isolated here. There are no residences, just businesses, all long closed. You could ram him, get him out of the truck and move on with very minimal risk of being seen."

"Amateur hour this wasn't," Ortega added, hands in his pockets, shaking his head. "This was a well-executed takedown."

Dick scratched the back of his head. "What the hell did Sam see?"

"I don't know, partner," Mac answered. "But I think we need to go up to Rogers and find out."

10

"STANDARD BEHAVIOR FOR A CRIMINAL DOUCHE BAG."

They'd gotten more information on Terrence Orr, via Paddy and his contacts in the Narcotics Unit. While Narcotics did not have Orr under an active investigation, he was thought to be a player.

"That's a little different than before," Dick suggested as he opened a new file folder on Orr.

Paddy nodded. "I talked to *more* guys, particularly Weed and Martinez, who have the best street intel. They say Orr is seen around from time to time over on the east side where he apparently has accumulated a fair amount of drug real estate. Weed also said—"

"Hold on a second," Mac interrupted, shaking his head. "We have a Narcotics cop named Weed?"

"Well...yeah," Paddy replied with a little smile. "His last name is Weidenbacher. He's a buddy of mine, good cop, who just so happens to have a very apt name for his current line of work. In any event, *Weed* also talked with some friends over in the Minneapolis Narcotics Unit and they've seen Orr around on the north side in what used to be considered your old buddy Charlie Boone's drug real estate.

However, for the most part his home base is over here on the east side between Payne Avenue and Arcade Street."

"Orr has some history of violence to him," Dick noted, looking up from the file. "He did his prison stint for assault. There are also some other gun charges. Hell, he got expelled from Johnson High School back in the day for bringing a gun to school."

"He does," Paddy answered. "But then Weed said something else interesting."

"Which was what?" Ortega asked.

"Orr has all of this territory yet there have been almost *no* killings. The streets are very quiet and they have been for some time."

"That doesn't compute with a guy with this kind of history," Dick reasoned, not buying it.

"Do we have Détente?" Mac asked. "Maybe a truce?"

"I don't know about that," Paddy replied. "The guys just said that there haven't been any drug murders, no fights over territory. It's as if everyone is all getting along and singing Kumbaya, especially on the east side. And you know, despite what people see on the news about murder being up in areas around the country, that is not necessarily the case here. The body count is down."

"It's true," Dick added. "Business has been down from a homicide standpoint."

"You almost make that sound like a bad thing," Mac asked incredulously.

"No, it's not," Dick answered flatly. "All I'm saying is your cousin is right, business *is* down recently."

A copy of Orr's file made its way around the group. "I think Payne and Arcade must be home to him," Rock observed. "He went to Johnson. Payne and Arcade are his stomping grounds, his native habitat if you will."

"Which means he's likely got friends over there," Mac offered. "Friends who will be watching his back, and watching for *us*."

"The narcotics guys gave me an address for a small house he supposedly owns on Clear Avenue just east of Payne, that he's been known to lay his head at, but they also say he is pretty mobile, moving around from night to night," Paddy added. "He'll usually ride with a crew of guys. Word is he also sits at a table at The Payne Reliever and likes to watch the girls dance."

"We'll take the strip club," Riles and Rock volunteered in unison.

"I'm shocked!" Mac mocked with a big grin. "Just shocked. I'm sure if Orr is there the two of you will feel the need to conduct close-in tight surveillance from inside, to keep an extremely close eye on him."

"A perk of the job, baby," Rock retorted gregariously.

"To serve and protect, my boy. *To serve and protect*," Riles added merrily and then to Rock said, "let's go."

Dick ordered Cruz and Carson, two young and new detectives, to take the house on Clear Avenue. Mac watched as the two rookies lethargically departed. He'd noticed their almost sleepy looks while the group had been discussing matters and looked to Dick. "No offense, but those two don't look too bright."

"Most detectives when they first start out aren't—you included, by the way."

Mac snorted his disagreement.

"Arrogant much?" Dick chastised. "They'll get smarter looking...eventually."

As for Rogers, Dick wanted a closer look at the location where Shead stopped but also had a place to potentially find Kline. He assigned Double Frank and Kurt Fisher to the auto repair shop on Rice Street. "That's where I found him. That's where it looks like Sam found him. That's where you'll find him."

"It's Saturday night," Double Frank noted. "The place is probably closed."

"They have fuel pumps," Dick answered. "If he's not there, try this." Dick handed him a yellow sticky note. "It's a rental house that aligns with the address on his license. If he's not at the auto repair place, you might pick him up there."

While Dick briefed the chief and Captain Peters on the investigation Mac, Ortega and Paddy waited outside in the warm pleasant humid air of the early evening. It was a beautiful night, not a cloud in the sky. In Mac's mind August was Minnesota's best summer month. The heat and humidity of July was generally gone, yet the air was comfortably warm. Just a little stickiness remained during the day, but the nights were ideal to be outside or on the lakes. It would have been a great night to be out on the back patio, having a little bonfire and a couple of beers.

"How's Jenny?" Mac asked Ortega.

"She's great, just great. I texted her about you earlier. She says we have to have you over to see our new place."

"How about kids? How many do you have now?" Mac asked.

"Still just my son, Robby, although Jen is four months pregnant."

"Congrats man, to both you and Jenny."

"Thanks. How about you? Any kids?"

Mac shook his head and related his recent change in marital status. "Down the road we'd both like to have kids, so we'll just see."

"I love hanging with my boy," Tommy replied. "He's got daddy's wheels and his hops."

"I assume you have him playing something?"

Tommy nodded. "Basketball. He loves basketball and he's got a little game, even at nine. I'm six-foot, but you know Jen is five-eleven and she has brothers who are in the mid sixes. Robby is pulling from a very good gene pool. He's going to have some size."

"How about football?" Paddy asked.

Tommy winced. "I'd like that, but Momma has been reading about CTE so she's not too keen on that. I'm playing the long game there. You can pick up football later on when you get to high school, especially if you're a good natural athlete which I think Robby will be." He transitioned topics. "This Orr sounds like a guy we ought to be getting very acquainted with."

"Agreed," Mac answered, nodding.

"With Orr, if they find him do they take him in?" Paddy asked.

"It's Dick's call but ... what's the hurry?" Mac asked in reply. "I mean, what do we really have on him? What do we really know?"

"Not much."

"We have *less* than that," Mac replied. "All we have is his criminal file, prison record and the notations from Sam's notebook. It's not yet a compelling case. I'd rather watch him for a spell and see where he goes, what he does and who he talks to. I know this investigation is about finding Sam's killer, but Kline has a history in the drug trade. Orr is suspected to be in the drug trade, along with some violence to him."

"So?" Paddy asked.

"Shead was just trying to figure out what happened to

this Luther, but what if he stumbled onto something a little bigger than that?" Ortega asked.

Mac nodded his agreement. "Paddy, Sam Shead saw something that night he was *not* supposed to see. He wrote down Kline's name, Orr's initials and license plate number and 'The Avocado'. I find all of that very interesting. Dick, Riles and Rock are just more narrowly focused on simply finding Sam's killer."

"Mac, is that such a bad thing?" Paddy asked questioningly.

Mac shook his head. "No, not at all. All I'm saying is this might, and I emphasize *might*, all be bigger than just Sam Shead and Luther Ellis."

Dick pushed his way through the doors and everyone fell in behind. As they walked over toward Dick's car Paddy asked, "It's Saturday night. Do we really think anything will be going on up there?"

"Only one way to find out," Dick answered. "It could be the first of many trips up to the sprawling metropolis that is Rogers, Minnesota."

As they reached the car Mac stopped them. Dick had a black Ford Taurus with dark rims. The car screamed police, not to mention cramped discomfort. Mac looked over to Dick. "We need a different set of wheels tonight. Let's at least take my Lincoln MKX."

"You just require rich Corinthian leather at all times, don't you?" Dick needled.

"I'm willing to donate my private resources to the common good," Mac rejoined. "Bring your police radio along. Besides, I'm a *far* better driver and navigator than you."

"Nah," Dick replied with a snicker, "I just like it when you serve as my driver slash bitch."

"Finally, *finally* we reach the ultimate truth."

They departed downtown St. Paul a little after 8:00 p.m. taking Interstate I-94 west toward Minneapolis.

"This is a nice ride," Dick remarked as he perused the interior of the MKX, his first time in the car. "How'd you pick this?"

"Well, it's a long story..." Mac's last Minnesota-based vehicle, a Yukon, perished while he was working a case up in the oil fields of North Dakota. He'd taken the insurance settlement and purchased the MKX, fully loaded with every possible upgrade, because it was a little smaller and fit better in his snug St. Paul garage. That, and Sally liked driving it. He figured it could be her car, if and when they moved back. "And, if for no other reason, I just kind of liked those Matthew McConaughey commercials. They were odd, but cool. So I bit and went to check an MKX out and liked it. It's a comfortable ride, although it does make me feel like just a bit of a poser."

"If it makes you feel any better," Dick replied, "I've always thought of you that way."

"Of course, if I were a true poser I wouldn't have you in the passenger seat," Mac shot back. "I'd put Ortega or Paddy up here and dress up the look and stick you back behind the tinted glass."

"That hurts. That really, really hurts."

"Do you two always do this?" Paddy asked from the back, bemused.

"*Yes!*" they answered in unison while laughing.

It took them a bit over a half hour to make their way around the 94/694 loop through the cities and up to Rogers northwest of Minneapolis.

"It's still light out," Dick remarked, the sun still hanging in the western sky as they exited the interstate.

"Then we'll be able to still see a little," Mac suggested. Following the GPS coordinates, Mac motored through the warehouses, navigated the street through a small grove of trees and then past a development of high-end houses to his left before reaching an intersection.

"Take a left," Paddy stated.

Mac took the left turn, drove ahead and then started up a gentle hill.

"And...stop," Paddy ordered.

"Here?" Mac asked as he reached the top of the hill. "Right here? Really?"

Paddy looked left to the freshly paved street leading into the housing development that was under construction. "I bet he parked on that street to the left. Pull in there."

"*Okay*," Mac responded skeptically, turning left onto the new street and pulling over to the right side and parking.

Once parked, they all exited the MKX, took a long look around and were left to scratch their heads. "So he sat in this position, or at least his phone did, for sixty-four minutes?" Mac asked. "Doing what?"

"Yeah," Paddy answered. "That's what the GPS data says. I mean, I can show you..."

"No, I believe you, cuz," Mac answered. "It's just damn peculiar because it doesn't seem like there is anything around here to look at. This area is as benign as it gets."

To their south there was the development of higher-end homes under construction with perhaps half of the possible lots filled with finished houses, with the remaining plots in various stages of development.

"These big houses don't exactly look like places that would attract Kline or Orr," Paddy remarked.

"I'd agree," Dick answered.

As a group they walked out to the main county road,

then turned to their collective left and looked to the west, down the other side of the hill. On the south side of the road was another industrial park area with a mixture of offices and warehouses. On the north side of the road was an open field and then the local high school.

"Does he sit up here and look in on those warehouses?" Paddy asked. "I mean, they have to be a good half mile down the road."

"I know for a fact that Sam was a good photographer, had himself a top-end Nikon with a long telephoto lens, and that the camera was not at his townhouse," Dick reported.

"Still," Paddy mused, "it seems if that was his target there had to be a closer place to set up shop and observe without being seen."

"This isn't making any sense," Ortega stated, shaking his head and doing a three-sixty look around. "I mean, what is *here*? Nothing that I see."

Cover was the issue, Mac thought. Sitting parked on this part of the road with a camera or a set of binoculars and conducting surveillance would have left Sam exposed. It would have looked odd and again, what was it he would have possibly been looking at? Mac turned all the way around and looked back down the county road to the east. There were some interspersed homes visible on larger multi-acre plots of land. Farther to the southeast he could make out some blue water that he knew was Diamond Lake, but that was as far as a mile away. He knew that farther still down the road was a public golf course that he'd played back in the day. There just wasn't anything in that direction that made sense.

He turned back to his left and walked across to the north side of the road. From that vantage point he looked out over a smallish tree-line defining the property's edge and then an open field to a large sprawling two-story ranch-style house with a circular driveway in front of it, well-tended gardens and a cobblestone sidewalk. Mac glanced farther to his left and noticed a small cluster of four mature trees maybe thirty to forty feet off the road. Cover was an issue here on the road, but what if he went down to those trees? There seemed to be something of a path through the mix of high grass and buckthorn down to the tree grouping.

"Where are you going?" Tommy Ortega asked.

"To check something out," Mac replied as he made his way down the narrow trampled path running through ankle-high grass down just a slight incline to the cluster of trees, all mature oaks. In the center of the tree cluster there was a small bare clearing, a dirt patch of sorts. When he reached the edge of the dirt clearing, Mac stopped. Even in the fading light he could see there were markings in the soil. Footprints. Large footprints. Mac crouched down and took a small flashlight out of his sport coat pocket and illuminated the area.

The others had followed. "What do you see?" Ortega inquired.

"How big were Sam's feet?"

"Big. Size twelve, thirteen maybe," Dick answered as he looked over Mac's shoulder. "Big like those."

The view to the left would have been through two trees, up nearly ten feet in elevation to the road. Because of the arrangement of the trees and the elevation of the road, he couldn't have seen anything directly to the west. However, when Mac peered to his right, there was a wide opening in the trees that looked out over the field directly to the front of the large two-story house. Carefully, Mac made his way to the other side of the patch and he noticed three small circular markings in the dirt in a triangular formation, all perhaps a foot apart. "Tripod?" Mac asked aloud, illuminating the markings with his flashlight.

"Could be," Dick answered, nodding. "Put the camera on the tripod and snap away?"

"But the only thing to see is that house," Mac replied skeptically. He turned to his cousin and tossed him the keys. "Do me a favor. Go back to the truck and then grab—"

"The binoculars. Right," Paddy answered as he ran off back toward the MKX.

"Do you think this is where he was sitting?" Dick asked after a quiet moment of contemplating the view.

Mac shrugged his shoulders. "He would have cover."

"Yeah. He could park his truck on that street on the other side of the road, get in here and in the dark, he'd be pretty much invisible," Ortega added. "But what is so special about this spot?"

"Here you go," Paddy said as he returned with two pairs of binoculars, one pair night-vision and the other regular, along with a camera case.

Mac took the binoculars and raised them to his eyes, first scanning the house left to right and then the property beyond the house.

"What do you see?" Dick asked.

"I see a nice well-maintained house," Mac muttered in response. "Back behind the house is a dirt road that leads into the trees and I think I can maybe see a structure in there. It's tough, we're pretty much out of daylight."

"It could be a barn," Dick observed, using the night-vision binoculars. "I can kind of make out a corner of a building, maybe a barn."

Mac scanned back to the house. There were interior lights illuminating the main level, although the curtains were pulled over all the windows. To the right side was what looked like a multi-stall garage nosing out from the house to the east. There were two SUVs parked in front of the garage. As he panned farther to the east he followed the long asphalt driveway out to the property's far eastern edge and a tall iron gate, which was closed. In fact, Mac noticed that there was also a white-railed fence that surrounded the entire property. He moved his view back to the iron gate and made note of the surveillance camera perched high on the ornate archway, focused on the short driveway in front of the gate.

"It's Saturday night, pretty quiet," Paddy stated. "I mean, what is likely to happen?"

"Not much," Ortega answered skeptically.

"Let's sit for a while and see," Mac suggested as he took the night vision binoculars from Lich and did another sweep across the property.

Dick looked down to his phone. "Kline is on the move, Fisher says. Getting onto I-94 and heading...west."

"Maybe he's coming here," Paddy offered. "Then we'd know for sure what we should be looking at."

"Then I'd stand corrected if that happens," Tommy replied with a smirk.

Five minutes later Mac muttered, "We have company." He peered back to the east. Headlights illuminated the iron gate as it slowly opened and the large SUV pulled through the gate and took the long driveway, approaching the house and pulling in front to the circular driveway and stopping at the front door.

Once the SUV stopped, two men came out the front door of the house. With the front exterior lights of the house turned on Mac could make out some detail.

"What do you see?"

"Two men. One African American, the short one. The

other may be Caucasian or Hispanic. I think Hispanic, but hard to tell. Getting out of the SUV we have..." Mac adjusted the focus on the binoculars. "Three men. I make one Caucasian and two African Americans."

"What kind of SUV is that?" Ortega asked, not having binoculars.

"I think a Toyota," Mac replied. "And at that size it's probably a Sequoia."

The rear tailgate of the Sequoia was raised open. The two African American men who'd arrived in the SUV pulled black duffel bags out of the back and then the whole group moved inside the house and closed the front door.

"What do you make of that?" Dick asked.

"I don't know what to make of the duffel bags but...I do note two surveillance cameras underneath the eave. One directed toward the driveway and the other looks like it's directed toward the house."

"In other words, seeing who's coming and who's going," Dick thought out loud. "Any others?"

"Look toward the garage to the east. There is one hanging down from the eave, pointed out at the driveway and then..." Mac panned away toward the light pole that provided illumination for the driveway in front of the garage. "There's one up on the light pole, focused on the garage doors, it would appear." Mac followed the driveway back out to the iron gate and noticed that there too, along with the camera focused on the road leading into the property, was a camera focused on the driveway inside the property.

"Someone's watching."

"Yeah," Mac answered. "The more I look around the property the more the whole place just says go away."

"But do you think this is what Shead was looking at?" Paddy asked.

"I'm a believer," Ortega affirmed.

Mac and Dick shared a look and a nod.

"I think so, kiddo," Dick said. "I think so. So tomorrow or first thing Monday, I want you to find out who owns this house."

"I'm on it."

Five minutes later the front door opened again and everyone filed back out of the house. The five men chatted for a few minutes along the front walk before the three men who'd arrived in the SUV got back in.

"Can you get the plate on the SUV?" Dick asked.

"I'm trying to," Mac answered, adjusting the focus, but they were just a little too far away and at a difficult angle. "Maybe if he turns my direction when he leaves," he mumbled as the SUV pulled forward and turned hard left toward him. "Shit!" Mac bitched. "He turned so fast I couldn't even make out one letter or number."

"I can run back to your car," Paddy offered.

"No," Dick replied. "I suspect we might be back now that we know this is here."

They watched as the SUV took the circular drive and drove through the opened iron gates and left the property.

Dick's phone beeped again. He reached inside his pocket. "Fisher says Kline is on I-94 in Brooklyn Park, driving west."

"Let's see if he comes this way, shall we?" Mac suggested.

Ten minutes later they had their answer. It wasn't what they expected.

"Shit," Dick complained. "Kline passed the Rogers exit."

That didn't compute. "I wonder if he made Double Frank's crew," Mac stated. "If he had something to do with

Sam's murder he might be keeping a tighter watch on his six."

"Could be," Dick responded. "Or it could be he's off to someplace else. Let's catch up and find out."

They all hustled back up the hill to Mac's MKX. Mac started the engine and pulled forward, quickly accelerating. "How far behind are we?"

"Six or seven miles," Paddy replied from the back seat. "I'm on with Fisher. Kline is in his black Tahoe in the right lane, cruising five above the posted."

"I hope there's no cops around," Mac blurted as he burst into an intersection on a long yellow, the light going red as he was in the middle, turning left onto Highway 101. A minute later he was accelerating down the entrance ramp to west Interstate 94. He looked over to Dick. "Maybe clue in the Highway Patrol that I'm going to be flying."

"I'm on it," Dick replied and reached for his radio. A minute later, "You're cleared."

Mac pushed the accelerator down, watching the needle make its way past ninety before he eased off.

Paddy's information from the Narcotics Unit proved accurate. Terrence Orr was in fact sitting inside the Payne Reliever at a table in the corner and sipping a drink. When they'd located Orr, Riley ordered Carson and Cruz over from Clear Avenue as another set of eyes. Over the last two hours Riles, Rock and then Cruz had each taken a turn inside the club. For that time, Orr sat at his table conducting brief meetings with people who came in and then left while two of his men kept watch, keeping others away.

"Cruz says he's still at that table taking the occasional

visitor and then talking on cell phones that one of his goons hands him," Riley reported.

"And if he has a brain, it's a burner phone so once the minutes are up, they ditch it and there's no record," Rock answered. "Standard behavior for a criminal douchebag."

Ten minutes later Carson called, "Orr looks to be packing up."

Not a minute later, Orr and his two men came out the front of the Payne Reliever and jumped into an older model Toyota 4-Runner.

"What's with the old 4-Runner?" Riles asked. "I wonder what happened to the Yukon?"

"The 4-Runner probably belongs to one of the goons," Rock replied. "Let's see where he goes."

From the Payne Reliever, Rock followed Orr south on Payne Avenue and eventually onto Interstate 94 west. The group rotated the direct tail, keeping several vehicles back in the traffic. It was assumed by the group he was heading over to north Minneapolis, where it was thought Orr also had business. The 4-Runner skipped every exit.

"Now where do you suppose he's off to?" Rock asked as he passed Carson's unmarked sedan to take the lead on the tail.

"I don't know," Riles answered, equally confused. "Let me check in with Lich."

~

"Do we have a meet?" Mac asked, now only two miles behind the group tailing Kline. They were still on Interstate 94, but now well out into Minnesota farm country.

"Could be," Dick answered and then to Riley he said,

"Where are you now? Uh-huh...Uh huh...Okay...Keep us updated."

"Where?"

"Riley said Orr is just passing Brooklyn Boulevard, still driving west on 694."

"If they get to the 494/694 split in Maple Grove and Orr stays to the right toward St. Cloud, we'll know this could be something."

Five minutes later, Riley reported that Orr had stayed right.

"He could be on the way to the house," Dick posited. "He could be going to Rogers. Maybe we should have stayed."

"We could try and swing back," Ortega offered. "Go back to that perch and see what's what."

Mac shook his head. "Nah, something is up. Kline skipped Rogers. Twenty bucks says Orr will too."

"Give me two-to-one odds," Dick replied.

"Done."

Less than ten minutes later they had their answer. "Orr just blew past Rogers," Dick reported, dramatically handing Mac a twenty. "The rich get richer."

Mac caught the back end of the group just short of St. Cloud.

"Kurt, we're right behind you," Dick reported.

"Our boy is a quarter mile ahead, right lane, the Tahoe that's...signaling. It looks like St. Cloud is our destination."

St. Cloud sat a comfortable hour northwest of Minneapolis. A college town of nearly 70,000, it was best known as the home of St. Cloud State University. The city itself was sliced in half by the Mississippi River, with the downtown core such as it was, sitting on the southern side as the river meandered to the southeast. Five minutes, three street changes and multiple stop lights later, Kline had pulled into a parking spot in the heart of the downtown St. Cloud business district. Double Frank drove past Kline and made a loop to the right around the next block ahead, eventually settling into a parking slot in an open-air lot to the northeast with a view of the back of Kline's Tahoe.

"What's he doing?" Dick asked as they approached the street Kline had turned left on.

"He's sitting and waiting," Fisher reported.

"Ask Fisher if that's the street where you find The Red Carpet, The Press and Hubie's," Mac asked, digging into his fond memories of visiting St. Cloud in his college days.

"Affirmative."

"Okay, I have an idea." Mac passed the turn on the left, went one more block and instead turned right and made a loop back and around, eventually finding a diagonal parking slot a half block west of the street Kline was parked on. "Kline is parked right around that corner to the right."

"What's he doing now?" Dick asked Fisher again via the radio.

"The two of them, Kline and his driver, are just sitting there," Fisher replied. "The car is running, but they aren't moving."

"What's he waiting for?" Paddy asked.

"Two things maybe," Dick answered. "One, they might be trying to determine if they were followed and two—"

"Orr," Mac answered. "The question is which bar they're meeting in."

"You're the Encyclopedia of Minnesota Bars, what do you think?" Dick asked back. "Which bar?"

"The Red Carpet is a night club and skews younger," Mac replied. "I've been there many times, although not much since college. Orr and Kline might not blend in demographically. The Press is music, noise and again, plays to the younger set. Again, not a fit."

"And Hubie's?"

Mac paused for a moment, collecting his thoughts, "If memory serves, Hubie's is a straight-up blue-collar working-man joint. There is a bar in the middle with booths down either side." He bit his lip, thinking and then looked to Dick, whose expression told Mac he was thinking the same thing.

"Riles, where are you at?" Dick asked into the radio.

"We're two miles from the exit for 75, probably ten to twelve minutes from your location, if that's where we are indeed going."

Dick looked to Mac. "What do you think?"

"Hubie's," Mac answered, looking left, contemplating their options. He evaluated his own attire, along with that of his compatriots. Ortega was dressed in khaki pants with a blue and white stripe button down shirt and more casual dress shoes. Paddy and Dick were in suits.

"It would be better to beat them inside if they're being *this* cautious." He looked to Paddy in the backseat. "Reach back behind you. There should be an Under Armour golf pullover and white Titleist golf hat, hand those up." A sport coat wouldn't be the best look in Hubie's. A golf quarter-zip and hat might blend better. "Tommy, ditch your tie and sport coat and run your hand through the hair, mess it up a bit."

"Are we going inside?" Ortega asked as he pulled the knot on his tie loose.

"Yes," Mac replied as he put on his golf hat. Then he looked to Dick as he opened the door. "Text me if they go into The Red Carpet or The Press instead."

"What do you think?" Neil asked.

Jockey Mike, his driver, nodded. "I think *we're* good."

Neil surveyed the street and the people loitering in the area a bit more. This was the bar district for St. Cloud. It would allow him to blend in on a Saturday night. It would also allow anyone following to blend in. Was he followed? He didn't think so. Jockey Mike, born with eyes in the back of his head, didn't think so.

"Keep an eye out. I think we're good, but with all that has been going down, you just never know."

"I'm on it," Jockey Mike answered as Neil slipped out of the truck, pulled a baseball cap down low, and stuck his hands in the pockets of his blue nylon jacket as he crossed the street to the sidewalk for St. Germain Street. At Hubie's he pulled open the front door and stepped inside. The bar was about three-quarters filled. Patrons were generally in groups of three to four, either occupying the booths on the left or right walls or space around the long bar. Along the left side he spotted an open booth which he quickly appropriated. He ordered a Miller High Life from the waitress, scooped up a small basket of popcorn out of the nearby popcorn machine and then waited.

Ten minutes later, T.O. came into the bar, baseball hat pulled down low, hands in the front pouch of his hoodie.

"Why the meet up here?" T.O. asked after his whiskey arrived. "We couldn't meet somewhere in the cities?"

"I wanted an out-of-the-way place."

"Mission accomplished then, but why?"

"So we could talk alone."

"About what?"

"Listen," Neil started, looking down at the popcorn basket, "you need to watch your back. The police are investigating the Shead murder hard and word is that they think it may have something to do with that Luther Ellis deal. A detective named Lich came around when Luther went missing, asking about him, about his money issues and that apparently I was someone who could direct Luther to people who would loan him money."

"And you gave him my name?" Orr asked angrily.

"*No*," Kline replied calmly. "I pointed him in *other* directions. Your name never came up. But now one of their own is dead. Whether he was an ex-cop or not is irrelevant, he was one of them. And his old partner was this cop, Lich, who is leading the investigation. I gotta think they will be visiting me any day now. Now, I was nowhere near all that action, but that doesn't mean I won't feel heat."

"Ya telling me you're going to fold?"

"No," Neil answered with a small smile and shake of his head. "They have nothing on me. But you were involved and you showed up the night they took him down."

"So?"

"So watch your back. The people you and I both work for wouldn't think twice about doing you. And listen, the reason Luther had to go, the reason this Shead was poking around in the first place, was because *you* let Luther see parts of the operation."

"I didn't let him see shit."

"But he followed you, right? You let him follow your ass up to Rogers, did you not? That's how he got there to begin with, correct?"

T.O. shook his head bitterly because it was true. "What are you saying?"

"I think you might want to think about putting together some cash and getting out of town," Neil stated before looking down at his beer as a man passed their booth.

"Aw man," T.O. moaned. "Really?"

"Look, you're my friend and I owe you for watching my back in prison. Consider this me returning the favor. I could be wrong, but I see trouble coming for you. I think the reason they had you help on Shead *was* Luther Ellis. The reason Luther Ellis was an issue was because of you. I'm not ripping you, dude, I'm just explaining the reality. Luther disappearing drew Shead's attention. That's what started all of the dominoes."

The two of them sat quietly for a moment, each taking a moment to reflect.

"Look, T," Neil continued, "my point is that the police are poking around. It's only a matter of time before your name comes up. If the police get onto you, the people we work for will view you as a liability. We've seen what they do to liabilities."

~

Mac and Tommy Ortega were positioned on a barstool on the front right corner of the bar. Mac wasn't carrying so he ordered a beer. Ortega was so he ordered a club soda with a lime.

"Tell me a little more about wife number two," Ortega asked. "She works in the White House?"

"Yeah, her name is Sally Kennedy. She's a senior advisor to the President himself," Mac replied. "She works just down the hall from the Oval Office."

"Really? Tell me more about that."

"I do have to say it's pretty cool," Mac answered and started talking about Sally until Kline came in the front door.

"How'd you meet her?"

"She was the county prosecutor on a case I was investigating. We worked closely on the case—it involved the murder of a local television reporter and the prime suspect was Senator Mason Johnson. You remember him?"

"I sure do. That was your case, huh?"

"Yeah, Lich and I. Sally was the prosecutor. She was divorced about a year at the time, as was I. I guess we'd both healed enough and were ready to jump in and give love another shot. One thing led to another and the rest is history."

"You're happy? She makes you happy?"

"Very," Mac replied as Kline came in the front door.

"Here's asshole number one," Ortega mumbled while sipping from his soda.

Kline took a booth on the opposite side of the bar. Mac casually peered at Kline over the top of his cell phone while slowly nursing his beer. His quick appraisal of Kline was that he was cautious, maybe even a bit suspicious, constantly peering around the bar, looking for familiar faces or prying eyes.

"He's a little paranoid," Tommy remarked as he too pretended to read from his phone. "Eyes are darting everywhere."

Orr swaggered in ten minutes after Kline, dressed in all black; black hoodie, black jeans, black shoes and black ball cap. And as he sat down Mac noticed the small bulge in his lower back; he was carrying. "You see that?"

"Yup," Tommy answered. "He's not doing a good job of hiding it."

"I don't think he wants to."

"With conceal and carry, he doesn't have to." After a few more minutes of observation Ortega remarked, "Pretty animated conversation between those two."

Carefully, Mac took some video of Kline and Orr talking

while continuing to pretend to be engrossed in his phone. Given the dimmer lighting inside the bar he wasn't sure the video would be worth anything, but it was a little less obvious than taking pictures, although he'd quickly managed two of those as well.

He shot Dick a text: *Orr-Kline having drinks. Animated conversation. Orr strapped.* Then he sent Lich a copy of the video he'd taken along with two photos. Then his phone, sitting on the bar, buzzed and Sally's picture appeared on the screen. "Speaking of my wife," Mac stated with a smile, reading the display.

"It's actually not bad timing," Tommy replied with a sly smile as he sipped his club soda, checking out the screen as well. "And...hey, I've seen her on TV. That's *your* wife? Dude, seriously? Talk about out-kicking your coverage."

Mac laughed as he answered, "Hey, babe."

"Hey yourself," Sally answered. "Guess what? I'm on a plane to the Twin Cities."

"Now?" Mac asked, happily surprised. "Right now?"

"Yes, we got back to D.C. early. There were a couple of business friends of the President from the Twin Cities on the trip. They let me jump on their Lear back to the cities. We just took off so we'll be landing in about three hours. Can you pick me up?"

Mac checked his watch and assessed his situation. He was a bit tied up. "I think so."

"You *think* so?" Sally replied, surprised and then heard the noise in the background. "Where are you?"

"Let's just say I'm working," Mac replied quietly. "I'm helping Dicky Boy on something."

There was a laugh on the other end. "Are you playing cop?" she teased. "Are you engaging in a little surveillance or something?"

"Yes, in fact I am," Mac replied seriously.

"Really?"

"Yes," and then he added quietly, "as always, you have impeccable timing. I'm looking at my targets right now. Your call is helping me. Way to go, babe."

"You're having fun, I can tell," she stated, not joking this time.

"I don't know about fun," Mac replied, not admitting that the adrenaline was flowing. "It's keeping me busy. Plus, you remember a buddy from high school I've talked about from time to time? Tommy Ortega?"

"Yeah, football buddy. Why?"

"He's moved back here and is now a St. Paul detective and, even better, he's sitting right next to me working this with me. So yeah, maybe I am having a little fun."

"Good, I'll have to finally meet him then. But look, about this investigative detail, can you get off it in a few hours? I mean, I assume you're working for free." Then she spoke quietly, as if she'd turned away from someone or was cupping her mouth. "I bought a little something in Paris to show you. I mean, there's not much to it, but—"

"I will be at that airport to pick you up."

"I thought so," she cooed and then hung up.

"On her way home?" Tommy asked.

"Yeah, so these two assholes better not sit here all night."

The whole time he was talking to Sally he'd never took his eyes off Orr and Kline, as they continued to talk and the conversation wasn't light.

So what were they talking about that had them so animated? Could he get a better idea? *I'm not someone they recognize,* Mac thought to himself, *not with the beard, longer hair and golf hat. What do I have to lose?* He reached inside his pocket and took a twenty out of his money clip and held it up to draw the attention of the bartender, who quickly approached. "I'd like another Lonely Blonde."

"Wouldn't we all?" the bartender quipped with a smirk.

"That's way too easy," Ortega quipped. "And not even fresh."

"How many times a night are you using *that* line?" Mac asked the bartender, grinning. "Be honest."

"Obviously too many," the bartender answered with a shrug, guilty as charged. "Another Lonely Blonde coming right up."

Mac glanced to Tommy. "I'll be right back."

"Be right back? Where the hell are you going?"

"To get a closer look."

"What? How?"

"Watch."

Mac made his way to the left of the bar and the narrow walkway between the booths and the bar and walked unhurriedly, his left arm hanging low, the phone in his hand recording. He feigned being stuck behind one of the waitresses who was waiting for her drink order, two feet short of Kline and Orr's booth, holding his phone low, looking away from the two men yet listening in as best he could.

"I think you might want to think about putting together some cash and getting out of town," he heard Kline say.

"Aw man," was the reply of Orr.

The waitress moved out of the way and Mac had no choice but to keep walking past the booth.

~

"As your friend, I'm telling you that you need to think about that," Neil pressed. "If I were you, I'd think of taking a long vacation and immediately."

"Man, I'm not that liquid right now. A lot of my money is tied up."

"Seriously?" Kline asked, surprised. "Doing what you do, that's *not* a good idea."

"I don't want to do this forever, but you know me, I like to have some fun."

"The clubbing and all the women can only lead to trouble. I've tried to tell you that time and again."

T.O. exhaled. "Look, I know you have. I appreciate that. But right now, I don't have a lot of loose cash. I can put my fingers on maybe ten grand. But if I gotta get out of town, I need more, *a lot more*. Can you hook me up?"

Neil sat back in his booth and eyed up T.O. His friend was a protector in prison and on occasion, out of prison. But the man ran way too fast and loose. His danger meter never seemed to function. Seeing two or three moves ahead was not a tool in his toolbox. Orr thought helping with Shead would *gain* him favor with his bosses. Neil knew otherwise. Helping with Shead made him a fall guy if shit went sideways. T.O. didn't see that. "Look T.O., I'm saving too, but I can come up with a little something that will help get you going right now. I could get you some more later. What other sources do you have?"

T.O. sat back and folded his arms across his chest. "I have some loans out, four people, they're all past due and the points have been building. I've been thinking they needed a motivational intervention to get them to pay up."

Neil nodded and took a pull from his beer. "I know it's against your nature, but I'd take what I could get right now and call it good. Get that. I can probably scrape up ten grand for you by tomorrow night."

"Ten grand, that's it?" T.O. protested. "Neil, I ain't going to get far on that."

"It's a start," Neil replied calmly, wanting to help his friend. "Listen, I get you ten, you come up with another ten, you close some of those loans and it gets you on the road. You go call and collect on these others and put together whatever you can *for now*. This is just to get you out of town until we see how much the heat is going to be turned up. Who knows, I could be completely wrong and you're back here in two weeks and the worst thing that happened is you took a little vacation."

"I hate running so lean, you know."

Neil nodded in agreement. "I hear you. Look, let me get you ten, I can do that. How about I meet you at DeAndre's over in Minneapolis tomorrow night? Say 11:00 p.m.?"

"You really think they'll come after me? You really think they think I'm a risk?"

"I don't know, brother. I just don't know," Neil replied, shaking his head nervously. "But they were willing to take out Shead to protect business. To further protect, they may be looking to tie up other loose ends and from where I sit you, my friend, look like a loose end."

"That could be you too, you know."

Neil nodded. "Oh, trust me, I've thought about that, but they went to some length to keep me out of the Shead and Luther situations. The reality is, I'm more integral to their overall operation, so I think I'm good for now. However, the last month or two have me thinking a fresh start somewhere else might not be the worst idea."

"I can get out of town, but where do you suggest I go?" Orr asked. "I have some people down in Chicago."

Neil shook his head. "So do they."

"Then where?"

Kline shrugged and thought for a moment, taking a pull from his beer. "You know, I have some friends down south,

El Paso way. If I bail, that might be where I'd go. My friends down there, they can hook you up with some work. It's not a garden spot, but you lay low in El Paso for some time, let this all cool down and then maybe you can make your way back home."

~

Ortega smiled upon Mac's return as he went around the bar and scooped some popcorn out of the machine and then made his way back. "So Obi Wan, what did we learn?" he asked as he reached for some kernels.

"Orr's making travel plans."

"Hmpf," Ortega snorted as he nodded. "You don't say."

Orr left the bar first, with a little less swagger and a lot more worry, Mac thought. Five minutes later Kline pushed himself up out of the booth and made his way out the front door, peering around suspiciously every step of the way. Mac and Ortega waited until Dick sent word that everyone had pulled out of downtown St. Cloud and were on their way back to the Twin Cities before they made their way out of Hubie's. As they walked back to Mac's SUV, they listened in on the video Mac took when he walked by Kline and Orr's booth.

"Rock and Riles, along with Carson and Cruz are on Orr. Double Frank and Fisher are on Neil," Dick reported when they were both back in the MKX.

"Take a listen," Mac ordered Dick as he jumped into the backseat. Paddy was now behind the wheel.

Dick listened to the playback of what Mac recorded when he was by the booth.

"Kline is telling Orr to get out of town," Dick remarked. "Intriguing."

"That's right," Mac replied. "And there's one very good reason I can think of that Neil would tell him to do that."

Neil jumped up into the passenger seat for the Tahoe. Jockey Mike was nervously peering around the area.

"What are you looking for?" Neil asked.

"If anyone is watching us."

"Why?"

"Because I think T.O. had himself a tail rolling out of here. I saw what I thought was an unmarked police car pull out from back down the street the minute T.O.'s boys pulled away. I think there might have been a Ford Explorer that followed as well. It was dark colored, probably black with dark rims and it looked police. Big white guy in the passenger seat and an even bigger black dude in the driver's seat."

"I see," Neil answered as he sunk down in his seat and started checking the rearview and side mirrors. "What about us?"

"I *think* we're clean," his driver answered. "I've been looking and I haven't seen anyone else."

"Okay, just the same, let's watch carefully on our way out of here," Neil answered and then reached for his phone. "And I better warn T.O. he has company."

11

"THAT'S SOME REAL SOLID DETECTIVE WORK RIGHT THERE!"

Neil was right.

When T.O. thought about it, the wily Neil was *almost* always right. The police were indeed on him, but why? What did they know? He trusted Neil. He didn't really think for a minute that Neil gave him up to the police. However, for some reason, the police *were* on him.

But was it for Shead? For a while as he drove back into the cities last night he wondered if it was simply because of what he was doing with his crews on the streets. He had a lot of territory now, both in St. Paul and even a little in Minneapolis and that might have been what was triggering the sudden interest in him, although upon further thought, he doubted it. Dead bodies were what usually drew the attention of the police. However, he was under orders *not* to leave bodies. If someone had to go they could be dealt with but not *loudly*, unless otherwise approved and that sort of approval hadn't come in quite some time. Another crew violated that rule six months ago. That crew was now gone, albeit quietly and partially at his hands, and now he had their real estate. So he kept his guys quiet and just kept working and there'd been little attention from the police until now. If he was the subject of interest, Neil was right, the people they worked for could decide he was a burden they no longer wished to carry.

So it had to be Shead. That damn Luther. Neil might have been right about a lot of things, but one thing he was wrong about was Luther. Orr was getting the blame for Luther, but it was Neil who sent Luther to him in the first place.

He should have just said no.

Luther was a bad risk, a very bad risk. But they'd been friends in prison and that warranted some consideration, so he loaned Luther the money. Then when it was time to repay the loan, Luther couldn't come up with the money. He didn't beg for more time or looser payment terms. Instead he said, "I've been watching you T.O., you and those people you work for and that house up in Rogers. I've seen it all following you around." Luther had set him up.

T.O. went to Neil with the issue. "I think we have to do something about this."

Neil ran it up the ladder and a day later passed the word back that Luther had to go. "You know what to do."

The next day T.O. and his crew took Luther and disposed of him *quietly*.

Orr peeked through the shades. Down the street he could see the black sedan still parked a block away. It had moved twice, but was still on the same side of the street. He looked back to his left, up the street. He thought there was another unit that was watching earlier, but he couldn't spot that one right now. It still might be out there. Undoubtedly there would be a unit watching the back of the apartment building, although he had no visual access to determine who and where they were.

There was a stirring behind him. "Baby, what are you doin'?" the sleepy voice from the bed asked.

"Just go back to bed," he replied flatly as he reached for his cell phone. He had a way to handle this.

Sally's plane touched down at 1:30 a.m. and they were home fifteen minutes later. She had indeed bought a very little something and it had stayed on a very little time.

At 6:30 Mac's phone started buzzing. "Cripes," he muttered as he rolled to his left to see the name on the display. It was Dick. "Yeah?" Mac asked, lying flat on his back, his eyes barely open.

"Listen, Ortega and I just got in and sitting on my desk was the final autopsy report. There is some interesting information from forensics on the plastic glass shards from over on Burns where we think they took Sam. Are you coming in?"

Mac glanced to his right to Sally, who was awake and had rolled over and was now looking at him with half-open bedroom eyes. *God, she's beautiful,* he thought. "You know what, partner? You and Ortega are on your own for now."

"But..."

"But Sally's home and I haven't seen her in a week, so..."

"Is she lying right there?"

"No, she's in the spare bedroom, dumbass," Mac replied while Sally stifled a laugh.

"Say no more."

"I'll catch up with you guys later."

Sally leaned in and kissed him lightly. "It feels good to be here," she said happily as she draped her right arm across him.

"These days I feel like we're having this scandalous long-distance relationship where we get to secretly meet maybe every couple of weeks in some out of the way hotel."

"Like we're having a naughty tryst?"

"Exactly," he replied, wrapping his right arm gently around her. "I really kind of miss having you around on a day-to-day basis, if you know what I mean."

Sally laughed. "Sorry, nature of the job right now."

"I understand," Mac replied quietly. "It doesn't mean I have to always like it."

"I don't like it...either," Sally answered seriously, softly caressing his chest. "Once a day I wonder if I should have said yes to this. I mean, all joking aside about scandalous secret trysts and all, this is hard on you. On us."

"Don't. Don't wonder," Mac answered. "Look, when you took the job at the White House I knew what that meant. When you accepted this promotion I knew what it meant. And what did I say to do?"

"Take it," Sally responded quickly. "You didn't even hesitate. You said it was a once in a lifetime opportunity that I had to take."

"Right," Mac answered, "I don't want you worrying about me or us, because both will be here when the mid-terms are over and when the first term is over. I'll be here and we'll go from there."

She leaned up and kissed him. "Thanks."

He laid his head on the pillow and lightly ran his fingers over Sally's back.

"What are you helping Dick with?"

"Just a case, a homicide. Do you remember a detective named Sam Shead?"

"Yeah, vaguely."

"He was murdered," Mac answered and quickly

explained the case. "He was Dick's partner before me. They were close friends and I know Dick is thinking if he'd have pushed harder on this thing the first time Shead might still be alive. So Dick asked me to help. What could I say?"

"And you're back in action."

"Yeah," Mac replied a little indifferently. "It's okay."

"Just okay?" Sally asked, sitting up. Upon a brief moment's study of Mac's expression and tone she immediately understood. "Oh wait, I get it. You're not running it. God, you are such a control freak."

"*I know, right?*" Mac readily agreed, fully acknowledging his own character flaw. "I've been accustomed to being the boss. Now I just offer suggestions and insight, but nothing is *my* call."

"You were in the bar on surveillance."

"Yeah, because I took Ortega and we bolted inside before Dick could really think about it. I just decided we were going in."

"And that's why you were excited."

"Excited?" Mac asked, not following.

"Oh, trust me, I could hear it in your voice last night," Sally replied, a little grin on her face. "There was an excitement in it. Like you were back in the game—you were operating, as you like to say, and when you're doing that you feel—"

"Alive," Mac finished the thought. "I did get a little rush, I suppose. And working with Ortega is just so unexpected. It is so good to see him. It's like we haven't skipped a verbal beat, you know, falling right into our old joking routines. He's such a happy-go-lucky, lively person and that's a...good thing for me to be around. Keeps me loose, kind of like Dicky Boy does too."

"You need that."

"Yeah, I do. So working with him, Dick, Riles and Rock, it's like old home week. I just wish all of that didn't involve investigating the death of Dick's friend. Getting the rush in that situation feels kind of...not quite right."

"Are you going to keep helping?"

"I don't know, we'll see," Mac answered. "It all depends, I suppose."

"On what?"

"How long are you here?"

Sally sighed. "Unfortunately, only until about 4:00 o'clock today. Then I'm on a plane back to Washington for two days for around-the-clock meetings with Judge Dixon on the mid-terms and then back out again. I'll hopefully, and I emphasize hopefully, be back in D.C. next weekend. I should be home for about a week and then we're gone again for eight or nine days on a trip to Asia."

"Really? I was hoping you'd be around tonight."

"What's tonight?"

"I have this dinner for that investment opportunity McHugh and Forbord are getting me into that I told you about. We meet the other investors, do the social hour thing, have dinner. It's at the Minikhada Club over in Minneapolis. I was hoping you could come. Most importantly, I wanted to show you off. Secondarily, I wanted you to suffer through one of these dog and pony shows like you make me do."

"Sorry, you know I'd love to," Sally replied disappointedly.

"I understand," Mac replied. "So basically, what you're telling me is I have you for about the next nine hours and then who knows when."

"That's right," Sally replied as she rolled fully on top of him, leaned down and kissed him lightly. "So what would you like to do with the time?"

At 6:00 a.m. Dick was up, alert and back in early with Paddy and Ortega. Riley and Rockford were in as well, having begged off watching Orr a little before 3:00 a.m. for a few hours of sleep.

"Where's Mac?" Rock asked as he dropped himself into his desk chair, half awake, pulling the plastic top off his Styrofoam cup to let the air cool the coffee.

"Sally flew into town late last night so he's a little tied up for now."

"I bet he's tied up," Rock replied with a sly grin and his deep rumbling laugh. "Is Sally the handcuffs type or more the leather straps around the bed posts Dominatrix kind of girl?"

"I'm not even touching that one," Riles replied with a smiling yawn and then he looked to Dick. "You're perky. What has you so fired up?"

"The forensics report," Dick answered, holding it up in his right hand. "You guys remember those plastic pieces we recovered over on Burns Avenue that we thought looked like a front headlight?"

Everyone in the group nodded.

"Out of those fragments and shards there were two slightly larger intact pieces. Inside one of them was a serial number. It's a match for a front headlight from a GMC Yukon. Now, what asshole currently under surveillance has a Yukon registered in his name?"

"Terrence Orr," Riles answered and then his eyes brightened a little more. "Ah, yet last night Orr was going around in that old 4-Runner."

"Could it be because the Yukon is currently out of commission and getting repaired?" Dick asked. "Plus, Mac and Ortega did a little slick sleuthing last night up in St. Cloud. Mac heard Orr and Kline talking, and it sounded like Kline was suggesting to Orr he leave town, so he's looking to run."

"Really?" Riles asked, eyebrows raised.

"Yup," Ortega replied, pouring himself a cup of coffee. "Orr did not leave the bar last night a happy camper."

"Are Carson and Cruz still on Orr?" Dick asked.

"Yes," Riles answered. "Ever since Orr's boys dropped him off last night at that apartment building."

"Give them a call."

A minute later Riley had them on speaker. "What's the situation there?" Riles asked.

"Quiet," Cruz replied. "Orr is still inside."

"Where? With who?" Dick asked.

"We think he's in a second-floor apartment that's rented to a woman he sees on occasion," Riles replied. "Word is she's one of the girls who dances at the Payne Reliever."

"And he's still inside?" Paddy asked.

"As far as we can tell," Cruz replied.

"Stay put," Dick ordered. "We're on our way over." Then to the group he added, "It's time to bring Orr in for a chat."

~

Neil had no hobbies and few outside interests. So while most people would avoid working on Sunday and taking a day of rest, Neil preferred the opposite, to go into the office. Often, on the way in to work he liked to stop at a small coffee shop along Rice Street a mile or so from the repair shop.

The lady working the order counter recognized him. "I

assume you want your usual? Two medium black coffees, room for cream in one?"

"Yes," Neil replied. "And I'd also like two breakfast sandwiches as well."

"Coming right up," she replied and then added, "by the way, your friend is over in the corner. He said if you came in I should send you over."

"My friend?" Neil asked questioningly. He glanced back to his right and viewed White sitting at the corner table with a newspaper and cup of coffee. Felix was with him, on his phone. He picked up his two coffees, took one out to Mike in the Tahoe and then came back inside.

"You couldn't meet me at the repair shop?" Neil asked quietly. He always thought it odd they never met at White's office. In fact, he had no idea where White's office was or where either of them lived.

White shook his head. "It's for your protection. If the police are watching we don't want to give them anything to see. You go to work, do your job and go home. They'll lose interest if there is nothing to see and no faces beyond workers and customers in the shop."

"Have you noticed anyone paying attention to you?" Felix asked.

Neil shook his head. "Not me. Mike and I have been watching and I think *we're* clean."

White picked up on the emphasis on *we're*. "You're clean? Who's not?"

"Nobody."

"*Neil*," White pressed. "Who's not clean?"

Neil sighed. "T.O.," he replied reluctantly, cursing himself for his verbal fumble. "I'm worried for him. I met up with him last night for a drink up in St. Cloud."

"Why St. Cloud?" Felix asked.

"An out of the way place," Neil replied quickly and didn't wait for a follow-up. "In any event, I went inside Hubie's while Mike stayed in the Tahoe and was watching outside. When T.O. left, Mike thought he might've had a tail on the way out of town."

"Did he see anyone? Any particular police?"

Neil shook his head. "He saw a car that followed T.O. that looked like a police sedan to him with two men in it and then a Ford Explorer, so two vehicles that Mike thought could be the cops. It could be that we're just being paranoid."

"I see," White answered casually, but Neil could see a fleck of concern in his eyes. "Did you tell Orr this?"

"Yes, I warned him that he might be being followed. I also told him it might be a good idea if he got out of town for some time."

"And what did he say to that?" White queried.

"He fought it at first, but then agreed and he's going to leave. I told him I'd help him with some cash so I'm meeting him later."

"How much are you giving him?" Felix inquired.

"Ten thou. Just enough so he can get somewhere and get started. He's pulling together what he can as well."

"I see," White replied and then his eyes drifted past Neil, who turned to see the lady working the counter approaching the table with a white paper bag holding the breakfast sandwiches. After she was out of earshot he asked Neil, "Where is Orr going?"

Neil shook his head. "I don't know. I'm sure someplace where he has some people he can trust, who can put him up and maybe get him some work."

White nodded, appeared to think for a moment and then looked over to Felix. "I think Orr leaving town for now is a good idea. We should help T.O. and add another ten to that."

Felix sat back and pondered for a moment before nodding lightly. "It probably is a good idea to get him out of here."

"Okay then," White said, turning back to Neil, "we'll get that for you and have someone deliver it to you at the shop. What time are you meeting him?"

"Tonight around eleven."

"Okay, someone will stop by the shop later today. Now, you better get going."

Neil nodded, picked up his coffee and sandwich bag and left. Once he was gone White exhaled. "The police are onto Orr."

Felix nodded. "I'm on it."

~

"What do you mean he's not there?" Dick growled, hands on hips, standing very close to young Detective Carson. "That doesn't work for me, Detective!"

"What do you want me to say? Orr's not in the apartment," the dejected rookie detective replied, head down, kicking at the pavement. "We went in and he's not there. I don't know what happened."

"Are we checking the other units?"

"Cruz is doing that now. But I don't think he's there."

"I thought you said the building was quiet?" Dick replied, stepping back and looking up at the three-story rectangular brick apartment building. "You said nobody was coming or going."

Carson simply nodded. "That's right."

"You're sure?"

"Yeah, I mean other than a refrigerator delivery there's been nothing."

Ortega, who'd been looking away, snapped his head back to Carson. "A refrigerator delivery? Really?"

"Yeah, just before Lich called a van pulled up and they unloaded a box for a refrigerator. A few minutes later they came out with another box and left."

Dick pinched the bridge of his nose. "On an early Sunday morning?"

"Yeah."

Dick shook his head and looked to Paddy, who instinctively knew what needed to be checked.

"Find the super and ask. I'm on it," Paddy answered. Ten minutes later Paddy had an answer. "The building superintendent says there was no refrigerator being delivered this morning."

"Of course," Dick answered and then glared at Carson, "because refrigerators don't get delivered at the ass crack of dawn on fucking Sunday mornings! You two idiots got made, and Orr pulls this weak-ass refrigerator delivery bit and slides out right under your noses. That's some *real* solid detective work right there." Dick disgustedly wiped his forehead. "Cripes, what next?"

"Sorry, Dick," Carson answered sheepishly. "We...we screwed up."

"Geez, ya think?" Dick answered, annoyed, with his hands on his hips. "Look, I don't want to hear about sorry. How about you find that partner of yours and the two of you go up and work over this chick Orr was banging and see if you can get a lead on where we can find him."

With his head down, Carson turned and walked toward the apartment building.

"Well, shit," Riles muttered. "Dick, Orr might have made

those two. He also might have made Bobby and me, so don't be too tough on them."

"Shit, I know," Dick answered, shaking his head, angry with himself for blowing his stack and upset at the fact Orr was gone. "But Orr might be able to close this thing for us and now he's in the wind, knows we're looking for him and he's already thinking of blowing town. Hell, at this point he might be as good as gone."

"Are we still on Kline?" Riles asked, leaning against his car. "I mean, if Orr made Carson and Cruz, Kline might have made you guys."

Dick looked to Paddy, who'd read his mind. "And?"

"Kline is at work," Paddy answered. "Double Frank is looking right at him."

~

"Thank you," Neil replied with a small courteous wave to a customer as he closed the cash register when two familiar faces entered the store. With a head nod, the two followed Neil back to his office.

Juan handed a white envelope to Neil. "This is from White."

Neil quickly checked the contents and saw the money inside in a mix of twenties and hundreds. It appeared to be ten grand. "Looks good."

"And there's one other thing," Juan added. "Mr. White and Felix want to make sure you're not followed. Here's what we're going to do."

~

Mac took Sally to the Sunday brunch downtown at the St.

Paul Hotel. After brunch, they drove over to Como Park, took a leisurely stroll around the lush green of the Como Park Conservatory and then later devoured a late lunch in the shade on their back patio. It had been a relaxing day; so relaxing in fact that in talking and catching up with each other they completely lost track of time and had to scramble to get her to the airport in time for her flight.

"So by Friday you'll be back?" Mac asked with a big smile.

"I should be," Sally replied, grinning. She then gave him the customary two kisses and was off to catch her flight.

While making his way back home from the airport he checked in with Dick.

"Are you still on Kline?"

"Yes," Dick answered. "Double Frank and Fisher and another unit are at the shop and Kline is inside. Problem is we're still hunting for that slippery son of a bitch Orr. Any chance you could help us on that?"

"I probably can later," Mac answered. "I have a dinner for this investment I'm getting into. I'll try to get out of it as quickly as I can and when I do, I'll call you."

~

"Is that the little driver guy for Kline?" Fisher asked, his hand draped casually over the steering wheel as he watched the small guy slip out the back door of the repair shop and get into the Tahoe.

"That's him," Double Frank replied as he sat up in the passenger seat and popped a Tic Tac into his mouth. "Kline should be out any minute."

"Or not?" Fisher replied with confusion as the little man

started the SUV and pulled away from the back of the shop. "Do I follow?"

"Is he by himself?"

"Yes."

"Follow him," Double Frank suggested while jumping on the radio to the other two-man crew watching the shop telling them to hold their position and report if they saw Kline.

Fisher and Double Frank followed the Tahoe as it motored its way down the familiar route to Kline's house. When the driver arrived there with the Tahoe, he was alone. He parked the Tahoe and then jumped into a beat-up Toyota Corolla.

"Stay with him," Double Frank ordered.

Ten minutes later they'd followed the driver to a two-story apartment building on Concord Street in South St. Paul. The driver parked and walked alone into the apartment building.

Double Frank reached for the radio and called to the unit still monitoring the repair shop. "Is there any sign of Neil Kline?"

"Negative. The lights are off and the shop is closed."

"What the hell?" Double Frank muttered, looking to Fisher.

"I think we just pulled a Cruz and Carson."

~

The dinner event started with cocktail hour at 5:00, followed by dinner at 6:00 and then an investment talk after. Mac arrived fashionably late at 5:30 and discreetly slid in the side door to the Lakeview Room and immediately went to the bar. Anticipating he might be catching Dick later, he ordered a club soda with a lemon and then stepped out onto the patio of the stately Minikhada Club. The country club, situated on a small hill west of Lake Calhoun and just southwest of downtown Minneapolis, provided for a panoramic view overlooking first its expansive private pool and then the sprawling beach and reflective blue waters of the lake farther to the east. If he pivoted slightly to his left, he had a remarkable view of the glistening modern glass skyline of downtown Minneapolis. As he sipped his club soda and soaked in the landscape there was a light tap on his left shoulder.

"I was getting worried you weren't going to make it," Mike McHugh greeted with a smile and handshake.

"You know me, this is not my kind of thing," Mac answered in a low voice, looking back inside to the clubhouse. "I mean, I see the who's who of Twin Cities wealth and finance is here."

"Indeed," McHugh replied.

"Isn't the tall guy with the blue sport coat and lime green dress shirt the new soccer team owner?"

"He is."

"And I see the billionaire trio is here—the Hendersons, the Grants and the Bergers, along with several from the trust fund brigade."

McHugh chuckled. "You've certainly noticed all the people who inherited their money. Although there are plenty here who've also earned it the old-fashioned way."

"I thought in this crowd inheriting it *was* the old-fashioned way," Mac retorted and then gestured to their right. "Who is the couple in the corner talking to old man Berger?"

"Oh, those are the Rosarios."

"The ones that own the Isla Mujeres restaurant chain?"

"Yes, Ernesto and Valeria. They are very nice folks."

"Sally *loves* Mexican food, particularly *their* Mexican food. We've singlehandedly made them millionaires. Too bad she couldn't have been here tonight."

As Mac scanned the room, by rough count he thought there were at least fifty different people mingling in the Lakeview Room. Mac considered himself quite comfortable, and by most any measure, wealthy. However, he well knew that his net worth was a small rounding error for pretty much everyone else in the room.

"I would have thought all of those White House and political events Sally drags you to that involve donors and whatnot would have made you more comfortable around moneyed folks."

Mac shrugged. "I've learned to make the small talk, smile at the right time, laugh at the lame jokes and do my duty, but it's really not my thing, you know."

"I do," Mike answered. "This has become mine and Kent's scene a little bit. We've gotten more accustomed to it. We've been let into the club, so to speak, but I don't view many of these people in the way I view you."

"And how is that?"

"As a good friend," Mike answered with a smile. "As for everyone else"—he gestured with his drink glass—"I'm useful to them, they're useful to me. I'm using their money and they're using mine and together we all hopefully do better."

"Hopefully."

"Kent's waving us over to that table in the corner. We should head inside."

Mike led Mac over to a table with four open chairs and they all sat down. Interestingly, they were being joined by the Rosarios, who took seats across the table. Mac ended up sitting next to a very attractive woman who looked vaguely familiar to him. She was perhaps in her mid-forties, dressed in an elegant black evening dress with her hair swirled up above large diamond earrings and a necklace.

"Gentlemen, I'd like to introduce you to Laura Peterson," Kent stated. "Laura, these are my business partners Mike McHugh and Mac McRyan."

When she shook Mac's hand Laura stopped and gave him an additional glance. "McRyan. Why have I heard that name before?"

"Probably his book," McHugh suggested. "He wrote a bestseller about a police investigation he was involved in during the last presidential election."

"Ah yes, I know the book," Laura answered with a wide smile. "That was you? You were a detective here once?"

"And he was also our third investor in the Grand Brew coffee chain," Kent added. "Mac's investment put us over the hump at that time."

"And Ms. Peterson," Mac replied, "you own the line of grocery stores. The Ready-Fresh Foods stores, right? My wife and I like to shop there."

"Yes, that's my company," she answered with a smile. "I'm so glad to hear you like it."

"It's the store brand items we just love," Mrs. Rosario piped in. "Truth be told, we wish we could sell some in our restaurants." She made a quick playful look around the room and then leaned in and said quietly, "We just love that Salsamole at home."

"My wife loves that stuff too," Mac added enthusiastically.

"I'm always glad to hear of satisfied customers," Laura answered with a big smile. "Thank you." And to the Rosarios she added, "You know, we could talk about getting that into your restaurants. We could both make out on *that* deal."

Valeria Rosario's eyes lit up. "Oh, we need to talk then."

With Mike and Kent there, Mac could unwind and enjoy the dinner and found the post-meal presentation interesting, informative and potentially lucrative. Their table, along with Laura Peterson and the Rosarios, also included another couple named Bourne, who turned out to be big Golden Gopher hockey fans. They recognized Mac's name from his University of Minnesota hockey days and that led to much of the dinner and post-dinner conversation revolving around hockey, a topic that was comfortably in Mac's wheelhouse.

"This really beats the political talk. I get so tired of that," Mac said in a massive understatement.

"I love hockey," Laura Peterson stated. "Of course, I was born and raised in Chicago, so I'm a Blackhawks fan."

Mac looked to Forbord with a smile. "And you let her sit at our table?"

"That's why I make sure I set aside my company's tickets for those games at the X," Laura added. "I go to four or five games a year and love it. The game is so fast."

"Now Laura, who do you go to those games with?" Martha Bourne asked. "Is there a Mr. Peterson?"

"No, there is no Mr. Peterson," Laura answered with a smile.

"A boyfriend, perhaps?" Martha persisted.

"Martha, seriously," Steve Bourne objected, "quit it, dear." And then to Laura, he said, "I must apologize for my wife. She's a hopeless romantic. If I didn't know better, she's thinking she has someone you should meet."

"Oh Steve, stop it."

"I knew it," Martha's husband replied and everyone had a good laugh.

Around 9:00 the party started to slow as people began to filter out of the Lakeview Room. "Mac, we're thinking of taking the group for a night cap. You care to join?" Kent asked.

Mac was thinking that sounded like a good idea when he checked his phone. A text from Dick had him slumping with an exhaled sigh. "Kent, I'd love to, but it looks like I have a friend who needs a helping hand."

12

"NOT A BANNER DAY."

After he snuck out in the morning, T.O. gave his two boys the day off once he picked up his repaired Yukon. He wanted the Yukon for traveling purposes; it was comfortable and it also contained a special hidden compartment for storage.

Discreetly, he made his way around St. Paul to collect on his outstanding loans. It burned him to no end to accept mere cents on the dollar, but if Neil was right, he needed to take what he could get on his four outstanding ones. He accepted what his clients had on them. He didn't forgive the balance as he expected to collect on the total at some point in the future; so as he said to one of his clients named Petey, "I'd suggest you keep socking it away. I *will* be back."

"What about the points?" Petey asked. "Twenty points, is that just going to keep going?"

"We'll call the balance fifteen grand and leave it there. You're paying me ninety-six hundred so you'll owe me the balance on the fifteen, but no more points."

"When are you going to be back?"

That was a good question, one for which he didn't have

an answer. But at least from the loans he was picking up twenty-eight thousand, four hundred in running money, which amounted to nearly seventy-percent of the total he had out. Add that to the ten grand Neil was delivering later and he was starting with a little over thirty-eight thousand.

It was a good starting point. However, T.O. didn't exactly tell Neil the whole truth the night before. He was plenty well equipped to run.

T.O. had watched enough of *The Sopranos*. Tony kept a stash and T.O. realized after his prison stretch and he started making some good money, thanks to Neil and Mr. White's hookup, that it might be a good idea if he started doing the same. However, he didn't have a dog kennel or garbage can or pool house floor to bury his cash in. He always thought those places were terribly insecure anyway, although they made for good theatre. Instead, he simply maintained a small storage locker which he visited once a week to make a deposit.

Inside the storage locker he kept a waist-high combination safe. Inside the safe were bundles of cash and two emergency credit cards along with three Berettas, his gun of choice. Next to the safe was a large duffel bag. Inside the duffel bag was a bulletproof vest, along with a sawed-off shotgun that had never been used and several boxes of ammunition.

T.O. counted out the cash he had on hand in the safe, which amounted to a little over one hundred thousand. He slowly shuffled through the stacks of cash, counting out the dollars and then placed the stacks into a black duffel bag. Did he want to take it all? He gave that some thought before deciding to leave thirty thousand in the safe, which would leave him some starting money depending when he got back to town. In all, he'd be running with nearly a hundred thousand. Not necessarily Tony Soprano money, but it would allow him to be relatively comfortable, especially in a place like El Paso. He figured he could live cheaply down there and if Neil's contacts came through with some paying work, he'd be just fine.

His pocket buzzed and it was Neil. "I have the ten for you, plus another ten from the bosses."

"I like it."

"Meet me at DeAndre's at eleven."

T.O. sighed in relief. Things could be worse. Now he would be leaving town with over a hundred thousand dollars and if Felix was adding an envelope, that was a good sign, both in the short and the long-term. He exhaled a sigh of relief and reached for his phone. Tiana had texted him earlier that he hadn't been by in a couple of months. El Paso was a long drive and a little time with her might take the edge off. He texted her back. There was time for a stop on the way out of town.

"What happened?" Mac asked as Dick and Ortega dropped themselves into the MKX. "Where the hell did Kline go?"

"I don't know," Dick sighed. "He obviously made us."

"Orr too," Mac replied, shaking his head. "Not a banner day."

"To say the least."

"We had a lot of vehicles in the mix last night up in St. Cloud. We might have stubbed our toe there," Mac mused. "So where to?"

Tommy handed him an address to plug into the GPS.

"And this is for where?"

"One of Orr's girls who goes by the name Lacey," Ortega answered. "She's a dancer."

"We're sitting on his known girlfriends, I take it?"

"And his house and the Payne Reliever as well. We're hoping maybe he stops before he leaves town. We have guys spread out on like six different women."

"And Kline?"

"He hasn't been seen since he slipped out of the repair shop."

"Any idea how?"

Dick shook his head. "No, but Double Frank and Fisher are feeling pretty sheepish about it."

"Did you go after them like you went after Cruz and Carson?"

"How'd you know about that?"

Mac gave him a look as if to say *are you serious?*

"Right, I should have known. Half the department's last name is McRyan."

~

T.O. parallel parked the Yukon along the street, pulled his hood over his head and while peering around, walked down the sidewalk to Lowry Avenue, made a left and walked a block to the side entrance to DeAndre's Joint. He went in the side door and saw Neil sitting at the far corner of the bar.

Orr sat down on the open stool to Neil's right. Without saying a word Neil reached inside his coat pocket and slipped one and then the other white envelope under the bar rail. "Twenty grand, ten in each," he whispered quietly.

T.O. looked down and quickly thumbed open the envelopes to see the cash and nodded his approval.

Kline was drinking a Wild Turkey. He held up his glass

and two fingers and two drinks were immediately delivered by the bartender. "When are you on the road?" he asked.

"Before the sun rises in the morning. I've got two bags packed with all I need."

"You're not leaving right now?"

Orr shook his head as he took a long drink of the Wild Turkey. "I have one last stop to make."

Neil snorted a knowing laugh. "What's her name?"

Orr smiled as he raised the Wild Turkey to his lips. "Tiana. I gotta get one last bit of that before I leave." He took another long drink. "So when I get settled down in Texas, do you have a number I can call to get hooked up with some work?"

Neil nodded and slipped T.O. a small white slip of paper. "Call that number in a week or so, mention my name and they'll arrange a meet. But listen, keep the profile low. You can still be reached down there. If you run into any trouble, get your ass into Mexico."

"I hear that. Thanks," Orr answered as he downed the last of the whiskey. "Are the boys with the Outfit okay?"

Neil nodded, taking a light sip from his drink. "The money says yes."

~

"There's Orr's truck," Tito pointed from the front passenger seat as the Yukon pulled onto Lowry Avenue and motored east.

"Follow," Felix ordered from his perch in the backseat.

~

"This is a shit detail," Cruz moaned bitterly as he raised his bottle of Diet Coke to his lips.

"We earned it," Carson muttered in reply, slumped down in the passenger seat, the police radio turned low. He checked his watch and it was just after midnight on a Sunday night, or by now a quiet Monday morning.

"So is this building complex apartments or townhouses?" Cruz asked. "I mean, they look like apartments—windows out of only two sides, small, maybe two-bedroom units."

"The sign for the complex says Como Townhouses, so they're townhouses."

"But what makes an apartment and what makes a townhouse?"

"How the hell should I know? Carson answered grumpily, sitting up in his seat. He gestured toward the building. "Maybe it's the fact that you own these. The file says she owns her unit, number three. You don't generally own apartments, you rent them. You don't typically rent townhouses, you own them. Also, apartments tend to have secured entrances. These building units do not. Hence, townhouse."

The Como Townhouses were kitty-corner from their current perch. Each building contained eight townhouses, four on the first floor, four on the second. Cutting through the middle of the building was an open entryway for all eight units, with stairway complexes and landings for the second-floor units. Their target, Tiana Callaway's townhouse, was the upstairs unit in the front left corner. They could view both the front windows and left side windows from their location.

Tiana was described as an ex-girlfriend of Orr's. "Does a

guy like this really have an ex-girlfriend?" Cruz had asked Dick earlier.

"I don't know, I don't care, just sit on her house and see if he shows."

"And if he does?"

"No hero shit. Call it in, we'll get people there and take Orr in."

T.O. parked his Yukon in the narrow alley a block from Tiana's. There was no sense taking any chances at this point. After he slipped his Beretta into the back of his pants, he pulled his hood up and slowly walked down the alley. This was the rare alley that had a turn in it rather than simply running straight for the whole block. An odd quirk, he thought as he turned and could see the townhouse complex ahead. As he came out of the alley he jogged across the street, through the rear parking lot and quickly up the stairs to the second-floor landing and to Tiana's unit, where he knocked lightly.

It took a moment but then he heard rustling and the light above the door was turned on and then the door opened. "Hey T.O," Tiana greeted with a big smile and her thigh-length black silk robe loosely tied, exposing a hint of flesh.

"Hey, Tiana baby," T.O. answered with a smile while stepping inside and slipping his hoodie off his head.

"It's been awhile. I'd thought you'd forgotten about me," Tiana cooed as she ran her hands up his chest and then wrapped her arms around his neck.

"We got lights on suddenly!" Carson stated urgently, quickly alert. "That's her place, isn't it?"

"Yup," Cruz replied, raising a pair of binoculars to his eyes.

~

"I'm glad you pinged me," T.O. said, pulling away from Tiana and moving into the small family room to the left.

"What are you doing?" Tiana asked.

"Just checking on something," he replied as he tweezered open the curtains and peered out at the street.

Tiana turned on the overhead light.

"*Turn that off!*"

~

"That's him!" Carson pointed. "In the front window, that's him."

~

"Shit!" T.O. growled as he turned and made for the back door.

~

"I think he's making a run for it!" Cruz bellowed as he opened the driver's side door. "That prick isn't getting away this time."

"Lich, ya there?" Carson yelled into the radio, up and out of the car now, running after Cruz who was already across the street, heading for the open entryway between the two sides of the building.

"This is Lich. Carson, what do ya got?"

"We have Orr. He's running from Tiana Callaway's townhouse, we're in pursuit! Send back up!"

"Orr, you better stop!" Cruz yelled, as he ran through the open entryway and could see their mark on the other side of the parking lot, heading for an alley. "Dammit!" he growled as he made his way between two parked cars.

"We're on our way!" Dick's voice declared over the radio.

"Copy," Carson replied as he dodged his way through the playground when his left foot dropped and then he felt his leg give way and heard the loud snap. "Ahh shit! Ahh Shit! Ahh Shit! Fuck! My leg! My leg!"

"What happened?" Cruz yelled looking back, hopping up and down.

"I think I broke my fuckin leg!" Cruz replied, reaching for his throbbing left ankle, seeing the hole in the ground he'd stepped into. *"Go!* Get that fucker! Go! *Go!"*

T.O. ran at a full sprint into the alley and reached in his left pant pocket for the key fob of the truck. He glanced back and could see the man chasing was in the street, perhaps forty yards back.

He turned the corner and the truck was thirty yards ahead. First, he looked down and hit the lock button and then the start button twice. The truck lit up and started. Next, he hit the unlock button. But doing all that had slowed him down.

Taking another glance back, he could see the cop was turning the alley corner and was closing fast.

T.O. skidded to a stop at the side of the truck and reached for the door handle when his attention was drawn to his left. He saw the flash and heard the pop. "What the he..."

Cruz felt the shot whiz by his head. He dropped, rolled to his left as the second shot buzzed by. He popped up on his right knee.

T.O. threw his hands up and yelled, "*Don't shoot!* It's not..."

It was too late.

A shot hit him in the torso, then one sliced right through his neck and he slumped back against the Yukon, suddenly unable to breathe.

Cruz popped up onto both of his feet and moved forward, his hands and gun lowered. He could see Orr laying against the Yukon with blood flowing out of his wounds.

Then he saw movement past the truck.

Boom! Boom! Boom!

The policeman went down.

Felix quickly jogged over to him and peered down. One of the shots hit the policeman in the head, just above the left eye. He was dead.

"The other cop is still down on the ground, injured, but is trying to get up now." Tito's voice reported calmly into Felix's earpiece. "You need to get moving."

Felix ran back to Orr who was fading fast, gasping for breath, the blood flowing out of his throat. He wouldn't last. Felix put his gun in Orr's right hand, raised it up and squeezed the trigger, firing one last shot in the policeman's general direction. Orr, dead weight in Felix's arms now, slumped down to the ground and then to a facedown position. Felix flipped up the back of Orr's black hoodie and took the gun Orr had stuffed behind his back and stuck it in his jacket pocket. Then out of Orr's other coat pocket he pulled out another gun, a Beretta, and stuffed it under the Yukon's driver's seat.

Felix ran back up to the other end of the alley as house and garage lights started popping on, dogs barking in backyards and the neighborhood, once peacefully asleep, was now jolted awake. He could now hear sirens rapidly approaching in the distance. At the end of the alley Jorge pulled the van to a stop, Tito slid open the side door and Felix leapt into the van as they sped away.

13

"A DEAD COP IS TOO HIGH A PRICE TO PAY FOR THIS."

Mac skidded to a stop along the street as Carson was hopping along, practically dragging his left ankle along the asphalt.

"What happened?" Dick yelled, up and out of the passenger seat.

"I don't know," Carson screamed. "I just heard a lot of shots fired in the alley! In the alley! *Cruz is in the alley*! He hasn't come out!"

Mac immediately had his gun out and a flashlight in his hand. He crossed his right hand with the gun over his left, which was holding the flashlight. Briefly he glanced back and Ortega and Dick were right behind him. The alley ahead was clear but there was a sharp left turn framed by the patchwork of wood privacy fences and single and double detached garages.

At the left-hand turn in the alley, Mac crouched down along the side of a garage wall and peered left around the side. He could see one body on the alley floor and another slumped against a running SUV farther down. "Not good," he muttered to himself.

Carefully, Mac moved around the corner and forward, peering ahead with the flashlight and gun as he approached the first body lying on the alley floor. It was Cruz. Mac saw the hole in his forehead. He quickly checked for a pulse just to be sure, but he was gone.

"Aw shit!" Dick groaned as he reached Cruz.

Mac pushed himself up, and along with Ortega the two of them pushed forward, deeper into the alley. Scanning with his flashlight Mac zeroed in on the SUV, which he recognized as a Yukon. It was running. There was a body lying face down on the left side. When he reached the body, Mac crouched down and with his flashlight illuminated enough of the man's left profile to be able to tell it was Terrence Orr. Ortega leaned down to check for a pulse. He looked over to Mac and shook his head.

"*Sweet*," Mac muttered disgustedly as he stood up and looked back to Cruz lying on the ground and Dick on the police radio, then back down to the dead Terrence Orr. "Tommy, you just can't make this shit up."

Two hours later Mac yawned as he was leaning against his MKX, his arms folded, a half-consumed bottle of Sprite in his right hand. In the aftermath Mac, Ortega and Dick secured the alley, Tiana Callaway and her apartment. With an officer dead and the investigation already involving a former cop, the chief brought the Minnesota Bureau of Criminal Apprehension in to investigate. Within the hour the BCA had a team onsite. The agent in charge, a man named Olson, had already taken Mac, Ortega's and Dick's statements; not that they had much information to provide as everything they'd seen was the aftermath.

Dick came walking back over, having just finished talking to Carson, who'd just completed giving a statement to Olson and was now being loaded into an ambulance, his leg immobilized. Riley and Rock joined while Double Frank and Fisher had also arrived on the scene.

"What happened?" Mac asked Dick.

Dick shook his head while scratching the back of it. "Cruz and Carson were parked down the street from the townhouse. It had been quiet, completely dark, when all the sudden a light went on outside of Tiana's unit. Then a minute or two later the lights come on inside and Carson said they saw a man looking out the front window that looked like Orr. Apparently, Orr saw them too and took off. They both ran after him and that's when Carson was calling me on the radio."

"What happened to Carson?" Riles asked.

Dick pointed back toward the townhouse complex and the playground. "He was running through the playground when he stepped into a hole and snapped his left ankle. He went down in a heap. EMT says he probably has multiple fractures of the ankle."

"And Cruz kept going, I assume," Rock speculated.

"That's what Carson said. He told him to. They weren't letting Orr slip away again on their watch is what he said. Carson saw Cruz run into that alley after Orr and then he heard a bunch of shooting for a few seconds before everything went stone quiet and Cruz didn't come back out of the alley. Carson pushed himself up at that point and was basically hopping toward the alley when we rolled in here."

"Cruz gets into that alley. Orr throws down. Cruz responds and they both end up dead?" Double Frank asked, shaking his head. "I mean, seriously?"

"It's what it looks like," Ortega answered with a head nod. "Cruz was shot in the head and Orr was hit in the throat."

Mac looked past everyone to the ambulance that was pulling away. "How's Carson doing?" he asked Dick.

"How do you think?" Dick replied, looking at the departing ambulance. "His partner is dead and he feels like he didn't have his back." Dick shook his head. "And to think, after they lost track of Orr earlier I put them on this Tiana Callaway because I never thought he'd show up here. She wasn't one of his regulars. I figured this could never get fucked up."

"It's dark, he's running, he's on the radio, there's no lighting in that playground area," Riley stated sadly. "It's nobody's fault. They were doing their job. Sometimes shit just goes bad."

"Well, the BCA has it now. They'll work it," Dick stated. "I talked to one of the BCA guys. He says in searching the truck that Orr had another gun under the driver's seat, two duffel bags of clothes, and in a compartment in the back there's thousands of dollars in cash. He was getting ready to leave town so we were right about that."

"There was a pretty good chance Orr did Sam," Rock declared. "He was up to his eyeballs in it and was looking to run. In my mind, the prick got what was coming to him."

"Yeah, but did we have to lose Cruz to do it?" Dick replied in anguish.

"Not bad for an ad lib," White offered when Felix finished his description of the events.

"I was stuck in that alley. There was no way to explain my presence there. I don't think I had a choice but to take them both. I'm very lucky the cop took Orr first."

"Quick thinking, cousin," Javier's voice bellowed over the phone. "Very quick, indeed."

Felix shrugged, nodded and then took a drink of Patrón. "Everything they need to hang Shead on Orr is in and on that truck. Plus, he shot an active duty cop this time so I have to think that the police will be dying to put it all on Orr and close the investigation."

"We shall see on that," Mr. White answered cautiously. "We'll see if this story holds. And I still have concerns that Neil Kline is somewhat exposed."

"Perhaps it will be advisable for you to reach out to your contact on the force and find out if that's the case," Javier suggested. "Offer him another inducement."

"Let's let this run its course for a few days," White counseled. "And then I'll do just that."

14

"A THIRD PERSON WOULD."

"Shamus, another round," Mac bellowed as he gestured to himself, Dick, Rock, Riles, Ortega and a few others surrounding him at the bar.

Shamus was Mac's uncle and the man in charge at McRyan's Pub. Mac was part of the fourth generation of McRyans that had worn the uniform of the St. Paul Police Department. Being a policeman in St. Paul was the first family business.

The second family business was the spacious three-story McRyan's Pub located on West Seventh Street on the southwestern edge of downtown. The pub was considered first and foremost the bar of cops. If you were there it was the safest place in the city, often filled with off-duty officers having a post-shift drink and bite to eat. It was also a popular watering hole for hockey fans given it was located a mere two blocks from the Xcel Energy Center, the home of the Minnesota Wild.

Like most bars, it was heavily decorated to reflect the interests and passions of its patrons. Consequently, the main original bar in the front was adorned with historical St. Paul

Police memorabilia, including vintage car doors from patrol units with the St. Paul Police logo emblazoned on them which hung on short chains dangling from the high ceiling. The rest of the three floors of the vast pub were filled with hockey memorabilia commemorating the sport's long, colorful and celebrated history in the city. A private meeting and party room in the basement called Patrick's Room, located behind a hidden door, paid homage to St. Paul's and the bar's infamous history of violating prohibition. In that spirit, the private room was adorned with black and white photos from that notorious and colorful era.

With Mac's oldest niece now waiting tables, the family was up to five generations of McRyans that had worked at the pub. For his niece and many other McRyans, the pub funded college education and provided wages for high school and college-age members of the McRyan family. It also served to help those McRyan family members who'd retired from the force, such as Shamus, who wanted or needed to supplement their police pension. As a result, between active and retired cops and their kids, there could be double digit McRyans on the payroll working in every part of the bar operation. It was like a mini-family reunion every night.

As was always the case anytime an officer was killed in the line of duty, there was the gathering at the Pub, an Irish Wake, regardless of your heritage or faith. Only cops were allowed in the main bar tonight as Rafael Cruz's picture was hoisted upon the wall in remembrance. The once capacity crowd had long been filtering out of the bar and at the late hour, it was now only Mac and his buddies huddled at the far corner of the long stretch of deep mahogany.

"Jen wanted me to tell you again how good it was too see you last night," Tommy said as he sat down next to Mac.

"It was good to see her and your son. He's a very polite young man."

"Jenny gets all the credit."

"Nah, that takes two parents, buddy. I enjoyed it as well. We need to do that again when Sally is back here. I really want her to meet Jen. I'm pretty sure they'll hit it off."

"Speaking of which, how much longer are you in town?" Tommy Ortega asked.

"Friday noon," Mac answered, "Then I'm on a plane back to D.C. Sally is home for a week before she goes back out with the President to various locales in Asia. With her new gig, I need to be available whenever she is."

Dick had been missing from the group for a while, but now made his way back.

"Where were you?" Mac asked, taking a drink of his bourbon.

"I just got off the phone with Olson from the BCA. He gave me a preliminary on their investigation."

"And?" Riles asked, reaching for his next Grain Belt Nordeast, his tall beer glass foaming commercial-like on the bar.

"They can't determine for sure who started shooting first," Dick stated. "But, based upon an examination of the weapons, Orr took six shots with his Beretta Px4 and Cruz took three with his Glock-17, so on that basis, they think it's likely Orr drew first. Based on the dirt on his clothes and markings in the light layer of dirt on the cement of the alley pavement, they think Cruz dropped and rolled, so that would appear to be an—"

"Evasive action," Rock finished.

"Correct. So Cruz does that because there are shots fired. He returns fire. Orr keeps shooting. They hit each other fatally. Cruz took his to the forehead, Orr to the throat, although he was also hit in the right upper chest."

"That's kind of what I thought it looked like when I was in that alley," Mac had replied with a nod.

"The tally on the money he had with him was a little over one hundred eight thousand, along with two duffel bags full of clothes. So as we suspected he was going on the run. And there are a couple of other things."

"What's that?"

"He shot Cruz with a Beretta, but they also found another Beretta tucked under the driver's seat in the car. They ran ballistics on it. Guess what it matches up to?"

"The slugs in Sam Shead?" Riles asked.

"No way," Mac replied in disbelief.

"Way. A perfect match," Dick replied with a nod. "And upon my asking, they took a longer look at the Yukon Orr was driving. It had new headlights, a fresh grill and bumper on the front-end, all brand spanking new."

"Because his Yukon was used to take down Sam," Rock suggested.

"That would be the logical guess," Dick replied. "In any event, that probably closes Sam's murder. Gun, truck and he's running. I mean, Orr probably had help from some of his buddies, but he took down Sam."

"You're probably right," Riles replied with a nod. "Have you told Nikki yet?"

Dick shook his head. "I talked to her the other day and told her that I thought I was close to having some answers."

"When will the BCA release their findings?" Rock asked.

"It'll be a few days until they do it officially, although Olson said he'd have a copy over to me tomorrow. I guess I'll give it a look, but it's case closed," Dick answered and waved down Uncle Shamus, who was still lingering behind the bar. "Tequila."

"Tequila?" Shamus asked questioningly. "You?"

"It's for Cruz."

"Copy that."

While he waited for the shots to come, Dick took a drink of his tap beer as Riley started regaling Rock and Ortega with a story. After a moment Dick glanced to his right at Mac, who was resting on a stool, slowly nursing his drink and staring off blankly in the distance. "Anything on your mind?"

"No." Then after a moment Mac turned to Dick. "Why do you think that?"

Lich looked at Mac as if to say *are you serious?* "This is me you're talking to. I've seen that far off look before. It generally causes my ass to pucker."

"You know, it's probably nothing," Mac replied with a shoulder shrug.

"I'm all ears," Dick pressed. "What gives?"

Mac thought for a moment. "Two things about that BCA investigation."

"Which are?"

"First, the gun. You're telling me that Orr still had the gun he shot Shead with?" Mac asked, incredulous. "That makes him dumber than a box of hammers."

Dick cackled. "I agree, but he still had it. Buddy, sometimes we get lucky. You said two things. What's the other?"

"Kline. What was Neil Kline's role in all of this? I mean we never really got around to him. It feels to me like he's somehow getting off the hook here. We were watching him, but in the end we never *even* talked to him. He was warning off Orr. Warning him off what? What did or does Kline know? What's his role in our little drama?"

It was Dick's turn to ponder in quiet for a moment before he took a small sip from his beer. "You know, Mac, maybe on that fateful night up in Rogers, Kline was just in the wrong place at the wrong time the night Sam saw him and Orr together. And it was really Orr, not Kline, who was the issue all along and who Sam was following."

"Yet, like Orr, Kline eluded us on Sunday too," Mac countered, unconvinced. "I mean, he snuck away from the repair shop, leaving his driver behind. He didn't walk out the front or back door, someone snuck him out. Why? What was he doing that he didn't want anyone to see?"

"I don't know. He wasn't at that Tiana Calloway's place, we know that. Double Frank and Fisher were watching Kline's house and he showed up at home about five minutes before Cruz and Orr held their Aaron Burr-Alexander Hamilton duel in that alley. You can't be in two places at once."

"That's true, but it just feels like a...loose end," Mac responded, perturbed, taking another pull from his drink. Kline didn't sit right with him. Orr was a thug and was working for someone operating a criminal enterprise of some kind that perhaps Luther, and then Sam, stumbled onto. Whatever that enterprise was it was no longer of interest to his four buddies to his left, since Sam's killer seemed to have been found. If it were Mac's call, he'd keep digging to learn more because there was more out there to be learned. But it wasn't his call and he could tell that his old partner was quite content with the current result. Maybe he needed to be too. Besides, he was on a plane back to D.C. in a day. Mac smiled. "Screw it. Sam's murderer was found. He's dead. Case closed."

"Yet you still have that unconvinced look."

"Maybe it's just my cynical nature."

"Or *maybe*," Dick suggested, handing Mac a shot of tequila, "it's that you haven't had enough to drink yet."

"I'll drink to that."

Everyone, Mac included, had far too much to drink. An Uber got Mac home while cabs or cops got the others to their humble abodes. The next morning, rather than call Uber for a ride back to the Pub, Mac decided to purge the tequila and other alcohol toxins from his system by putting on his jogging shoes and making the five-mile run from home down to the Pub to pick up his MKX. As he was driving back, sipping his bottle of water and wiping sweat from his brow, his phone rang. The call came up as simply a phone number on the display, but it was a Minneapolis 612-area code. "McRyan."

"Mac, this is Charlie. Are you still in town?"

"Yeah, until tomorrow, why? Are you calling in *another* favor?" Mac asked, needling.

There was a hesitation on the other end of the call.

"Charlie?"

"Mac, are you involved with that Orr investigation?"

"Kind...of," Mac answered haltingly, caught off guard by the solemn tone on the other end of the line. "What's going on, Charlie?"

"I don't know if it's anything, Mac. It may not be, but I think I have something you should at least see involving that case. Can you meet me at my office?"

Mac went home, quickly showered and dressed and made his way over to north Minneapolis. Along the way he made a stop at a Grand Brew to pick up a cup of coffee for himself and two extras. Ten minutes later he was parking on the east side of the street and got out with the two extra cups of coffee in a cardboard carrier. With a broad smile, he walked toward the big man patrolling the front of a nondescript one-story brown brick office building, part offices, part hardware store.

"Mac, is that you, my man?" Vincent, one of Charlie's massive bodyguards, greeted with his deep low voice and a friendly fist bump. "How are you, my brotha? I almost didn't recognize you with the beard, the flow, looking all very stylish I must say. And you brought coffee, a latte?"

"I know what you like, Vincent," Mac replied with a smile. "I have one for Victor too. Is he around?"

"He's out patrolling. You know us, we like to walk around with a little flex and make our presence felt, especially since the boss pretty much owns everything businesswise around here now. But don't worry, I'll let Vic know you brought him a treat." Vincent tipped his head to the right. "The boss is expecting you. You know the way. We'll be watching your ride."

"Thanks."

Mac indeed did know the way. The office space on the first floor of the building at one time housed a small law firm. Years ago, the attorney, a street lawyer with the last name of Riley essentially moved his law practice down into the basement not long before he sold the building to Charlie. Cleverly, he'd placed a sign at the building's edge that said: "Lawyers Entrance in the Rear," along with an arrow pointing to the walkway leading to the back of the building. Charlie, a man with a robust sense of humor, found the sign highly amusing if not also a bit instructive, and never had it removed. Mac smiled as he made his way past the sign and around to the back to the landing and narrow cement stairway down to the entrance on the lower level. At the bottom of the steps he was admitted by another bodyguard. "He's in the office down the hall."

Mac walked down the dark yet familiar skinny hallway

into a large room that occupied nearly half the basement of the building.

"Mac!" Fat Charlie greeted warmly, getting up out of his chair to come over and shake hands. "Good to see you."

"Hello, Charlie, you're looking well."

"I'm feeling well," Charlie answered with gusto and as Mac assessed him. The man was indeed looking healthier than ever. Fat Charlie Boone as a moniker was no longer remotely accurate. At one time, Charlie's six-foot frame was carrying nearly four hundred pounds. When Mac first met Charlie some years ago he'd just undergone gastric bypass surgery. Since that time, Charlie continued to slim down to easily now under two hundred pounds. Some of the slimming was for health and some was for legitimacy. Back in the day, Charlie was a bigger than life personality who dressed flamboyantly with loud suits, gold chains and wild hair in a manner that reminded one of the boxing promoter, Don King. These days Charlie was strictly low key; conservative dark suits, his hair cut short with distinguishing flecks of gray, particularly in his well-trimmed beard where there was an almost whitish strip of hair covering his chin. Now he looked and spoke more like Morgan Freeman. "I'd offer you a drink, but I see you're drinking coffee."

"I had a late night," Mac answered as he sat down.

"No doubt toasting to the life of officer Rafael Cruz at your family's establishment, I'm sure," Charlie answered, well informed as always.

"And on that point, now that I'm here, what is it you wanted me to see, Charlie?"

Charlie looked over to a chair in the corner. One of Charlie's sons that Mac recognized walked over to the table with a laptop computer along with another man dressed in blue jeans and a red untucked golf shirt.

"Mac, you know my son Jameel, of course. This other man here is DeAndre. DeAndre and I own DeAndre's Joint across the street."

"Okay, so what's up?"

"Well, on Sunday night you all had this Cruz and Orr business over in St. Paul. However, before that all went down, this Mr. Orr was across the street at DeAndre's."

"Okay," Mac replied. "Is that what we're here to talk about?"

"It's more, see," Charlie answered and then pointed to DeAndre.

"I saw the picture of Orr on television yesterday," DeAndre reported, taking a seat at the table. "And I recognized him from being in our place on Sunday night. I was tending bar and I served him a couple of drinks. So I guess for whatever reason, I decided to look at the surveillance footage from that night in case something went on that I should be worried about."

"And I assume you saw something?" Mac led.

"*Maybe*," Charlie answered cautiously and then gestured to his son. "Show him."

Jameel turned the laptop toward Mac and pushed play. The video was not hi-definition, but Mac could easily make out Orr as he came into the bar and took a seat at the bar next to... "Neil Kline," Mac muttered softly. The video now had his attention.

"You know who that man is?" Charlie asked.

"Yes. Yes, I do."

Kline and Orr talked briefly and ordered drinks. After the drinks were ordered, Kline reached inside his jacket for a white envelope and then another. In both cases his hands dropped below the bar rail, but from the movement of his right arm it was clear he handed both envelopes to Orr. Orr looked down and appeared to evaluate the contents of each and then nodded in satisfaction before he slipped the envelopes inside the front pouch of his black hoodie. For the remainder of the time Kline and Orr conversed until Orr got up, shook Kline's hand and departed. Given the time on the monitor, it was clear that after leaving DeAndre's Orr drove directly to Tiana Callaway's. Mac had Jameel replay the beginning a couple of times before sitting back in his chair.

Mac looked over to Charlie and pointed to him. "What do *you* think?"

"I don't know if I *think* anything, specifically. But he's in my bar getting two envelopes, most likely with cash and then about an hour later, if that, that man ended up dead. I saw that, and it...smelled to me of something."

Mac suspected Charlie *thought* more than he was saying and Mac needed to work it out of him. "We think he was leaving town."

"What was he doing in St. Paul then?"

"Meeting up with a girl before he left it seems," Mac replied. "He was a bit of a hound dog apparently. But in his truck there were two large duffel bags of clothes and money, a lot of money."

"How much?"

"A little over a hundred eight grand in his truck."

Charlie's eyebrows raised. "Those envelopes were not thick enough for a hundred eight thousand, Mac."

"No, they weren't," Mac agreed. "Still..."

"Still...what?" Charlie asked.

"Still, I'm not sure it means anything. I mean, the shooting in the alley looks like it was between Orr and Cruz. Cruz was chasing Orr, Orr turned and fired, Cruz returned it, they both hit each other and they're both dead."

"Why was Orr leaving town?"

"I suspect because we were interested in him for the Sam Shead murder and he seemed to be sensing that as well. We had evidence indicating he was involved somehow and maybe the other guy in the video too. It's interesting because we lost Orr earlier that day and we lost this Neil Kline as well. We actually had two cops watching Kline's house and he got home a few minutes before all the stuff with Orr went down in that alley."

"So he was leaving town, yet thought he had time for a little extra pussy before he bailed?" Charlie asked.

"Yeah," Mac replied. "That's what it looks like, anyway."

"If I were afraid of being caught by the cops I wouldn't have been making an extra stop on the way out of town. I'd have gotten out of town," Charlie stated, shaking his head. "Unless..."

"Unless what?" Mac asked.

"Unless the police were not who he really feared," Charlie speculated. "Maybe he feared someone else."

"Like his employer?"

"Right," Charlie answered. "Do you have any idea who this Orr worked for?"

"No," Mac answered, shaking his head. "We were just starting in on that when we got onto Orr and literally forty-eight hours later he's lying dead in that alley, along with Rafael Cruz."

"What's this Kline guy's story?"

"Not sure, Charlie. He's hooked up with Orr somehow. They were in prison together out at Stillwater. Their paths seemed to cross often. I suspect they worked for the same employer."

Charlie sat back into his chair, folded his arms and stared up at the ceiling, deep in thought. After a moment to collect his thoughts he said, "Look, Mac. I kind of know of this Orr. Word on the street was he was operating over here on the north side, up in the area around Patrick Henry High School. There were some others who had that area for quite some time. I knew them, they knew me and knew I wouldn't put up with any shit. We had an open line of communication. They didn't mess with what I was trying to do here on the north side and in return, I largely left them alone. Then one day they were gone and the word I got was this Orr was now the man in charge and everyone on the street reported to him. In all of that, I got the sense that Orr wasn't the real boss, someone else higher up was."

"Who?" Mac asked, his interest piqued.

"Here's the weird part—I could never find out," Charlie replied. "He worked for someone, but nobody either knows, or if they do, they won't say. Orr wouldn't say. I sent Victor and Vincent over for one of their chats and all that entails. Orr wouldn't cough it up. He was respectful, business-like and said repeatedly he didn't want trouble and if there was any, that they or I directly could reach out to Orr and he would handle it but his bosses...he wouldn't give them up. I mean, Mac, they dragged him out of the cities to a place I have. Nobody had an idea where he was. Vincent put a damn gun to his head. Yet, despite all of that, Orr wouldn't give it up."

"Who puts that kind of fear in someone?"

"I don't know, my friend," Charlie answered seriously. "I'd say, though, it should give you some insight as to why he might have been running. Now, you mentioned this Kline fella. Who'd be higher up in the organization? Orr or Kline?"

Mac took a long drink from his coffee and thought for a moment, contemplating their background, at least as much as he knew about them. "Hard to say for sure, Charlie, but their history says Kline. Orr is muscle for hire, working the streets. Kline is smarter and he's operating a business." Mac took another look at the video and looked back to Charlie with a little grin. "What are you thinking? I know you're thinking something."

"You know what I see in that video?"

"A payoff?" Mac asked.

"Correct, my man, a payoff. I used to have envelopes like that delivered to people as payment, payoffs, rewards, bonuses, what have you. You said Orr was found with a lot of money, over a hundred grand. Whatever Kline passed over to him in DeAndre's was probably a nice little chunk of that but nowhere near that total amount. Perhaps the rest was his own or from different sources."

Mac nodded. "It could be a payoff. Or...or..." Suddenly he thought of the gun in the truck, the Beretta. "Or a damned setup." The gun in the truck. Why would Orr still have the gun in the truck? Was he that stupid? After Shead's body resurfaced, was he so stupid as to have kept the gun? Especially with the police on him? If you're eluding the police, don't you dump that gun? That didn't make sense unless...it was a setup. Mac's mind suddenly started racing. "I gotta go."

"Mac, what is it?" Charlie asked.

"You know what? Thanks, Charlie. I'm glad you called on this, *really glad*." He gestured to the computer. "Can I get a copy of this footage?"

A half hour later Mac made his way up to the Homicide Unit, which was largely empty. Only Paddy and Ortega were present. "Where is everybody?"

"Riley and Rock are off today. Double Frank and Fisher are checking out a home invasion. Dick was in earlier, but

I'm not sure where he's off to now," Paddy answered. "What's up?"

"Did the BCA send Dick their draft report?"

"Yeah, there's a copy on Dick's desk. Why?"

Mac picked up the report and started flipping through it. If it was a setup, what would be the evidence of that in that alley beyond the gun? How could it have gone down? As he flipped to the third page, which had the ballistics report he found a possible answer.

"What are you doing here?" Dick asked, walking back into Homicide.

"Do you two have a free hour?" Mac asked Dick and Ortega, who both nodded.

"Why?" Ortega asked.

"We need to go back to that alley and look at something."

"*Why*?" Dick asked guardedly after a moment of considering Mac's expression and body language.

"I'll explain while we drive over." Mac looked over to Paddy. "You want to learn something?"

"Sure."

"Good, you can make it four of us. Grab your gear, a camera, a tape measure and some orange cones."

Twenty minutes later the four of them were back in the alley. On the way over Mac explained his meeting with Charlie and what he'd learned. All of them were skeptical. "By now, I know it's better to hear you out," Dick acknowledged warily. "But I'm now starting to feel my ass pucker."

The crime scene tape was long gone so Mac parked the MKX where Orr's Yukon had been parked. He double and triple checked to make sure he had it located in the exact spot, at one point moving his truck two feet back based on crime scene photos and the diagram.

"Mac, what are we looking for? What are *you* looking for?" Dick asked.

"This," Mac replied, standing by his open driver's side door. "So what we think happened is Orr sees Cruz and Carson out on the street and flees, right?"

"Yes," Dick replied.

"He runs through the parking lot and playground, across the street and into the alley and then takes the left turn because he'd parked his Yukon here, correct?"

"Yes."

"And when you and I and Tommy got into this alley and found both dead bodies, the Yukon was running. How do you explain that?"

Dick shrugged, not fully into Mac's line of thinking yet. But Ortega was working it through his head. Tommy looked back down the alley and then to where Mac's MKX was parked. "Key fob? Automatic start?"

Mac nodded. "Right. He's running, he hits start, he gets to the car and then what?"

Tommy looked at Mac quizzically and then back down the alley. "He shoots at Cruz...right?"

"I think that's what we're supposed to think," Mac answered. "I think that's what we're *supposed* to see."

"But you don't think that's what happened?" Dick asked, hands casually in his pockets, starting to engage.

"If I'm Orr and I'm ahead of Cruz, and the truck is started and the door is open, why do I stop, turn around and start shooting at a cop?"

"Because he thought Cruz would catch him?" Paddy asked.

"How far back is Cruz's body?" Mac asked Paddy. "Walk it off."

Paddy looked back to a small orange cone that referenced where Cruz's body was found. He walked it off with his stride. At six-feet tall his stride was a yard, give or take. Mac's cousin took twenty-five strides to the cone and then walked back. "Twenty-five yards or so."

"Exactly, so why shoot at Cruz?" Mac asked. "Why shoot at a trained police officer who is going to fire back when you can get in the truck and pull away? I mean, think about it. How far away is Cruz from *his* own vehicle?"

"Hmpf," Paddy snorted. "From here, two blocks, maybe more."

"Right, so if Orr just gets in the damn Yukon—"

"He's gone, or at least has a hell of a head start," Paddy concluded.

"I think that too," Mac replied. "Now he'd have to ditch the truck and get another set of wheels, but for him he'd have that taken care of in an hour by calling one of his boys. He'd be on his way before we could track him down."

Dick shook his head. "But Mac, Orr has the gun in his hand. He has the gun that killed Cruz *in his hand.* He was tested for gun powder residue, he had it on him. I mean, he fired the damn gun. I agree, it was stupid. You said it yourself the other night, he's dumb as a box of hammers. I'd have gotten into that truck and hit the gas, but Orr didn't."

Mac looked at Dick, then Ortega and then finally to Paddy, who was soaking it all in, and then back to Dick. "Are you sure Orr fired at Cruz?"

"Mac, Dick's right. Two words—gunshot residue," Tommy replied. "It's right here in black and white in the BCA report."

Dick piled on, "You explain that and I'll open up my mind to an alternate theory."

"Okay," Mac replied and then posed a question. "How

well do you guys know your ballistics, particularly for a Beretta Px4?"

"I can read a report," Dick replied curtly.

"How far does a Px4 eject a shell casing?" Mac asked.

Dick gave it a moment's thought. "Six feet, give or take as I recall."

"That's about right," Mac answered and then waved for them to follow him while he carried another orange cone away from the MKX at about a thirty-degree angle deeper into the alley past where the truck was parked and set it down near the fence and a garbage can. "How far is it from this cone to my SUV?"

Paddy walked it off; it only took six strides, which would be six to seven yards. "That's roughly twenty feet."

Mac opened the BCA investigative report to page three and pointed to the alley diagram drawn by the BCA investigators. "Why are five shell casings from that Px4 found right here then? A Px4 ejects its shell casing six feet or so. We're twenty feet away."

"Why would Orr shoot from there?" Paddy asked.

"He wouldn't," Mac answered, shaking his head. "A third person would."

"A third person?" Dick asked. "You're saying another person was in the alley."

"No way," Ortega replied reflexively but with some doubt when he added another, quieter, "no way."

"Had to be," Mac answered with conviction. "These shell casings say so. Orr wouldn't run past his already running and unlocked vehicle by another fifteen to twenty feet and then turn around and shoot. That makes no sense. *No sense.* Plus, he was found at the driver's side door, *with it open* anyway."

"But again, explain the gun powder residue," Dick pressed, not yet agreeing with Mac. "He *fired* the gun."

Mac nodded, "I don't dispute it."

"Then how do you explain it?" Tommy asked.

Mac flipped another few pages until he reached Carson's statement. He handed the page to Paddy. "Read the passage in the third paragraph."

Paddy took the page and began reading.

"Officer Carson was lying on the ground, his left ankle broken. He witnessed Detective Cruz continue pursuit into the alley. It was dark, the lighting was poor in the alley and he lost sight of Detective Cruz. Then he heard shooting coming from the direction Cruz had run. Carson heard two shots fired and then a break of a second or two. Then there were three shots fired. Then a second or two later he heard two or three more shots and then silence. Some seconds later, he wasn't sure how many, but within an interval of several seconds he heard one last shot.

As Paddy read the passage, Mac could see Dick and Tommy were starting to grasp what actually happened. "Some seconds later he heard—"

"One last shot," Dick finished the sentence. He looked past Mac to where the first five casings were found. "Mac, the third person shoots from over there. Maybe he was crouched down behind that garbage can. He's waiting on Orr."

"Yes," Mac replied. "But then Orr has pursuers."

"And the third person is screwed," Dick stated. "How do I explain my presence here? I can't run myself. I can't hide, there's a police officer coming."

"So what do you do?" Mac asked.

Dick paused for a second, taking the whole scenario in. "Mac, whoever this guy is, he was pretty cool under pressure."

"Yes, yes, he was, partner," Mac replied with a nod. "Because he quickly calculated that his only chance was to kill them both and make it look like he was never here."

"So he takes two shots at Cruz because he knows Cruz will return fire," Tommy stated, fully tracking now.

"And Cruz does and he kills Orr," Mac continued. "But then Cruz, seeing Orr down, lets his own guard down."

"And our third guy blasts him three times," Paddy continued, taking three steps forward from the hiding spot. "In the darkness of this alley, Cruz would have never seen him back here."

"I agree. I was in this alley. There was very little light other than the yellow lights of the truck and the lights on the poles at either end of the alley. Cruz wouldn't have seen him, or if he did, it was too late," Mac noted. "So then what happened? We have one more shot unaccounted for."

"It's the one that explains the gunshot residue," Dick answered, shaking his head, now fully understanding what Mac was seeing. "Because our guy comes over to Orr, who's now dead or immobilized, puts the gun in his hand and after a few seconds he fires the *one last shot*, leaving the gun in Orr's hand."

"And," Mac added, "the report places one last shell casing just a few feet back away from the Yukon."

Paddy shook his head in admiration. "Pretty cool, cuz."

Ortega laughed, astonished. "Shit, Mac, I'd have never seen this."

Dick wasn't as entertained. He was vexed. "How the hell did you figure this out?"

"It's the other gun under the driver's seat," Mac replied, shaking his head. "You told me the BCA ran ballistics and it was a match to the slugs they pulled out of Sam. I couldn't believe the luck of it all. I mean, it tied up the case so perfectly. You had Orr, you had the Yukon, we know he's running. It all fit perfectly. *Too* perfectly. When I saw that video footage of Kline sliding the money to Orr and the idea of a setup popped into my head, well… what happened in this alley suddenly played a lot differently in my mind. When I read the report back in the homicide offices and saw where the shell casings were found, then I had a pretty good idea what we were seeing was not what really happened."

"So our really smart guy took it a step too far then," Dick suggested.

"He did," Mac answered. "If he wouldn't have put the Beretta under the driver's seat, I don't think any of this would have ever occurred to me."

"So now what?" Ortega asked.

"I suppose you want to reopen this thing," Dick asked.

"That's not my call," Mac answered. "Orr was involved in Sam's killing, no question. He probably killed Luther Ellis. He was a thug. His death is a favor to society. You can call it good and let it all rest and nobody will be the wiser. But know this. There was someone else in this alley and that person killed Rafael Cruz."

Dick, Paddy, Ortega and Mac explained it to Chief Flanagan.

"We are not letting this go," the chief growled angrily, picking up the phone.

Flanagan and Dick went over to the BCA to meet with Olson and his boss. While neither was thrilled with their work being checked, when Dick explained how it all could have gone down they quickly came around.

"Sorry that it looks like we went around your back," Dick stated solemnly. "We obtained information you didn't have and we wanted to see if it made any sense before we brought it to you. I'm just glad we could do it before the report was finished."

Much of the rest of the night was spent laying out the investigative approach and lines of communication. The BCA would continue to focus on the Cruz shooting in the alley. St. Paul Police would continue to investigate the broader case of Orr, Neil Kline, Sam Shead's murder and wherever that led. Both agencies would support the other whenever needed.

"So where do we start?" Dick asked Mac late on Thursday night once all the powers that be were on board.

Mac grimaced.

"What?"

"I'm on a flight to D.C. in the morning. I've seen my wife like four days in the last month. She has five, maybe six relatively clear days in D.C. before she starts traveling again. I *have* to go home."

"Let me get this straight," Dick replied, looking stunned. "You stir all this shit up, *all* this shit, and now you're leaving? Takes balls, man."

"God, I'm sorry...I'm so, so..."

"Here's a steaming pile of shit, Dick," he barked. "Now you go figure it out, that's what you're telling me? That's what you're leaving me with?"

"I know, geezus," Mac replied, anguished and stammering. "But I...just, I...gotta...I mean she has this new job, she's on the road all the time and it's only going to get worse with the mid-terms coming up. I don't get to see her and we're newly married, and...man, I know I'm on really thin ice here..."

"Unbelievable!"

"I know," Mac replied with a hang dog expression,

unable to even look Dick in the eye. "I'm leaving you hanging...and..." Then Mac heard light chuckling. He looked up.

Dick was flashing a cheesy grin under his big bushy mustache. He'd gotten him.

"You asshole," Mac snorted.

"I got you!"

"*You asshole!* Here I'm feeling all guilty and shit."

"Well, you should, shouldn't you?"

"And I do."

"I know," Dick answered with a knowing nod and a big grin. "Go home and see that pretty little thing of yours. You know, this was not your responsibility to begin with. You were just helping us out, me out. You, Mac, are not on the job in St. Paul. We are and we got this."

"You sure?"

"Yeah," Dick answered, waving Mac off. "It's not like we don't know how to do this, superstar. I know this will be of some surprise to you, but we've been functioning pretty well without you. High case clearance rates, low homicides. Hell, the stats are better since you left."

"I didn't mean to imply..."

"Maybe you were the problem."

"You know I wasn't suggesting you couldn't do it without..."

"I know we're just simpleton cops and all..."

"Would you just shut the bleep up?" Mac replied playfully.

Dick just laughed. "I'm kind of having fun jacking *you* around for once."

"I can tell."

"Look, you know as well as I do that this could take a while. There's going to be a lot of *watching* of Neil Kline. We need to take a closer look at the house up in Rogers. Hopefully, Kline starts driving around again and we can see where he's going and start looking at those places and people. And, while I have to think about it a little more, it might be time to get Kline's ass in here and start asking some questions," Dick replied, forming the outlines of his investigative plan. "But let me ask you this, hotshot. Since Sally is on the road a lot, will you come back here to help out at some point if this thing heats up?"

Mac didn't hesitate. "You know I will."

15

"I SEE THE MEXICANS, THE TRUCKS, THE POWDER, THE MONEY."

Thursday nights were payday and Jockey Mike received his envelope from Neil. The envelope was five hundred light.

"What's this?"

"Mike, you know the money I gave to T.O. I'm not getting that money back. I take a hit, so *you* take a hit."

"But Neil, seriously. I'm barely scraping by as it is. You had ten grand for T.O. You can't spare the extra five hundo for me?"

"Be glad I only held back the five."

It wasn't always this way for the diminutive one they called Jockey Mike. What he truly missed were the horses. When he was on his mount, in the race or simply hanging around the track, life was good. He'd race in the summers out at Canterbury and then for the winters he'd go south, usually racing at Gulfstream Park in Miami. He'd get four to five races a day and he had a good enough track record that he generally rode good mounts and made a little something for himself. And then just like that, it was over.

The end came during the Twin Cities Cup race at

Canterbury. He was caught up in a grouping of five horses jockeying for position as they all came around the final turn. His horse, *Jane's Lily*, had plenty left in the tank, but he was caught on the inside against the rail and was behind two horses plus one on the right. He was boxed in. Then as they were in the straightaway, he thought he saw a sliver of an opening to the right. He leaned and yanked with his right hand and the horse responded, but in a flash the opening was closed by another horse making a charge from the back. The horses rubbed hard against one another and in the process Mike was knocked off balance. As his horse jerked hard back left away from the contact, Mike was leaning too far right, lost hold of the reins and was thrown from the horse onto the track. He was trampled by all the other trailing horses.

He broke both of his legs, his left arm and worst of all, his back and just like that, he was done. For jockeys there was no union, no retirement plan and no continuing medical coverage. What there was plenty of was pain, the searing kind permanently in his neck, back and legs.

Mike never graduated high school. He'd turned sixteen and left home for good for the horse life. There were no other skills to fall back on after he couldn't ride. All he was left with was the pain in his neck, back and legs. There was a meager disability check that was far from enough to continue to keep his health insurance. He applied for Social Security Disability benefits and was denied repeatedly, but he still had his pain and a growing addiction and dependence on painkillers. It was a fix he became more and more desperate to placate and which became more and more difficult to do without any money.

One night he broke into a small medical clinic looking for Vicodin, Percocet, any form of pain medication. He was easily caught, arrested, convicted and sent to Stillwater. In prison his cell was next to Neil's. If there was one other skill that Mike possessed, it was excellent hearing and because of his diminutive size and frail appearance, he had an ability to sneak around and hear things without anyone noticing. In prison it was overhearing guards' or cons' conversations and sharing them with Neil, who in turn knew how to spin it to his advantage and make a buck on the inside. Neil gave Mike a little spiff off the action, but the spiff, just like the envelope he received tonight, was not much to speak of.

"Listen, Mike. If you're dissatisfied with your working conditions feel free to go try and find another job," Neil retorted bitterly. "I won't have trouble finding a driver, particularly one who isn't a fucking cripple."

He didn't want to take any more pills. He was trying to stop as he was starting to get stomach pains and he suspected the years of painkillers were eating away at his insides. So he'd been trying other pain relievers. Tonight it was whiskey while sitting at the bar, catching some of the late-night Twins game against the A's.

He sloppily held up his glass. "Another, please."

"Are you sure?" the smaller female bartender asked. "You've had a lot, *a lot*."

Mike just held up his glass.

"You look sad," the woman asked as she filled his small tumbler. "What's got you down?"

Mike just started talking, and talking, and talking, "I really just miss the horses. I miss riding them, getting to know them, shoeing them, washing them. I really wish I could go back to that life. I'd give anything to go back to it."

"How'd you get the job you have now? The one you said where you drive."

"I work for a guy I knew in prison, I helped him there,

I'd hear things and feed him the information. I'm kind of good at it. I'm a little guy, not even five feet tall and nobody ever pays me much mind. I'm a threat to nobody." He took a sip of his whiskey. "You know, I'd hear what the guards were saying, I'd hear what the cons were saying and I helped him move product through prison."

"Product?"

"Drugs, other contraband. You wouldn't believe the stuff that moves through a place like that."

"I've never been to jail, prison, what have you," the bartender replied. "But I would think those skills made you really valuable to him. I bet they still do."

"Hah!" Jockey Mike laughed and shook his head in bitterness. "You'd think so," he added angrily. "Jack shit is what he pays me."

"Really?" the bartender replied.

Mike nodded, taking another drink. "He pays me enough to get by and he has access to all the painkillers I need. But what I really want to do is get clean, get off them, maybe see if I could get some therapy for all my pain, but he won't help me. All he cares about is the people he works for."

"What do those people do?"

He shook his head. "It's better that you don't know. But you know what's funny? They think I don't know, but I know exactly what they're doing. I see the Mexicans, the trucks, the powder, the money. I hear the conversations, the whispers and the promises. I see and hear it all."

"That sounds like really nasty work. Quit," the bartender suggested as she wiped down the bar in front of him, picked up his drink and put it back on the coaster. "If you don't like it then quit. Walk away and find something better."

"I wish I could," Mike replied, shaking his head and

taking a sip. He held up his glass for another refill but the bartender shook her head.

"I have to cut you off."

"Really?"

"Yes, I'd feel terrible if something happened to you. I'm going to get you a cab, on the house."

Mike looked at her in surprise, shocked at the kindness of the gesture. "Can I ask what's your name?"

"Denise," the woman answered as she wiped the bar, "although everyone around here calls me DeNasty."

"Why? You seem really nice," Mike said sincerely.

"I know, *right*?" DeNasty answered with a big smile.

"So Denise," he asked. "You said I should do something different, how about you? Do you like what you do or do you dream of something else?"

"What, you think I'd give up all of this?" DeNasty replied with a big smile, waving around the now nearly empty bar. "It's a job, it pays the bills and the people I work with are like family."

"I wish I had that."

"Go find it."

"I had it once, but I can't ride anymore," he replied as he plowed back the last little drops of the alcohol in his glass. "I just can't, I'm too broken down. But man, I miss the horses. I love the horses and they...they loved me."

Fifteen minutes later DeNasty, with the help of BTG and Heavy G, poured the ex-jockey into a cab, handing fare to the driver. They both watched as the cab pulled away.

"What was his name again?" BTG asked.

"I'm not sure I caught it," DeNasty replied. "I sure hope he finds his way back to the horses though."

16

"IT'S NOT MAGICAL, IT'S SURGICAL."

White slowly twisted his drink glass on its circular cardboard coaster with a bit of unease. The police had faded away for a week and things seemed as if they were getting back to normal. But now he sensed they were back and with more intensity. That feeling was confirmed when Fisher called for a meet, and undoubtedly another envelope.

"They've been back on it since yesterday. Lich, Riley, Rockford, the chief's boys think they're onto something," Fisher reported as he took a quick look at the contents of his envelope. "They don't really know exactly what they're onto yet, but they know they have the scent of *something*."

"What are their suspicions?"

Fisher nodded. "They suspect drugs, a drug operation of some kind, but they haven't actually seen any yet. However, they look at the backgrounds of guys like Luther Ellis, Terrence Orr and Neil Kline, and drugs is what naturally springs to mind. If it walks like a duck, looks like a duck, smells like a duck, it's a duck."

It was Sunday night and the crowd was sparse in the

small dimly lit bar in River Falls, a small college town a half hour east of St. Paul, across the St. Croix River and located in the gently rolling countryside of far western Wisconsin. The two of them occupied a small back booth and spoke in low voices.

"What happened on the Orr case? I thought that was closed," White asked quietly with his drink glass close to his lips.

"It was. We had the funeral for Cruz and word was the BCA was ruling it a good shoot, that the two of them did each other in. Orr looked good for the Shead murder, particularly because of the gun they found in his Yukon, among other things. It was case closed."

"What happened then?" White asked pointedly.

"Hey," Fisher answered defensively. "I don't have any control over those things."

"I understand, but what happened? *What changed*?"

"There is one other person who's been involved in this case you may not know about."

"Who?"

"Have you ever heard of a guy named Mac McRyan?"

White's eyes darted up to meet Fisher's and he slowly nodded. If you followed the St. Paul Police Department at all, which White did, you knew there were many McRyans in it and that Mac McRyan was the most notable of them. "I didn't think he was a St. Paul cop anymore. I thought he lived in Washington or something like that."

"He's not a cop, at least officially, and he does live in Washington, but this is home and he visits from time to time. McRyan, like Shead, is an old partner of Lich. McRyan was home from D.C., had some free time and as a favor to his old partner was helping in the background on the Shead thing. Apparently, McRyan found some footage of your boy

Kline slipping a couple of envelopes to Orr while the two of them had drinks at DeAndre's Joint."

"How'd he get that?"

"I don't know. But something on that footage caused McRyan to take another look at that shooting in the alley. Whatever it was he saw convinced the powers that be that there was a third person in that alley and that the third person killed Cruz. That's why all the new heat now—a dead cop. Flanagan is now convinced they don't have the guy who killed Cruz. I'm just telling you, Flanagan"—Fisher shook his head warningly—"he won't let that go. The chief has given his boys a green light to use whatever resources they need. And..."

"And?"

"I think they're just getting warmed up."

"What do you mean?'

"For starters, there is a plan to haul Kline in, maybe as soon as tomorrow."

"I see. What else?"

"They've been *carefully* eyeing the house up in Rogers again. I don't know what you have going on up there, but you might want to consider vacating it as soon as possible, tonight if you can. A move is going to be made on that real soon, again maybe tomorrow."

"Anything else?"

"They have a GPS readout for Shead's last few nights before you did your thing on him. They got it from his cell phone. They're tracking his stops as it looks like he was following either Kline or Orr, but probably Kline."

"What have they found?"

"Nothing yet as best I can tell. Shead's stops were in commercial areas so they can't isolate exactly where he stopped so obviously your people need to be careful. But like I said, Flanagan is all in on providing resources so more and more people are going to be assigned to this. He may even start reaching out to other agencies. The BCA is already assisting, particularly in further evaluating the Orr and Cruz shooting. Lich, Riley, Rockford, and if McRyan comes back and helps, you know as well as I do that those guys are all rock solid. If there is something to be found, they *will* find it. So you need to make some moves here, and make them quick." He downed the last of his drink and started to slide out of the booth.

"You'll keep me informed, of course," White demanded.

Fisher stopped and patted the envelope inside his coat. "If you keep these coming, yes."

"I think we've been quite generous," White replied, not liking a shakedown and his tone said so.

Fisher snorted his own disapproval and then turned dark. "Now you listen here, White. That was *before* you killed a cop. It's one thing to feed you a little information every so often, help you avoid our attention and keep your organization below the radar, but this shit just got real. I didn't sign up to help you kill cops."

"That was extremely unfortunate. That was not...part of the plan."

Fisher gritted his teeth. "No more fucking dead cops, you understand? No. More. Dead. Cops." He slid out of the booth and stood up. "I'll reach out if I get anything new."

White watched as his contact exited out the back door. Felix had been sitting at the bar fifteen feet away, nursing a drink of his own. He slipped into the booth.

"You look...worried," Felix stated, taking the measure of White.

"Too much attention," White answered with a weary sigh. "This is starting to feel like Chicago."

White had been with the organization for nearly fifteen years. At the start his last name was Bruce, not White, and he was just a street lawyer in Indianapolis. His practice was mostly criminal defense, although he handled the occasional business matter that arose for the small businesses located in the neighborhood where he had his office. Back then Felix found himself in some difficulty with the police in Indianapolis on a drug distribution charge. White craftily raised issues with the probable cause the police relied upon to search the trunk of his car. Once the evidence was thrown out by the court, Felix was a free man on his way back to Chicago to further establish and operate his cousin and uncle's drug operation.

In Chicago, for what Felix and Javier had in mind in the long term, they needed a willing and experienced legal hand. They approached White, promising him a generous salary to handle the legal interests of one client, a client operating in an extremely non-legal environment. There would be no shortage of work and quite adequate pay.

"Make no mistake about what we're doing," Felix said, "it is risky for me, and for you, but there is a reward too."

White was more than a bit leery of the criminality they were asking him to wade into. Once he jumped in there would be no turning back. However, as wary as he might have been, he was more tired of the year-after-year, month-after-month and day-after-day struggle to pay the bills not to mention the constant hustling for new clients. He took the offer. White changed his last name from Bruce to Black, became the consigliere and never looked back. The moniker White would not come for some time.

The first eight years in Chicago, the operation purred along under the radar as it grew and prospered. Felix was not afraid of getting bloody, but not long after he arrived in

Chicago, White prevailed in convincing him and Javier, and later even Helena that less could be more. "Why make a scene to show how tough you are?" White asked pointedly after one particularly bloody night.

"Then they fear us and will not mess with us," Javier explained.

"It's how it's done," Felix added in agreement. "You have to fight for this business. There are no 'legal' rules. You want it, you take it. That is what they must fear. Get in line or be gone."

"Fine," White answered. "But then you need to fear the police. You do all that killing, the police will learn who you and your people are. It won't be long before you'll have a target on you and then how far will you get? You want to try to run a multi-state drug operation while doing life in prison? Good luck."

"What do you propose?" Javier asked that night.

"Why all the killing? Why all the bodies for show? I think you strike more fear in people if they know that if you don't get your way, they will just disappear. They don't know when. They don't see you coming. Just one day they were there, the next they were not. You want sinister? What's more sinister than a ghost who makes people vanish?"

"Like what, magic?"

White shrugged. "It's not magical, it's surgical. Your product is the best on the market and supply is *not* the issue. Getting your product on the street is and you're going to war to get it out there. It's getting awfully costly to do business that way. Why not try working with these people first? Making business alliances to get our product out on the streets is better, it makes us safer and lets others take the heat."

"Just roll up and talk business?" Felix asked skeptically.

Back then Felix was a soldier and a fighter. He did not yet have the seasoning to see it was all just business.

White saw it as a business. "Yes, it's business. We're in business to make money, so are they. So we form partnerships."

"And what if these people don't want to be partners?"

"If they don't get on board then they disappear. You identify who you need to eliminate. Then rather than making a huge show of it, you instead very carefully plan your attack and in the middle of the night, when the person you're after is vulnerable and alone, you grab them. You take them somewhere else, get what information you need out of them and then bury the body in the countryside or dump it out in the middle of Lake Michigan or the Chicago River, someplace nobody will ever find it. Then the next day you go to that person's turf and his people and you explain that their world just changed."

White won the argument that night and Felix and Javier gave it a shot. It worked. The organization flew well below the radar for years in Chicago. Javier could visit often from Mexico and later, when Helena was brought into the operation, developed an ingenious way of transporting their product to Chicago, a method they used to this day.

Structurally, over time White developed a siloed operation whereby only himself, Javier, Felix, Helena and a select few others knew the entire operation in the Upper Midwest. The product was delivered from Mexico to a processing facility well outside the city. Once the raw product was processed and repackaged, it was filtered through others before it was distributed to the street level by one group of people. Their street level crews would sell, collect and then hold the money until yet another group arrived, which was responsible for money collection. They would bring the money to scattered legitimate businesses throughout the city. The legitimate businesses were used as fronts to launder their earnings. What money couldn't be laundered through the businesses was then delivered to a location for accounting, bundling and eventually, shipment back to Mexico. That money was eventually filtered back to Helena who would invest it. This was largely the arrangement in Chicago, although it was used to a smaller degree in some other cities including Milwaukee, Des Moines, Kansas City and the Twin Cities.

For eight years nobody in Chicago had an inkling of who was behind the operation that over time became responsible for over sixty percent of the drug traffic in the city and its suburbs. Then one night some new members of a street-level crew lost their cool, ignored the rules and started shooting during a beef over territory. In the end there were three dead bodies, a stash house full of heroin, coke and meth and a couple hundred thousand dollars. There was significant media coverage of the dead bodies as well as the drugs and money. White and Felix moved quickly to isolate the problem, but then sure enough, a similar incident happened two weeks later: dead bodies, lots of drugs and big money found at another house. The political and law enforcement leaders in Chicago started asking where was it all coming from.

The Chicago Police and DEA started digging, working their way through the street level until they caught a break and got a level above the street and then caught onto two of their fronts.

"They have the smell of it now," Felix remarked at the time to Javier.

"And they're just going to keep coming," Helena added and then looked to White. "What do you think?"

"I think we walk away from it."

"The whole thing? This is home."

"I understand, but the risks of staying are only going to become greater. At this point the police don't know anything about you, Javier, or Felix or Helena or me. But if we hang around long enough, they just might and then what? I think we have enough time to safely take in our last shipment here at the processing location and then we shut the doors. The fronts where we're collecting and filtering the money, we walk away from them and let the guys running them sink or swim without us. Who knows, they might make it on their own. As for the main cash drop house, shut it down and move everything out. We move our entire base of operations to another city."

"And what of Helena's business?" Javier asked.

"In time she will need to move too. That can happen more slowly and methodically and it has to, but then again, that's the slower part of the whole operation anyway."

"I hate giving up Chicago," Felix complained.

"I'm not saying you give up Chicago or at least your market share, far from it," White replied. "There is nothing wrong with our product—we just find a new way to deliver and distribute it here with some new people between us and the street so we're further insulated. I've been thinking as we've gotten bigger we needed that anyway, which is why only a few of us know the whole operation. Others only know their part of it. But in my mind, our base of operations must move. The longer we stay, the more at risk we are. So I say we move, split the remaining operation up into smaller units and put people in charge of those groups. We'll set up shop in another city and coordinate supply of Chicago from there."

By that time, given the overall success of the operation,

White's counsel was almost always accepted. Two months later their base of operations moved to St. Paul.

Upon his arrival, White needed to find some people to help run the operation down on the street when a local criminal lawyer White had befriended mentioned his client by the name of Neil Kline. "He's just gotten out of Stillwater. He did five years, but he could have gotten out sooner or not gone at all if he'd have flipped, but he didn't. Neil kept his mouth shut. Shit, he ran drugs through that prison for four years and nobody could prove he was doing it. If you need someone who is good on the street and knows the players, he'd be a good place to start."

Neil was as advertised. He recruited their crew to run the stores where the money was filtered through. Kline knew who had the drug territory, particularly in St. Paul and discreetly introduced Felix around. Felix in turn made deals with crews to distribute the product. If there were crews who didn't go along, the White Solution as they called it, was implemented. The crews that wouldn't do business disappeared and new ones more amenable to Felix's terms took their place.

It operated just like Chicago. Until now.

"You're really worried?" Felix asked for confirmation.

White nodded. "We're drawing far too much attention all of a sudden and I fear it's only going to get worse." He explained the state of the investigation and that Flanagan was pouring into St. Paul Police resources. "They're going to haul Neil in for questioning, probably tomorrow, and they're very interested in the house in Rogers. And with Neil pinned down and the police having some idea of the locations of some of our other storefronts, we're losing room to maneuver. And with the next big shipment coming here in ten days or so, we must protect that. More than anything else, we have to protect the supply line."

"You sound like you think we need to leave."

"I hate to say it, but we have to start thinking about it and at least planning for that contingency, especially after that shipment comes in," White answered, nodding. "We really do."

"I hate the idea of doing that again."

"Trust me," White sighed, "so do I, but I feel like it's getting too risky to stay. We've moved before, we can do it again. After six months of transition it'll all be good. But look, in the meantime we shut down the house in Rogers, *tonight*. You call up there and tell them to load everything into the vans. There isn't a lot of money out there right now, but what there is goes in the van, along with the equipment, the money counters, the supplies, anything they can move. If it takes multiple trips, it takes multiple trips, but get it out."

"What about those two safes?" Felix asked. "We need big trucks for those."

"Don't worry about them. They were both purchased with cash out of state years ago. Load up everything else, wipe down the house and leave. We'll find another place."

"I'll take care of it."

"No," White counseled, "*you* don't go anywhere near there, you just convey the instructions. Let *them* take care of it. You and I need to be very careful with all this police attention going on. Our profiles get even lower now."

"And what about Neil?"

"I'm calling him and we need to lawyer him up right now. We need to protect him...and ourselves."

17

"THERE'S AN OLD SAYING: YOU PLAY IN THE DIRT, YOU GET DIRTY."

"Is Double Frank ready to roll?" Rock asked, checking his watch.

"Yup," Dick replied. "He, Ortega and Fisher, Olson and a couple of his boys from the BCA and the Rogers Police are gearing up right now and they're thinking they'll roll in a half-hour at ten. We need to go now."

Monday morning right at 9:30 a.m., Dick and Paddy, along with Rock and Riles and two patrol units pulled up to Rice Street Auto Repair. In front of a shop full of customers Rock asked Neil Kline to accompany them downtown.

"Am I under arrest?"

"Rather than that," Rock suggested, "I think we'd just prefer that you come and have a chat all nice and polite like."

Kline was smart. He didn't resist in any way and simply asked if he could call his lawyer.

"Sure," Dick replied. "Make the call right now. Here's where he can show," he added, handing Kline a card. Once the call was made they left the repair shop.

The lawyer, a well-regarded downtown St. Paul criminal

defense lawyer by the name of Byrnes was waiting at the Department of Public Safety when they arrived.

"What, Byrnes was waiting for the phone call?" Rock bitched. "From this ass clown?"

"Everything tells you something," Riles replied, slipping a piece of Dentyne into his mouth. "Do you really think Neil Kline has high-quality defense counsel on speed dial who will just appear at the drop of a hat?"

"No, but whoever... he works for does."

"Exactly," Riles replied. "So who exactly is that?" Pat patted Dick on the back. "Maybe Dicky Boy here will be able to find out."

"Let's all find out," Lich replied as he opened the door into the interview room.

"Why am I here?" Neil demanded irritably with what Dick thought, upon a moment's reflection and evaluation, was feigned exasperation. The only real surprise for Neil Kline was that he wasn't brought in sooner.

"I'll get to that," Dick replied, getting comfortable, flipping his notebook open. Riley sat to his right while Rock leaned against the wall behind them, his hands in his pockets. "Tell me about your job. Who do you work for?"

"Rice Street Auto Repair."

"No," Dick asked, "I mean, *who* do you work for? Who owns it?"

"I do," Kline replied indignantly. "I bought it five years ago."

"Five years ago, you got out of prison, Neil," Dick stated. Dick and the boys knew that Kline's name was on the papers and tax return. They were also smart enough to know that a front never had the name of the organization that really owned it anywhere on the paperwork. You had people like Neil for that. "What, you rolled out of prison after five years and suddenly had the downstroke to buy an auto repair shop? Come on, who really owns it?"

"I do," Neil responded indignantly. "It's my place and I've worked damn hard at it."

"How the hell would someone like you have been able to afford to buy a gas station?" Riles asked. "A street drug dealer who does five years in Stillwater, walks out of prison and four months later he owns an auto repair shop?"

"I had a lot of money saved up before I went in prison."

"Dirty drug money, no doubt," Dick snorted.

"Who cares? Think what you want, Detective. I had the money, the bank took it and the shop was mine. That's how those things work."

"And what kind of background did you have that suggested you'd be able to make that work?"

Neil smiled. He had a record, they all knew he had a record and to anyone it would seem odd that he not only owned an auto repair shop but had any clue how to operate it. "I worked in the machine shop when I was in prison and picked up some skills. I know motors and engines. I like cars. I do well with people. I have some business savvy. You know you can get business experience in school or out on the street. Mine wasn't from no book."

"I see," Dick answered and then took a shot. "Pick up that business savvy running drugs?"

Kline snorted his disapproval. His attorney interrupted.

"Detective Lich, move on or this is going to be awfully..."

"Why am I here?" Kline barked, not letting the lawyer finish. "I'm not answering any more fucking questions until I know why the hell I'm here."

Dick sat back and folded his arms. "Neil, you know why you're here."

Kline stared right back. "No, I don't."

It was all part of the game, Dick thought as he replied, "Terrence Orr."

"T.O.? All I know about T.O. is that he's dead."

"Really? That's it?" Riles asked, eyebrows raised, arms folded. "Bullshit. You know more, a *lot* more."

"Look," Kline replied, sitting back in his chair and folding his arms over his chest. "T.O.? That dude always knew how to find trouble. I'm not the least bit surprised he went the way he did."

"I can't say that I totally agree with that assessment," Dick stated, leaning forward with his elbows on the interrogation table, clasping his hands in front of him. "In fact, I think T.O. was probably pretty surprised at how he went."

Neil was about to respond and then stopped, a hint of confusion on his face.

"I got you thinking now just a little, don't I?" Dick needled. "Now on T.O., Neil, you do realize that you're the last person he ever spoke to?" Dick placed still photos from the surveillance video out on the table for Kline and the lawyer to see. "I can bring in the video if you'd like. But the time stamp in the upper corner puts your little meet here at DeAndre's at 11:22 p.m."

Kline chortled. "What, I can't meet up with an old friend? Please."

"And was this the first time you'd met him as of late?"

"I'd see Terrence from time to time."

"Time to time?"

"Yeah."

"Not daily or anything?"

"No, not at all."

"You're sure about that?" Dick asked. "I mean, absolutely sure? Just time to time is all?"

"I'm sure if you've done any checking at all, you'd know that he and I were in prison together. He's a friend."

"A felony friend."

"Is there a law against that? He paid his debt too. The problem for T.O. was he didn't get his life straightened out. I *did*."

"How was it that you came to meet him at DeAndre's?"

"What does that matter?" Kline asked, again looking to his lawyer. "What does it matter that I met him there? I didn't shoot him"—he turned back to Dick— "you guys did. DeAndre's is in Minneapolis. The shooting was over in St. Paul. He said he was going to a girl named Tiana's house. I assume that's where you found him."

"I need to know why he was where he was," Dick answered calmly. "Just because he was shot doesn't mean I don't need to know why he was there. In any murder investigation..."

"Hold on," Neil interrupted. "Murder investigation? What murder investigation?"

"Well, let's see. We think your buddy T.O. was involved in the murder of a former police officer named Sam Shead. His name arose, along with yours I might add, in the disappearance of a man named Luther Ellis. You remember that, don't you, Neil?" Dick said. "That's where our paths first crossed a few months ago."

"What does any of that have to do with me? Or with T.O.?"

"Look, Neil. I asked you a question a minute ago. Why were you meeting Terrence Orr at DeAndre's in Minneapolis and why were you slyly slipping him white envelopes full of cash?"

"Yeah, nothing *suspicious* about that?" Rock suggested,

leaning back against the wall rolling a toothpick around in his mouth.

Kline looked to his lawyer who leaned in to whisper to him. The lawyer nodded his head and Kline turned back to Dick. "He needed some help."

"What kind of help?"

"He wanted to leave town."

"Was that you suggesting he leave or was this his idea?"

"His."

"Really?" Dick replied skeptically, certain Kline was the one who suggested it. "You sure about that? You sure you weren't the one suggesting that?"

"No, I didn't suggest it, I questioned it."

"Why?"

"Because it seemed things had been going good for him."

"Really?"

"Yeah, so I didn't initially understand why he wanted to skip town."

"Okay, I'll bite. Why?" Dick asked, his skepticism showing. "Why did a tough guy like Terrence Orr feel the need to leave town?"

Neil shrugged and sat back in his chair, arms folded. "All I know is he just wanted to leave and he needed some help."

"So would that help be the twenty thousand of help in the two white envelopes you handed to him?" Dick replied, showing two more still photos of Kline handing the envelope to Orr. The envelopes were in a back compartment of the Yukon, along with the rest of the money Orr was taking with him. "Again, I've got the video if you want to see it."

"So what?" Kline answered, nonplussed.

"There was twenty grand combined in the two envelopes."

Kline shrugged. "It was a loan."

"A loan?"

"Yeah, a loan."

Dick was dumbfounded. "Neil, let me get this straight. You own this auto repair shop, which, in the unlikely event the whole thing is on the up-and-up, probably provides a modest income. Call me a skeptic, but let's just say I don't buy you're taking enough out of it to be able to come up with twenty thousand dollars *in cash* for a loan," Dick stated.

Kline's lawyer leaned in again and whispered something in his client's ear. Kline nodded and returned his gaze to Dick. He was careful. "T.O. was a friend. He said he was in some trouble and looking to leave town. I wanted to help him. He was a good friend in prison, a protector, I felt I owed him so I stretched for him."

"Did he tell you why he was in trouble?"

"No," Kline replied. "He said he didn't want to get me involved."

"Yet here you were making a loan," Dick replied skeptically. "You loan him twenty gees and you don't ask him why he needs it?"

"What do you want me to say?"

"The truth is always good," Dick retorted, trying to bait Kline. "How about you try that?"

Kline had a response he wanted to give, but he was also canny and his lawyer was lightly reaching for his left arm to steady him, which seemed to have the desired effect. After a moment Kline sat back just slightly, paused, exhaled and then responded. "Look, I don't know what T.O. was mixed up in. I know that he was never one to shy away from fast money and I don't think he necessarily avoided his old life after he got out of Stillwater. He took a different path than I did."

"Oh, you're just all hard work and perseverance," Dick mocked.

Kline ignored the jab. "So it sounded like T.O. got on the wrong side with some bad people and he needed to get out of town and needed some money while he ran and got himself settled somewhere else."

"When did he ask you for this loan?"

"The day before."

"Saturday?" Dick asked. "He was shot on Sunday night. So in a mere twenty-four hours you came up with twenty thousand dollars in cash? Where did you get the money?"

"I had it."

"Where did you go get it? It sure as hell wasn't a bank."

"Like I said, I had it."

"In your mattress? Buried in the backyard? Coffee can on top of the fridge?"

"I had the money. Is it illegal for me to have a lot of cash?"

"No, it's just not believable," Dick answered.

"Enough!" Kline's lawyer admonished. "How or where my client got the money is of no relevance."

"Actually, it is," Riley replied flatly. "Where the money came from is quite relevant because, Counselor, we don't believe for a minute it was your client's money."

"How do you figure?" Neil asked.

"We'll come back to that," Dick stated. "So did your *friend* tell you where he was going?"

Kline shook his head.

"Is that a no?"

"No, he didn't tell me."

"Well, did you ask?"

"No."

Dick guffawed out loud and looked first to Riley and Rock in mock shock. "Can you believe this guy?"

"No," Riles and Rock each replied quickly, shaking their heads, chuckling.

Dick turned back to Kline. "So let me get this straight. Orr is leaving town with twenty grand of your money and you didn't even ask where he was going? Really? You really expect me to believe that, Neil?"

Kline shook his head. "I didn't ask."

"Why the heck not?"

"Because if the people looking for him came to ask me where he was, I wouldn't know."

"How would they know to come to you to begin with if you have no idea who T.O. is having issues with?"

Kline snorted. It was a good question and boxed him in a little, so he deflected. "I have learned over the years that at times, the less you know the better."

"These people are *so* dangerous that someone as bad as Terrence Orr feels the need to run, yet you're willing to give him twenty thou? In cash? I mean, again, where does a guy like you come up with twenty grand in cash?"

"You ever heard of a safe? I'm a saver, I don't live extravagantly," Neil retorted. "And I believe in cash. A lot of people lost their shirts in '08 because their money was in the market. Mine was in cash. I didn't lose a dime. I believe in cash, I keep loose cash and so I got him the cash."

"Twenty thousand?"

Kline nodded. "It was a loan."

"Got any loan papers?" Riles asked.

Neil shook his head. "T.O. would have paid me back, and..."

"And what?"

"Well, it is kind of cold to ask, but since T.O. is dead I'd like the money back."

"I can see how broken up you are about your buddy's death," Riles needled.

"Yeah, one can just see the tears in his eyes," Rock added sarcastically. "You want a tissue?"

"It's evidence," Dick stated and then added something Kline wouldn't know. "It's all part of the hundred and eight thousand in cash that was found in his Yukon."

Kline couldn't hide his surprise.

Riles seized on it. "One hundred eight thousand four hundred dollars. Now if he had that much money, why did he need a puny loan for twenty from you?"

"Somebody got *plaaaayed*," Rock added mockingly.

"Of course," Dick suggested, leaning forward. "I suspect your buddy T.O. got the other eighty-eight four we found in a compartment in that Yukon doing work for the same people who financed your repair shop purchase."

"Detective, I'm still waiting for you to give me some evidence of that," the lawyer demanded. "And until you do, my client isn't going to dignify that with a response."

At that moment there was a knock on the door. "Well, perhaps Counselor, we'll have that evidence right here," Dick stated, knowing the knock was for the expected update on the raid of the house in Rogers.

An aide handed in a sheet of paper to Rock who read it and did a double take. He handed the page to Riles who lightly shook his head and then handed it to Dick. The sheet was a report from Double Frank that simply stated: *The Rogers house was empty. Nothing inside other than some furniture and two large safes. Nothing else. Nobody else. No vehicles, no money, no drugs. It was cleaned out. Forensic team says house has been wiped down.*

It was a gut punch.

Kline sensed something was amiss. "My shop runs like a well-oiled machine. We're busy, we do good work and I have a lot of satisfied, repeat customers. In fact, I'm looking at buying another shop."

"So you want to build an empire?" Rock asked.

"Not an empire, Detective, just a regular normal life."

Suddenly, Kline sounded almost convincingly sympathetic. How dare people question how hard he worked?

In all actuality, none of the three detectives questioned his work ethic, only who he worked for. Today, Dick realized, especially with the failure up in Rogers that they didn't have enough to get the answer to that question. The whole conversation reminded Dick of the one he'd had with Sam Shead. If you want to squeeze, you must have leverage. Dick was coming to the realization that they didn't have enough yet.

"Detectives, unless you have anything else?" Byrnes the lawyer counseled, sensing that things were at an end. "I think we're done here."

"Perhaps, Counselor, we're done for now," Dick replied with a light nod. "We viewed this as a get-acquainted meeting anyway."

"Figures," Neil bitched, looking over to his lawyer. "You do your time, but you're never really free."

Dick chuckled, as did Riley and Rockford.

"Something funny?" Kline asked.

"Just your little pity party over there," Riles remarked in return. "There's an old saying: You play in the dirt, you get dirty."

"I'll keep that in mind," Kline replied derisively.

Dick made a show of closing his notebook and putting

the evidence photos back in a folder. "Neil, I want to leave you with one little thought."

"What's that?"

"You know on the Sunday Terrence Orr was shot, we were watching both you and Orr. Funny... Orr slipped away and so did *you*."

"I have no idea what you're talking about."

Dick just smiled as if to say *really*? "Now, either you came up with it on your own or you had some help, but you skipped out of the shop hidden somehow. Orr slipped out of an apartment building on that Sunday morning with, what I must admit, was a pretty good little ruse of his own."

"So what if he did? Heck, so what if I did?"

"Well, it could matter if the whole point of slipping you away was so that someone would know where to find Orr," Dick stated. "Perhaps because they knew you were already meeting, or that you could contact him and arrange for a meet."

"And even if you already have eighty-eight thousand and change to go on the run with, another twenty grand..." Riles suggested.

"Is another twenty grand," Rock finished.

"So that cash was an attractive inducement to get Orr to a place where someone knew they could find him. We think maybe it's because someone wanted him found."

"So T.O. got himself an extra twenty thousand," Neil shrugged. "Perhaps he played me."

Dick smiled, a big broad grin underneath his bushy mustache. "Oh Neil, you weren't played just by T.O. Oh, no, no, no. You were played by *both* sides." Dick stood up and got ready to leave, but as he reached the door, he looked back. "By the way, you don't really think it was just T.O. and Detective Rafael Cruz in that alley, do you?" Dick let that hang in the air for a moment before smiling. "We'll see you around, Neil."

~

"What do you mean nothing?" Dick barked into the phone in disbelief.

"Dick, there was nothing in the house," Double Frank replied sheepishly over the speaker phone. "It was cleaned out. No clothes, no food, only a few small pieces of furniture and that's it. Forensics has been working their way through the house, but it's been wiped down."

"What about those safes?"

"Down in the basement there were two American Security safes, seventy-two inches high, big ones," Double Frank replied. "They were closed when we came in."

"We brought someone in to open them up," Fisher added. "They were empty. They were situated in an area with some metal shelving units, all of which were empty. Whatever it was that was here, Dick, is gone."

"And what was going on up there last night?" Riles asked.

"From what the BCA guys are saying, nothing terribly unusual. A few vans came and went, that was it," Ortega answered. "But vehicles have come and gone each night."

"Vans," Riles mused looking over to Dick. "That's what was different, the vans."

"More space in a van," Rock added.

"Look, I'll call if we get anything from forensics, but brace yourself," Double Frank warned. "It doesn't look good."

The three of them retreated to the break area in search of sodas.

"You know what else was the case?" Riles offered as he dropped himself into an orange plastic chair at one of the round tables. "Kline wasn't the least bit fazed by us, maybe other than when we told him about the hundred grand that was found in Orr's truck."

"Because he or they saw us coming a mile away," Dick replied disgustedly, grabbing a chair of his own. "They saw us up there watching somehow. We'd pulled back quite a way from that house yet we still must have been spotted. So there's that calamity. And as for Kline, he clearly knew we'd been paying attention to him."

"Hence the lawyer being so prompt to arrive," Rock added, contemplating his vending machine selections.

"Shit," Dick bitched. "I feel like we're back to square one again."

Riles shrugged, not as bothered. "Maybe so, maybe so, but I'll tell you one other thing. Kline knows we don't believe this whole I work hard, I've earned everything I got, I saved my money bullshit for that repair shop. He's too smart for that. Right now, however, he knows we have no evidence against him, no leverage, but he knows we don't believe that line of garbage for a minute."

"No, you're right about that," Dick replied. "Kline is savvy enough to recognize this probably isn't the last of it."

"And I'll tell you one more thing," Riles continued, pointing at Dick. "Your last little statement in there about the alley and that it wasn't just Orr and Cruz in there, that statement..."

"Got him thinking a little," Rock finished the thought as he opened his bag of Funyuns from the vending machine. "It's got him thinking we either know he set his friend up or he is now realizing he was used to set up Orr. And if he was used to set up Orr, what's to say that..."

"His employer wouldn't set him up too," Riles agreed with a smile. "You can bet he's thinking on that, at least a little."

"Well, that could prove useful if we can find something to make him think on it a little harder," Dick replied. "The problem is, right now he fears his employer more than he fears us."

~

Neil went back to the lawyer's office. White was waiting.

"And?" White asked.

"It went fine," Byrnes the lawyer replied as he sat down into his high-backed leather chair behind his expansive desk. "Based on what you prepped me for, I think they actually had a little less than I'd expected."

"Really?"

"Or they were keeping a couple left in the chamber for later," Byrnes added as he casually folded his left leg over his right. "I don't think this is over. They maintain interest in Neil."

That caused White to frown. Neil being tied down to the repair shop was impinging on their operation. If Neil was watching over the retail fronts and other parts of the street operation, White and Felix didn't have to face that exposure. That was Neil's key role and right now he was benched, sitting still at the repair shop under constant police watch. "Is there anything we can do to get them to back off?"

Byrnes shook his head. "They can *watch* all they want. If they harass him that's another story, but as of now they've just been watching. From where I sit Neil needs to behave himself and he'll be fine. Eventually, if they're unable to develop any probable cause to obtain a search warrant to rummage through the shop or conduct any sort of electronic surveillance, they'll get tired of watching nothing happening and eventually will drift away. My advice is to just be patient."

White looked to Neil. "I guess that means sit tight."

Neil exhaled and slowly nodded his head. More time caged up at the shop. Then he looked back to White and asked, "What happened to T.O. in that alley?"

"What do you mean?"

"Detective Lich made a comment to the effect that it wasn't just Orr and the cop in that alley," Byrnes explained and then looked to Neil. "I think he was jerking your chain. A little face-saving maneuver on their part since you'd given them nothing."

White nodded his agreement. "Neil, T.O. screwed up. He should have just left town after he met with you and got the money. If he had he'd be alive. He didn't—he fired at the police and they of course returned it. He's dead. It's nobody's fault but his."

Neil kept his gaze on White for a moment, trying to get a read on the man. The problem was that White was aptly named, always opaque, both in color and expression. Was he telling the truth? Neil couldn't tell. "So I guess I'll head back to the shop then."

"Yes," White answered. "Keep your eyes open. I'll be in touch."

18

"GIVING HIM TEN GRAND WAS LIKE YOU OR I GIVING A DOG A BONE."

"Should we have one more glass of wine?" Mac asked Sally as he pulled the key out of the deadbolt for the front door of their brownstone townhouse in Georgetown. They'd walked the three blocks back from their favorite little Italian restaurant and the night was still young enough for a nightcap.

"For sure," Sally replied, "It's a beautiful night, let's sit on the back patio."

"What would you like?"

"We had red for dinner, so how about a glass of Chardonnay?"

Mac went to their wine fridge in the kitchen and reached for a perfectly chilled bottle, expertly opened it and poured two glasses. They sat on the lounge chairs and enjoyed the comfortable warmth of a mid-August night.

"So what time do you leave on Friday?" Mac asked.

"We're actually leaving later in the afternoon."

"And the first stop is Tokyo?"

"Yes, a day to travel, two full days there, then to Seoul for two days before we go to Beijing for two more days, and then a stop in Hawaii for a visit to Pearl Harbor for a little over a day on the way back, so it'll be a heck of a trip."

"Pretty cool, babe. You do get to travel to some pretty interesting places in your job," Mac replied.

Sally nodded as she took a small drink of her wine. "We do, but we're working, and on this trip we're working *a lot*. We'll be handling both the politics of the trip with the diplomatic corps, not to mention evaluating the ever-changing landscape for the mid-terms so, unfortunately, I don't think there will be a lot of downtime for sightseeing."

"That's okay," Mac replied. "Just make a list of all these places. We'll go back and see them after you're done with politics."

His wife smiled brightly and toasted his glass. "Just the two of us. That would be awesome."

"We'll do it," Mac replied as he reached inside his pocket for his ringing cell phone. "It's Lich, it can wait."

"Nah, answer it," Sally replied, totally relaxed in the lounge chair. "Put it on speaker."

"Dicky Boy, what's going on?" Mac answered breezily. "Sally's here too."

"Counselor, how are you?" Dick greeted warmly. They spent ten minutes idly talking about life in general. Sally had a big soft spot in her heart for the round mustached man and she absolutely adored Dot.

"So I know you didn't call to shoot the shit with my wife. What's up?" Mac asked.

"We're stuck," Dick answered, explaining how uneventful their interview with Kline was and that they came up dry on the house in Rogers. "I had hoped that by bringing in Kline at the same time we went for the house we'd shake something loose. That plan failed spectacularly."

"The house was empty?" Mac asked. "Absolutely empty? How can that be?"

"Zip, zero, nada. Not even a fingerprint to be found."

How could that *possibly* be? Mac wondered and it got his mind racing in a couple of new directions, directions he did not like. "There was nothing in the house at all? Nothing?"

"The only thing left behind were the safes. Your buddy Ortega traced them back to their original purchases. The original buyers sold them for cash five and four years ago respectively. It appears they were sold to the same guy as both sellers agree on the general description of a middle-aged white guy of medium height with thinning hair. Neither seller had a name and in fact couldn't even remember if they asked for one. In both sales it was a straight cash transaction. No receipt, no sales slip, nothing."

"And what was the house situation? Ownership? Rental? What?"

"Rental," Dick replied. "It took us a week to track down the owner who was out of the country traveling. He's a retired guy living down in Tucson, Arizona. He built the house fifteen years ago thinking growth would keep coming out that far and make the house and its big plot of land a little goldmine for him. Instead it's been a white elephant. He's been renting it out for five years."

"To who?"

"A company, A&B Enterprises. An electronic funds transfer was made monthly for rent to the owner's account from a bank in the Cayman Islands and it's all paid up through this month. The owner would come up here in the summer and check on the place and everything looked fine. No damage, well-maintained and all."

"Did he recall who he rented it to?" Sally asked.

Dick laughed. "Yeah. Shockingly enough it was a

middle-aged white guy of medium height with thinning hair. The owner couldn't recall the man's name. He just said he represented this A&B Enterprises and they were looking for a long-term home to rent for an executive."

"Probably the same guy who bought the safes," Mac answered. "Is there a signature on the lease?"

"Yes," Lich replied. "It's a complete scribble, though. We're having an expert review it, but honest to God, it's just a big squiggle. The owner had a phone number we could call. I had Paddy follow up on that, but it goes to an answering service located down in Texas. We left a message."

"But since the house is cleaned out that message will not be returned," Mac answered, finishing off the house line of inquiry. He moved to another. "Did you get any of the plate numbers from vehicles doing the drop-offs?"

"We got them for three SUVs. We've been watching them, but right now, all three are parked and haven't moved in three days."

"In other words, they know they've been identified and they're not..."

"Leading us anywhere. We have the names the vehicles are registered to. None of the names have records. In fact, in two circumstances the vehicles are registered to women over the age of sixty."

"Okay, so you have that, which isn't much. Could be down the road. What other moves are you making right now?"

"We're still watching Kline, although I'm not sure what that's worth at this point. He knows we're watching so he's not doing anything."

"I'm not sure that's worthless," Mac answered. "In fact, I disagree with that."

"Why?"

"Let's just say that before you were watching Kline, what he was doing was making these stops. Now he's not. And in fact, now there are three other vehicles that appear to be grounded."

"So?'

"Kline is out of action. These other vehicles are idle, but that doesn't mean the stops they were all making don't still have to be made. Someone else is doing it."

"Yeah, I follow you there," Dick replied. "That's why we're going back through the GPS from Sam's phone to try and figure out where Kline was stopping when Sam was following him around."

"Again, assuming that was who Sam was following," Mac cautioned.

"Duly noted," Dick responded. "But I think that's what Sam was doing. You remember the one night we looked at, there were several stops in St. Paul and another couple in Minneapolis. However, all the stops were in commercial areas with several possible business options so we can't really tell where it was Kline, or whoever Sam was following, may have stopped. There are also homes and apartments in each of these areas, so it's proving difficult to know where the stops were made or what Sam was looking at and surveilling. So as I sit here at my kitchen table having myself a High Life, I'm calling you because I could use some outside thinking on this."

Sally had just been listening to the conversation, soaking in the information and then asked, "What do you think these guys are up to?"

"Drugs, right?" Mac suggested, offering at least one answer. "This whole thing sounds like a drug crew of some kind, don't you think? I mean, the rental property and anonymous name, no useful names on the vehicles; Neil Kline and Terrence Orr and their criminal histories and backgrounds. The whole thing says drugs."

"We think so," Dick answered. "That would fit the background of the players involved. It might fit with the activity we saw at the Rogers house, where it looked like money drops were being made. However, we haven't seen any drugs. Maybe, just maybe, some money and even that's speculative since all we've seen for sure is duffel bags. I mean, you think about this. We've done a lot of work and we really don't have much to show for it."

"You need to identify the drug players then," Sally mused, looking to Mac. "If this is drugs and money and this Kline guy was making stops at these places, it could have been to pick up money, to check in on the operation, whatever. But St. Paul isn't *that* big of a city. The Twin Cities isn't *that* big of an area, so the drug players should be..."

"Identifiable," Mac finished the thought and smiled. "You're pretty damn smart."

"That's what I keep telling you."

"We've been using the wrong people," Mac added, shaking his head. Sometimes solutions can be so simple.

"Or the wrong resources," Sally replied.

"What?" Dick asked through the phone. "I can't follow what you two are saying to each other."

"Dick, is the chief still giving you whatever resources you need?"

"Yeah, why?"

"Maybe we've been using some of the wrong guys. Instead of using Homicide guys to watch these areas, pull guys from the Narcotics Unit, put them in surveillance vans and let them see if they recognize anyone in these commercial areas. Paddy has friends in that unit. Ask him who knows their stuff and get some of those guys involved. Maybe the Narcotics guys see a recognizable face or two and then you work it back from that angle."

"That's not a bad idea," Dick replied appreciatively. "We'll do that first thing tomorrow."

"Keep the pressure up, buddy," Mac added. "Something will pop."

"Will do," Dick answered and then shifted gears. "Say, I know your beautiful bride is sitting there and all..."

"Flattery will get you everywhere, Dick," Sally replied glowingly, "But I know where you're going with this. He can come back Friday night."

"Four days, man," Mac added. "I'll get back on Friday night and I can give you a hand for like a good week. How's that?"

"I'd appreciate that."

Sally pushed herself up from her lounger. "I'm going to head inside. Chat for a while if you want," she said as she kissed him on the cheek.

Mac did in fact have one other thought running through his mind but waited for his wife to get safely inside. "Listen, Dick, one other thing."

"What's that?"

"Watch your back."

"Why...do you say that?" Dick asked haltingly in reply, catching the warning tone of Mac's voice.

"The house was completely empty. There is one other possible reason that happened." Mac paused for a moment. "They were tipped off."

"You think someone is talking. A cop?"

"Come on," Mac replied, "it has to have at least occurred to you."

He could hear Dick sigh on the other end of the line.

"Yeah, it has," he replied reluctantly. "I guess I just don't want to believe it's possible."

"It might not be possible. I have no evidence, only suspicions," Mac replied. "That suspicion is just an alternative explanation for what happened. The house being completely empty when there had been traffic in and out of there up until that point in time? It's like they knew you were coming and when. Think about it. To have that large a house cleaned out and wiped down completely? How would they know?"

"Still," Dick replied. "If someone is talking..."

"They're talking to the people who killed Rafael Cruz," Mac replied darkly. "Like I said, watch your back. And perhaps tighten the circle around this thing to people you know you can trust. Riles, Rock, the chief, Paddy, perhaps Double Frank."

"What about your buddy Ortega?"

"You can trust him," Mac replied.

"How do you know? I mean, you haven't seen him in a long time."

"That's true," Mac responded. It was a fair point. "Keep things tight. Don't loop him into the circle if you have doubts. But take my blind spot for him out of this. Logically, he wouldn't be right for a mole. He's only been with the force three months after moving back here from Denver. He's barely had time to settle in. And look, again, I might be *completely* wrong about this."

He heard Dick exhale a sigh on the other end of the line. Dick loved being a cop, being a part of the brotherhood. And more than that, he simply loved other cops and they all loved him. He was the infamous Dick Lick, one of the most popular guys on the force. The last thing he wanted to believe was that a fellow cop, one of his guys, could be dirty. "This is all I need. A fucking rat."

"We don't know for sure," Mac answered. "It's a guess on our part. What evidence do we have? Look, I'm not there right now. I'm the quintessential Monday Morning Quarterback tossing around suspicion bombs from a thousand miles away. I may be, and probably am entirely full of shit, but...I just don't think you should entirely discount the possibility. Give it some thought."

"I will."

"What's the story on that DeVonte Rice trial?" Mac asked, changing topics. "Where is that at?"

"The defense rested today. Closing arguments are tomorrow and then it goes to the jury."

"What do you think about what happened there? Now that the trial has finished, do you think those two blew it?"

"I don't know, buddy. I've been on that traffic stop before, you know? You have too. It's intense, you're trying to keep your wits about you, but there are a lot of crazies out there carrying guns. DeVonte Rice just led a police chase. Is he on something? What was he running from? Is he a guy who feels like he's in a no-win scenario? Does he have anything to live for? You don't know any of this at that moment when it's you and him. So even though the car is surrounded with cops and he's going nowhere and any resistance on his part is futile, if he has a death wish do you want to be the one cop he gets before everyone else draws? His hands disappear from sight and you...react," Dick replied, but there was an air of doubt in his voice.

"But?"

"I hate all the second guessers out there who've never done this job questioning those who do it, but in this case," Dick paused and exhaled a heavy sigh. "In this case, I personally think these two guys screwed up. Go to jail for life screwed up? No. But they blew it and killed an unarmed man."

"Is your view universally held?"

"No," Dick replied. "I'd say it's about fifty-fifty, though. For the most part, we all try not talking about it because when you do it tends to get a little edgy, if you know what I mean. We have to have each other's backs so if you come out and say those two shit the bed, someone is going to be back in your face pretty quickly."

"How has the trial gone?"

"There has been a lot of back and forth. The Minneapolis cops have Carl May and Joe Freeland representing them. They are as good as defense counsel gets around here other than maybe Lyman Hisle. The news accounts suggest they've chiseled some cracks into the prosecution's case. You think with all that video of the incident that these guys would be toast, but the reality is that this happened at night. It was dark, so you can't see what Rice does with his hands. So it really comes down to what the cops say they saw and how believable it is."

"If these guys get off, then what?"

"Then we'll need to keep our heads down because I think it'll be rough. Black motorist shot by two white cops. It's all caught on video and he wasn't armed. If they walk, I fear what might happen."

"Come on, it's Minnesota, how bad could it get?"

"Mac, you're not on the street much these days so maybe you don't get it. What happened with DeVonte Rice has played out around the country repeatedly in other cities. So while you have visions and memories of Minnesota Nice, the reality is that right now it's tense on the streets. Relations between us and many of our citizens are not what I would characterize as warm. Trust in us is at an all-time low among certain segments of the population. Hostility, on the other hand, is at an all-time high. Here and everywhere. These two walking would not make it better."

"What happened with the police today?" Jockey Mike asked Neil. His boss was gone for much of the day.

Neil glanced to the right to his driver and, upon thought, friend. For all his business savvy, social skills and networking, Neil occasionally thought about the fact that he had few people he could truly call friends. He didn't have many people he could call up who would be willing to go out for a drink, maybe a meal, catch a ball game or just hang out. There was no family to speak of. There were only the people who were useful in some way that he needed to operate his part of the overall machine for White and Felix and that was pretty much it in his life. He had few people to confide in. T.O. was one, but he was gone now. Reality was, Jockey Mike was about all he had. Jockey Mike was always there at his side, at his beck and call. *Maybe you should treat him a little better,* Neil thought to himself. In any event, he was in the mood to talk and Mike was ready to engage. "They asked a lot of questions. I didn't give them many answers. For the most part the detectives ended up frustrated, especially because when they raided the house up in Rogers there was nothing there."

"So White and Felix must know you were hauled in then, right?"

Neil nodded. "Yes. In fact, they'd been expecting it."

"Were they okay after it was all over?"

"Yes." Neil nodded and then thought for a moment. "I guess they seemed to be."

The two of them sat in silence for a bit, taking in the preseason football game on the corner flat screen of the sparsely populated tavern.

"I know the cops have been watching the shop. I assume that's why we've just been staying there all the time."

"Yeah, that's right. Are you getting bored, Mike?"

"I don't know," the little man replied. "Somewhat, I guess. I mean, all I do is sit around and wait for you to need to go somewhere. If you're not going anywhere, I don't have much to do but sit around the shop and read stuff."

"Me too. I feel cooped up."

"Did all of this have something to do with that guy, the ex-cop who was watching us that night?"

"Yes, that's a big part of it. I think that's why the police have been watching the shop again, so there is that."

"It seemed like they were watching, then they weren't and now they're back again. I mean, I think they are. I do what you tell me, I keep my eyes open and each day I seem to be able to find the cops who are on watch. They change up their cars or trucks or SUVs, but I seem to be able to pick them out. But why is it they seemed to stop and now they're back again? That's what I can't figure."

Neil nodded as he reached into the popcorn basket for a handful of popcorn. Jockey Mike was observant as ever. "You know what, Mikey, that is odd. You know what else was odd? They were asking questions about T.O."

"T.O.? Why T.O.?" Mike asked, surprised. "Why would they ask you about that?"

"I guess because I was the last person to talk to him. Before he was in that alley in St. Paul, I was meeting up with him at DeAndre's Joint in Minneapolis."

"The afternoon you snuck out of the shop? That day you told me to leave at six and just go home?"

"That's right."

"What did you talk to T.O. about that made you have to sneak out?"

"Getting out of town, Mikey. I suggested to him the night before that he get out of town for a while since he seemed to have attracted so much attention from the cops. I don't think T.O. saw it, but I did. I could see that he was a potential liability if he hung around with the police starting to hound him. We've seen what White and Felix do if someone causes problems."

"The person disappears."

"That's right. I was worried T.O. would suffer that fate."

"Did T.O. have something to do with that ex-cop they found in the river?"

Neil snorted and smiled at how Mikey had worked things through in his own right. "I think the less either of us know on that point the better, don't you agree?"

"If you say so."

"I just try to keep my head down and do my job, like I've always told you to do," Neil counseled. "But T.O. didn't always do that. And because of that, I suggested to T.O. that he take a long vacation until the heat died down around here. He said he needed some money to run." Neil shook his head with a little disgust. "As it turns out, he didn't really need it."

"He didn't?"

"Nope," Neil replied and then with a wry smile added, "the police said they found over a hundred grand in a compartment in his Yukon the night he was shot."

"He was a scammer. He even scammed his friends," Mike retorted. "He played you."

"So it appears, because I put together a little for him and I also had some money for him from White and Felix."

"They paid him?" Jockey Mike asked in surprise.

"Yeah."

"How much?"

"Ten grand."

"Hmpf," Mike snorted and took a sip of his beer.

"What are you snorting about? I thought it was good they put the money on the table."

Mike shook his head. "Neil, what's ten thousand dollars to those two? I'm not blind. I know when we were driving up to Rogers those duffels were full of serious cash, thousands and thousands of dollars. I mean, we made those runs for what, four years? Probably closer to five? Hell, it was millions upon millions. It was probably dangerous, you and I by ourselves, driving around with that money. So ten thou?" Jockey Mike shook his head in disgust. "Ten grand is nothing to White and Felix. To you and me it would be something, it would be significant, a little cushion in our lives. For them, it's nothing. *Nothing.* Those two probably walk around with that much in their pockets all the time. Giving him ten grand was like you or I giving a dog a bone."

He had Neil thinking now and his mind drifted back to the interview with the police and what the fat detective, the one named Lich, said to him as he left the room. "I wonder."

"Wonder what?" Mike asked.

Neil opened his mouth and then stopped. The issue of T.O. in the alley and the shooting was something he needed to work through in his mind before he talked it out, even with Mike, so he backed away from the issue for the time being. "I don't know, just the whole kind of questioning about T.O....I didn't expect that."

"I don't know why the police would want to talk to you

about T.O. either," Mike answered. "I mean, he was killed in that alley by the police, right? I read in the paper T.O. and the cop shot each other. That's what happened, isn't it?"

White turned left up into the driveway and pulled behind the house and into the detached garage. He powered down the garage door, went to the side door of the double garage and peered outside. Had anyone followed?

He was getting a little paranoid. It appeared that Kline was as far as the police had gotten and according to the lawyer, Neil gave them nothing during the interrogation. He'd handled it like a pro, the lawyer reported. So as of right now, between the results of Kline's interrogation and his own internal sources, White felt positive the police knew nothing about himself personally or their overall organization yet. But, as he continued to scan out the window for any followers, White also knew that the police were aware that White and Felix and their organization were out there. Lich and his merry band of detectives were on the hunt. That thought occupied his mind as he exited the side door of the garage and walked in the shadows of the trees to the back door of the house. Once inside he turned on a light switch for the thin lights mounted under the kitchen cabinets. He went to the fridge and reached inside for a beer and tossed his keys on the counter. He stepped into the living room, sat at his desk and turned on the desk lamp, then nearly jumped out of his chair, *"Geezus!"*

Felix was sitting casually with his legs crossed in the armchair in the corner of the living room.

"I hate when you do that," White complained, sitting

back in his chair but eyeing the second desk drawer where his gun was loaded and ready.

Felix spit out an evil laugh. "Relax, if I was here to do you any harm I'd have never let you turn on that light."

"Still, I damn near had a heart attack," White replied, wiping his brow. His crafty counterpart feared no one and would kill anybody without giving it a second thought. For Felix, killing someone was as emotional as flipping on a light switch.

"Hey, you're the one saying we need to move around all stealthy and shit so...here I am."

"And why are you here?"

"Kline. How did it go?"

White exhaled and relaxed back into his chair. "According to the lawyer, fine."

"Is it over?"

White shook his head. "The police, and in particular this Lich, got nothing out of Neil. But Neil and the lawyer got the distinct sense the police viewed this as an initial confrontation. There could be more to come."

Felix shrugged. "If we keep Neil where he is for now there will be nothing for the police to see."

"True, but there is one other thing that the police said to him that bothered me and I'm worried might get Neil thinking."

"Which is what?"

"The police questioned Neil quite a bit about Orr and about the night when Neil gave him the money."

"So we gave Kline the money to give to Orr. As far as Neil knows that's what we did. And we know the police have suspicions that there was a third person in the alley. But even if they have those suspicions, they have no way to know it was me."

"The police don't, you're right. But the police certainly left Neil with the impression that there was someone else in that alley and there would be only one reason for that person to be there."

"Again, so?"

White paused and clasped his hands in front of him. "Do you think Neil Kline is smart?"

Felix nodded. "Yeah, pretty smart."

"Okay, then let me ask you this. If you're Neil, and the police get you thinking that there was a mysterious third person in that alley, what do you think he starts thinking about?"

That statement got Felix's attention. After a moment he said, "Go on."

"Neil is smart enough to realize that this third person was there to kill Orr, not a *cop*," White stated. "I mean, Neil was suggesting to Orr that he get out of town. Orr was his friend, he was worried about him getting in trouble with the police. Or..."

"Or what?"

"Neil was worried Orr would be in trouble with us."

Felix fully understood where White was going now. "Is Neil a problem?"

White took a drink from his beer and thought for a moment. "I don't think so, as long as we don't give him any reason to fear us. He's stuck in that repair shop for now, not moving, not doing anything and drawing police attention. While it impacts our operation in that you and I must get closer to the street level, with the police fixated on Neil, it does give us a little bit of room to maneuver. He's taking the hit for us. We just need him to keep doing that until we get the next shipment in. No matter what happens, we must hang in here for at least another week to ten days until that gets here. After that, I think we need to leave."

"And if that happens, what about Neil?" Felix asked.

"He's good with people, has good contacts and has shown an ability to develop them. He could prove useful in a place such as Kansas City."

"And what if he doesn't want to move? Neil is good with people here. What if he doesn't want to move to say, Kansas City? What then?"

"He will."

"But what if he doesn't?" Felix pressed.

White sighed and slowly shook his head. "If he doesn't come with us, we can't leave him behind."

19

"IT'S LIKE THEY FORGOT US."

It was closing in on 4:00 a.m. Only light traffic passed overhead on wet Interstate 35 leading south into downtown St. Paul. The Wednesday workday commute into the cities was two plus hours from the starter's gun. The chosen meeting site was in the middle of a construction zone of mechanical equipment: haulers, trucks, concrete mixers, mounds of soil and rock and large steel and concrete spans for the highway expansion being constructed above his head. The thick humidity and a light rain only added to the ideally murky meeting conditions.

White waited patiently, a tumbler of coffee in his right hand, his large black umbrella in his left. Felix was a hundred yards away, concealed under a tarp, providing protection if necessary.

He heard footsteps from his left and turned to see Fisher as he approached, hands in his pockets, baseball cap pulled way down low, wearing a raincoat with the hood pulled over his head.

"You sure know how to pick spots," Fisher remarked bitterly.

"Perhaps you'd prefer to meet out in the open?" White asked derisively.

"No, I would not. I can't imagine anyone ever wanting to be in this spot at this time of night," the detective answered while holding his coat open enough for White to see the gun in the shoulder holster. "It's not my service weapon."

"I should certainly hope not," White replied as he held open his own raincoat so that his contact could see the envelope in his coat pocket, and the fact that White was unarmed.

Fisher nodded. "I'll take that off your hands."

"In a minute," White replied curtly. "First, what do you know?"

The detective shrugged. "Right now the investigation is fixed in neutral. Kline was a dead end. The house was a dead end. We're continuing to push the investigation, although I have to admit I'm not as close as I once was."

"Why not?"

"Lich is using some other people from the Narcotics unit right now."

"To do what?"

"One of the things that led Lich to Orr was that we got the cell phone records for Shead and the GPS readout of where he traveled the night you took him down over off of White Bear Avenue. Lich and McRyan found that crash site and identified some of the debris as being from a Yukon like Orr owned."

"You've told us that already."

"Yes, but where this all leads is back to that GPS data. They think, and I would assume they are correct, that Shead was following Kline that night, and other nights. They're trying to figure out where Kline stopped. They're trying to catch the scent on you that way."

"I see. And have they had any luck?"

The man shook his head. "Not as far as I've seen or heard. I've seen nothing but long faces from Lich, Riley and Rockford."

"And what was this route that they have for Shead following Kline?"

"They have three nights of data and it's pretty much the same loop route each night. Payne Avenue, down south on Robert Street, to the far end of West Seventh and then into Minneapolis. But again, we have the route, but we don't know where the stops are happening."

"I see. And what of me? They have Kline, but have they any idea about me or any other people in our operation?"

"Nah," Fisher responded, shaking his head confidently. "I've seen nothing and I'm still close enough that I'd know if they had. If they had that, I would have reached out and told you. Kline is as high as they've gotten."

"And you'll let me know if they get any further than that?"

Fisher simply nodded.

White inclined his head as well, reached inside his coat for the envelope and handed it to Fisher, who quickly checked it, turned and walked away.

A minute later Felix rolled up in White's Cadillac and the two drove off.

"What did we learn?"

"That we need to be very careful around our retail shops," White answered.

"Do they know where they are?" Felix asked with concern.

"No, not yet anyway." White explained what Fisher told him. "They have some concept of the general areas but not which ones are ours. And it appears there is one they don't really have that was not part of Neil's regular route, the bar over on White Bear Avenue. We need to adjust before they get smart here."

"So what do you suggest?"

"Get the word out. Money is no longer delivered to the shops. We've stopped having it go to Neil's. Now it doesn't go to *any* of them."

"Who picks up the money then?"

"I suggest you and some of your best boys do it, and do it very discreetly. Coordinate out of the back office of the bar on White Bear Avenue."

"If I'm doing that, then I'm going to need something of a list," Felix replied. "Because damn, we have a lot of crews."

Detective Weidenbacher yawned and stretched from the swivel seat in the back of the white surveillance panel van and poured himself a cup of coffee from his well-worn steel thermos. His narcotics partner, Detective Jay Martinez, sitting up front, was unloading their camera from its carrying case.

This kind of assignment was the norm for the two of them. They'd both been on the narcotics beat for years. Unlike their drinking buddy Paddy McRyan, to date neither seemed all that interested in doing anything else or advancing. They both liked being in the field wearing tennis shoes, jeans and hoodies to do their jobs.

Weed looked out the back window a half-block to the south to the string of storefronts that occupied the west and then east side of Payne Avenue. There were twelve separate businesses in total, small retail operations that included a drycleaner, a small law office, an accounting office, two restaurants, one Vietnamese and the other a small deli sandwich shop, a small corner convenience store, a furniture repair shop, a beauty salon, a real estate office, a small independent coffee and donut shop, a bar and finally a tobacco shop that Weed often frequented for his favored cigars. Those were just the retail locations. There were also two apartment buildings in the immediate vicinity and numerous modest houses. The only place they really didn't need to watch was the elementary school, whose parking lot they were perched in.

Martinez was short and stout, a former wrestler. He took a seat next to the thin and lanky Weed's left and tested the camera. "I'm ready to take pictures. Of what, I have *no* idea."

"Lich says we observe the activity in the area, snap photos of people going into and coming out of the businesses, the apartments or the houses and most importantly, of anyone that we, as trained narcotics officers, might recognize from our part of the world."

"Rah," Martinez replied as he took a photo of a woman stepping inside the corner convenience store. "I think the Homicide boys are grasping at straws on this one."

"Lich says the guys we're trying to find were responsible for Cruz."

Martinez raised the camera to his right eye. "Let's hope we grasp the damn straw then."

Dick walked past his usual booth and into the small meeting room in the back of the Cleveland Grill where Dot had a private table waiting for him. As usual, she had the newspapers waiting and today, two pots of coffee. Usually, he preferred the peace and quiet at 5:30 a.m. but today, he wanted to meet offsite with Rock, Riles and one more.

"Good morning, Chief," Dick greeted, standing up as Flanagan approached.

"Sit down, sit down," Flanagan waved at Dick as he took a chair opposite of him. Once he sat down, the chief quickly surveyed his surroundings. "You know what? I haven't eaten in here in a long time. Too long a time."

Dot beelined right over to the table to greet the chief, pour coffee and chitchat for a few minutes. She too realized that the chief had not been into her restaurant in a long time. She teased him mercilessly about that very point, particularly as Rock and Riley arrived. "These two come in all of the time and support me," she needled, winking at the two big men. "But their boss, the chief? Not lately. I must say, I don't feel so served and protected."

Flanagan put his hands up in mock surrender. "Dot, *I promise* my next trip will be very soon, and with my wife. Heck, I'll bring the grandkids, the whole Flanagan family. You'll have to fill this room with tables to serve us all."

"You better."

"I promise."

Everyone had one last laugh before Dot scampered back up to the front register to greet another one of her regular customers.

"So where are we at?" Flanagan asked.

Dick gave him an update and then tossed in one other nugget, the nugget that caused him to want the chief to join them. "We think there could be a rat."

Flanagan was taken aback. However, he knew the men sitting around the table wouldn't throw out such an accusation without a damn good reason. After a moment the chief asked, "What evidence do you have?"

"The house up in Rogers. It smells. That place was just *too* clean," Dick answered. "It was way too clean. The logistics of that do not add up."

"That's it? That's not much."

"Chief, the three of us have been talking about it," Riley added quietly, no doubt the most respected of the three by Flanagan. "It's thin. We don't have a name, at least yet. We just have suspicions but we wanted you to know that. Rafael Cruz was killed in that alley by a third person. That person wasn't there to kill Cruz, he was there to kill Orr. Orr and Neil Kline both evaded us that day when we were watching them. Now, it's one thing for one to sneak away, but both? How did they know to evade us? How did they know they needed to? It's certainly possible it was us not doing a good enough job of concealing ourselves while watching. Or, could it be that someone got a tip?"

"And Kline," Rock added. "He wasn't surprised when we showed. Instead, he was ready to go when we brought him in. And with top-notch legal talent waiting for the call. Hell, the lawyer beat us back downtown."

"So Kline knew it was coming," the chief surmised.

All three nodded.

"What do you boys want *me* to do?"

"For one, I'd like to move the investigation out of Homicide to an offsite location," Dick replied. "I was thinking the old Fourth Precinct building down there on West Seventh. I believe it still gets used from time to time on projects. It's still a department-owned building, correct?"

The chief nodded. "Done. What else?"

"We have a list of other cops that have had some contact with the case, including our names. We were thinking you could perhaps have a quiet off-the-record discussion with some folks in Internal Affairs and see what they might be able to do or if any of these names have appeared on their radar for any reason."

"I see," the chief replied, scanning the list of names, twenty-three in all. "You boys sure about this?"

The three of them looked at each other. Riles spoke for the group, "Chief, yes and no. Yes, we think we should have this checked out. No, we really, *really* hope we're wrong."

"Anyone been by?" Leon asked back inside the house as he peered down to the alley below from his tattered lawn chair resting on the rickety balcony of his second-story perch.

"Nah, man. Quiet. Nobody today, nobody yesterday," JuJu responded. "It's like we been abandoned or something."

"It involves money, Ju. They be by in time."

"I know, I know. But man, I don't like it cause we sittin' on like over thirty thou I bet today, maybe even a bit more. I get a little nervy with that kind of coin sitting here. We don't have a lot of muscle hanging about."

Leon flashed his eyes to his .38 sitting on the table.

"Yeah," Ju replied. "I got one of those too. It don't mean I want to have to use it."

"Can't be afraid."

"I ain't, but all the same it'd be nice if someone rolled by and took this off our hands."

"And the count? We on?"

"It's correct. It still cooking down there?"

"Sure is," Leon answered. "We're doing good, our crews are tight. We've resupplied like six times today. Rico and Reggie have been by twice, in fact."

"How is supply?"

"It's getting down, way down, Ju," Leon replied. "So I'm with you. Hopefully they'll be by soon."

JuJu looked at his phone. The rule was no phones for business. If you needed resupply you ordered it in advance when Neil's guys would come around to pick up the cash. On occasion, JuJu would run it over to the store on Payne instead of waiting for pickup because he needed to reorder more quickly. On occasion, he'd broken the rules and called Neil when they were short. But Neil was strictly off limits right now.

"I tell you, Leo, we get to about six and nobody's been by, we're going to need to make a run."

"Okay, man."

~

"Have we heard from anyone?" Rock asked, sitting on the long table, his feet resting on the seat of the chair. With the move offsite, they had to spend much of the day moving the case files and equipment, setting up computers and linking up with the department. "No," Dick shook his head, sifting through some papers. "No familiar faces, at least thus far. Guys are going to start transmitting the pictures they've taken so that we can take a look and see if anything pops."

"This is like looking for a needle in a haystack," Rock remarked bitterly.

"If we knew what the needle looked like," Riles added. "I'm all ears if you have other ideas," Dick replied with a sharp look.

"Nah, this is what we have to do," Riles replied skeptically. "But what is our end game here? Is it we find someone we recognize and hope to what? Pop them with dope and money and then get them to talk?"

"Maybe," Dick answered. "Or maybe we just follow them around and see who they associate with."

"If Sam was following and stopped as many times as he did, this is a pretty big operation," Rock remarked. "An operation with a lot of crews. I mean, there are stops in Minneapolis too."

"And the narcotics boys know nothing about this?" Riles inquired skeptically, looking back to Dick.

"It's interesting, they sense there is someone out there, but they operate a little like us. Without bodies, without disputes over territory, they are having a hard time getting in. And the captain of that group, Schroeder, says there is another thing that happened. A lot of the visible players are gone. They're trying to figure out who the new players are."

"Gone? Gone how?" Rock asked.

"Nobody knows for sure," Dick replied. "They're just gone. It's not the first time I've heard that, either. When I was trying to hunt around and figure out what happened to Luther Ellis a few months ago, there was this street kid—I think he went by JuJu—who said if guys cause trouble they just end up gone."

"What are we up to now?" Leon asked.

"I count nearly forty thou," JuJu replied, admiring the cash in the duffel bag. He and Leon were getting a percentage of the net as a sort of commission or bonus, sometimes known as points on the package. Of course, you didn't get any commission if you didn't have any product to sell.

"Man, this is jacked up," Leon moaned. "I can't believe nobody's been by. And Ju, we damn near outta supply. It's gonna be dark in a few hours and we gonna miss the night action if we don't get some shit soon."

"Fuck it, then. Tell our boys down the street to keep working. We're taking the money in. It's like they forgot about us."

Weed sat back in the swivel chair and yawned while running his right hand down his face. He checked his wrist; just after 7:00 p.m. "Long day, Jay."

"Yup," Martinez replied, watching while also checking his phone. "The Twins won."

"What is that, four in a row?"

"Five. They're only three games out of the wild card for the playoffs. I would not have anticipated that for this year. I thought .500 would be a miracle."

"Sano can flat out rake, man," Weed answered. "And he's picking it pretty good at third."

"For sure. How much longer do we have to go here?"

"A couple of hours, I suppose," Weed answered. "Six or seven of these places are still open."

"Long day."

"But plenty of overtime."

"I hear that," Martinez answered and raised the binoculars to his face. "Hmm."

"What?" Weed asked, turning to look out the back and raising his own set of binoculars.

"West side of the street, walking down the sidewalk, who do you see?"

"Oh, wait. Is that..."

"That's fricking JuJu and Leon Fulbright, coming right down the sidewalk plain as day. They got out of a Jeep

Cherokee. I haven't seen those two boys in quite some time," Martinez stated, having quickly exchanged his binoculars for his camera and was clicking away. "They are heading inside that donut shop."

"And they're both carrying themselves backpacks," Weed observed.

Given their angle, they could see inside to the counter of the donut shop. "Did you see JuJu drop that backpack off his shoulder?"

"Looked heavy."

The two narcotics detectives observed the discussion at the register. Then JuJu and Leon followed a man toward the back of the store. "I'm tempted to jump out for a better look," Jay suggested.

"Sit tight," Weed replied, his binoculars still to his eyes, "They're coming back out and JuJu has a little slip of paper in his hand."

"And the same backpacks. It looks like they're jumping back into the Jeep."

"I'm following," Weed declared, grabbing his keys and phone and his own surveillance backpack, putting his binoculars inside with another camera. "You sit tight."

Weed jumped out of the surveillance van and right into his personal vehicle, his old beat-up black Chevy Blazer. He turned left onto Payne Avenue just as JuJu and Fulbright pulled away from the curb and headed south along Payne before taking a left onto Phalen Boulevard. Phalen was a busy road that sliced its way northeast through St. Paul's east side. He hung back a couple hundred yards and chuckled at the irony as he approached the junction with Maryland Avenue, the Bureau of Criminal Apprehension on the corner to his right. JuJu turned right onto Maryland and proceeded another six blocks to White Bear Avenue where he waited at the stoplight. Weed was three vehicles back.

Martinez called. "Where are you at?"

"Turning left onto White Bear Avenue off Maryland. Hang on, I'm putting you on speaker."

"You want any help?"

"Not sure yet. I don't know if I have anything."

Weed followed JuJu, who took the left onto White Bear Avenue and drove north several blocks until he reached the junction with Hoyt Avenue, where he took a quick right and then an immediate left turn in behind the Polar Bar where there was a small parking area. Weed turned right into the Kwik Trip station just short of Hoyt and pulled around behind the station and car wash and was able to see JuJu and Fulbright take the backpacks in the back door to the bar.

This was as far as Weed could go. JuJu and Leon Fulbright would recognize him were he to go inside. Instead, he started taking pictures.

"What the hell are you doing here?" Tito growled at JuJu and Leon. "What were the orders?"

"To sit tight," JuJu replied. "Except we've been sittin' tight three days and nobody has been by. We're sittin' on all this cash, not a lot of security and we're pretty much out of shit, so what we supposed to do?"

"Follow fuckin' orders, you dumbshit," Tito growled.

"Well, shit," JuJu replied.

"Leave the money. Someone will be by with a resupply in time. Don't show up here again, you read me?"

"Yeah," JuJu and Leon both replied quietly.

Tito took a breath. He had two good workers in front of him just trying to do their job. "Look, I know you're trying to do right and"—Tito looked to the bag on the desk—"that's good work, that's good money for three days so I like what you two are doin'. But from now on, follow your orders and we'll get to you. You two understand?"

JuJu and Leon nodded meekly.

"Now get on outta here."

~

Weed snapped photos as JuJu and Leon stepped out of the back of the bar and passed a patron on the way in, without the backpacks they'd been carrying. "You two are walking just a little hang dog, I'd say."

He kept snapping photos of JuJu and Leon as they got into the Jeep Cherokee and pulled away. Weed put his camera down and followed.

~

"Cripes," Tito moaned as he took another look inside the duffel bag. At least the two corner boys weren't lying; they had the cash counted and bound with a proper slip inside.

"How did those two even know to come here?" Felix asked, stepping into the back office from another office across the hallway.

"I guess Big Wayne at the Donut Shop sent them this way so someone might need to have a conversation there," Tito answered. "This list of crews you gave us didn't have those two on it. Nobody had been by in a few days to either pick up or resupply them. Those two are doing good work. There's over forty in here."

"Great, forty thou and they came here," Felix answered, suddenly paranoid and looking out the windows.

White walked inside and took in the obvious discomfort of the room. "What did I miss?"

Dick, Rock, Riley, Double Frank, Fisher, Ortega and Paddy looked at the photos.

"I remember that kid," Dick said as he examined the photos taken by Weidenbacher and Martinez. "I talked to him a few months ago. His name is JuJu, right?"

"That's his street name. He's been in the drug trade for years," Weed answered. "Generally, pretty smart on the street. He was popped for possession once and it was a number of years ago. Same thing on Fulbright. They're pretty savvy and stay out of sight most of the time. They're the kind of guys a good drug crew needs. But if I didn't know any better they dropped off something and in my experience, that was probably a money drop of some kind. And I think it was out of the ordinary too, because they went from the Donut Shop to the Polar Bar."

"But they left the Polar Bar empty-handed, right?" Dick asked.

"That's right," Martinez responded and then flipped to another set of photos. "Because, if you work for a crew the money goes one place and the drugs come from another. Three hours after JuJu and Fulbright got back to that house, we have this SUV that rolls down the alley and stops for a moment and out of the house comes..."

"Fulbright," Weed answered. "And there goes a new backpack inside so I'd say they've now been resupplied."

"Most likely," Martinez added. "I mean, you don't see the

drugs. The boys in that Tahoe could have been returning the backpacks that were dropped off at the Polar Bar, but I really doubt it. These two are running that little bit of territory around there."

"Do we have probable cause to execute on the house? Maybe flip these guys?" Riles asked.

"Only one way to find out," Dick answered, checking his watch. "We go see the county attorney in the morning. In the meantime, let's get some people watching these guys. Maybe develop that P.C. a little better."

"Heck, it might make more sense to just watch for a while," Ortega suggested. "See who else comes by or who they talk to."

"That's a...thought," Paddy replied but then stopped.

"What is it?" Dick asked.

"A text I just got..." Paddy answered as he broke away from the group.

Dick looked over to Ortega. "That might be an idea worth thinking about, Detective. However, what I really want is to know what the story was with the money drop at the Polar Bar."

"I agree," Riles nodded. "The money goes to the higher-ups. Those are the people we're interested in."

"Hey, guys, I think you might want to see this," Paddy reported and found a remote control for the television up in the corner.

"What is it?" Rock asked.

"The jury verdict is in on the trial for the DeVonte Rice shooting."

"And?"

"Not guilty, on all counts."

"Seriously?" Riles asked in shock. "Not guilty? Of all charges? Everything?"

"All charges," Paddy replied. "They announced it ten minutes ago."

"I know we don't all agree on whether these two screwed up or not," Dick stated, "but I have to say I'm shocked. All charges." He whistled and shook his head. "All charges."

"I can't believe they announced it tonight," Riles observed. "That was a *really* bad idea."

Rock nodded his agreement. "For sure, this is going to set the cities on fire."

"It already has," Paddy added as he changed the TV to Channel Eight. "Outside the Hennepin County Courthouse there is already a riot. Someone threw a Molotov cocktail and burned a police cruiser."

"Buckle up, boys," Riles suggested. "The next twenty-four to forty-eight hours are about to get rough."

20

"YOU'LL DEAL ME TO SAVE YOUR ASS."

It started three years ago.

Fisher caught a homicide that involved the killing of the head of a local drug crew. As the case got rolling and a few leads were developing, he was approached by White one night while he was sitting alone, nursing a post-shift beer at a quiet local bar.

"If this case didn't move in a certain direction, I could see that it worked to your benefit," White proposed quietly. "I know *you* could use some assistance, Detective. Let me help."

The man clearly did his homework. White knew that Fisher was recently divorced at the time and was being crushed with child support and credit card debt, such that he was looking at personal bankruptcy. The envelope of cash that White dangled with thousands of tax free dollars unreported and, more importantly, unknown to his ex-wife was simply too hard to pass up. The case in question was a drug dispute over territory with one street dealer dead. What did the case or its outcome really matter? It was just one criminal dirtbag offing another.

The problem was, once someone like White had you on the line, he wasn't about to let go. He owned you.

At first it was a meeting every so often. White would ask some questions and Fisher would provide answers. It was usually about whether investigations had been opened on certain matters. Often, it turned out there was no investigation. "It's pretty hard to investigate a homicide without a body, especially when there are open homicides where there is a body," Fisher would often report. White would give a little nod of approval and then hand over the envelope full of cash.

But now Shead, and even worse, Cruz, were dead. Flanagan was making every resource possible available. White and his crew, including the big Hispanic named Felix, were on borrowed time. And Fisher knew he too was exposed. If White were caught and arrested, Fisher knew it was inevitable that he would go down with him.

He reached the alley and stopped at the edge and peeked left around the corner. He was vulnerable and there was no backup. And this meeting, in this location, at this time and on a night filled with so much turmoil, had all the makings of an ambush. White was out there somewhere, hiding in the shadows, where the man truly seemed to live his life. The Felix guy that always seemed to be around was no doubt nearby.

Fisher patted his left chest, feeling his gun in the shoulder holster. There was a second small Smith and Wesson strapped around his left ankle, not to mention his switchblade. He reached inside his jacket and pulled out his gun and held it down low and just back from his body. His gait was deliberate and his posture wary as he methodically picked his way down the narrow alley, keeping his head on a swivel, making sure nobody was coming up from behind. As he moved forward, he was mindful of maintaining some semblance of cover as he maneuvered his way through the maze of garbage cans and dumpsters.

"The gun won't be needed, Fisher," White's voice called from the dark as he stepped out from an entryway.

"We just met and now you've called me again. And tonight, of all nights no less," Fisher muttered peering around, his gun still hanging low in his right hand. "What gives?"

"I understand your wariness, but it's unnecessary, for me *and* for you. Besides, with all the unrest tonight from that jury verdict, the demonstrations and rioting in Minneapolis, the police's attention is directed elsewhere. Nobody cares about the two of us tonight. It is the perfect time to meet."

Fisher approached warily, closing the gap between the two of them, the gun still hanging down low as he noticed the small spiral cord running up White's neck and to the earpiece in his ear. Someone and probably more than one someone was watching. "Just the same, I'm going to frisk you."

"Feel free," White replied and held his arms out.

Fisher frisked him. Not finding a weapon, Fisher exhaled and relaxed slightly and holstered his weapon.

"It appears our relationship has changed," White said lightly.

"Yeah, well, you've got some real trouble now."

"Do tell."

Fisher explained what Lich and his boys now possessed. "They don't know exactly what they have yet, but they will eventually and eventually will come soon," Fisher warned. "They have these pictures of these two drug runners for you guys, but they have photos of *you* walking into that bar. Now they don't know it's you, but in time..."

"What else?"

"They have pictures of all of the vehicles parked there and all of the license plates. It's only a matter of time before they start tracking all that down. That includes the Infiniti sedan you were driving and all the SUVs your boys are driving. Now, I'm sure you have those registered in phantom names and all that, but each day they get another piece and brick by brick they get a little closer."

"Give me an example."

"They are all over JuJu and Fulbright. If they flip those two, who knows where it might lead."

"Those two know nothing."

"You're not hearing me," Fisher snapped back. "They're onto you. Maybe not you, maybe not your Mexican buddy who's always around, but they are onto your operation and if they're onto that, soon they'll get onto you."

"So if I'm hearing you right..."

"You need to leave town fast."

White leaned back against the wall and nodded slowly. "That would be convenient for you now, wouldn't it?"

"Yes and no," Fisher answered, his arms folded over his chest, but his eyes darting around, scanning the area. "After all, your leaving is going to make me a lot lighter in the pocket. Unless you go completely to ground, completely out of sight and shut down what you're doing, I don't think it can last much longer. It just can't. Lich, Riley and Rockford, the chief's boys, now have a thread and they're going to pull and the whole thing could come apart. So you need to act or you're going to have serious trouble. Heck, from where I stand you already do."

"And of course, you're worried that if we go down we'll take you down with us."

"Damn right," Fisher replied bluntly. "I know you won't

protect me. You'll deal me to save your ass, especially with a dead cop and dead ex-cop on your hands."

Fisher was near the it's either them or me point. And White couldn't help but notice how close Fisher's hand was to the opening in his coat. The detective could pull his gun and White would be done and he'd have a fair chance of evading Felix and his men, depending on whether he had a vehicle close or not. That was no doubt what the detective was thinking about as the two of them eyed each other up. White had been contemplating how much to tell Fisher and decided he needed to get Fisher to stand down.

"I think I can put your mind at ease, Detective. I have no more interest in being in police custody than you do. We *are* pulling out. In about five days or so we'll be gone. We just have to take care of one last piece of business, but it's a *big* piece of business. Until then..." White carefully and slowly reached inside his coat and pulled out another envelope. "I may need to be able to call on you just to stay a step or two ahead." He gently handed the envelope to Fisher.

Fisher quickly checked the inside of the envelope, thumbing through the crisp hundreds inside. It was thicker than usual and he looked back up to White. "What's the story with the extra?"

"I added twenty percent," White replied evenly. "And there could be more for you before we leave town as long as you continue to be available. Are you able to stay close to the investigation?"

Fisher nodded as he stuffed the envelope inside his coat. "I'm on the team. Double Frank is tight with Lich, Riley and Rockford. I'm supposed to sit with him on the house just off Payne Avenue where this JuJu and Fulbright are slinging and watch. You obviously understand why we are. Lich will be looking to flip those kids and once they do flip, because they always do, undoubtedly they will lead Lich and company back to the Polar Bar and that donut shop."

"I see. Is there anything else?"

Fisher shook his head. "I may learn more later tomorrow as we're all supposed to meet at the 280 Grille for burgers and then we're probably going out for drinks, and undoubtedly this investigation will be a big topic of discussion. So I'm still in the loop. However, with all that went down tonight it'll be interesting to see if that impacts what we're doing. Hell, we could all be suiting up in riot gear tomorrow for all I know."

White pulled a little slip of folded paper out of his white dress shirt pocket and handed it to Fisher. "We're taking precautions as well. This is a number you can reach me at temporarily. It's a burner phone and I'll probably dump it within a day or two. You will call me with updates, correct?"

"If there is anything to report, yeah. But we only talk face to face," he added as he patted his chest.

"I always pay, Kurt, if the information is good," White answered.

Fisher turned around and left the way he'd arrived. White leaned back against the wall, watching as Fisher looked back several times as he went. The pressure and paranoia was starting to get to the detective. He liked the money but he wanted it all to end.

After Fisher turned right at the end of the alley, White left his covered perch and walked to the north end of the alley. Felix pulled up and White jumped into the Navigator.

"I'm sure you heard, but we now have confirmation that the Polar Bar is off limits." White counseled and explained what he'd learned from Fisher. "The police will be all over that place. Fisher is on the team and will be close to Lich and the rest of those guys at least for the next eighteen to twenty-four hours."

"We're running out of places to operate from," Felix replied bitterly after hearing the explanation. "I'm worried about the shipment and the rest of the operation."

"We were right to make the decision to pull out," White replied. "We take care of the last shipment and we leave. Tito and Jorge will lay low for a few months and then take over here." He looked back and checked the rearview as well.

"Where should we go now?"

"As for meeting places, my office is still good for the time being, I think," White answered. "Only you, Tito and Jorge know where it is. Let's go there and talk this out and figure out our next move."

The two did just that in the early morning hours, the sun rising in the east. The television in the corner was turned to the local news. The only story being covered was the demonstrations and rioting from the night before.

Announcing the verdict just before 10:00 p.m. was a colossal blunder. Without much warning of the announcement, the Minneapolis Police had been caught flat-footed and undermanned. The large crowd gathered at the courthouse for the verdict immediately expressed their outrage. Demonstrators set two police cars on fire and overturned three others in downtown Minneapolis in the area surrounding the Hennepin County Courthouse and Minneapolis's City Hall.

News of the verdict quickly spread through social media which led to more people, demonstrators and troublemakers quickly descending on Minneapolis. As the crowd metastasized, it moved towards the downtown core and became more virulent. Windows were shattered along

Nicollet Mall and three retail stores were firebombed and two others looted before the Minneapolis Police could finally restore some semblance of order around 1:30 a.m. But just when the police thought they had some measure of control, the crowds flowing out of the downtown bar district between Hennepin and First Avenue merged and inevitably clashed with the demonstrators and the violence started all over again. Numerous skirmishes broke out with several reports of shots being fired along Hennepin and First Avenues. Two bystanders were shot and were hospitalized. Miraculously, no deaths were reported.

With the clock now reaching 6:00 a.m., the rioting in downtown Minneapolis seemed to have burned itself out. However, with the dawn breaking a new wave of demonstrations was rising throughout the broader Twin Cities, including one walking north along Interstate 35W, blocking and backing up the morning commute traffic into downtown Minneapolis. Several people were simply lying in the middle of the interstate.

The explosion of reaction to the verdict drew national attention and was the lead early morning story on the cable and television networks. Interspersed with the coverage of the demonstrations was a replay of the video footage of the shooting of DeVonte Rice on the highway a year ago. Local leaders of the African American community were taking the opportunity to get on camera and voice their outrage at the treatment of African American men by the police in general and via the verdict in particular.

Thus far, St. Paul had only been subject to a few small and relatively peaceful demonstrations. The city seemed to go largely unscathed, at least in part because the case was tried in Minneapolis and St. Paul Police officers were not the ones to shoot DeVonte Rice at the end of the chase. In fact, it was the St. Paul officers that testified to the fact that there was no gun in the car and that they didn't see any movements of the driver that the Minneapolis cops claimed they had seen.

The mayors for both cities, as well as the chiefs of police were pleading for calm now that order had been somewhat restored. The local television reporters, while indicating that order had been re-established, in the tone of their reports sensed that the calm could be short-lived and that more trouble could be on the horizon.

"You know, this is not the worst thing that could have happened," White remarked after having watched a half hour of the footage. "The police will be distracted and spending their time dealing with keeping the cities under control. They will be cautious with their actions." He looked over to Felix who'd been stroking his beard, watching the story in total silence. "What are you thinking?"

Felix pointed at the television. "I see an opportunity."

"To do what?"

"*Completely* distract the police and set this town ablaze. All of this and a few things Fisher said has given me an idea. I think I can get the police to completely forget about us and chase something else."

White took the measure of Felix and his demeanor change. After a moment, he understood exactly what Felix meant. "We better call Javier."

21

"SUMMER HOURS FOR DRUG DEALERS. RIIIGHT."

"Why is it men love morning sex so much?" Sally asked as she rolled her curvy naked body out of bed. Since she was leaving later in the day for an eight-day trip overseas, she didn't necessarily have to be in as early to work. That left some time for them to lounge around and one thing led to another.

"You didn't seem to mind it."

"No, I didn't. In fact, I very much enjoyed it," Sally answered with a big smile, leaning down to peck him on the lips. "But seriously, I'm curious. What is it? I mean, wasn't last night enough?"

"I don't really know. Maybe it's because I spent the night cuddled up next to your magnificent body and it caused me to wake up with a raging erection."

"You make it sound *soooo* romantic."

"I'm a guy," Mac reasoned. "Can't it just be as simple as you look ridiculously hot with amazing hair porn in the morning and it makes me want you?"

Sally cackled. "I'll settle for that, I guess," she said as she sat down on his side of the bed and cupped his face in her right hand. "And for the record, I still find the thick stubble and longer hair to be very sexy. It makes me amorous in the morning too."

"How much time do you have left then?" Mac asked, flicking his eyebrows while slyly moving his left hand to her thigh. "I mean, you're going to be gone for eight days."

"Not enough for what you have in mind," Sally replied, lightly slapping his hand away and then kissing him quickly. "Last night and this morning will just have to do there, stud."

"Killjoy."

"Hey, I gave it up twice. *Twice*—so go make me some breakfast," Sally ordered with a wicked smile as she walked naked as could be into the bathroom to turn on the shower.

It was Mac's turn to laugh out loud.

Twenty minutes later with the coffee maker percolating, Mac cracked four eggs and dropped them into the glass bowl, added a splash of milk and quickly mixed it together. With the small frying pan heating, he dropped in some of the egg mixture and let it start to slowly cook while examining the chopped ham, cheese, tomatoes and green peppers assembled on the cutting board to the left. ESPN's *SportsCenter* was playing in the background.

"Mac!" Sally yelled down from upstairs. "Turn to CNN. That jury verdict came in last night in Minneapolis. The cops were cleared of everything. There were riots in Minneapolis last night."

Mac scrambled for the remote and powered up the flat screen on the opposite wall. "Not good," he muttered as he watched the replays of the demonstrations, riots and resulting damage. "So not good."

He recognized the scenes along Nicollet Mall, the heart of

downtown Minneapolis, and from the bar district, places he'd regularly frequented over the years. This was not Los Angeles post-Rodney King verdict. Nevertheless, the damage was more than skin deep, would take several days to clean up and would undoubtedly leave a lasting scar on the Twin Cities. He let it play in the background as he prepared their omelets. As he watched he got a text from Dick: *I assume you've seen?*

Mac quickly responded: *Yes. Will call you in a bit.*

"Can you believe that? It's Minnesota. People don't riot like that in Minnesota," Sally proclaimed as she came charging into the kitchen, dragging her suitcase and shoulder bag. "Aren't you surprised they got off? They had the video. He was unarmed, there was the testimony of the two St. Paul cops that they didn't see any movements by Rice. I know those are tough cases to prosecute, but I'm still shocked."

"I'm a little surprised as well, although Dick warned me the other day about where the trial was going. He said the defense lawyers were effectively creating some cracks in the prosecution's case and the standard to find guilt in a case like that against an officer is awfully high. Clearly it was a tough one for the jury to decide. They deliberated for three days."

"Still, you see that video of the shooting and it looks just...awful. Don't you think?"

"I think it looks bad, really bad for the two officers who shot the motorist. But"—he hesitated for a moment—"you know, one thing a lot of people just don't understand is what it's like to be a cop and to be in that situation. People who aren't cops sit there and analyze the situation from the comfort of their couch, desk or bed and say what idiot would try to shoot with four cops standing outside his car and more on the way. He wouldn't, so why do the cops have to shoot him?"

"That's what I'm thinking."

"Except here's the thing, babe," Mac answered as he worked the edges of the omelet loose with a spatula. "I've been on that traffic stop before. You have a split second to act. It could be you or him, so if you think the person has a gun and everyone—and I mean everyone—does these days, that adrenaline starts flowing and if that guy twitches the wrong way—"

"A cop defends himself," Sally answered.

"When you're a patrol officer you have a simple thought every day. You just want to get through your shift, hopefully help a few people along the way and get home to your family at the end of the day without anything bad happening."

"The motorist probably had the same hope."

"Really? The guy led everyone on a high-speed chase," Mac replied sharply. "I think he has a pretty damn high degree of fault here."

"Hey, hey, hey," Sally backtracked, her hands held up in surrender. "I was a prosecutor. I'm a friend. I'm just saying, the cop wants to get home but so does the citizen. I get it, I totally get it. *I've lived with it.* It's a hard, *hard* job—I know this and you know I know this." Sally took a drink from her coffee. "Maybe it's like you say. Sometimes situations just go bad. This situation went bad, sadly bad for everyone." She took another look at the screen and shook her head. "It certainly appears you'll be heading home into a hornet's nest."

"For sure," Mac answered as he plated Sally's breakfast. "But with all that went sideways last night, you can bet the police won't get caught with their pants down again. They'll be ready for the demonstrations and whatnot. I'm sure extra guys will be pulled on duty. I just hope all we end up with are demonstrations and not another fiasco like last night."

They quietly ate their breakfast while watching the news before he drove Sally over to the White House to drop her off. As he emptied her wheeled suitcase out of the back, she gave him a big embrace. "Do be careful," she said as she rested her head on his shoulder. "It could be dicey back home."

"I will."

She looked up, kissed him twice on the lips, pulled out the handle from her wheeled suitcase, threw her Michael Kors purse over her shoulder and she was off into the West Wing. Just like that she was gone for the next week plus.

Back at home, Mac called Dick. "What's the story?"

"It's shitty," Dick replied and Mac could hear the melancholy in his friend's voice. "What a disaster. Damn lazy dumbass county judge. They announced that verdict so late and Minneapolis was caught completely off guard. They weren't ready and well...you've seen the aftermath of all that. What a mess."

"How about in St. Paul?"

"We weren't ready either, I don't think, but since our guys weren't the shooters, people aren't quite as angry at the men on our side of the river. However, today is a new day and the anger hasn't burned out as far as I can tell, so we'll see. The tension in the air is pretty thick. Everyone seems to have this sense of foreboding, if you know what I mean. I'm sure the powers that be are not looking forward to sunset, that's for sure. Word is extra shifts are set for tonight. Lots of overtime to be paid to keep the peace."

"Has the chief had anything to say on this? I mean, other than the statement I saw him make on the news."

"Yeah, about that," Dick muttered bitterly.

"Uh oh. What happened?" Mac asked and then it hit him. "Wait, don't tell me. He's putting the brakes on things, isn't he?"

"Yup," Dick sighed. "We're suddenly very cautious here in River City."

"Really? You guys have the goods to move on that house, don't you?"

"I sure thought so, but higher powers seem to suddenly disagree."

"How so?"

"I'm not sure what comes first, the chicken or the egg."

"Meaning?"

"For starters, the county attorney was a little leery of the level of our probable cause. She thought it was thin. I mean, we have Weed following these guys with those backpacks. He tracks them to the bar, then to that house. An hour or two later they take delivery of a duffel bag. Of course, the attorney says we didn't actually see either money or drugs, but I'm like, seriously? What the hell else do you really think this all is? So I look to Flanagan for support."

"No go."

"He took our legs out from under us when he agreed with her and said that given what happened last night, the verdict, the reaction to it, he too thought we ought to get a little more."

"In other words, we don't need to be breaking doors down on allegedly weak probable cause the day after people rioted violently over the not guilty verdict of two cops who shot an unarmed man."

"Basically," Dick replied.

"Maybe it's all the time I spend around my wife, but I kind of get it politically," Mac answered evenly. "Last night is not one you want to double down on. It's probably a good day to exercise some restraint."

"Yeah," Dick sighed. "I do get it. I don't like it, I want to start moving on these guys, but I get it."

"So what's the plan, boss?"

"Doing what the chief said. We're watching the house. We're watching the Polar Bar. We're running all the license plates we have from the bar. If we get more evidence to tighten up the PC, I've been told we'll get the green light to go in. When are you getting back?"

"My flight will touch down at 5:15 or so. Any chance you can pick me up?"

~

"Where are these guys?" Double Frank moaned, taking another look at the pictures of JuJu and Leon Fulbright. "I haven't seen them around here all day."

"Who knows?" Fisher answered, putting another small handful of sunflower seeds into his mouth. "It's Friday. Maybe they have summer hours."

Double Frank laughed. "Summer hours for drug dealers. *Riiight.*"

~

Felix pulled up along the curb at the Southwest Airlines sign and his two old friends came strolling out of the sliding doors from baggage claim. He hit the rear tailgate button for the Navigator and the two men tossed their bags in the back. Sylvester took a seat in the front, Juan in the back.

"Good to see you both."

"Where to?" Sylvester asked.

"We have a stop to make," Felix responded. "Then we'll set up."

"Holy cow, the whole cavalry is here," Mac exclaimed happily as he exited the Delta Airlines baggage claim door to find Dick, Riley and Rockford waiting for him. "I feel so special."

"We were in the neighborhood," Riles replied, shaking Mac's hand.

Rock grabbed Mac's suitcase and tossed it into the trunk.

"Let's drop my stuff off at the house and then get to work," Mac replied.

A half hour later they were entering the Fourth Precinct building a little after 6:00 p.m. to find Paddy and Ortega sitting at a computer.

"Hey, cuz," Paddy greeted.

"Boys," Mac greeted, slapping his cousin on the back and high-fiving Ortega. "I see they have you two doing the grunt work."

"Those three donkeys couldn't turn on a computer, let alone use one," Paddy replied with a smirk.

"I know how to put your head through the monitor," Rock growled playfully. "That would be an effective use of it."

Riles got down to business. "Okay, hotshot. Any names popping on those license plates from the Polar Bar yesterday?"

Paddy grimaced. "I have a list, but none of the names really jump out at me. I've put together a file with all the plates and the DMV info for the drivers. I haven't gone deep on those people yet. I do know that the names in that file do not have criminal records, nor do the names pop in our system in any other way."

"Who owns the bar?" Dick asked.

"That's what I've been working on here the last little while. It looks like the owner is this woman," Ortega answered, handing Dick a file.

"Beverly Light? What's her story?"

"She's owned it for a long time, over ten years according to the Secretary of State records. Before that it was her father's place. As best I can tell, it's been in the family going on thirty years. If we could get a search warrant, we could dig into the financials a little more."

"Good," Dick answered, but he still had a perturbed look on his face. "Okay, so at least initially we have a clean list of people here. So what, pray tell, was going on at the Polar Bar yesterday then?" Dick asked the group.

Riles and Rock shrugged. They didn't know and didn't seem to possess any theories.

"Don't look at me," Mac answered. "I just got back. I don't know shit right now."

"Well, the Polar Bar was not on the routes driven by Sam Shead," Paddy offered.

"Does that lead to a theory, Young McRyan?" Riles asked.

Paddy nodded.

"Atta boy," Mac encouraged. "Let's hear it."

"Maybe the bar has nothing to do with it," Paddy suggested. "Instead, JuJu and Leon just went there to meet someone and drop the backpacks off. Weed didn't sit on the bar when those two left after the drop-off. Instead, he kept following those two. Whoever got those backpacks could have strolled on out of the bar after Weed left."

"But if they met someone, it was most likely someone

with one of the cars or trucks in the parking lot," Mac rejoined, scanning the list Paddy had printed. "So whoever got the money likely was there in one of those vehicles."

"That's true," Paddy answered, nodding. "I'll start digging deeper on all of that."

"You can dig tomorrow," Dick answered as he looked at his phone. "It's Friday night, you can call it a day. We've been going long hours and we all need a break. Are you joining us tonight, Tommy?"

"You know it."

"What about you, Paddy?" Mac asked.

"Ahh," Paddy hemmed. "You know, I have this..."

"What's her name?"

"Mia."

"Oooo," Ortega replied. "She sounds alluring."

"Mia, that name just makes her sound hot," Rock added.

"She is kinda hot, actually," Paddy replied sheepishly. "We have plans. I mean, I could break them I suppose if...I have to."

"Nah," Dick replied, waving Paddy off. "We'll see you tomorrow, but you will have to share the details."

Paddy didn't need to be told twice. He was out the door in two minutes.

"I gotta tell you," Dick said to Mac, "I kind of live vicariously through him. He gets more damn tail."

"He has the gift," Mac replied with a grin. "Always has. So what's next?" Mac asked Dick.

"You and I are going to Fireball to see Nikki. She's been texting and *texting* me for an update. With all that's been going on, I've been somewhat forced to put her off. After that, we'll meet these three jokers at the 280 and go out and solve all the world's problems."

22

"UNIVERSITY AND CROMWELL."

"University and Cromwell."

Dick had hoped that the next time he walked in the doors of Fireball and saw Nikki he'd have more progress to report. Instead, at this point he had far more questions than he had answers. What had been an investigation of Sam's death had morphed into a sprawling investigation involving not just his good friend's death, but that of an active police officer. Not to mention the fact that every time it seemed they caught a break it quickly dried up, only lending more credence to Mac's theory that there was a rat somewhere in the department. All in all, things were not progressing in what one would view as a positive forward direction.

"You came here to tell me that?" Nikki asked Dick.

"I told you I'd let you know how it was going. That included if it wasn't going well."

"I see," Nikki answered. "You're not giving up, are you?"

"Hell no," Dick answered quickly and with more bravado than he felt. "If anything, we're investigating this thing harder. It's just that it's about a lot more than Sam now and I wanted you to know that."

"Do you have anything? Anything at all? Anyone you think had a role in Sam's death?"

Dick looked to Mac. "What do you think?"

"Show her. What could it hurt at this point?"

Dick opened his file and took out some papers and photos.

"Sam was taking a close look at this house up in Rogers." He showed her a photo of the house. "Ring any bells?"

Nikki shook her head.

"I didn't think it would. Sam had a notation in his notebook about this guy." Dick slid a picture over for Nikki to look at. "The guy on the left is Neil Kline."

"Who is the short man standing next to him?"

"That's his driver."

"Driver?"

"Yeah, probably Gilligan to Kline's Skipper, we think," Mac added. "The driver's a nobody. Kline is the guy that matters."

"He matters with this guy," Dick continued, setting another photo down. "This guy is Terrence Orr."

"Isn't he the man who was shot in the alley with the St. Paul police officer?"

"With Rafael Cruz, correct," Dick answered.

"That has something to do with Sam's case?"

"Yes. Orr and Kline are friends, this much we know. Orr was known as, among other things, muscle for hire. As we understand it, he was also running some drug crews over here in St. Paul on the east side. We were very interested in him because we think he was involved in the abduction, beating, and killing of Sam. The night he was shot we were hunting all over town for him. That's why Cruz and he ended up in that alley. Cruz was chasing him."

"But then this Orr, I assume, shot at Cruz."

Here Dick was in murky waters. Mac shook his head just slightly and Dick had to agree. "That's what happened."

"You said you were hunting for this Orr?" Nikki asked.

Dick nodded. "I had men watching a place where he was staying and we gave the order to bring him in for questioning, but when my guys went to bring him in, he'd slipped out of the building. Of course, we were also watching Kline that day and he managed to slip away without us seeing as well."

"It seems they both figured out we were watching somehow," Mac added.

"So we lost track of both," Dick continued. "And it turns out the two of them met up late that night at a bar over in Minneapolis. It's a long story and not terribly relevant to you how we know that, but we do. Then after those two met, we stumbled onto Orr."

"How?"

"Rafael Cruz and his partner were watching the townhouse of this woman who was an acquaintance of Orr. I almost didn't bother having her place staked out, but we did. And lo and behold, Orr happened to show up there that night. Cruz and Carson saw him, they gave chase and you know the rest."

"What about this Kline?" Nikki asked, pointing to the picture on the table. "Have you questioned him?"

"Yes."

"And?"

"We got jack squat," Dick replied honestly. "Other than his name in Sam's notebook, Nikki, he hasn't done anything in the last two to three weeks that gives us anything to work with."

"And so that's where it's at?"

Dick nodded.

"But you're still going, right? You're not giving up, are you?" Nikki pressed.

"No," Dick replied. "But right now, we're kind of stuck in neutral trying to find a way forward."

"No leads."

"We have a couple that could lead somewhere, but there's nothing really imminent that I can give you."

"I see."

"Look, we're not done here, not by a long shot, but I wanted to update you and do it honestly," Dick stated and then asked, "Are you keeping your guard up for tonight?"

Nikki nodded. "I have extra security on. I even called Coleman and he's sending two guys over to stand post just in case. As far as I know there is a demonstration planned down at the Capitol and of course, there is some stuff in Minneapolis too. As for right here, I'm not anticipating trouble, but you never know what might trigger something. We're on the light rail line so I could see people having been at those demonstrations jumping off here, coming inside and stirring some stuff up. So the bartenders have all been instructed to issue the early cutoffs. If anyone causes even a little ruckus they'll be out of here and if we need to close the doors early, we will."

There was a knock on the office door and DeNasty and BTG stuck their heads in. Before Dick could say anything Nikki invited them inside. The pictures of Kline and Orr were still out on the desk. DeNasty gave them a quick look, and then stopped and went back to the photo of Kline.

"Hey BTG, isn't that our little guy from the other night?"

The tall, lanky bouncer finished grabbing a soda water out of the small fridge and then sauntered over. "Yeah, that's him. Man, was he a mess when we poured him into that cab."

"This guy?" Mac asked, pointing to the driver to Kline's left in the photo. "You're sure? You're absolutely sure?"

"Yup, that's him," DeNasty answered. "He spent a good hour bitching about his life and his job."

"He was in here? *Here*?" Mac asked again, almost in disbelief. "And *you* talked to him?"

"Off and on for an hour or so, I sure did," DeNasty answered.

"Really?" Dick asked and looked to BTG. "She did?"

"Yeah," the big guy answered. "She was talking to him. I was watching from my perch."

"Don't sound so shocked, *Dick,*" DeNasty barked. "You know, despite my nickname I do have the ability to be a shoulder to lean on and listen to people's sorrows every so often if it's not ridiculously busy. Which it wasn't that night."

"And you said he was bitching about his life," Mac asked, now engaged. "This guy bitched about his life."

"Yeah," DeNasty answered after a moment's thought. "He spent a lot of time complaining about his job. About how little he was paid by his boss."

"This is important, Denise," Mac said in a calm, quiet voice that masked the sudden jolt of adrenaline coursing through him. "Tell us *exactly* what he said. Take your time, but we need to know."

"Does this relate to Sam?"

"This guy"—Dick pointed to Neil Kline, to the right of the little guy in the picture—"Is named Neil Kline, and he's involved somehow in Sam's death." He then pointed to the picture of Orr. "Kline and this man named Terrence Orr were friends and we think business associates. Orr, we're pretty sure, was involved in Sam's abduction and murder. Just after Kline met with this man he got into a shootout in an alley with another police officer."

"The shooting that was on the news last week?" DeNasty asked. "My goodness."

"We don't know what these guys do or exactly what they're into," Mac explained, providing context. "So if this man you've pointed to was here in the bar and bitching about his job, his boss and his life, Dick and I need to know everything he told you about his job."

DeNasty nodded. "I remember he said that it was better that I didn't know what they did."

Mac deflated and looked to Dick.

"But," DeNasty continued, "he did say something to the effect that they..." She closed her eyes for a second and then nodded. "Yeah, that's right. He said they think I don't know but I know exactly what they're doing. Then he said something about the fact he wasn't stupid and said he sees the Mexicans, the trucks, the money, the powder. I see it all."

"Mexicans, trucks, money and powder," Dick repeated. "He said all of that? This little shit right here in the photo said all of that to you?"

"Yes," DeNasty answered.

Mac and Dick shared a quick *can you believe this* glance, and then Dick asked, "Anything else?"

She thought for a moment. "No, not really. He said he and this guy who was his boss were in jail together. He said he helped the guy in jail and that's how they became... connected, I guess."

"He doesn't weigh much, not much at all," BTG added. "Yet he was knocking back the shots. Hence the cab."

"Yeah. He said he was a jockey or something," DeNasty

added. "He kept saying he loved the horses, missed the horses. He went on and on about the horses. If he could just get back to the horses."

Dick and Mac gently pushed DeNasty for a while longer and walked her through the whole conversation with the driver again. They got the cab company name and planned to track down the taxi number, driver and where he dropped the man off.

"Do I have to go down to the police station now and make some sort of statement?" DeNasty asked.

Dick and Mac shared another quick look and Mac gave a light head shake.

"For now, no," Dick stated. "If this leads somewhere, then down the road we might need to put it on the record. I have good notes and obviously I know where to find you, so if need be we'll do this all formal style downtown at a later date, okay?"

"Okay."

Dick and Mac left the bar and stood in the parking lot for a moment trying to make sense of what they'd just heard.

"Mexicans, money, trucks and powder. What are we talking about here?" Dick asked.

"Mexicans, money, trucks, powder. What it means to me is that we might have a cartel connection," Mac answered seriously. "We have the cartel, a drug cartel, operating here in the cities. And it explains taking down Sam," Mac theorized, leaning against the car. "Local corner boys, even the gangs, wouldn't dare screw with the police or even the ex-police. But the cartel?" Mac just shook his head. "They just don't give a fuck."

"So Sam saw too much that night. Heck, maybe he saw who was behind the whole damn thing."

"The Avocado?" Mac asked.

"The Avocado," Dick answered, thinking back to Sam's notebook scribbles. "Sam met his demise later that night so he saw something. He saw the cartel and who was running it, the boss. We have to talk to this little man."

"We do, but stop and think about that for a second," Mac cautioned. "Think this through, Dicky Boy. If we approach that guy, unless he can't remember a thing, he'll probably know what?"

"He'd know it came from Denise in there."

"That's right. If these guys took down a cop, they wouldn't think twice about going after Denise or BTG or anyone else in there. So my point is—"

"We have to find another way."

Mac nodded. "Yeah. We have to protect those guys."

"And we might have a rat," Dick added.

"That's right. We need to keep this between you and I and maybe Rock and Riles. That's it until we figure out what to do with it and how to approach this driver without exposing Nikki and her friends."

"Well, let's think on it while we drive over to the 280 and meet up with those guys."

~

The 280 Grille was an aptly named all-night joint. Located on the corner of University and Cromwell Avenues, it was a half-block east of Highway 280, an odd, narrow four-mile state highway that slithered through the residential, industrial and commercial areas on the extreme western edge of St. Paul. State Highway 280 also was something of an unofficial border between Minneapolis and St. Paul, with the actual border running just a few blocks west of the highway.

This was a large reason why both Minneapolis and St. Paul officers were involved in the chase that led to the DeVonte Rice shooting. The 280 Grille, because of its proximity to the border between the two cities, drew cops from both towns. The cops often met at the 280 to quickly commiserate, get a hot cup of coffee or grab one of their legendary, reasonably priced burger bags for a late-night snack while on patrol.

Riles pulled the front door open for Rock and Ortega, who walked in to find Double Frank and Fisher already sitting in a back corner booth. There were four Minneapolis uniform cops taking a break, occupying a booth, one of whom Riles knew.

"How's it going on your side of the river today?" Riles asked sympathetically.

"Pretty rough, Riles. Folks are really edgy," a veteran patrol officer named Stevens answered as he slid out of the booth, having finished his plate of food. "We're expecting a tense night. My partner and I here are heading back out now. We're patrolling around the University of Minnesota tonight. That's an area that could have some activity."

"That's why you're here, huh? Getting a little fuel?"

"That's what we did," Stevens answered and then introduced Riles to the other two officers.

"A little petrol for you boys too, eh?"

"Burgers, tots and we'll be getting ourselves those big to-go coffees. What about you guys?"

Riles hooked his thumb at the back booth. "I guess we're lucky. We're all off the clock now. So we're heading out for some cocktails, but those burgers serve as an awfully good base."

"They do at that. Enjoy your night."

Riles bid Stevens a goodbye and left the other

Minneapolis cops to finish their burgers and took his seat in the booth opposite Rock.

"What's the good news?" Double Frank asked.

"Lich is on his way over here and he texted that he had some good news. A new lead on things that he cryptically said was complicated and will be a bit of a shocker."

"What, he's leaving us in suspense?" Fisher asked.

"I guess," Riles answered. "The other little nugget is Mac is back in town. That'll help too."

"I don't really know McRyan," Fisher stated. "I never worked with him when he was here. Is he really a good guy or is it an act?"

"Good guy," Riles answered, "real good guy."

"Always has been," Ortega added. "I've known him since elementary school, although until the last couple of weeks I hadn't seen him in some years. He carries himself a little differently now, in a kind of worldly way, but still seems to be pretty much the same good guy he always was."

Fisher looked to Rockford. "Is he?"

"He's gone kind of Hollywood on us and all," Rock started.

"That's kinda harsh," Riles replied in surprise.

"Let me finish," Rock said, holding up his hand. "I love the guy like a little brother, you know that. But, you must admit, Riles, he's gone Washington. Hell, Ortega sees it."

"I wasn't ripping him. It was just an observation."

"I'm not ripping him either. *But*, Mac's got money, the gorgeous wife, access to the President of the United States, Judge Dixon on speed dial, the fancy car and the Georgetown brownstone. He visits us from time to time, but he lives in an entirely different world now. He's different now. How could he not be?"

"You make that all sound bad, Rock," Riles retorted.

"Let me finish," Rock replied, holding up his hand. "I might have said all that, but let me tell you something else. If something, anything, ever happened to someone I cared about, that son of a gun is the one I'd want to investigate the case."

"He's that good?" Fisher asked Riles.

"We're all good cops," Riles replied, pointing to everyone around the table, "but I'm not too proud to admit that Mac is at a little different level. He just sees shit other people don't. And there is one other thing."

"What's that?" Fisher asked.

"Rock and Ortega aren't wrong. Our boy has gone a little uptown, but it's only natural given what's happened in his life. But let me tell you something, he is a warrior and a ruthless motherfucker when he has to be. If he believes he's right, he will not stop no matter what anyone else says."

"Oh yeah," Rock answered with a smile, nodding, "That's for sure. You don't fuck with Mac."

"He'll fuck you back," Riles replied with a big smile, which quickly vanished when he glanced to his left. "What the..."

Three men in black face masks burst through the front door. All three had assault rifles. They were coming right at them.

"Oh shit!" Riles exclaimed as he reached for his hip.

Juan was the key as the first one in. He took the uniform cops to the left, catching them in mid-bite and had two shots in each of them before they could even flinch.

Sylvester was the second one in and he went for the corner booth. The big white cop from St. Paul, Riley, saw them coming in the door. He was reaching for his gun while rising out of the booth.

Sylvester didn't hesitate. *Boom. Boom. Boom*, sending Riley flying backward over a table and into the wall.

He turned quickly back left. Ortega was nearly out of the booth, his gun up. The cop got one stray shot away before Sylvester unloaded, sending the detective down to the floor.

Rockford dove out of the booth low, seeking cover behind a table. Felix tracked him and unloaded, hitting him multiple times before the big cop crashed into a table, bringing it down on top of him.

Juan pivoted to his right to the corner booth and took a step forward. Fisher and Franklin were scrambling, stuck in the tight booth, trying to reach their weapons and escape. Juan kept his trigger depressed. He fired again and again and again, hitting the two cops repeatedly, immobilizing them. Then Juan twisted back to the two Minneapolis uniform cops. He shot the first one in the forehead. He turned to the second officer.

"Please," the officer pleaded, unable to move. "My wife just had a baby."

Juan shot him in the face.

Sylvester, walked to his right and around the table to find Ortega lying on his back, spitting up blood, gasping for breath.

"You... have no idea the hell that is about to...come down on...all of you..."

"Like I'm scared," Sylvester said coldly before shooting Ortega in the head.

Felix moved to the corner booth. Franklin was shot twice in the chest and there was another wound in throat and he was bleeding out. Felix shot him in the head finishing him off. Then he rotated to Fisher who was immobilized, his eyes frantic, gasping for breath after being shot in the chest multiple times. Felix stepped forward and put his gun to Fisher's forehead and said, "Sorry, Fisher. I guess you won't get to spend all that money," before he depressed the trigger.

Felix looked to his right to big Riley, his motionless body lying face down on the floor between the wall with the table lying on top of him. Rockford was motionless on the floor, a table and chairs lying on top of him. The sound of police sirens was audible in the distance.

"We gotta go! Let's go!" Sylvester warned urgently, gesturing toward the front door with his rifle. "*Right now!*"

Felix nodded, started backing away and yelled, *"That's for DeVonte! That's for DeVonte! That's for DeVonte!"* as he ran out the door.

~

"I haven't had a 280 burger in a long while," Mac said, salivating at the thought of one as they passed the exit for Snelling Avenue, heading west on I-94. "I'm feeling like a double, heck, maybe a triple. I went for a long run before my flight today. I have expansive caloric capacity available."

"I'll probably have a salad," Dick muttered and looked over to a shocked Mac, "Dot wants me to shed a few."

"Steak salad then," Mac answered. "You gotta get your protein, dude."

The radio came to life: "*Code 3, officer down, shots fired southeast corner of University and Cromwell.*"

"University and Cromwell," Mac exclaimed, looking over to his partner.

"Southeast corner. That's the 280," Dick answered, activating the lights and sirens. "Hang on."

"I'm not carrying."

Dick raised his left leg and reached down with his right hand and pulled his backup Glock-9 out of his ankle holster and handed it to Mac. Mac released the magazine, checked it and slammed it back in, chambering a round.

They were only a minute or two away as Dick hit the accelerator and powered west on I-94, with siren and lights. He took the exit to north on Highway 280 and then the immediate exit to the right for University Avenue. At the top of the ramp, Dick veered slightly right and then turned a hard left, fishtailing onto Cromwell and accelerated again north to the intersection with University and skidded hard to a stop at the side of the 280 Grille.

Along the side of the building, scrawled ominously over both the long run of tall windows in bright red paint was sprayed: *Remember DeVonte!*

"Shit!" Dick growled.

Mac opened the passenger side door and crouched down behind it for cover, scanning the interior. All he could see was blood and bodies. "Oh, man."

Detecting no motion inside, Mac, continuing to scan the interior quickly shuffled sideways to the left toward the front door, Dick to his immediate left doing the same. At the front door, Mac nodded and Dick pulled it open and Mac darted inside, gun up.

It was carnage.

"My God!" Dick croaked as he followed Mac in.

Pools of blood were everywhere. To the left were two Minneapolis patrol officers sprawled in a booth. They were both riddled with bullet holes, with execution kill shots to their foreheads. Hiding in a booth to Mac's right were two civilians, under the table, whimpering. Then he glanced left to the floor.

"*Tommy!*" Mac yelled, taking a step before sliding on the floor to him. He'd been shot in the head. Ortega's eyes were open and lifeless. "*No! No! No!*" Mac howled as he frantically checked Ortega for a pulse, for anything, for any sign of life but his friend was gone. "*God, no!*"

"*Mac!*" Dick exclaimed. Mac spun back to his right.

Dick was pulling a table off Rock, whose legs were slowly moving. Bobby moaned as Dick helped him roll over onto his back. "I'm hit bad, really bad," he croaked out, his right hand covering a wound in his belly. Mac could see that Rock was hit in the leg and left upper chest as well. Rock rolled his eyes to his right and grunted out, "Riles."

Mac looked past Rockford and saw a table lying on top of Riley. Mac leaped over Rock and grabbed the table and pulled it off Riles. "*Oh man. Oh man, oh man, oh man.*"

Riles was lying face down, motionless, blood all over the floor underneath him. Then Mac saw the big man's arm move, just a twitch and there was an almost imperceptible moan.

"Riles!" Mac exclaimed and dropped to his knees and rolled Pat onto his back. "Riles!" Mac screamed, slapping his friend's face, "Riles! Riles! It's Mac! Look at me! *LOOK! AT! ME!*"

Riles eyes fluttered open but when he tried to speak, blood spilled out of his mouth.

"Stay with me, buddy. *Stay with me.*" Mac roared, looking around for something to stop the bleeding. He yelled back to the kitchen. "We're police officers. We need towels and bandages right now!"

Two people, very scared, ran out of the kitchen with towels and rags.

Sirens were approaching the scene and two Minneapolis uniform officers burst into the restaurant with guns drawn.

"We need ambulances now*!*" Mac yelled urgently. "*Right fuckin' now!*"

"They're rolling," the patrol officer reported. "Be here any second."

One person from the kitchen kneeled next to Dick and started applying pressure to Rock's wounds. "Hang in there, Bobby! Hang in there!" Dick exclaimed as he searched Rock's body for more holes. He reached behind and felt more blood. He ordered one of the workers to put pressure on the belly wound. Dick took another towel and reached behind to apply pressure to the back wound. "I think we have a through and through here!"

The other cook kneeled next to Riles and looked to Mac. "What do I do?"

"Apply pressure with the towels to these wounds in the belly. Use both of your hands," Mac ordered.

The cook did as Mac instructed. Others streamed out of the back of the restaurant now that it was safe with towels and a blue box first aid kit. Mac needed an octopus there were so many wounds. He looked back up to Riles' face and saw the eyes roll back into the big man's head. "Riles! *Riles!*"

Mac checked for a pulse. There wasn't one and he leaned down to Riles' mouth. The big man wasn't breathing now. "Pull back," Mac ordered, pushing the cook away as he threw his left leg over Riles body and straddled him and began CPR. "Come on, dammit! Riles, *come on!*" Mac grunted as he counted out the compressions.

There were more sirens and two paramedics burst through the front doors while Mac continued to work on Riles and Dick looked over Rock.

"He's got at least four wounds," Dick reported to the first paramedic. "This belly wound looks the worst, he's bleeding front and back from it. Are you guys it?"

"More are on the way," the second paramedic replied calmly as he rushed past Dick and took a knee next to Mac.

Mac kept giving compressions. Then Riles coughed up blood. "He's back," Mac exclaimed, pulling his hands back from Riles' chest.

"Okay, let's get off him," the paramedic ordered. Mac quickly fell off to the side and then watched closely as the paramedic began assessing Riles. Another paramedic came in with two patrol officers rolling a stretcher behind him.

The second paramedic looked around Riley and the floor beneath him. "He's had to have lost a ton of blood."

"We need to get him to the hospital now," the first paramedic observed as he assessed Pat's airway and pulse while the other was checking the wounds, making a quick count. His assessment matched Mac's which was of five holes, two in the upper chest and three in the abdomen.

Riles was struggling. Mac squeezed his hand. "Stay with us, Riles*! Stay with us!*" he begged. Riles squeezed Mac's hand lightly and Mac looked to his face and his eyes were just open. "Come on buddy, hang in there," he uttered more calmly. "Bobby's over there alive. You two are both going to the hospital. Just stay with us, buddy!"

Mac looked back to see Dick, two paramedics and a uniform cop moving Rock to a stretcher. Once on the stretcher they quickly popped it up and rapidly pushed Rock out the door.

"Let's get this man on the stretcher," the first paramedic directed. Mac, the two paramedics and another uniform officer took positions. "One, two, three," the paramedic counted out and they all lifted Riles onto the stretcher. The paramedic quickly elevated the stretcher. "We have to motivate."

"Out of the way, coming through!" the other paramedic exclaimed.

"I want units in front and behind! Get their asses over to Hennepin County Medical Center," Dick ordered to the patrol officers who were out the door right behind the stretcher. Less than a minute later, two patrol units led out the ambulances with another two behind as more officers were arriving and securing the scene.

It had been a slaughter.

Mac looked to the two civilians who were now sitting up. "They just came in, these men had assault rifles and just started shooting," a man, pale with shock whimpered. "They just kept shooting and yelling, *For DeVonte! For DeVonte!*"

"Can you describe them?" Mac asked, leaning down while a paramedic tended to him.

The man shook his head. "They were dressed in all black, wearing black face masks."

"How many?"

"Three."

"Did you see them leave?"

"No," the man replied, blankly looking ahead. "No."

"We heard them leave," his woman friend said as she wiped away tears, her body still shaking. "I heard a vehicle pull away...but...we were hiding under the table."

"Did you see what they were driving? Which way they left?" Dick asked as calmly as he could. "Anything like that at all?"

"No," the woman replied quietly, whimpering. "I'm sorry."

More uniform cops were arriving on the scene.

"Guys, let's get outside," Dick said quietly, waving them out. "There is nothing more we can do in here. Let's not contaminate the scene any more than it already is. Let's get control outside and keep people back."

Mac looked back to his right and the far corner and slowly stepped that way. Double Frank and Fisher were dead, never even making it out of their booth. They both had gunshot wounds to their foreheads.

"They were executed," Dick pronounced quietly.

"They all were," Mac answered as he looked back to Tommy Ortega. His bottom lip started to lightly tremble as he made his way back over to his friend. He took a knee and gently reached for Ortega's right hand and took it in his hands, closed his eyes and silently said a prayer.

When Mac was finished, Dick laid a clean white towel over Ortega's face. "God help whoever did this."

"God won't," Mac answered coldly. "They're going to hell and we're going to deliver them there."

23

"THE AVOCADO IS THE KEY TO EVERYTHING."

"That was good work," Felix said as he slipped a cigar into his mouth and handed Juan and Sylvester their large yellow envelopes.

The two men, smoking celebratory cigars of their own, knew it wasn't necessary to check the contents. Back in the day when Felix first started with the Lazaro Cardenas family, he supplied crews in South Central Los Angeles. Juan and Sylvester were two of his early finds and they'd remained loyal and dependable ever since.

"The rest was of course wired to your preferred accounts," Felix added. "Someday soon the three of us are going to have to go somewhere and spend some of it."

"For sure," Sylvester answered before blowing out a big puffy plume of cigar smoke. "Juan and I have been eyeing up some fishing."

"Yeah?"

"Oh yeah," Juan replied in agreement. "Take a boat out of Encinitas."

"Well, once things die down around here and we get

things up and running in Kansas City, I'm in," Felix replied with a smile.

"Will they die down?" Sylvester asked. "Seems to me you've just whipped things up into a big ball of fire. They're going to tear the town apart looking for you, for us."

Felix nodded and smiled broadly. "*Exactly*."

The three of them were standing in the entryway to the back of a barn on a farm outside of Elko, a sleepy rural exurb resting on the far southern edge of the suburbs south of Minneapolis. The night sky was crystal clear, the air comfortably cool in the countryside with just the rhythmic chirping of the crickets disturbing the quiet. A silver bucket with Dos Equis rested at their feet.

Originally the plan was to have the two of them fly out in the morning back to Los Angeles. But with the expected heat, Felix was starting to think their remaining presence was needed.

"Are you two going to be alright hanging out at the farm here for a few days?" Felix asked. "I wouldn't mind you being around for security purposes when we take our last shipment. Once that's done, I'll get you on a plane. Of course, we'd be adding to those envelopes I just handed you."

"For this, I'm always happy to do my thing," Juan replied, holding up his yellow envelope.

"*Si*," Sylvester added.

"Good. We just have to ride this out for a few more days but your presence could prove helpful."

White came out of the small farmhouse and approached the group, reaching down to grab a beer out of the bucket. He'd been inside watching the news reports.

"And?"

"It's chaos and people are reacting as we'd hopes. A

master stroke really, Felix. The whole city is going to explode. The police all over the Twin Cities are going to be tearing the entire town apart looking for three shooters clad all in black, shooters they'll undoubtedly presume are black, avenging the death of DeVonte Rice. They'll rip the town to shreds trying to find them."

"Which of course, they won't," Felix answered.

"That's right," White replied with a nod. "African American community leaders, politicians, rabble rousers, all of them will be fighting the law enforcement onslaught. The media will go crazy." The lawyer and fixer snorted a chuckle. "Hell, Sam Shead, Rafael Cruz, the Polar Bar, Kline, JuJu and Fulbright, all of it will just be an afterthought."

"And by the time they get back around to it..."

"We'll all be long gone."

~

"I'd known Tommy Ortega since I was like ten years old, Sal," Mac said softly. "I mean, we ran everywhere together. In high school we played football and baseball together, we double dated to prom, we had our first beers together, we had a lot of firsts together. Just about anything I did, good or bad, he was there with me. He was there every step of the way when my dad died and now...Sally, he'd just gotten back to town and we'd reconnected and..." His voice trailed off.

"Mac, I'm sorry, I'm so, so sorry about your friend." Sally said. "Has anyone reached out to his family?"

"The chief and Peters went over to her house. They also had to go see Double Frank's wife too. It must have been awful."

"Any kids involved?"

"Double Frank's kids are grown, but Tommy had one son and a baby on the way."

"Oh my gosh, his poor wife."

"I know, I should go see Jenny...I should...I don't know what I should do."

"Is there any more word on Riles and Rock?"

"They're both in surgery. I guess Rock crashed on the ambulance ride over and the paramedic was riding on top, giving CPR when they wheeled him into the ER. They got his heart going again and rushed him into surgery. He was so shot up and Riles was worse. I mean, I saw it, I felt it, Riles...his heart stopping, Sal. His eyes rolled back. I was giving him CPR."

"And because you two made it there when you did, they might both survive."

"Sally," Mac replied quietly, "Dick and I were on our way there. Had we gotten there ten minutes earlier, heck, five minutes, Dick and I would have been lying on that floor. You'd have been getting the call from the chief."

"I know," Sally replied softly. "And selfishly, I'm thanking God I didn't. Look, I'm going to see if I can catch a flight home. You need me there and..."

"No," Mac answered, cutting her off. "No, no, no, not right now."

"But..."

"I appreciate it, I really do, you know I do," Mac replied sternly, coming out of his emotional stupor. "I don't mean this how it sounds, but Sal, the last thing I need right now is you here. You don't want to be here. You're not going to want to see me."

"Mac, what's going to happen?" Sally asked warily.

"Bad things," he answered darkly. He was angry, wanted

payback and didn't want her to be around to see it. "And that's why I think you should stay away."

"You're going after these guys, aren't you?"

"One of my best friends was assassinated. Two men who are like brothers to me are just hanging on. Five other cops were murdered in cold blood. I'm going hunting for these bastards and I don't plan on coming up empty. I don't care what it takes."

"Good," Sally answered forcefully. "You do whatever you have to do. Hunt them down like the animals they are."

He'd been worried about how his wife would respond. He should have known better. "I just can't believe this happened. I mean, I thought there might be some fireworks tonight, more demonstrations, maybe some more rioting, but this? Here? In St. Paul?"

"Why do you think they picked the 280?"

"St. Paul and Minneapolis cops were involved in the DeVonte Rice incident. Where can you find both Minneapolis and St. Paul cops on any given night? The 280."

"So you really think this was about revenge for DeVonte Rice?" Sally asked.

"Yea..." Then Mac's voice drifted off. Sally was driving at something. There was a purposeful skepticism in her voice. "Sally, what are you thinking? I can hear it in your voice. What is it?"

"I know the 280 is a cop place. I've been there with you. I've seen it. But I also think it was quite the coincidence that Riles, Rock, Ortega, Double Frank, Fisher...heck, for you and Dick to have been there. I mean, what are the odds that all the people working on..."

"The Shead case were there," Mac finished and his mind started racing. "Sally, that's a really...good thought."

With all that had happened, Mac had stopped thinking

about the case. His mind wasn't sorting properly and making connections that it should have been. Sally's insight snapped him out of that fog. "The odds are—" His voice drifted away. "You know what, Sal, they're damn long," Mac declared and suddenly a bunch of questions were running through his head.

"Mac, what are you going to do?"

"I'm going to figure this out."

A bloody mess, he'd left the hospital with Riles and Rock still in surgery to come home and change. It would be hours before they were out, but a nurse said, "They both made it to the operating room. That's always a good sign."

As Mac sat at the foot of his bed at 4:00 a.m., looking at his bloody clothes in a mangled pile in the clothes basket, he decided he needed to get back into the game—*in full*. That required a phone call to the chief. There was no preamble. "I want my badge."

"Done."

"Who is handling the 280?"

"Right now, Bonnie Schmidt and a new detective named Tommy Armstrong. Do you want them in?"

"Yes, make it 6:00 a.m. but at the old Fourth Precinct."

"Why there?"

"I don't want the people I'm hunting knowing I'm in the game. I don't want people hearing what I'm thinking and saying. Are there any more updates on Riles and Rock?"

"They're both still in surgery. I'll see you in a few hours."

Mac took a quick shower to get the blood off. He went to his closet and to his detective suits that he'd stored in clothing bags to protect them from dust. He pulled out a plain black suit and matched it up with a navy-blue pinstripe dress shirt. Dressed, he went down to the basement and his gun safe and took out his old Sig Sauer. He pulled out the magazine, checked that it was full and jammed it back in. In addition, he pulled out his Glock-9 and his ankle holster and strapped it around his left ankle. Next, he went to the closet next to the safe. Inside he took out a duffel bag and zipped it open to check its contents, which included his Kevlar vest, cuffs case, flashlight, spare magazines for the Sig and Glock and a switchblade knife, which he slipped into his pants pocket. He threw the big duffel bag over his shoulder.

He was at the old Fourth Precinct building just before 5:00 a.m. and was surprised to find Paddy already inside.

"You can always count on family," Mac remarked, prideful.

"I had to do something and...I didn't know what else to do or...where else to go," Paddy replied and then noticed the gun on his cousin's right hip. "Are you helping us now for real?"

"Yes," Mac answered, taking his coat off and throwing it over the back of the chair. "Let's get this thing organized properly."

"You're still working this thing? Not the 280?"

"Trust me," Mac answered and waved to the evidence on the table, "working this *is* working the 280."

"But the paint on the windows..."

"*Trust me.*"

Paddy took the measure of his cousin. "I'm with ya."

Dick had moved the investigation down to this building in the last few days after they'd talked about the possibility of a rat. Whatever case organization Dick had going back in the Homicide Unit was clearly out the window. While there was a white board and bulletin board available for use, for the most part the case evidence sat scattered on a long conference table.

"What a mess."

"Those guys are old school. They keep everything in their head," Paddy remarked.

"That doesn't work for me."

Mac was a self-acknowledged control freak and when he and Dick worked together, Mac always used a whiteboard, assembled the evidence and was dictatorial in how the information went up on it and was organized. He required order and he had to see a case visually to process, work, understand and remember it. As such, he needed things on a timeline and needed everything up in front of him to decipher what was going on.

So even though he had somewhat of a handle on the case Mac, with Paddy's help, started organizing. "It really starts with Sam Shead," Mac murmured.

On the top of the board he put a timeline of the events of the night Sam Shead went missing, the time he was parked near the house up in Rogers, his stop at Fireball and then the last location of his cell phone.

Next, Mac moved the timeline out two days to when Sam's body was found in the river. He included pictures of Sam's body along with a notation regarding the autopsy report and findings of white nylon fibers, consistent with those used for a kind of body bag. As Mac read that notation in his mind he envisioned the killers zipping Sam's body up in the bag, weighing it down so that when they dumped the body in the Mississippi it sank to the bottom of the river.

"But that didn't work," Mac said quietly. Had that occurred, they'd have no idea what happened to him. They wouldn't have known that he was interrogated, beaten and then shot. Heck, there probably wouldn't be any case at all.

"You interrogate to know what he knew? What he saw?"

Mac mumbled quietly. "So what did you see, Sam? Or maybe better, *who* did you see?"

"Do you always talk to yourself like this?" Paddy asked, somewhat amused.

"Yeah, don't you?"

They suspected Shead saw Kline and probably Orr, based on the notation for T.O. in the notebook, but was seeing either of them worth killing Sam over? That was highly doubtful, but there was the other notation in the notebook that Mac wrote on the whiteboard: *Who is The Avocado?*

"We've never really gotten anywhere on that," Paddy reported.

"I think it's time we do," Mac answered. "It triggered everything."

To the right of the timeline, Mac put up pictures of persons of interest. First was the now deceased Terrence Orr. Mac figured out that there was a third person in the alley when Orr and Cruz were shot. That third person shot Cruz because he had to, but his purpose in being there was to kill Orr. "You're there to kill Orr," Mac muttered, "but then along comes Cruz and on the fly...you shoot at Cruz, and he does your dirty work for you and kills Orr and then you kill Cruz and make it look like Orr was the one who shot him." Mac shook his head. "Not bad, even if it ultimately didn't work."

"Someone needed Orr dead."

"Yes, they did," Mac replied. "Why? And more importantly, who?"

At the bar in St. Cloud, Mac overheard Kline counseling him on getting out of town. Why? What did he know? Who did he know it about? What did he do? Was he involved in Shead's murder? Mac put up a picture of Orr's black Yukon along with the notation: *Front left bumper, headlight and fender, all new*. Next to that notation he placed a picture of the debris from Burns Avenue where they thought Orr's Tahoe was involved in the takedown of Shead.

Since that time, Dick had been searching for another way to figure out who they were after. This is where Mac had dropped out of the case, although he was getting the occasional update from Dick.

There was the house in Rogers. It was empty, which just seemed wrong to Mac from what Dick told him. They were watching the house from a very safe distance, yet somehow they knew to close shop possibly the night before the raid. Next to the picture of the house, Mac wrote: *Empty?*

"Mac?"

"Yeah?"

"On the house," Paddy hesitated. "I suppose I can ask you this, do you think..."

"They were tipped off?" Mac finished the thought. "I wasn't here when that all went down, cuz. But it sure seems possible."

"Whoever did that doesn't have just Rafael Cruz's blood on his hands. Now he has Ortega, and Double Frank and Fisher, those guys from Minneapolis and maybe Riles and Rock..."

"I know," Mac replied quietly as he reached for a photo, "I know." The photo was of Neil Kline.

Kline's interrogation went nowhere. As Dick said, it was as if he saw it coming and was completely prepared for it with high-priced legal counsel waiting for the call. That begged the question: how did Kline afford that? Who was paying the tab? And was he just a savvy con, was he tipped off, or perhaps was it both? "Did we have eyes on Kline last night?"

"Yes, Schmidt and Armstrong were on Kline last night. When it all went down, Kline and his little driver buddy were sitting at a bar having a drink ten miles away. But the chief pulled them off that to work the 280."

"So we have no eyes on Kline right now?"

Paddy shook his head.

"We'll have to fix that."

Mac placed three pictures of Kline on the board. One was a mugshot from five years ago, another was with Kline in his truck with his driver and the third was the picture Mac took of Kline and Orr at the bar in St. Cloud. "Kline is the key. We need to get him to talk."

"Those guys tried, Mac. Kline treated them like a minor inconvenience."

"Then we'll need to inconvenience him."

"How?"

"I'm working on it."

Mac's gaze lingered on the second Kline picture where he was standing with his driver outside of the repair shop. Kline's driver certainly seemed to know some things. Money, Mexicans, trucks, powder. That all said drugs to Mac; with the mention of Mexicans, maybe even a drug cartel.

He reached for a black marker, took off the cap and was going to add that to the board and then stopped. Right now, in his mind that was information that was too dangerous to leave in the open. It would put Nikki, Denise and BTG and everyone else at Fireball in danger. He put the cap back on the marker, but the more he thought about that information, the more of an idea began to form in his head.

"You two have been busy."

Mac and Paddy turned around to see Dick scanning the whiteboard. Chief Flanagan was right behind him.

"Any more word on Rock and Riles?" Mac asked.

"They're both out of surgery now," the chief replied tiredly. "They're both still in serious condition, but they think, they plugged all of the holes. One shot missed Riles' heart by that much," Flanagan added, holding his index finger and thumb an inch apart.

"What are their odds?"

"You can never tell with doctors. They hedge and cover themselves with all kinds of qualifiers, but after the surgeon's filibuster I sensed we should be guardedly optimistic, but neither of them are anywhere near out of danger yet. The next twenty-four hours will probably tell the tale."

Mac nodded and exhaled a sigh of relief.

"What do we have?" Dick asked, pointing to the whiteboard.

"Sorry, Dick, but if I'm going to work this full bore I have to start looking at the case in a way that makes sense to me," Mac explained.

Dick shook his head, unoffended. "I always liked it when you did this. I just can never make it look as pretty and organized as this."

"Mac, this looks an awful lot like the Sam Shead and Rafael Cruz investigation," the chief muttered, a confused look on his face.

"It is," Mac replied.

"I thought you wanted to investigate the 280 shooting."

"Chief, I am."

"How so?" Flanagan asked quizzically, not following.

Before Mac could answer Detectives Bonnie Schmidt and Tommy Armstrong, the detectives assigned to the shooting at the 280, came inside.

"How you guys doing?" Bonnie asked.

"We're fine," Dick answered.

"Let me tell you, it is not fine out there," Bonnie replied, gesturing out the window toward the city. "Have you seen the television?"

Mac had been so focused on the whiteboard he hadn't bothered to turn on the television. Bonnie grabbed the remote and flipped through all four of the local television channels, all with ongoing live coverage from outside the 280. CNN was also covering the story, using local reporters. The other news networks were starting to dig into it as well. The connection between the jury verdict and the shooting was obvious. With all the attention, a lot of people were eager to get on camera and not all were sympathetic.

"Cops got what they had coming," an anonymous Minneapolis northside citizen yelled into the camera for Channel Six. "That's for DeVonte Rice. That's for all the African American men who've been murdered by the police all over the country. They got what they had coming!"

"Cripes," the chief moaned, shaking his head. "I hope there aren't a ton of people like that guy out there."

Channel Six then flipped to Pastor Bobby Beal of the Mount Zion Baptist Church. "This violence has to stop," the pastor proclaimed quietly to the camera, citizens standing behind him. "Nothing good can come from any of this for anyone, our community, our citizens, the police. This must stop, the police, the retaliation. It can't go on. We have all lost. To begin to mend we must all come together, not tear each other apart."

"There's a sane voice," Mac replied. "He can help."

"Oh yeah," Bonnie answered as she changed to Channel Eight. "But not everyone's in such a conciliatory mood."

Lester Osmond with Twin Cities Civil Rights was not calm and cool-headed. "The cops have been getting off all over the country killing black men. DeVonte Rice was unarmed, and he was shot in front of God and everyone! We have it on tape—the police admit they shot an unarmed man. Yet, what happens? The jury lets these cops walk. Where's the justice? Where's the justice for DeVonte? Well, you know what? Maybe some people decided it was time to fight back. We're under siege from the police and when that happens, well, obviously some people acted. I don't condone it, but I understand it."

"That's *real* calming," Dick remarked.

The television reports continued. Mayors from both cities were pleading for calm and calling for the community to come together. Both cities would be imposing a curfew for at least the next couple of days. "Everyone has lost here," the St. Paul mayor stated solemnly. "And everyone needs to heal."

Everyone had seen enough and Schmidt turned off the television.

"Jurgenson and I are going to need to work and coordinate on this," Flanagan muttered, referencing his counterpart in Minneapolis. "I feel like ripping down every door in this city to find these guys, but everybody needs to keep their cool." The chief then turned back to Mac. "You said this shooting last night has something to do with Sam Shead. How? I don't see the connection. Hell, I've got DeVonte Rice's named spray painted all over the 280, Mac."

"I'll get there, Chief," Mac answered and then looked to Armstrong and Schmidt. "Tell me, who are we hunting for?"

"Let me show you," Armstrong replied, sitting down at a laptop computer and plugging in a flash drive. "We have the surveillance footage. Fair warning, it's rough to watch." Armstrong moved the mouse and pushed play.

The surveillance camera vantage point was situated over the front door with a panoramic view of the entire dining area that consisted of six tables in a triangle formation in the middle, resting between the five waist-high booths running along the walls on the left and right. The two uniform officers were sitting in the second booth along the left wall. Riley, Rockford, Ortega, Franklin and Fisher were in the back-left corner booth. Two of the tables in the middle were occupied by civilians, along with a booth along the right side.

At 9:21:14 three masked men in all black burst through the front door with automatic rifles. The first man came in, took the left side and took out the uniformed officers. The second and third men came in and went for the back-corner booth.

"Sweet Jesus," Dick croaked.

Riles charged out of the booth but was hit multiple times in the chest and sent flying backward over a table. Rock also leapt from the booth, trying for cover low behind a table, but he was hit multiple times too.

Ortega was next. He got his gun out and managed to fire one stray round before he was mowed down to the floor.

Fisher and Franklin were trapped in the booth and hardly able to move before they were gunned down. The third shooter then moved in and finished them off with head shots.

"It gets worse," Schmidt cautioned.

Shooter number two stood over Ortega. He looked down and they could tell that Tommy said something before the shooter shot him in the head as if it was no big thing. At the same time, the first shooter had moved back to the uniformed officers and shot both of them in the head, finishing them off. The whole sequence took barely thirty seconds.

"It was a mass execution, plain and simple," the chief growled angrily.

"Why didn't they finish off Rock or Riley?" Paddy asked.

"Providence. They must have assumed they were dead. They were both covered by tipped-over tables, not moving," Mac answered, peering close at the screen. "I mean, neither of them are moving. They're both lying face down."

"And time," Dick added. "They only had so much time to do what they needed to do before they had to get out of there."

Bonnie Schmidt's eyes were moist. "I've watched it five or six times now, but I just can't..." Her voice trailed off.

For Mac there were no tears, just anger for a moment, and then analysis. "Any better descriptions from the witnesses?"

Armstrong shook his head. "They were in full face masks, dressed in all black and everyone was ducking for cover. Same thing I think they told you. The only thing all of them said is one of the shooters repeatedly yelled 'this was for DeVonte.' And of course, they spray painted *DeVonte* on the outside of the building."

Mac re-watched the footage again. One thing that stuck out to him was the precision and almost professionalism of the three men. "Those were not some neighborhood boys out looking for revenge. Those are assault rifles. They're wearing body armor. They took the room down surgically."

"That's a three-man team," Dick added, "and that was clearly not the first time they all rock and rolled together. I agree with Mac, they had a plan going in. First shooter took the left, the next two took that booth and they ignored the citizens. They were after *us*."

"They went in there knowing exactly what they were doing and *who* they were after," Mac added and then looked back to the group. "*Exactly* who they were after."

"What do you mean?" Flanagan asked. "What do you

mean they went there knowing exactly who they were going after? Armstrong just told you that one of the shooters yelled, 'this is for DeVonte.'"

"That's what we're getting from the scene," Schmidt added. "Everyone heard it."

"Everyone was supposed to," Mac answered. "Everyone heard what the shooters wanted them to hear. It was all a diversion to get us looking away from what we've been working on."

"Wait, wait, wait a minute, Mac," the chief interrupted. "You can't think that this is because of Sam Shead?"

"It's not about Sam, Chief, but it's about what Sam *saw*. It's always been about what or who Sam saw. I keep running this whole thing around in mind and it's what this whole thing comes back to. His murder, the shooting of Orr and Cruz in that alley, and yes, the 280," Mac argued. "These shooters shot seven police. Five of whom are detectives investigating the Shead and Cruz case. The sixth, Dick, was on his way there with me, who you could argue is a seventh. I mean, if we'd been there five or ten minutes earlier, Dick and I would have been lying on that floor too! This was for DeVonte? *Bullshit*." Mac pointed to the white board. "This is all about *this* case."

"Convince me," the chief demanded. "Link it all up."

"Some of this you know, but let's start at the beginning. Months ago, Dick investigated the disappearance of a man named Luther Ellis."

"And he is who exactly?"

"Luther was a regular patron at the Fireball and he and Sam became friends," Dick explained, adding information about Luther's past to bring the others up to speed. "Luther got himself into some financial trouble and started going to old friends from prison for help, one of whom was Neil

Kline. Neil and Luther were also in prison with Terrence Orr."

Mac went over to the whiteboard and picked up the thread, "Luther's mom was having medical issues and was at risk of losing her house. Luther couldn't go to the bank and get a loan, he had no collateral, nothing to back it up with. He had difficulty finding consistent work and had limited income so to help his mom save the house he had to go off the normal market. Guys like Kline and Orr are off the normal market. Orr has been known to loan shark and Luther, in a jam, might have went there."

"What's the disappearance about?"

"Luther didn't have the money to pay back the loan but told Sam he had some dirt on whoever he took the loan from. He had some leverage," Dick replied. "And then Luther was gone."

"Gone?"

"Disappeared, Chief," Dick replied. "Sam asked me to dig into it, and I did for a few weeks. But Luther was gone, flat up and vanished. I worked his neighborhood, his haunts and talked to his mother, but nobody knew a thing. The only thing I had was the name of Neil Kline."

"Not Orr?"

"No, I didn't have that name at the time."

"I assume you questioned Kline at the time?"

Dick nodded. "You bet, but Kline gave me nothing. I had nothing to pressure him with. Hell, he was fairly convincing in expressing concern for his old friend and gave me the *If there's anything I could do, if I hear anything I'll call, BS.*" Dick took a drink of his coffee. "I'm pretty sure Kline has an idea of what happened or at least who is responsible for Luther's disappearance, but he's also pretty smart. He knows how the game is played so he said nothing and knew I had nothing.

So while the case was still technically open, I wasn't actively working it."

"But Sam was?" the Chief asked and then knowingly shook his head. "He wouldn't let it go."

Mac and Dick both nodded.

"Sam was working at Fireball," Dick stated. "It appears he was following Kline around in his off hours."

"And that's when we think he saw something he shouldn't have," Mac answered and pointed to a map. "We were able to use the GPS from his cell phone to track what he was doing his last night. He was up in Rogers and it looks like he was watching this house. After that he went back into St. Paul and stopped at Fireball for some time."

"Where, by the way, he accidentally left his notebook," Dick added. "Now, we all know Sam was a cryptic note-taker, but on that last night there were references to Kline, T.O. and then something called The Avocado. T.O. is Orr. We don't know who or what The Avocado is yet."

Mac continued. "But The Avocado is the key to everything. After Sam left Fireball he headed home. A little after 2:00 a.m. our last hit on his phone is over in the Battle Creek neighborhood. That's where we think Sam was abducted," Mac explained their theory of the takedown. "We found this debris from a front headlight. There were serial numbers on it which indicated the light was for a Yukon. In fact, for the year of Yukon owned by Terrence Orr."

"When we learned *that*, and that he was looking to skip town, we decided to bring Orr in, but then he eluded us," Dick explained, adding information about how Orr deceived them with the fake refrigerator delivery.

"And what about Kline? I assume you were on him?"

"We were until he also evaded us that day as well," Dick answered.

"Odd that the two of them needed to disappear, isn't it?" the chief asked.

"Indeed," Mac answered. "But Kline and Orr met up later that night. Kline slipped Orr twenty grand and then Orr went over to Tiana Callaway's. Well, we know what happened then. Orr and Cruz ended up dead in that alley. Now at that point, it seemed they had what they wanted. Orr was dead, shot by Cruz. But then I found this video of Kline slipping Orr the twenty thousand just before he went over to Callaway's."

"Neil claimed when we brought him in the other day that it was a loan," Dick added. "Which is total garbage."

"It was a way for whoever the third person was in that alley to get onto Orr and follow him. One way or another, Orr was going to be killed that night."

"Why kill Orr?" the chief asked.

"The only explanation is because he could hurt them," Mac answered. "And we were on him and sooner or later we were going to get our hands on him. So they took him out."

"But who are these guys?" the chief asked. "I get your theory. Do I buy it completely?" The chief shook his head slightly. "But I can see the logic in it. But then the question I keep coming back to is who? Who has the balls to do this?"

Mac looked to Dick, who nodded.

"There is some information I have not put up on the whiteboard."

"Which is?" the chief asked.

"This is all about drugs and this has the earmarks of a cartel, a Mexican drug cartel."

"A cartel?" the chief asked, his jaw agape. "Here. How do you make *that* leap?"

Mac made a quick decision on Armstrong and Schmidt. They'd had no exposure to the case so he thought it virtually impossible that either of them could be the rat. This was a risk, but he shared a glance with Dick who nodded, thinking the same thing. "This can't leave the room, does everyone understand? If it does, more lives could be in danger and if something happens to one of them, Dick and I are going to hold the people here responsible."

Everyone nodded.

Mac explained what Kline's driver said at Fireball. "Mexicans, powder, trucks, money. That says cartel to me and if you think about it, the cartel makes some sense. The cartel wouldn't hesitate to mow down a bunch of cops, not if they got in the way of their business. Not for a second. You see how they operate in Mexico, we've seen how they work in some other cities here in the U.S. They'll do what they have to do to protect their business."

"Of course, you have no way of proving this," the chief stated. "I mean, we don't have any evidence of the cartel, just a theory."

"Right now, yes sir, that's it," Mac answered, arms folded, leaning against a desk.

"So what do you propose to do, Mac?" the chief inquired in a tone that said he wanted something done.

Mac turned his gaze back to the whiteboard and to a picture of Neil Kline and the idea running around in his head, an idea that was *far* outside the bounds of legality. "I have an idea, Chief, especially for someone who is not on the force."

"So now you don't want your shield?"

"No," Mac replied. "My idea works better if I'm not yet a cop."

"Mac, we lost three men last night and two more are just barely hanging on. Minneapolis lost two good men. If you're right, these guys also killed Rafael Cruz and Sam Shead.

Nobody in this room ever heard me say this but"—he pointed to Mac—"the gloves are off. I know I'm going to be telling the troops today to keep their heads and I'm going to be on camera pleading for calm, but I don't give a shit if it's a local drug crew or a Mexican drug cartel or whoever. This shit will not stand. Am I clear?"

"Yes, sir."

"Then get to it," the chief ordered, checked his watch and headed for the exit, adding, "Keep me posted" as he walked out the door.

"So what's the plan?" Schmidt and Armstrong asked.

"I'm not telling you my plan for your own good. Your plan for now is to investigate the 280," Mac answered. "First, I don't think I'm wrong, but let's not put all the eggs in that one basket. See what you can find—scour traffic cameras, security footage, interview anyone possibly in the area of the 280 Grille last night. Maybe we get lucky. Second, forget you ever saw me this morning and not a word to anyone I'm even involved."

The two detectives smirked a little knowing smile, gave Mac a nod and they too headed out the door.

"So what is it that we're doing?" Dick asked, Paddy right behind him. It was just the three of them now.

"You two are not going to like it, but for the next twenty-four hours you're going to work this case from here."

"Hey, now wait," Dick protested.

"Mac, come on, you can't freeze us out," Paddy pleaded.

"You're both going to have to trust me," Mac counseled sternly. "I'm looking after your best interests here. If this shit I'm going to pull goes bad, you're protected and that is the way it's going to be."

Dick wanted to protest but also knew Mac and knew that once his mind was made up, there was little to no chance of changing it. "What is it then that you're doing that I'm not supposed to know about?"

"Calling in a few favors."

"I'm sensing a felony favor," Paddy muttered, shaking his head. "I hope you know what you're doing, cousin."

"I do."

"And what is it that you are trying to do?" Dick asked.

"Finding out *exactly* who the hell is behind all of this and Kline is the key. You said it yourself, we don't have any leverage on him. If we are going to turn the tables here, we can't play by the rules anymore. It's time to get dirty, *very* dirty."

Mac turned to walk away from Dick and took his cell phone out and punched up a number. There was an immediate answer on the other end. "I need a favor."

24

"THREE HOTS, A COT AND HORSES WOULD PROBABLY MAKE HIM FEEL PRETTY COMPLETE."

Jockey Mike sat in a chair in front of the beat-up metal desk, turned in the opposite direction toward the small box television. It was tuned to Channel Six, which was leading the ten o'clock news with continued coverage of the 280 shooting.

While the television played, Neil finished typing in the last of the data into the Excel spreadsheet for the deposit, saved the page and closed the program. He finished the deposit slip and it would be ready for the bank run in the morning. Normally, he'd have spent another hour or two further massaging the books, filtering money through before making the cash run up to Rogers. That procedure was no longer in play and with it, his role in the organization seemed to be diminishing by the day. Not only had neither White or Felix stopped by in days, there had been no contact from anyone. There was nothing but radio silence.

"Is there anyone out there watching?" Neil asked, looking to his driver.

"I've been peering around out there all day and tonight

as well," Mike replied. "Right now, I don't think so. There was someone yesterday, but today I haven't seen anyone."

Neil nodded. "With that shooting at the 280 Grille last night, perhaps the police are busy with much more important things. It's night out there. Things could get interesting."

"That's irrational shit, Neil. Going in there and killing all those cops, all to protest one shooting and one not guilty verdict. I mean, that's crazy."

"It's not just about that, Mike. I think it's probably about all the other shootings that have happened all over the place. But you're right. It's sheer madness. It's like they have a death wish or something."

"The cops are going to tear this town apart searching for those guys."

The two of them watched the Channel 6 local news, largely because Neil liked the look of the woman anchor, Andrea Rowland, a hypnotically beautiful brunette with inviting brown eyes, high cheekbones and just the slightest overbite. She'd brought her car into the shop one day when the check engine light for her BMW sports car went on and she was panicked she'd be late for work. She batted her beautiful brown eyes at Neil. "Can you help me out here?"

Neil had his guys drop everything. As his boys feverishly worked on her little sports car, he could barely take his eyes off her. "That might have been the best half hour of my life," he said to Mike after she pulled away. Ever since, Channel 6 was must-watch television in the shop. As Andrea reported on the shooting, the pictures of the St. Paul officers killed appeared on the screen. Neil froze.

"In addition to the two Minneapolis patrol officers who were killed, St. Paul Detectives Thomas Ortega, Francis Franklin and Kurt Fisher were shot and killed. St. Paul Detectives Patrick Riley

and Robert Rockford both remain hospitalized following lengthy surgeries for numerous gunshot wounds."

Jockey Mike saw the look on his boss's face. "Neil?"

Neil just stared at the screen, his mouth agape.

"What is it?" Mike asked. "You look like you saw a ghost all of the sudden."

"Uh, uh...nothing," Neil answered, trying to cover. "I'm... I'm not feeling that well. Maybe we should call it a night."

"No drink or anything?"

"Nah, just drive me home, okay?"

"Hey, you're the boss."

Neil set the alarm for the shop and locked the door and they jumped into the Tahoe and drove to Neil's house in relative silence. Fifteen minutes later, Jockey Mike pulled up in front of the house that Neil rented and they both piled out.

"Are you sure you're okay?" Mike asked. "Do you need me to get you anything?"

"No."

"You're sure? I mean, you look like you're going to be sick."

"Just pick me up at 6:00," Neil ordered, not even looking back as he quickly walked up the front sidewalk to the front door.

"Okay," Mike answered reluctantly. Usually Neil liked to hang for a little while, maybe have a drink but clearly not tonight. Mike put the keys for the Yukon in his pocket and pulled out the keys for his little 1997 Toyota Corolla parked two cars down. Mike jammed the key in the ignition and listened to the engine groan to life. The rust bucket of a car was twenty years old but the engine still worked well enough, and given what he made, Mike couldn't afford much more.

He pulled away from the front of Neil's house and took his usual left turn that would lead him back to Concord Street. At the stop sign he pulled to a slow rolling stop while he looked down at the car stereo, looking to change away from the commercial playing to another station when he sensed a flash of movement from the left. He looked up and a black panel van slammed to a hard stop in front of him. Then another truck pinned him in from behind.

He looked back forward and the panel van door flew open. Two masked men with guns jumped out and were immediately at the driver side door. One man pulled the door open, the other man quickly dragged him out of the car by the back of his shirt, took three steps and threw him through the open sliding door and into the panel van. Inside, another man was on top of him, putting duct tape over his mouth, followed by a pillowcase. The man then flipped him over like a pancake, pulled his arms behind him and started taping them together while another man had jumped inside and was taping his ankles.

"They have the car?" a voice asked.

"Yes," another voice from the front answered and he could feel the van accelerating away.

"We clear?" a voice from what he thought was the front asked.

"Looks good," another voice answered.

Nobody said a word to him as the van motored along. He could feel the van accelerating but not necessarily speeding down a street, what he thought felt like south. Then there was a turn, smoothly to the left, and then he felt the van accelerate, the engine roaring a bit more and he could tell they were elevating, driving up an on ramp. From that point, the van motored along smoothly and the men inside the panel van were quiet, saying nary a word.

The van continued for what seemed like an hour before he felt it veer slightly right and slow as it was descending, as if down an exit ramp. There was a turn at the bottom, what felt like a right and they drove for a few minutes before there was a series of turns, the last of which was onto a rough twisting road before the van came to a stop.

He heard the sliding door open. Down at his legs he felt the tape being cut loose. He was picked up and lifted out of the van and there was a man on either side of him, each holding him by the back of his biceps as he was pushed forward.

"There are two steps in front of you," one of the men grunted as they both guided him up the two steps. He took three more steps. "Another step up." With the last step, he felt as if he'd entered a building and then he was abruptly turned right.

"Now you're going down steps that are steep." The man who was holding his right arm led him slowly down the steps. "Last one's a little bigger drop."

At the bottom, he was walked straight forward until the man pushed him down into a chair.

"Sit still," the man grunted while he once again taped his legs to the right and left leg of the chair. The man then cut the tape off his hands behind him and then brought Mike's hands around to his front and rested them on the arms for the chair. The man then taped first his left wrist to the chair's arm, followed by the right. At least it was more comfortable than his arms behind him.

The pillowcase was yanked off his head. The tape over his mouth was ripped away and the man wearing a black snow mask left, slamming the door closed behind him.

Mike adjusted his eyes and tried to get his bearings. He was in a small, square cinder block room with a hint of musty air to it. He was seated in front of a small square metal table and there was an empty metal folding chair across from him. There was a single solitary bright light bulb hanging from the ceiling that was positioned over the center of the table.

"Good evening, Mr. Willows," an ominous voice greeted.

Mike looked to his right and emerging out of the dark corner of the room was a man. He was African American, tall, dressed in a black shirt and suit coat and wearing a dark gray fedora. The man slowly walked over and sat down on the table right in front of him.

"Who are you?" Mike asked.

"Does it really matter?"

"What do you mean does it matter? Of course, it matters. Who the hell are you and why am I here?"

"You don't want to know my name or who I work for. That is for your *own* protection. I can assure you of only one thing."

"Which is?"

"That if you answer my questions to *my* satisfaction, you have a chance, *a chance* of leaving this cellar alive. And if you don't..." The man let his words hang in the air for moment. "Well, use your imagination."

"What...do you want to know?" Mike asked hesitantly.

"For starters, who is your employer?"

"Rice Street Auto Repair."

The interrogator angrily leapt off the table and with all his force slapped Mike in the face, nearly sending his chair over sideways to the right. That was only stopped by the interrogator grabbing Mike by the throat with his gloved left hand, putting his own face inches from Mike's.

"*Don't you dare fucking lie to me again! Do you understand me?*" the interrogator screamed and then wound up and violently slapped Mike again, practically leaving his feet in the process, knocking the small man's head back before it snapped back forward.

Mike shook violently, sucking in big gasps of air, the pain searing through his head and neck. It was like when he'd fallen off the horse, that kind of pain jolted through his body. It took what seemed like an eternity before the pain began to dull and he could open his eyes and finally slow his breathing.

In the meantime, the interrogator had walked around the table and took the seat on the other side. As Mike finally opened his eyes, he found those of the interrogator lasering in on him. His eyes were piercing, his expression menacing, and when he finally spoke, his tone dark.

"Situation analysis, Mr. Willows. For you, it's grim. You are sitting alone with me at an unknown location, bound to a chair, your life very much hanging in the balance. Nobody knows where you are, *boy*. Nobody saw us take you and *you* have absolutely no idea where you are. You have no leverage, no bargaining power and nothing to negotiate with. I own your fuckin' ass." The interrogator let those words hang in the air. "Given your predicament, it would be extremely unwise for you to think me stupid, Mr. Willows. It would be ill advised for you to not answer my questions truthfully. For example, if all you did was work for an auto repair shop, there would be no need for me to have you here in this room duct taped to a chair. But we both know that while you *work at* an auto repair shop, we both also know that you do not *work for* an auto repair shop. So I would advise you to dispense with the bullshit."

"You don't understand," Mike replied, looking down and choking up. He was a beaten down and weakened man.

"What don't I understand?"

"These people," he started and then his voice trailed off. "If I tell you what I know, what I've seen and heard, they'll kill me."

The man leaned forward and his eyes narrowed. "It is 11:48 p.m., Mr. Willows. Therefore, whomever it is you are working for does not yet know you're missing. They have no reason to have concerns about you—yet. *Yet.* But the longer this takes, the longer you are gone and unaccounted for, the more suspicious the people you work for *will* become. You have a window of opportunity here, a very *small* window and I'm obviously very impatient. However, should you be truthful and forthcoming in the next minutes and seconds of your life, you have a chance, *a chance* to live. Should you not be forthcoming, then you need not worry about who you work for because you will not return to work for them. You'll die in this room. You wouldn't be the first and you undoubtedly won't be the last."

Jockey Mike snorted and shook his head.

"Play the odds," the interrogator suggested quietly. "Die tonight or tell me what I want to know and take your chances knowing that I work for someone who clearly intends to do your employer harm."

An hour later, the interrogator pushed himself up from the table, out the door, up the steps to the main level and then up to the second floor to find Mac and Fat Charlie waiting. They'd been watching via a closed-circuit feed. Mac was flipping through his notes. He now had an idea of who and what they were up against. That was the good news. The bad news was there was still a big hill to climb.

"Charlie, that was like old times," Tony Swinton said with a big smile as he sat down in an open chair, tilted his fedora back on his head and reached for the bottle of whisky and poured himself a small glass. "But man, you boys sure know how to pick them."

"You heard cartel and shit your pants, didn't you?" Charlie said with a chuckle.

"I kept my poker face," the interrogator replied with a head shake and wry smile. "But if this Willows is to be believed, and I'm inclined to believe the man since his fear was off the charts real, you've got yourselves the Lazaro Cardenas Drug Cartel right here in the Twin Cities. I assume that's a real cartel?"

"Google says it is," Mac replied. "They aren't perhaps as well known as many of the other cartels we've heard of, like the Sinaloa or Juarez. They're based out of the Michoacán state in western Mexico. They used to be part of the larger Gamez-Castillo Cartel but broke off from that years ago led by a man named Hector Alvarado."

"Well, okay then. This Lazaro Cardenas group is in the cities. And they're not just operating a little satellite outfit either, it sounds like they're using the Twin Cities as a base of operation for the Upper Midwest. Not only that, you get the CA-57s coming in from Los Angeles, for heavy muscle when needed." Tony shook his head and looked to Mac with concern. "Good luck to you. I'm just glad I get to go back to Louisville and regrow my beard."

"I suspected the cartel going into this but still, just to actually hear it is stunning. You're right, Tony, they're not just kind of here, they're based here!" Mac replied as he leaned against the wall with his arms folded, shaking his head in wonder. "The cartel basing part of their United States operation in the Twin Cities just seems so...not us. It's like we're too small for this."

"Well, the mob used to hide in St. Paul back in the 20's and 30's during prohibition, Mac," Charlie noted. "Hell, they hid in the basement of that family bar of yours, did they not? These guys would come up here and hide, conduct some business and when things cooled down, they'd go back to Chicago. Isn't that Patrick's Room a nod to that... what would you call it? Colorful, maybe sordid, history."

"Indeed it is, Charlie, indeed it is," Mac answered. "And in that context, I can see the logic of a cartel wanting to use the Twin Cities as a base. Logistically, the Twin Cities is a good place. It's on I-35 straight up from Mexico. It is also in a good position to move drugs east on I-94 into Wisconsin, and west on I-90 or 94 out to the Dakotas, and while it is a metropolitan area of over three million, it doesn't have the profile of Chicago. It's flyover country, sleepy, quiet and a little more under the radar."

"Too bad he doesn't know more about how they operate," Fat Charlie noted.

"He seems to know a few things," Mac answered. "He knows the drugs come from Mexico in refrigerated trucks carrying vegetables. He knows the trucks come five to six times per year, for large deliveries. He mentioned he'd heard corn, strawberries, guava, lemons, peaches and most interestingly, *avocados*."

"Why are avocados so important?" Tony asked, picking up on Mac's emphasis.

Mac explained the notation in Shead's notebook. "So who is The Avocado? We've been trying to figure that out. This might help. And he knows about the money."

"Yeah, where it gets delivered," Tony nodded.

"Where it *used to* get delivered," Mac replied and explained what happened when they searched the house. "And he also talked about these trucks that the money would get loaded into compartments on the roofs of the trailers, or at least that's what Neil Kline told him one time."

"But not the drugs," Charlie noted. "He hasn't seen that side of it."

"Are the vegetables and drugs at the same place?" Charlie wondered.

Mac shook his head. "I doubt it, but who knows? Little Jockey Mike Willows doesn't. He's never seen that part of the operation. He's seen the drugs go out of the fronts and the money come in. He's seen the money drop in Rogers. That's it. He says he hasn't seen the rest and I don't think he has."

"He's seen the key players though," Charlie stated. "This Felix is a guy you need to get acquainted with."

"Maybe he's this Avocado, Mac," Tony suggested, taking another sip of his drink. "He seems to be the boss man, so it could be."

Mac thought for a moment and then shook his head in doubt. "Maybe, but...I don't know, that doesn't feel quite right. But we'll see. He says this Felix shows up from time to time, not regularly, but he's around. He might be boss man locally, but is he boss man for the cartel? Would the head of the cartel ever be around?"

Charlie and Tony shook their heads. "Times change, but not in my experience, Mac," Charlie added. "Back in my day I had some cartel contact for drug supply. I made a few trips to California and one down to southern Arizona, but I never met the head of a cartel, just someone who had the ability to make a deal, a middleman. I was never big enough to warrant that kind of attention. That's probably who this Felix is. He's around enough that he clearly has some authority."

"And who's this Mr. White?" Tony asked. "He also seems to have a lot of authority. Maybe that's your Mr. Avocado."

"He said a lawyer of some kind," Charlie replied. "You need those around too."

"Well, if he's a lawyer he wasn't the lawyer for Neil Kline, that much I know," Mac answered, flipping through the notes he'd been taking. "That guy was a local pro."

"Again, like Felix, Mr. White just kind of shows up, no set schedule and this Mike has never been to White's office," Tony noted. "And he has only seen Felix in Rogers, at the repair shop or at another front, never anywhere else."

"So why did you see Kline's lawyer?" Charlie inquired.

"Kline was the last person to speak with Terrence Orr at DeAndre's," Mac answered. "He handed him those envelopes with the twenty thousand inside."

"Mac, this Kline runs the auto repair shop, but for some reason I get the sense from this little guy that Neil Kline is more important to the organization than just that. What is this Kline's background?"

"He did a nickel at Stillwater for drugs. In prison he had no official trouble, according to his file. However, unofficially he was suspected of running all kinds of contraband through Stillwater. His record, his background say he's a good middleman type with good people skills. He was in prison with Orr and then Orr was part of the operation until his untimely demise, perhaps with the assistance of Kline. He was in prison with this Jockey Mike. He was also in prison with Luther Ellis. I wonder if we started looking at the guys working at the auto repair shop, at the other front locations, if we can figure out what the other fronts are, if they'd have some connection to Kline. It's like he's the key guy in that regard."

"You can't run an enterprise like this without good middlemen," Charlie explained, a man with intimate knowledge of such an operation. "I loved guys like this Kline back in the day. Tony here was a guy like Kline, although in a different capacity. They created those layers between the top and the street. Now you had to take care of them because they would take a lot of heat, both in the organization and on the street. I bet this Kline has been a guy that has helped find people to create the layers and run the operation."

"And he's given some leeway," Mac answered. "After all, he has a driver like this Jockey Mike."

Swinton shook his head. "I agree that this Jockey Mike is pretty harmless looking, meek, small, hobbled, drug-addled. Clearly, this Kline character has something of a soft spot for him for some reason. But to let him know as much as he does, be around the operation as much as he is, is dangerous. I'd have never let someone this ... weak know anything."

"For Kline it's a blind spot," Charlie added and then gestured to Mac. "For you, my friend, he gives you a ton of information."

"Not that I can legally use any of it, at least not for an arrest or search warrant," Mac answered. "I'm sure the two of you appreciate the completely illegal nature of this. None of what this guy has told us would ever be admissible."

"You knew that going in," Charlie answered.

Mac nodded. "I did. But now at least I know what I'm looking for and I think I know how to use this. There is one thing I need Tony to go back in and do and that's ask Mike if he knows who the Avocado is. And keep your phone close while you do."

"I can do that."

Tony went back into the room to find Jockey Mike with his head slumped, sleeping. He was jarred awake by the slamming door. Tony sat down at the table. "I got a question for you. Do you know of anyone they call The Avocado?"

Mike looked at Tony and slowly shook his head. "I don't know anyone by that name."

"You ever heard of anyone referred to by that name?"

"No, sir."

"Does avocado or The Avocado mean anything to you at all?"

Mike thought for a moment and shrugged. "The only thing I know about avocados is that I think they probably come in those trucks."

"And again, how often do those trucks come to town?"

"Like I said before, five, maybe six times a year. I think they're coming soon. I heard Neil and White talking about it not that long ago, that the trucks are coming."

"When?"

"I don't know," Mike replied, shaking his head. "I think soon, but I don't have a date or anything."

"But soon?"

"I think so."

"What would be a sign that the trucks are coming?"

Mike thought for a moment, and then while looking away from Tony uttered, "I guess if Neil gives me the night off." He looked back to Swinton. "I saw the trucks once, but just once, and I think it was a little by accident. But occasionally Neil will give me the night off and early because he has to take care of some money stuff, he'll say."

Mac was watching the interview, itching to go into the room himself but knowing he couldn't do that. Instead he texted Tony a question.

"Besides the repair shop, where are the other stores that are part of the operation?" Tony asked.

"What do you mean?"

Tony stared the little man down. "What did I say before

about dispensing with the bullshit? I want to know where those storefronts are."

"The repair shop, there's a donut shop on Payne. There is..." Jockey Mike provided ten different locations. "Those are the ones I know about, that Neil has stopped at."

"Are there more?"

Mike shrugged. "There could be. I just don't know."

"You mentioned the trucks earlier. Describe the trucks," Tony ordered.

"They're white," Mike answered. "Plain white. They're the long-haul types, the refrigerator trucks."

"Plain white, no markings?"

Mike nodded his head.

Mac texted another question: *Besides Felix and White, anyone else show up in Rogers? Especially recently.*

"Mike, you've told me about Mr. White and Felix. Anyone else?"

"Like who?"

"Someone you haven't seen before? Somebody new, especially up at the warehouse in Rogers?"

"N..." Mike started and then slowed for a second, "Well, it was I want to say a couple of weeks ago, the last time we went up there, and Felix was there and then another SUV drove up with some people that I'd never seen before. I just kind of saw them while I was parked in Neil's SUV, waiting for him."

"Who were these people?"

"I don't know who they were. I never learned who they were. Neil never said."

"Tell me about them."

Mike shrugged. "I didn't get a great look, but there was a man and a woman, a pretty woman."

"White? Hispanic? Black?"

"The man was Hispanic-looking."

"How old?"

"Maybe in his forties, maybe a little older. He was older than Felix, I know that."

"And how did Felix respond to this man?"

Mike thought for a moment. "Respectfully."

"Like he was the boss?"

"Yes, I suppose. All I know is Felix nodded quite a bit while the man spoke."

"And the woman, was she the Hispanic's girlfriend?"

"I don't really know," Mike answered.

"Was she white, African American, Hispanic, Asian?"

"White, I thought, and pretty."

"Describe her."

"I only saw her for just a few seconds and only her head, really."

"What did you see?"

"She had dark hair, up in back. She looked nicely dressed, like she was wearing a dress of some kind. She had a necklace and long straight earrings that glittered. And she had nice eyes, big eyes, I remember that. I noticed her eyes."

"So the Hispanic man's girlfriend."

"I suppose, although I kind of thought maybe she was a boss, too."

"Really?" Tony responded, looking up from his notepad. "Why do you say that?"

"Because like I said before, Felix is intimidating to be around. I always feel like he could decide to shoot me at a moment's notice, or anyone else for that matter. He doesn't give a shit about anyone, *anyone*. But *this* man and *this* woman"—Jockey Mike shook his head—"he gave a shit about them. He stood tall, at attention and respected them."

"What kind of SUV did they roll up in?"

"An Escalade, I think. A black Cadillac Escalade."

"And you'd never seen these people before?"

"No, it was the first time."

"I see."

"And you haven't seen them since?"

"No."

Mac sent yet another question: *Did Neil see them*?

"Mike," Tony asked, "did Neil Kline see these people?"

"Please don't make me get Neil in trouble," Mike pleaded. "Please."

"I don't see Neil here," Tony responded, sitting forward, staring Mike down. "Neil can't help you here. I'm only going to ask one more time. Did Neil see these people?"

Mike's head drooped down, slowly shaking as he exhaled. "Yes. He was standing near Felix, maybe ten, fifteen feet away so he saw them, was part of the conversation."

Mac looked over to Charlie. "Sam Shead saw someone much higher up the food chain."

"If not the boss, someone very close to the boss. The boss of this Felix and Mr. White, I'd say."

That gave Mac another thought and he texted Tony another question.

"So Mike," Tony asked, "that night you saw these people show up in Rogers, there apparently was someone else watching up there. Do you know anything about that?"

Mike snorted. "Yeah, there was some cop or ex-cop up there watching."

"And what happened to that ex-cop?"

"Are you a cop? Are you a fucking cop?"

Lightning quick, Tony exploded out of his chair and slapped Jockey Mike with the back of his right hand. "Tell me about what you know about the ex-cop! Tell me right now! I'm not going to ask again!"

Mike groaned from being slapped again and meekly looked up, blood streaming from his nose and mouth. "I know that he was killed. I heard Mr. White come to the store and tell Neil that was taken care of."

"And how did they take care of it?"

"All I know is T.O. was involved."

"Terrence Orr?"

"Yeah," Jockey Mike replied. "That ex-cop was hanging around because T.O. let Luther, another guy we all knew in prison, get over on him. Luther saw some things he shouldn't have and T.O. took him out."

"What did they do to Luther?"

"I don't know," Mike answered. "I just know Neil told me Luther wouldn't be coming around anymore."

"I see."

Tony waited to see if any more questions came. Mac texted a message a minute later: *I think we're good.*

"What is going to happen to me?" Mike pleaded, sniffling, blood running down from his nose and pooling above his lip. "What's going to happen to me?"

"Honestly I don't know yet, Mike," Tony answered, sitting back in his chair, his arms folded.

Jockey Mike began to weep. "I got nothing if I don't have this. Nothing."

Tony got up from his chair and took out a hanky from his back pocket. He staunched the bleeding from the nose, tilting Mike head back for a moment or two. "Besides this, what have you done?" he asked.

"I used to be a jockey."

"Ahh, hence Jockey Mike. What happened, why did you stop doing that?"

Sniffling, his eyes teary, Jockey Mike explained. "I got hurt." He described his accident at Canterbury. "I was done after that, but I loved it when I could work with the horses. I just loved being around horses, riding them, caring for them, getting to know them." He paused, his eyes moist. "I wish I could go back to that, back to the horses." The faucet opened and Jockey Mike began to sob and shake.

Tony took one last look down at the shell of a man bound to the chair. He cut off the tape that was holding his left hand to the chair and handed him the hanky. "Hold that up under your nose, tilt your head back and the bleeding will stop. I'll be back." He made his way back upstairs. "What do you guys think?"

"At least now I know what Sam saw. He saw the boss, or someone very close to the boss and described him or maybe her, as The Avocado," Mac stated excitedly. He'd always thought Sam saw something important and now he had a pretty good idea of who from a hierarchical standpoint with a general description.

"How can you know?" Tony asked, not yet following.

Mac looked over to Charlie, who answered the question. "Because there are *five* dead cops from the 280 Grille last night, plus Cruz, plus Shead, an ex-cop," Fat Charlie answered. "You don't go to this extreme because little ole Neil Kline or fierce Terrence Orr is there. You do it because someone else has been *seen*, someone who wasn't supposed to be *seen* and them being *seen* is a huge issue."

"Boss man. You think it was the cartel boss man?" Tony pressed.

Mac shrugged, but positively. "Why not? The drugs come in, the money goes out. You heard Jockey Mike in there describe the money. If he's to be believed, it's millions and millions and *millions* of dollars. If these guys are running drugs throughout the Upper Midwest, are running drugs and drug money through these front businesses, then the boss man, even a cartel boss man, may show up from time to time to look in on his operation. Maybe that's what Sam saw."

"But there is no way to really know."

"Ah, but there is," Mac answered. "Neil Kline knows."

"How are you going to get him to talk about that?" Charlie asked. "As you said earlier, none of this is admissible."

"True that. Nevertheless, it has all given me an idea or two," Mac answered with a wicked smile. "Neil Kline will talk. It's only a matter of time."

"In the meantime, what do we do with this guy?" Tony asked, gesturing to the monitor. "You can't send him back to these guys. He'll end up dead, either because they figure out he talked or if this is the cartel, they just decide to purge everyone around here and move on."

"Well, what does he want?"

"You heard it, he'd like to just go away and be around horses again," Tony answered, some sympathy showing.

Charlie caught the tone in Tony's voice. "You want to help him, don't you? Man, you've gone legit and you've gotten so soft."

Tony shrugged. "I can always use someone who's good with horses. I don't think little old Mike here needs much. Three hots, a cot and horses would probably make him feel pretty complete."

"Not yet, though," Mac answered coldly. "Not yet. If he leaves now, suspicion is raised and I need these guys feeling like they're in the clear."

"How long do you need?" Tony asked. "I'm not a cop, but a police investigation of something like this, the time it takes to get up on it, monitor, surveil and build your case, that could take weeks. Months."

"That's right," Mac answered. "If that's the way I intended to do it."

"But you don't, do you?" Charlie answered with a smile.

"No," Mac answered. "If these guys pulled the 280 shooting, how long are they really going to stick around? They're not going to go to war with us unless they have a death wish. This is a one-time kind of move. They're not going to stay much longer."

"If you're right, they might already be gone," Charlie suggested.

"Maybe," Mac answered. "But little Mike here mentioned those trucks and a delivery that *might* be coming. Now, if our little jockey friend is to be believed, the cartel has been running a large drug operation based here. You don't move that with a snap of the fingers. It takes time, logistics and you need somewhere to move the operation to. With another shipment coming, if one is coming, they probably want to handle that first before they pull up stakes."

"So you think they pulled this 280 job to distract you guys long enough to get in this last delivery and then get the hell out of Dodge?"

"Only one way to find out."

"Which is what?"

"Ask Neil Kline."

"Okay, fine," Tony replied, "but again, what do I tell our little friend here?"

"Tell him he needs to go back to work and act normal and, if things work out, in a week to ten days someone will pay him a visit with an offer he'll find hard to refuse."

Mac and Charlie watched on the video monitor as Tony went back into the room. "Mike, if you do as I say this could work out for you."

Charlie looked over to Mac. "You know, if he lives, are we really going to do this? Have him go down to Tony's place?"

"If we're men of our words, yes."

"Okay, fine. But now that you have all this information, what are you going to do?"

"I have a couple of ideas."

"These guys are parasites, Mac. I know that sounds ironic coming from me, but there were rules when I operated. My people never put a gun on a normal citizen who had nothing to do with my business and we sure as hell never messed with cops. As for people who were in the trade, even then drastic action was taken only as a very last resort." Charlie was angry and there was a darkness in his eyes Mac had never seen. Old Charlie was talking. "Mac, the cartel? These guys? They have no rules, no morals, they have no respect for life, for people. They just kill. They're just tearing up our home, yours and mine."

"You want blood."

"Don't you?"

Mac's look in reply said it all.

25

"IT'S AN EVOLVING PLAN."

With a midnight to 5:00 a.m. curfew in place, the night after the 280 was quiet and uneventful. Yet as Felix drove through downtown St. Paul, then past the State Capitol building just to the north and then along Rice Street, he could see the heavy police presence. By his rough count, he'd passed six patrol units plus two other cars that might have been unmarked units, and if he had to guess, probably another one or two were hiding in the near vicinity of the repair shop as he passed it on his right. A mile farther north he slowed and turned right and parked along the curb of the side street.

Felix sat with the engine off for a moment, peering intently in his rearview mirror for a moment, determining if anyone followed. He saw nothing of concern. He lowered himself out of his Lincoln Navigator and crossed the street and entered the coffee shop via the side door. At the counter he ordered himself a French Roast and then found White sitting back in the windowless corner, reading a newspaper, a tall cup of coffee and small empty plate with muffin remnants on it sitting on the small square table in front of him.

"A quiet night?" White asked.

Felix nodded as he took the top off his coffee to let it cool. "Slow for the obvious reasons, but the back of the Navigator is still quite full. Where should I take it?"

"Out to the farm in St. Michael. They'll count it, wrap it and get it ready for transport. I just got confirmation, the trucks are crossing the border. They will be here in two days on Tuesday night."

Felix nodded and turned to see Neil Kline come into the coffee shop. Kline ordered a quick coffee and made his way to the back table.

"Did you have company behind you?"

"We were looking, but we didn't see anyone. I had Mikey do a couple of double backs and quick turns. We didn't see anything."

"Good," White replied and then took the measure of Kline. "Neil, are you feeling alright?"

"Yeah, why?"

"Dude, you look pale, white like a ghost," Felix remarked.

Neil took a sip of his coffee. "I think I feel fine."

"Sleep okay?" White inquired.

"Yeah, I guess."

White himself took a long drink of his coffee and then swirled his cup in his hand. "Are you stressed?"

Kline looked down at his own coffee, not making eye contact, but he nodded. "I'm stuck in that repair shop with the police all over me. How do you think I feel?"

"It'll work out, Neil," White counseled. "You just need to sit tight."

"How much longer?" Neil asked. "I mean, how much longer are we going to operate this way?"

"Not much," White answered. "We are changing some elements of the operation."

"How? In what ways?"

"With the authorities showing such interest in you, I think the less you know the better. We'll bring you up to speed when the time is right. Just keep watching your back and let us know what you see."

"About that. How do I reach you if I need to?"

"Call the lawyer with this phone," White answered, handing Neil a new burner phone. "He will relay your call to me. Talking to the lawyer makes things privileged. In the meantime, keep a low profile, stay in the shop, keep a close eye on the area around the shop and don't be out after work. Just go home. Don't do anything to draw any attention. Did you go home last night?"

"Yes."

"Keep doing that. Just take it easy."

Neil nodded.

"Okay, off to work with you then."

Kline picked up his coffee and headed out the door of the coffee shop.

White looked to Felix. "You're worried about him."

"I'm worried about everyone," Felix answered.

"He was in that coffee shop a long time," Martinez reported into the radio while parked on southbound Rice Street, a block north of the coffee shop. He and Weed were following Kline, but to mix it up they were in separate vehicles. Their own vehicles.

"Too long just to grab a cup of joe," Weed agreed, replying. "I assume Kline is going to the shop. I'm going to linger and see who comes out."

"Mac, here's the Judge," Sally said and then he could hear her handing her cell phone to the great man and her direct boss.

"Mac boy, how are you?" Judge Dixon, Senior Counselor to the President of the United States greeted warmly. During his press conference yesterday from Tokyo, President Thomson expressed grave concern about what was going on in his home state. Judge Dixon, the President's closest confidant and advisor and a Minnesotan in his own right, had been checking in with Sally. These men owed Mac more than one favor. He was about to take advantage and was using Sally as the go-between.

"I'm fine, Judge," Mac answered as he pulled to a stop in front of Flanagan's house just before 6:00 a.m.

"You're on the case now?"

"Officially, I will be in about five minutes. Unofficially, I've been working it overnight, which is why I'm calling," Mac answered. "I need your help. This is what I know." Mac explained quickly about what he'd learned from Jockey Mike. "I have an idea of how to take these guys down, but to do it, I'm going to need some federal resources and I need you to make it happen."

"What do you have in mind?"

Mac explained. His plan required the assistance of two federal agencies and he didn't have time for a bunch of bureaucratic red tape. He needed what he needed, he needed it now and he needed to be able to *control* those resources without question, so the order had to come from the top.

"Daring, I like it," the judge answered. "Let me make some calls. I will be in touch."

Mac hung up and hit the doorbell.

The chief opened the door, freshly shaven and ready for the day. Mac was not. "Mac, you look like..." The chief was going to say hell but then stopped and looked Mac over more carefully. Yes, Mac's beard was scruffy and loose, his hair mussed and his dress shirt, suit coat and pants all wrinkled with just a hint of grime. It was clear Mac had pulled an all-nighter. For most people, that would mean their bodies would be lethargic; there would be bags under their eyes and a weariness to their demeanor. Mac exhibited none of those traits. The chief could see it in his man's eyes. He wasn't tired. Rather, it looked as if he was just getting started.

The chief waved him inside and into the kitchen and poured them each coffee. "What do you need?" the chief asked.

"For starters, my badge," Mac answered.

"What else?"

"We're going to put a target on someone." Mac explained all that he'd learned overnight. "The one thing you can't do, Chief, is mention this Jockey Mike's name to anyone. I mean anyone. Other than you, the only person I'm telling about this is Lich."

"I assume this information you obtained wasn't voluntary?"

"No, sir."

"And you got this how?"

"You told me the gloves were off."

"Yes, I did."

"Then I did what I had to do, and used who I needed to use to figure out who is behind all of this."

"So now we know we have the cartel operating here." The chief shook his head in disgust.

"For the last few days we've suspected that was the case," Mac replied. "Now we know. Now we know who is behind killing a bunch of cops and they did it to distract and divert us from what we *were* investigating, which is Sam's murder and what he saw up at that house in Rogers."

"Do you really know that, though?" the chief pushed. "I mean, I get your deductive reasoning here. I see the logic. But be honest, you still don't have that answer for sure. This Jockey Mike doesn't know they pulled the trigger at the 280."

"Have Lich or Armstrong and Bonnie Schmidt made any progress on the 280 investigation?"

"No."

"Do they have any new witnesses, any new leads, anything that points to others in the community?"

"No."

"The footage is out on television now. Has anyone called in any leads? Has anything at all popped?"

"No," the chief answered, slowly nodding. "No. Look, I'm not arguing with you. I'm not fighting you, but I can see what you're thinking, what you're feeling here. You're angry."

"And you aren't?"

Flanagan gave Mac a stern look. "Come on."

"Sorry."

"You're angry," the chief continued. "Now I've always said you were really good in a storm, but this is about family to you and me. And you're going a hundred miles an hour in one direction here. I said the gloves were off, but don't—"

"Turn into what I'm chasing," Mac finished the thought. "Don't worry about that. But Chief, we aren't going to get these guys by playing by all the rules either." Mac explained his theory, that there was only a short window of time left. "They'll be gone. We can't let that happen."

"Agreed." Flanagan shifted gears. "This Jockey Mike, he was there the night Sam was looking at this house in Rogers. But this Mike doesn't know what Sam saw?"

"I think it's more about *who*, Chief," Mac answered, calmer now. "It's about who he saw. Sam saw some people that night and Mike says they killed Sam because of it. And we know that they tortured Sam to find out what he knew and who he might have told before dumping him in the river. Jockey Mike saw these people and could perhaps identify them but doesn't know their names or who they were. He just saw them for a brief period."

"Are they the people running this operation?"

"I believe that's possible, if not highly likely," Mac answered. "Like I said, my guy didn't know their names or recognize them, but they were both shown great respect by this Felix, so they are higher up the food chain for sure and their identities are important enough to go to this extreme to protect. What he does know is that it's the Lazaro Cardenas Cartel, so I have someone getting me information on that."

"Who?"

"I've called in a favor or two."

"I bet you have," the chief replied with a snort. "What else?"

"They're running money and drugs through the front businesses, and we have a list of them now. The money comes in there and the drugs go out, and that's just locally. It appears the operation is far bigger than that, covers a broader territory but is based here. Another interesting thing is this Mike guy said that if they need muscle, they contact the CA-57s out in California and guys will fly in."

The CA-57s were a well-known and violent Hispanic gang based in South Central Los Angeles. "Those bastards," the chief replied in disbelief. "Vicious."

"As vicious as they come. I suspect we'll find that there is a CA-57 and Lazaro Cardenas cartel connection. I will bet you some CA-57 boys were in town the other night for the 280. I think we need to be checking flights in from and back out to LAX, Orange County and maybe San Diego."

"So you believe this guy? He's on the level?"

Mac nodded. "He told us what he knows. Of that I'm positive. He wasn't left much of a choice."

The chief looked at Mac severely.

"Not...much of a glove was laid on him. Now threatened? Perhaps led to believe there could be severe consequences if he failed to comply?" Mac shrugged, unbothered.

"And who did this?"

"You don't want to know."

"But you were there?"

Mac nodded. "But I wasn't a cop at that time."

"Good luck with that one," the chief replied with a skeptical snicker. "You know, Mac, this shit could get out of control. Cartel, drugs, money, killing cops. You know what I should probably do is call the FBI, Homeland Security, DEA, build a task force and go to work on these guys."

"No," Mac replied. "No. Once you go down the federal path and give them control, this thing takes months and the guys who shot our people, Riles, Rock, everyone will end up cutting some deal if we get them at all. I have a better and quicker way."

"Thought this out, have you?"

"It's an evolving plan," Mac replied. "But yes, I have thought it out."

"Then you better get to it."

26

"WHAT NEXT? YOUR WEAK-ASS VERSION OF THE ZAPRUDER FILM?"

Neil leaned against the doorjamb and watched as two of his staff assisted customers at the service desk. To his right, the three repair bays were filled and technicians were working on two cars and a large pick-up truck. The repair shop was humming along and as he stood there, Neil thought that for not knowing a ton about cars and trucks, he'd done a pretty decent job running the shop. These days, even without the drug money, the shop would run fine. If White and Felix moved out of town, Neil wondered if he could make the shop go. His place was doing a good *legitimate* business.

He heard rustling behind him and turned to see Jockey Mike coming in the back door. His driver had made a quick lunch run just down the street to Jimmy Johns. Back in the office Mike sat the sandwiches on the desk, along with chips and Diet Cokes, yawning while doing so.

"Why were you so tired?" Neil asked and then took a longer look at his driver. "Why are you *still* so tired?"

"What do you mean?"

"You were practically asleep when I came out of the

coffee shop this morning, you were sleeping in the back office much of the morning. I mean, we had an early night last night," Neil stated as he unwrapped his sub.

"Sorry, long night," Mike answered as he struggled to open a bag of kettle chips. "I couldn't sleep. My back was just killing me for some reason."

Neil waved his hand and Mike sent the chip bag over, which Neil opened for him. The sound of police sirens filled the air, getting louder and then stopping in their area.

"What's going on?" Neil asked as he pushed himself up from the desk and went out to the front desk of the repair shop. Coming in the front door were two uniformed officers along with two more plainclothes officers behind them, one man and one woman.

"Are you Neil Kline?" the first uniformed officer asked.

"Yeah?"

"You need to come with us," one of the plainclothes officers stated as he chewed on a toothpick.

"And you are?" Neil demanded.

"Detective Armstrong and to my left is Detective Schmidt. We're with the St. Paul Police

Department Homicide Division."

"Am I under arrest?"

"You can be if you want to be," Armstrong answered matter-of-factly. "I can put you in cuffs, stick you in the back of the squad car, make a nice big scene of it. In fact, it wouldn't bother me a bit to do that."

"Or," Schmidt added, "you could not be a jackass and simply join us for a short little ride downtown for a talk with a friend of ours."

"Homicide? What homicide?" Neil demanded.

"Let's just go outside and get in the car," Armstrong counseled.

"I want to call my lawyer."

"It'll be the first thing you can do when you get downtown," Schmidt answered.

~

Neil Kline was put into interview room number two. As expected, Byrnes, the lawyer, arrived quickly. Mac let them stew for an hour before Dick led them into interview room number two.

"You again?" Neil asked. "What, still asking questions about Luther Ellis? You ever find him, by the way?"

Dick smiled and shook his head. "No, although you know what happened to him."

"I'm pretty sure you know about a lot of things, Neil," Mac added as he barged into the room. He'd cleaned up and was attired in one of his sharp black suits, bright white dress shirt and a striped black tie. It was as sharp and high-powered a look as he could cut.

"You see," Dick stated, sitting down, casually crossing his legs, an evil smirk on his face, "you fucked around with me before, *twice*. But him"—he gestured with his thumb to Mac—"you can't fuck around with. He fucks with you."

"Oh really," Neil replied cockily. "And you are?"

"Mac McRyan," Byrnes replied warily. He'd been in the room with Mac before. There was obvious respect in the lawyer's voice. "Last time I checked you weren't a St. Paul cop, Mac."

Mac unbuttoned his suit coat to reveal his badge clipped to his belt. "Any questions, Counselor?" Then Mac turned to Kline, leaning down on the table to Neil's right. "You can already hear it in your lawyer's voice, Neil, can't you?"

"Hear what?"

"Your lawyer is wondering what the hell has my shit bird client gotten himself into that would draw *my* interest?"

Neil snorted. "Nice suit."

"Hmpf," was Mac's initial reply as he stood back up and started pacing the room. "Neil, you should have your lawyer Google my name."

"Do it," Dick added. "I mean, shit, he's every bit as responsible as millions of voters for putting the President in the White House."

Neil looked over to his lawyer and casually asked, "Is that true?"

The lawyer simply nodded. "What do you have, Mac?" the lawyer asked. Byrnes was a pro. He had no intention of letting his client speak, but Mac was making it obvious he had some things to say. A good lawyer listens. Mac hoped his client would too.

"Counselor, your client is fucked and he doesn't even know it."

Kline smirked confidently.

The lawyer kept a poker face, simply asking, "How so?"

"Let's take the police killings at the 280. He knows who's responsible for that. He knows because, by the way, Counselor, I'm pretty sure it's also the same people paying *your* bill," Mac declared, going big right away, setting a heavy tone. He then leaned back down on the table into Neil and said with a quiet menace, "And here you are now in the lion's den, corridors full of cops checking you out. And I've made sure everyone out there, and I mean *everyone* knows you were involved."

"I don't know anything about that," Neil answered back hotly. "I'm not crazy. I had nothing to do with that. I was nowhere near there." He looked to his lawyer. "I have an alibi for that very time, at least twenty people would have seen me. I was at..."

Mac plowed through. "Now, did you pull the trigger?" He shrugged his shoulders, shook his head and slipped his hands into his pockets. "Oh, I don't think so. I don't think you have the stones to do that. But someone with that drug ring that you work for sure did."

Neil laughed—but nervously, a nervousness that confirmed Mac's point. Yes, there was a drug operation and yes, Neil knew they were capable of such acts.

"Yeah, *that* drug ring," Mac added quietly, leaning over again, getting closer and staring Neil down for a moment before standing back up and pacing around the interview room some more. "I know a lot about the drug ring and I'm learning more by the day now that we know what to look for. I know that drug outfit killed Luther Ellis. I even know why—it was because he had something on Terrence Orr." Mac eyed Neil when he said it. There was a flinch, ever so slight, a flinch of *how the hell would he know that?* Neil still didn't look overly concerned or scared, but he was sitting up in his chair, a little less confident. Mac was on the right track. He turned his back to Neil and continued.

"Neil, I know that drug outfit killed Sam Shead. I know that on a Wednesday night, a little over two weeks ago they saw Sam watching you, Terrence Orr and some other very important people up at that house in Rogers." Mac turned to face Neil and nodded. "Yeah, that's right, I know that. We know that Sam saw someone very important up there that night. You know how I know? Because I have his notes from that night. It's funny really, because that drug ring you work for tried like crazy to find them. They searched his house, I'm sure they searched his truck and then they interrogated the hell out of him before they killed him with three gunshots to the chest."

Dick, on cue, pulled out the photos from Sam's autopsy. "While the damage was extensive, it minimally involves two broken hands, ten broken fingers, six broken ribs, two broken ankles, a shattered jaw and two broken orbital bones." Dick slid the list across the table, "As you can see, the list of damage is rather lengthy. I've only provided an estimate, of course."

"The short form answer to that is they beat the hell out of him, Neil," Mac continued, "they tortured him. Why? Because he saw someone important. You know who I think he saw?"

Neil just snorted and folded his arms.

"He saw the boss," Mac stated confidently. "Or bosses, as his notes mention two people, a man and a woman up there in a Cadillac Escalade. Now, unfortunately we don't yet have their names, but we'll get them eventually. Hell, I bet I get them from *you*."

"Get what?" Neil bitched.

Mac just kept going, pacing the room. "So, Sam saw something he shouldn't have, so they killed him and then they killed another of your friends, Terrence Orr. Heck, you set him up."

"Oh really?"

"What, you think you didn't when you slipped him that twenty grand?" Mac asked. "You don't think that allowed your friends with this drug ring to get a bead on Orr? I mean, why else sneak you out? And don't tell me you think it was just Orr and Detective Cruz in that alley?" Mac laughed openly. "It wasn't, Neil. It was someone from your drug operation that was in that alley, waiting for Orr, waiting to take him out. I'll bet they were going to kill Orr, throw his body into a truck or a van and go bury it in the woods or dump it in the river, just like they did with Sam Shead. But it didn't quite come off that way. Now some of that is speculation on my part, but you know what is true, Neil?"

"What's that?"

"You set up your friend to be killed, Neil," Mac teased. "You see, a night before you and Orr met up in St. Cloud at a bar. I know, I was inside that bar. I was sitting right across the bar watching the two of you talk, right alongside St. Paul Detective Thomas Ortega, one of the men murdered at the 280, and also, by the way, one of my best friends from childhood."

"And for the record, Neil," Dick added with a growl, "Sam Shead was one of my best friends."

"You two were making plans, Neil," Mac continued. "I can just tell when two criminal douchebags are sitting there making plans. In fact, I think those plans were for Terrence Orr to leave town. Now why would Terrence need to leave town?" Mac asked rhetorically. "Dick, could it be because he was part of the crew that killed Sam Shead?"

"I sure think so, Mac," Dick answered, pulling out some more pictures.

"You see," Mac continued, "we used the GPS from Shead's phone. We tracked him over to Burns Avenue and there was a collision along there. We reconstructed it and these photos here show debris which is for a headlight on a Yukon. Dick, who drove a Yukon?"

"Terrence Orr. The Yukon in this picture."

"Dick, when Orr's Yukon was found in the alley after he was killed, what did we find regarding the grill, headlights and fenders?"

"That they were all brand new. It was clear they'd just

been replaced, especially when compared to the rest of the truck."

"Neil, Terrence Orr was part of the crew that killed Sam Shead. But then we got onto Terrence and what happened to him?"

"Your detective shot him in the alley," Neil replied. "I read it in the papers. T.O. shot at him and he returned fire. They both died. T.O. was stupid and your guy died a hero, killed in the line of duty. But you know what I didn't read in the papers was anything about some third shooter on the grassy knoll. What's next, your weak-ass version of the Zapruder film?"

Mac and Dick laughed.

"Hey, that was pretty good," Dick remarked with an evil smile but then the smile vanished. "But not true."

"What is true is that there was a third person in that alley, Neil," Mac needled. "He was there. I can prove it easily. You know why we haven't gone public yet? Because we've been coming after *you*. There was a third shooter in that alley. Who do you suppose that was?" Mac let his question hang in the air for a moment and watched as Neil looked down and away from Mac. There was a crack in the facade.

"Neeeiiiilll," Mac mocked lightly as he moved to the side and set his hands back down on the table, leaned into Kline and spoke quickly. "That third shooter was part of that drug ring, wasn't he? You're not completely stupid, Neil. I can see you're putting it all together in that head of yours. You're starting to realize that he was in that alley waiting to take out Orr after *you'd* lured him with twenty thousand dollars in walking money. They had you set him up so they'd know where he was. They were going to kill Orr, why? Because he was a liability. He was a liability on Sam Shead. He was a liability on Luther Ellis and who knows on what else. That's what these people do with liabilities, Neil," Mac stated. "They. Eliminate. Them."

"Detective, step away from my client," the lawyer ordered.

Mac held his gaze on Neil for an extra moment before slowly shifting his eyes to glance at Byrnes. Mac snorted a small laugh before slowly standing up, but he didn't leave Kline's side. "Fine. But all of that isn't even your biggest problem, Neil. You know what your biggest problem is?"

"What?"

"Your biggest issue is that drug ring you work for also killed those five police officers at the 280 the other night. The takedown on Orr didn't go exactly as planned. We've been applying pressure to that operation you work for and I think we were getting a little too close. So what did they do? They went after the cops who'd been tracking Terrence Orr. These parasites you work for made it look like some sort of revenge shooting, preying on the tensions in the country, using the unfortunate shooting of DeVonte Rice and the not guilty verdict on the two Minneapolis officers as the motivation, but we know better."

"It wasn't a revenge killing," Dick said coldly. "It was cold-blooded murder. By the people *you* work for."

"That's what these people you work for are, this drug ring. Well, actually it's a *cartel.* This cartel you work for, they're murderers."

"You have any evidence of that?" the lawyer asked.

"I'm not in front of a jury, Counselor," Mac replied quickly. "I'm merely explaining the environment in which your client lives."

"What's your point, Detective?"

"My point, Counselor, is that your client is the next Terrence Orr."

"Is that a threat?"

"That's reality." Mac turned to Neil and moved in again, this time in almost a whisper. "You're a liability, Neil. We've been spending some time watching you and you know what I think? I think you know too much. You're the last link, the weak link, the last liability. It's only a matter of time before *you* go down. If you're lucky they'll put you down like Orr, with a bullet. If you're unlucky you'll go down like Sam Shead. But either way, brotha, sooner or later, and I'm betting on sooner, you're going down. They killed Orr because he was a liability. *You're* a liability. How long until they move on you?"

Mac let his last comment hang in the air as he pushed himself up and away from the table and walked behind Dick and leaned against the wall, his arms folded, observing Neil.

The lawyer sat back. "It's a great story, Mac. And I read your book so I know you can spin a yarn. But it's long on narrative and short on evidence against my client or this *phantom* organization you speak of."

Mac shrugged, leaning comfortably against the wall. "Suit yourself, Counselor. I have the benefit of knowing things you don't or that I'm sure your client or the people actually paying your bill have omitted telling you. The reality is, however, that your client, assuming you actually view Neil as *your* client, has one good option available and that's to tell me everything and we see what we can do. I don't think your boy here pulled the trigger, I don't think he's a murderer. What he does possess, however, is a lot of information that could help me and is worth something to me. Of course, if his employer has a clue, they too know he's full of information. So the question is whether your client decides to help himself before his employer decides he's too big a liability to leave walking around out on the streets."

Dick started putting the pictures and other evidence back into a folder while Mac stood up and went to the door, opened it and held it open.

"What? I can just leave?" Neil asked, surprised.

"Your lawyer is right, I don't have enough evidence yet to arrest you," Mac answered. "The question you have to ask yourself is whether you can stay alive long enough for me to get it. But know this, Neil. There is only one person who can save your ass right now, and that's me."

27

"NO LOOSE ENDS."

Neil's lawyer drove him back to his law office in downtown St. Paul where White was waiting in a windowless conference room. The lawyer and Neil provided White with a recap of the interview. The lawyer then departed so White and Neil could talk privately.

"This McRyan is no joke," Neil exclaimed nervously. "I Googled him on the way back over here and you should too because he is coming after you, after Felix, after all of us."

"This is not the first time we've had a cop, a police department, a federal agency become involved in our affairs," Mr. White replied dismissively. "This is part of our business and we know how to handle it, which is to change up our operation and we're doing that."

"I don't know," Neil replied, shaking his head in doubt. "This McRyan didn't put much evidence on the table, but he *knew* things. He had notes that Sam Shead left behind. So tell me, how'd those get missed?"

"I don't know. Interestingly though, other than you and Orr he revealed no other names."

"No, he didn't."

"That's right," White replied. "Because he doesn't have names or other key information. He's fishing. Look Neil, I've looked up McRyan too. He was a St. Paul detective some years ago but now lives in Washington D.C. because his wife works in the White House for the President of the United States. To come after our organization would require a lot of time and effort that I seriously doubt he'll be willing to put in. And that assumes we wouldn't be changing up our operation and we are."

"And the people who run it?"

White nodded. "And the people who run it, but Neil, you should realize by now how valuable you are to us. The stores are run by your people. As we adjust, we're going to need you to find us more good people. That's your value to the organization. You just need to ride it out. This game we play is not without risks and this is one of those tense times, but we'll get through."

"You'll get through, I'm sure," Neil replied with some bitterness. "But what about me?"

"You've drawn attention right now, sure," White replied with an unworried tone. "That's why we've reduced what we're having you do, just working the repair shop until this blows over because we need you, Neil. It's why we're protecting you."

"You really think this is going to blow over?" Neil asked. "This McRyan guy, you think he's just going to let it blow over? Jesus Christ, he thinks you, we, had something to do with the 280 shooting."

White snorted and shook his head skeptically. "Again, did he put any evidence of that on the table?"

"No."

"Right, because he doesn't have any."

That was the wrong answer and Neil caught it. "Saying

he doesn't have evidence isn't the same thing as saying we didn't have something to do with it. Did we?"

White didn't respond.

Neil pressed the question. "Did you guys go and do that?"

Again, White didn't respond.

"Oh man," Neil groaned, shaking his head. "Are you guys crazy?"

"Look Neil, sometimes decisions are made that I don't always agree with and you have to protect yourself and eliminate your liabilities."

"Like T.O., for instance?" Neil asked sharply. "Tell me that extra ten thousand you gave me wasn't an enticement to make sure he showed up at DeAndre's."

Again, White didn't respond.

"I guess McRyan was right about that, wasn't he?"

White stared Neil down, choosing his next words carefully. "Neil, you want to be very careful right about now. You know who you work for. Don't sit here and tell me you're shocked that certain decisions get made and actions get taken."

"When's that decision coming on me? When will I be considered too big of a liability?"

"If you keep your head down and your mouth shut, it won't. There is one thing you are that Terrence Orr wasn't."

"Which is?"

"Valuable. You would be wise to remember that."

An hour later, White returned to his law office to find Felix inside waiting.

"How did it go?" Felix asked.

White sat down in his chair behind his desk and closed his eyes for a moment. "Not well." He recapped his discussion with Neil. "He suspects we did the 280 and T.O. I can sense him turning. And he senses our questioning his loyalty. He thinks we're going to do him in." White slowly wiped his face with his hand, suddenly feeling tired and worn. He was getting tired of the killing. Unlike other circumstances where they'd decided to take action, in this case he really liked Neil, but business was business and they were in survival mode now, trying to run out the clock. The lawyer exhaled. "Neil will not be coming with us."

"Then Neil will have to go."

White slowly nodded. "No loose ends."

28

"LATHER, RINSE AND REPEAT."

Neil threw back the last of his whiskey while Mike did the same with his beer.

"Need another one, Neil?" Irv of Irv's Bar asked.

"No, not tonight, Irv," Neil replied evenly. "I'm turning in."

Neil and Mike walked out the front door of Irv's and looked up in the sky at the fireworks. "Where are those coming from?" Mike asked.

"The State Fair, I think," Neil replied as he opened the passenger door to the Tahoe. "There's fireworks sometimes after the Grandstand concert. If I recall correctly, tonight was a Def Leppard and Journey doubleheader. I bet the fair crowd was huge tonight, being Sunday and all, probably well over a hundred thousand."

"That many people, even with all that's happened around here?"

Neil thought for a moment. "Minnesota folks are pretty resilient, pretty stoic types. They mourn and then they move on. Besides, with all the crowds the State Fair is a safe place to be."

"I haven't ever been to the fair," Mike stated.

"Really? I thought every single person who ever lived in this state went to the fair. You've never had real cheese curds, a pork chop on a stick or deep-fried Twinkie?"

"No."

"Dude, you've missed out on a significant cultural experience."

"What about me says cultural experiences?" Mike replied. "So, are we heading home?"

"Yeah," Neil replied as he suspiciously looked around.

"I didn't see anyone behind us on the way over here," Mike stated, reading Neil's mind. "It was clear behind us."

The parking lot for Irv's was sparsely populated, seven other vehicles by Neil's count and Como Avenue in front was quiet and no other cars seemed to be parked in the vicinity. "Yeah, I guess you're right," Neil replied and lifted himself up into the passenger seat. "I'm bushed."

Neil sat back in the passenger seat, closed his eyes and slowly massaged his temples. The interview with McRyan, the uncomfortable talk with White, his strong suspicions that T.O. was killed by Felix and White and wondering when the next shoe would drop with the police... All of that was swirling around inside of his head. He was starting to think it might make sense to take everything he had and run.

Jockey Mike pulled straight out of Irv's parking lot and then turned left onto Como Avenue. A few blocks east there was an unexpected roar of an engine behind them. Neil turned around and saw a truck right behind them, without its lights on. This approach had an eerily familiar look and feel to it. "You need to hit it, Mikey! *We gotta move!*"

It was too late. The truck already pulled to their left and was roaring past them about thirty feet and then angled hard right in front of them, cutting them off. Jockey Mike had no choice, braking hard but still careening into the front of the pick-up truck.

Then there was another truck behind them, a panel van, right on their tail. They were pinned.

"Shit!" Neil growled and looked to Mike, whose eyes were wide with panic.

The passenger door was yanked open and Neil was grabbed around his neck and dragged out of the Tahoe.

"Lo puso en la furgoneta! Lo puso en la furgoneta!"

Neil understood Spanish well enough to know that meant. *Put him in the van.* The men did just that, throwing him into the back of the panel van. "Let's go! Let's go!" the driver yelled in Spanish. Neil could feel the van speeding away.

"Ve rapido! Ve rapido!"

The van roared to life and Neil felt it make a hard U-turn, heading back to what he knew was the west. A man jumped on top of him while still another tied up his legs. They flipped him over onto his stomach and yanked his arms and hands behind him and Neil heard the unmistakable sound of duct tape ripping, then felt it being wrapped around his wrists and ankles. They flipped him back over again and duct taped his mouth. He knew this was exactly what Felix did to people when he wanted them to disappear. He'd call in his cartel friends and away the person went, never to be seen again.

The driver yelled, *"Creo que tenemos un policía detrás de nosotros*!" There was a police car behind him.

"Shit, take a right on Snelling!"

Then Neil heard the siren and could see the blue and red of the emergency lights reflecting on the interior ceiling of the van.

"*Mas rapido! Mas rapido!*" yelled the man holding him down.

He felt the van turn sharp left and then it came to a hard stop, sending him careening forward, slamming headfirst into the hard back of the driver's seat. He was dazed but could hear the sirens rapidly approaching and the flashing blue and red police lights became brighter.

The van door was ripped open and the two men who'd thrown him into the van leaped out and started running. The driver did the same, leaving the van running. As he looked out the opening for the sliding door he could see people cautiously approaching, the onlookers unsure of what they'd just witnessed.

"They ran through the gates and into the fair!" a voice yelled and then a pack of uniformed police officers sprinted past the van. He could hear more sirens approaching and saw more flashing lights. Two more officers sprinted past the van, portable radios in their hands. *"Lock it down! Lock all the entrances and exits down!"* he heard a voice yell.

He lay in the van, helpless and bound, unable to move, a nervous sweat running down his face.

"Get back! Everyone get back!" a familiar voice bellowed and he could see two more uniformed officers now standing in front of the onlookers, waving them back away from the van. Then as he looked out the sliding door opening he saw a now familiar face. Lich turned to look inside the van.

And then another newly familiar voice stuck his head around the corner. "Well hello, Neil!" greeted McRyan, who then looked to his partner. "Dick, it sure is a good thing we were watching after him, don't you think?"

"I'm pretty sure Ol' Neil here thinks so."

"I bet you just pissed your pants and shit your drawers,"

McRyan needled as he snapped open his switchblade knife to cut away the duct tape.

At the old Fourth Precinct Building Mac stood with his hands in his pockets, observing Neil Kline through the one-way glass. Fourteen hours ago, Neil sat in an interview room downtown. Back then he was cocksure, a lawyer at his side, confident in his knowledge that the police had no leverage on him.

The tables were now turned. Neil had been in the room for nearly three hours now, a police guard outside the door. Food and coffee had been brought in for him, but Mac strategically let him sit and stew and contemplate his new reality.

Standing to his left was Dick. Standing to his right was Jon Erickson of the Drug Enforcement Agency. The Judge had indeed been a man of his word. Erickson had been hot on the tail of the Lazaro Cardenas Cartel in Chicago when it up and disappeared five years ago without so much as a trace. He and the DEA wanted another shot and were willing to play by Mac's rules to get it.

Also joining them in the observation room was Chief Flanagan and Captain Peters, along with Paddy, Schmidt and Armstrong.

Mac turned to Erickson. "Are your guys back now?"

"Yeah," Erickson smiled in return. "Once they got into the State Fair they ran down as far as the Midway before pulling up. Once they caught their breath they had a good laugh with your boys. After that they enjoyed a little tour around and scored some cheese curds and beers at a beer garden. No sweat." Erickson took a sip of coffee. "Now, the question is whether this little abduction stunt of yours actually worked?"

Mac nodded. He'd used the method he suspected was used on Sam Shead in the hopes that Kline would recognize the signature. The question was would he buy it? Would he now believe that his employer intended to kill him? It was time to find out.

"Mac, I know you say this guy didn't pull the trigger, but if this piece of shit knows who killed Franklin, Fisher, Ortega, Cruz and has Riles and Rock in comas, you get it out of him. Do you understand?" the chief demanded.

"Yes, sir."

Mac exhaled and took one last drink from his coffee cup. "Let's go see if this guy has wised up."

"*It's about time!*" Neil barked when Mac, Dick and Erickson entered the interrogation room.

"Really, Neil?" Mac replied sarcastically, shaking his head as he sat down in a chair across from Kline. "That's your opener? *We*"—Mac waved around the room—"we all save your ass and all I get is it's about time? How about a thank you?"

"Well..."

"Shut up and listen, dumbass, because you are in a world of hurt right now." Mac clasped his hands in front of him. "Hey, do you maybe want to call your lawyer first?"

Neil looked down.

"Oh wait, you haven't yet. Could it be because they paid for him? They did, didn't they?"

There was no response.

"What did I tell you was going to happen? Your bosses clearly want you dead. That takedown sure looks a lot like the one they pulled on Sam Shead, probably on Luther Ellis and who knows how many others. It appears to be their go-to move, wouldn't you agree, Detective Lich?"

Dick nodded confidently. "We hear stories about guys being there one day and gone the next. They just disappear. Poof, they're gone." Dick turned back to Neil. "That was almost you."

"I bet that's how they do it," Mac added pointedly. "They roll up on the guy, pin the truck in, drag the person out and throw them into a getaway vehicle. Take them somewhere, interrogate, beat, kill and then dump like it's a checklist. Lather, rinse and repeat."

"Those guys that did it," Dick suggested. "It wasn't their first rodeo, that's for sure. It was very systematic."

"They were very good. Heck, they almost slipped away from us," Mac said in admiration. "The experience was evident."

Neil looked down and shook his head and Mac knew it to be true, all of it.

"Here's the deal, Neil. You have a pretty narrow window here to do a little something for yourself."

"Like what?"

"Like save your life," Mac replied.

"You don't understand."

"I don't understand what?"

"If I talk to you. If I tell you what I know, I'm dead."

"*If you don't, you're dead!*" Mac shouted, pounding the table with his fist. "If you don't tell me what I need to know right now I'm throwing your ass back out on the streets. How long do you think you'll last? I mean you can run, but if this is the cartel and they want to find *Neil Kline*, they'll find Neil Kline."

"Did you catch those guys who took me?"

"Not yet. We're still hunting. They got into the State Fair. You know, a hundred thousand plus people on a beautiful summer night with a big concert and fireworks. I only had so many cops..." Mac let his voice drift away. After a moment he leaned forward, his forearms on the table, hands clasped. "Now, there is a door number two. You tell me about the entire operation, tell me everything I want to know and we can protect you."

"What, the St. Paul Police Department can offer protection?" Kline waved his hand dismissively. "*Riiight.*"

"Me?" Mac retorted, leaning back shaking his head. "No, I can't provide you long-term, *life-altering* protection." Mac gestured with his right thumb to the man leaning against the wall to his right. "But he can."

Kline looked to the left to the thin man with straight black hair leaning against the wall. "Who are you?"

"Jon Erickson with the Drug Enforcement Agency. I might be able to help you with witness protection, but I need to hear what you know first. Like Detective McRyan said, we know we're talking cartel here. Which one?"

Kline looked down, his arms folded, lightly rubbing his bottom lip with his right index finger, contemplating his situation. After a minute of quiet thought and one last big sigh, Neil looked up. "Lazaro Cardenas. It's the Lazaro Cardenas Cartel."

Mac, Dick and Erickson exchanged a quick glance. Kline confirmed what Jockey Mike had told Mac and Erickson's eyes said he was very keen to be in. *Now they were in business,* Mac thought.

"Okay, Neil," Mac stated. "Let's talk about the operation. Who's in charge of it?"

"Locally, it's this guy named Felix."

"Felix have a last name?" Erickson asked, having now taken a seat at the end of the table.

"Calderon, I think," Neil replied. "I think I overheard that one time."

"You work for the guy and you don't know his name?" Dick asked in disbelief.

"Have you met the guy?" Neil asked in complete fear. "You don't ask him questions. You do what he says and hope he leaves you alone and you keep breathing."

"He's a killer then," Mac noted, not in question form.

Neil turned his gaze to Mac and slowly nodded. "He does it for fun."

"Did he kill Luther Ellis?"

Neil shook his head. "No, they made T.O. do that one, although I'm sure Felix was involved."

"Any idea where the body is?" Mac asked.

Neil shook his head. "I just know they took care of the problem."

"Did this Felix kill Sam Shead?"

"I'd bet on it," Neil replied quietly. "I mean, they didn't necessarily share that with me, but I know that a day or two later I was told that he would no longer be an issue. I've heard that before and *I know* Felix handles those situations. That's his job."

"Was Orr involved in that too?" Mac asked, seeking confirmation from his line of questioning from their last session.

"Yes. They made T.O. help since it was his fuckup that drew Shead's attention in the first place. In the end, I'm pretty sure they set up T.O. in case they needed a fall guy. I could see that coming a mile away. T.O. didn't, but I did."

"You said they told you that Shead would no longer be an issue. Who told you that, this Felix?" Erickson asked.

"No," Neil replied with a shake of the head. "White told me that."

"Who's White?" Mac asked and then looked to his right to Dick who nodded and started reaching inside a folder.

"Felix is the man in charge overall here in the cities, but Mr. White runs the businesses."

"The fronts?" Dick asked.

Neil nodded. "Yeah. He's the one who oversees that part of the operation. I hired a lot of the guys working at these stores. Guys I knew over the years who were in the trade, so to speak, who had the ability to move from the street into more of an environment like that. We'd distribute the drugs out of the fronts and take in the money. Some of the money would be filtered—"

"Laundered, you mean," Mac finished.

"Whatever you want to call it," Neil replied. "White set that up and taught me how to do it and then I taught some others how that worked so the money could be siphoned through many different businesses."

"And what about the money that didn't get laundered through the businesses?"

"That went up to the cash house in Rogers."

"And this Mr. White ran all of that?"

"Yes."

Mac looked over to Dick who slid a bunch of pictures in front of Neil. They were pictures from the Polar Bar, a coffee shop from yesterday morning and from numerous days at the repair shop. "Are this Felix and White anywhere in these pictures?"

Neil sifted through the photos. "You have them a few times here as it turns out. This is White walking into the Polar Bar." Neil smiled. "That must have been the day you got onto JuJu and Leon, because whoever took these photos was focused on those two and seems to miss White, as all you have here is the back of him walking in."

"Do we have any of his face?"

"Right here," Neil replied, sifting through more of the pictures. "This older guy walking out the side of the coffee shop, wearing the black fedora is White. And this bigger guy walking out after him, the Hispanic, is Felix. I met them at that coffee shop. We did that a lot."

"How do we find them?" Dick asked.

"You don't," Neil answered with a wry laugh. "They find you."

"What?" Erickson asked. "You don't know where they live? Where they work out of? You don't have any way to contact them?"

Neil shook his head, his arms folded. "No. They'd stop by the shop once a day to check in, answer questions and give instructions. Each week I'd get a new number to reach Mr. White, but I was only to use the number in case of emergency. There was a general rule, no business of any kind by phone. It was all face to face. They were constantly afraid of electronic surveillance. No phones, no texting, period."

"You don't know where either of these guys lives or has offices?" Dick asked, incredulous.

"No," Neil answered with a head shake. "The operation was siloed, if that's a word. That's the term White used. I had my part of the business, which was my repair shop. The fronts and I coordinated distribution and money at the street level. Until recently, until all this trouble started, I was going around and picking up the money at night from some of the other shops that we didn't launder, as you call it, and delivered it up to the house in Rogers, but that's as far as I went."

"And what would they do with the money up there at that house?"

"Store it in big safes and wrap it in stacks about so high. Then every so often, four, five, maybe six times a year, they'd load it all onto these big semi-tractor trailers."

"To go where?"

"I assume Mexico."

"Would the money be in bundles? Stored on pallets? What?" Erickson asked.

Neil gave a wan smile. "I saw it a couple of times out at the house. Back in the woods there is an old barn where they would do the loading. The tops of the trailers are hollow. There were these metal plates on the roof of the trailer that could be unscrewed. Based upon how far I saw a guy's arm go down in there one night, I bet the compartment is at least a couple feet deep, probably a little more. They'd take those plates off, store the money inside and then put the plates back on and off the trucks would go."

Mac looked over to Erickson who was thinking the same thing. "The drugs come into the country in those compartments, high off the ground," Erickson mused. "Bring the drugs in and take the money out the same way."

"I think so," Neil offered. "But I don't know for sure. I never saw the drug part of it, ever. I don't know if those compartments allow them to get across the border or if the drugs are loaded after they cross the border. I just don't know."

"They didn't unload the drugs up at that house though, did they?" Mac asked Kline.

"No. That was done somewhere else."

"Where?" Dick asked.

Neil shrugged. "I don't know. Like I said, it's a siloed operation. I never was where the drugs were unloaded, whether it was coke, heroin, weed, meth. We sell it all, but that all happened somewhere else. I never saw it."

"You never saw it, but what do you know about it?" Mac pushed.

"Just that there's a place where the drugs are delivered, but I swear to you, I don't know where that is. I do know based on what I saw a couple of times when money was loaded on the trucks that those compartments on top were empty, so the drugs were delivered somewhere else first."

"When do these deliveries take place?"

"Every so often. I know one is coming soon."

"When?"

Neil shook his head. "I don't know when, exactly, but it's been like ten, maybe eleven weeks since there was last activity with the trucks, the money and a new influx of supply, so it's due. The trucks are going to be coming. White said so a few weeks ago."

"Tell me about the trucks," Mac asked. "You said they were refrigerated?"

"Yeah, I think so."

"What did they look like?"

"White. They were white semi-tractor trailers—truck and trailer were both plain white."

"Any markings on the outside?"

Neil shook his head. "None that I ever remember seeing. Plain, generic, wouldn't-give-it-a-second-look white."

"And they were refrigerated. Any idea what they were carrying? I mean, if the drugs are stored in those panels on top, I assume something else was inside the trailers. They were delivering something."

"I think vegetables," Neil answered. "Again, I never saw that part of it. I remember asking one time why the trucks were refrigerated and one of Felix's men said they were for the vegetables."

"What kinds?" Dick asked.

"I have no idea," Neil answered. "I suppose whatever would come from Mexico."

"The Lazaro Cardenas Cartel is based out of Michoacán state," Erickson added. "It's a big agricultural state on the west side of the country. In that part of Mexico they grow corn, strawberries, peaches, limes, mangos, avocados, wheat, sugar cane...stuff like that."

"Much of which could be delivered in refrigerated trucks," Dick noted, "including..."

"Avocados," Mac replied, picking up the train of thought. "Neil, do you know of anyone who's referred to as The Avocado?"

Neil crinkled his nose and shook his head.

"You've never heard that reference?" Mac pressed.

"No, not at all. Why?"

"I'll get to that in a minute. So you don't know where the drugs are dropped off, but the money comes to the house in Rogers."

"Yes, or it..." Neil closed his eyes. "Shit."

"What?" Mac asked.

"You know this too now, I guess, but the money *did* go to Rogers. However, after you guys started showing interest in our operations, Mr. White said we were changing up. The money wouldn't go up to Rogers anymore."

"Where was it going?" Dick asked.

"I don't know. Remember, siloed operation. Since you guys started watching me they've started phasing me out, telling me to sit at the repair shop until you guys lost interest. In the meantime, they were changing up so there is a lot going on now that I don't know about."

It was Mac's turn to have his stomach churn. He'd been basing his whole theory that Neil would be able to put him onto the people in charge of the operation. Yet Neil didn't know where they lived, worked out of and now didn't know where the money was going. He identified the cartel, what they were doing and how they were doing it, but the details on the key parts of the operation were getting light.

"Neil, how do we figure this out?" Mac asked. "You're giving me some pretty good information but now you're telling me they're changing up and you have no idea where to or what they're now doing?"

Neil just shook his head.

"Well shit," Dick muttered disgustedly. "You're not much good to us then, Neil."

"What do you want me to say? I'm telling you what I know. I can't tell you what I don't know."

Mac pushed himself up from the table and started pacing around the room. Neil had confirmed a lot for them, but Mac was expecting more from this. He *needed* more from it. They knew who most likely killed Sam and Luther Ellis. But what about the 280? Mac turned and looked to Neil. "What do you know about the 280?"

"I know they did it."

"Anyone tell you that?"

"Not direct like, no, but Mr. White as much admitted to it after you had me in here earlier. Mr. White and I had a talk. I asked him about the 280 and he said something to the effect that you eliminate your liabilities. I guess they thought that by doing the 280 and killing those cops who'd been after T.O., you guys would be far more interested in chasing after that and less interested in them."

"Any idea who did the shooting?"

"I'm sure it was Felix that was behind it. I think that guy would live for something like that."

"Would he pull the trigger, though?" Mac pressed.

Neil nodded. "Like I said, Felix had no issues with

killing. They killed people all the time. Killing to Felix was like you or I brushing our teeth. No big thing."

"You said they killed people all the time?" Dick asked. "Who? When? Where? I'm a homicide cop. It's been fairly quiet the last couple of years."

Neil smiled. "Because there is another rule—you never leave a body. Mr. White told me that. You can take people out, but it doesn't mean you leave a body. Bodies bring cops and attention. If someone wasn't cooperating, Felix and some guys would go out and..."

"Pull a maneuver like they tried tonight?" Mac finished. "Pull a maneuver like they did on Sam Shead?"

"Yes. We've been operating five years. Took over lots of drug real estate. If someone didn't go along with us, Felix would take care of it and the real estate would be ours."

"Felix have other muscle?" Dick asked Neil.

"Yeah, he had his own guys. But if things were going to get messy and he didn't want to expose his guys, he'd call out to California and the CA-57s would send some guys up here. You've heard of the CA-57s right?"

Everyone nodded.

Neil shuddered. "Felix is menacing, but those CA-57 guys were downright scary. Jockey Mike, my driver—where is he, by the way? Is he okay?"

"We have him," Mac answered. "He's safe, resting in a room down the hall. So, the CA-57s?"

"Mike and I went out to the airport one time to pick two guys up. I seriously thought I was going to shit my pants. These guys were...frightening. They were all tatted up with shaved heads, bulging muscles and they had these small, dark, lifeless eyes. I'm not sure I took a breath the entire time they were in the truck."

"For the 280, if Felix did this, he'd have brought guys like that in?"

"I'd bet a lot of money on it. His guys here are tough, but shooting cops?" Neil shook his head. "I don't think they'd have the stomach for it. But these guys I picked up at the airport, shit, they wouldn't give it a second thought. They'd kill anybody."

"And he'd bring these guys in when?" Dick asked, leading.

"To take or help take people out. I think sometimes they'd interrogate them because all of a sudden we'd know things about certain crews, issues, internal politics, drug connections, things like that and I'm sure they got it from these guys before they... disappeared."

"Any idea how they disposed of the bodies?" Dick asked, taking notes.

Neil shook his head. "I assume they were burying them in the woods somewhere, but I don't really know. I have a habit of knowing things, knowing people, knowing what's going on. I see things and I get what's happening. But that having been said, you work for these guys you keep your head down, do your job, and you don't ask a lot of questions."

"Neil, you don't strike me as a terrible guy. I question your chosen profession, but you don't seem like the blood-thirsty type. Why even work for these guys?" Dick asked.

"Because when I got out of prison, Mr. White showed up. He knew all about me, my prison record, what I'd done on the streets, my contacts, what my skills were and background. He offered me a job and more money than I'd ever been paid. Nobody else was offering me a job, at least not for that kind of money." Neil shook his head. "Now look where it got me."

Dick flipped open a laptop and turned it around to face Neil. "This is the footage from the 280's surveillance cameras. Watch it."

Dick pushed play. Neil watched it, wincing at the brutality of the killings. "God, it was over just like that," he croaked as he watched the three men exit the 280.

"Do you recognize anybody?"

Neil reached for the computer and hit play again, watching closely the footage of the men moving around the restaurant. He shook his head. "I think Felix is the third one in the door based on how he moves. You can see that the shooter is left-handed and Felix is a lefty. The body type is right for Felix and the movements look familiar, but...the head is covered with that mask so...I can't say for sure, but I'd bet that's Felix."

"How about the other two?" Dick asked. "Could they be CA-57 guys?"

"It's possible," Neil answered, "but I don't really know them. I haven't seen them in action. I just picked them up at the airport that one time and I never wanted to see them again."

Mac leaned against the wall and shook his head. He'd gambled big and was coming up too light. He'd staged the abduction of Neil to get him to talk. Erickson wasn't there with just witness protection; it was his guys who abducted Kline and put him in the van. Mac set it up for them to drive to the entrance to the State Fair so the men could "escape" into the mass of the Sunday night's crowd at the fair. They had Neil and he was talking, but based upon what he had told them, the operation was changing up. Neil didn't know where to find either Felix or this Mr. White. And now that Mac had taken Neil off the streets, they'd undoubtedly be spooked even more. They might even pull out of town altogether.

Mac sat down at the table and looked through the evidence they had in the file and stopped on a picture of Shead's notebook. He thought back to what triggered all of this. "Neil, the night they saw Shead watching the house from up on that hill, who else was there?"

"Who else?"

"Yeah," Mac replied and looked to Dick. "Remember I told you last time we shared a room like this that we found Sam's notebook. There was a notation in there that he saw you, T.O., which we assumed was Orr and then someone Sam described as The Avocado. Who is The Avocado?"

Neil thought back to that night and then blurted out, "I suppose it could be Javier Alvarado."

"What?" That answer got Erickson's attention. "Javier Alvarado was in this country? A cartel head was in this country? Here in the Twin Cities?"

Neil nodded. "Yeah, I saw him a few times over the years at the house up in Rogers. I assumed he wanted to make sure the money was going where it was supposed to."

"Are you sure?" Erickson asked. "Are you absolutely sure?"

Neil nodded.

"Why are you so skeptical?" Mac asked Erickson.

"Because Javier Alvarado is not exactly a household name. His father Hector was kind of flamboyant, was well-photographed and it wasn't a real secret where he lived. But after Hector died and Javier took over, he went to ground to a certain degree, much lower profile. Thus there are few pictures of him in existence, at least that people have identified him in. I think the DEA's most current photo is like seven or eight years old. I mean, I'm just wondering how the hell he even got into the country."

"Well, I don't know what to tell you," Neil replied. "But I know who I saw. Mr. White confirmed it for me once. He told me not to talk to him. I asked why and he said just don't, that's the boss man from Mexico."

"Give me a minute," Erickson said as he left the room. He was back five minutes later with two photos. "Is this the man you saw?"

"Yes," Neil answered without hesitation. "His hair is a little longer now in the back and there are a few wrinkles, but that's the man I saw."

"So that's who The Avocado was, I guess," Dick stated. "Hmpf."

"I guess so," Erickson agreed. "That would be a reason to kill your old friend if he saw *this* guy."

Mac stood up and paced around the room in thought and then stopped and turned back to Kline. "Wait a minute. How the hell would Sam know that he was looking at Javier Alvarado?" He looked to Erickson. "Didn't you just say there are few pictures of him? That the DEA's photos, which I'm looking at here, are several years old."

"Yeah," Erickson replied and then he got it. "That's a good point—how the hell does your friend know this is Javier Alvarado?"

"He probably didn't," Mac replied and then turned to Neil. "Who else was with Javier? There must have been someone else."

Neil nodded. "Yeah, there was...a woman, a pretty woman."

"Do you have a name?" Dick asked.

"No."

"Describe her." Mac asked.

"Like I said attractive, strikingly pretty, but then again she was with Javier Alvarado. What do you expect?"

"And tell us about her."

"Dark black hair that was stylishly up like women like to wear it, darker skin it seemed. She was white, but she seemed to have darker skin. Maybe she was a little tanned—it is summer. She was wearing some expensive jewelry."

"Hispanic?" Dick asked, jotting notes.

"No, not necessarily," Neil replied, sitting back and closing his eyes. "Could have been, I suppose. Maybe it was her eyes, she had these big attractive eyes. I'd felt like I'd seen her somewhere before."

"Up at the house?"

"No, I want to say in the... newspaper."

"You read the paper?" Dick asked.

"Yeah, I read the paper," Neil replied tartly, "the business section. These guys paid me decently. I took that money and invested it and I followed it daily. I just remember thinking that I'd seen her in the paper recently is all."

"Which paper?"

"The *StarTribune*, I think," Neil replied. "I read it every day, front to back."

"And recently? How recently?"

"The last month or so," Neil answered and then pondered for a moment. "Yeah, the last month or so."

"So 'The Avocado' was in the paper... The avocado... avocados," Mac mumbled, thinking, "avocados...avo... cado..." And then it hit him. "No way," he blurted as he reached for his phone. "No way, no way, no way."

"What?" Dick asked.

"It can't be...can it?" Mac muttered as he started searching, going to the *StarTribune* website's search bar and quickly tapped in a name. The article popped up as item number one in the search. It ran in the business section twenty-seven days ago and detailed the massive success of a local company whose hit product was sweeping the nation. Mac and Sally loved the stuff, ate it all the time and were pumped when they started being able to get it out in Washington.

"Refrigerated trucks," Mac muttered, shaking his head and smiling. "You need refrigerated trucks to transport avocados. Avocados come from the Michoacán state. They're Hass avocados actually, considered the best in the world," he reported. "They're the vital ingredient in one of the hottest products on the party snack food market...Salsamole."

"I love that stuff," Dick exclaimed.

"Everybody does," Mac answered with a big smile. "Salsamole is the brainchild of this woman." Mac held up his phone for Neil to see.

"That's her," Neil said, pointing at the phone. "No doubt. She was there that night with Javier."

Mac shook his head in disbelief and looked to Dick and Erickson, holding up his phone for them to see. "Say hello to The Avocado. Laura Peterson."

29

"BUT IT'S NOT ROMANCE, IT'S FAMILY."

Laura Peterson. Unbelievable.

Mac burst out of the interview room with renewed energy. He found the chief, Peters, Schmidt, Armstrong all in shock, but that's not who he was looking for. Where was Paddy? Mac pivoted to his left to see his cousin already at a laptop.

"I'm already with you, cuz," Paddy stated when Mac came over to his desk.

"Everything you can find on Laura Peterson. Full history. If you need help and by that, I mean some manpower, just say so."

"I can get you help too," Erickson added. "DEA, FBI, whatever you need."

"I'm on it," replied the younger McRyan with the gift for the paper trail, his fingers rapidly dancing over his laptop keyboard.

Mac was back in the interview room and they spent another two hours going through everything with Kline. They went back to the beginning and worked forward from

Luther Ellis, to Sam Shead, to Terrence Orr, to the 280, the drug operation. Then they reviewed Javier Alvarado, Mr. White, Felix, the people Neil knew Felix had probably killed and finally, back to Laura Peterson. Mac worked Neil over again and again on that point to make certain of it. While ninety-nine-point-nine percent certain Neil was being fully truthful, Mac nevertheless was having a hard time wrapping his mind around the Laura Peterson angle.

They all took a break from the interview, the rising sun filtering through around the outer edges of all the pulled window shades. Kline sacked out on an old, musty brown couch in one of the spare offices along with his driver. Armstrong and Schmidt made a quick run for beverages and something to eat.

The group reconvened twenty minutes later after clearing their minds, stretching and splashing some water on their faces. With the adrenaline from the interview fading, Mac was slumped down in a chair, exhausted and yawning; the coffee, the cold water, the hot water, all ineffective in re-energizing him.

"Why would Laura Peterson get mixed up in this?" Dick asked.

"That's the question Peters and I keep asking too," Chief Flanagan replied as they all sat in an empty office that the chief commandeered, drinking coffee and diving into a box of sticky gas station donuts.

"She's rich, what does she need this for?" Captain Peters stated. "I know what Kline is telling you, I've been watching. And he's believable and credible, but it doesn't make any sense."

And there was another thing that made the chief wince. "Can you just imagine the flesh- eating lawyers she'll sic on us if we go down this road?" Flanagan shook his head.

"We're getting ahead of ourselves here," Mac counseled through a yawn. "We're not charging her, Chief. That's not on the table, not with what we have. But what we do have right now is more than enough to take a good long look at her and start building a case. Erickson and I have been talking about this from a drug standpoint and we can paint a picture where it could make some sense."

"Actually, it's really a good possible setup," Erickson, the DEA agent, added.

"How so?" the chief and Peters asked almost in unison.

"I've got Paddy researching Peterson as we speak," Mac reported. "However, I did just a little ten-minute search on her and about her Salsamole product here on my phone. There was an article in *Skymall* magazine six months ago about her, the product line she has and how she gets her avocados from Mexico—Michoacán state. If Kline is to be believed and Laura Peterson is involved, then her role must be the trucks. They're hers. They come into the country from Mexico, transporting the vegetables, like avocados, up here for all her grocery products. It's not a stretch that the drugs are also transported in those trucks and then return to Mexico with the cash."

"And she gets out of this—what?" the chief asked.

"What anyone else would want," Erickson answered, "money. Lots and lots of money."

"But like the cap said, she is already rich, isn't she?" Flanagan asked in reply.

"But how did she get so rich?" Paddy asked as he opened the door. "How did Laura Peterson become so wealthy and one of America's rising women entrepreneurs?"

"I assume you're about to tell us," the chief answered, pointing to a chair for Paddy to sit down in. "Go."

"Laura Helena Mendes Peterson is forty-five years old.

She was married once to Steven Peterson, a man fifteen years her senior. He died fourteen years ago of cancer. They had no children. I found a number of articles about her, a few from when she was in Chicago and then later ones from the newspapers and magazines here in the Twin Cities and a few national hits as well. One article from the *Chicago Sun-Times* indicated that at the time her husband died, she owned a small Mexican restaurant up in Lake Forest, a suburb up north of Chicago. The article indicated that she owned the café, cooked and even waited tables and that the signature item was an appetizer that was a salsa guacamole mix served with tortilla chips."

"Nachos?" Dick asked.

"Basically," Paddy answered. "Her late husband owned part of a small investment consulting business at the time of his passing. Between some life insurance and the interest in the consulting business, which she later sold, this article indicated she was comfortable, had a few million in the bank. It was at that point she sold the café and started her own food line."

"Not bad," Dick answered. "Now, I'm no businessman, but is that enough money to jump start her to where she is today?"

Paddy shrugged. "I don't know, I'm not a businessman either."

"I kind of am," Mac answered. "The answer is I don't think so. She would need a cash infusion from somewhere, some investors probably."

Paddy nodded and flipped to another page. "The next kind of hit on her comes four years later. At the time, she was still in Chicago and her food line, including her best product, the Salsamole, is starting to take off locally. Here's the kicker, the article discussed how she has spent a lot of time in Mexico looking for the best avocados she can find."

"Hass avocados?" Mac asked, knowing the answer.

"Correct, and that she's having them shipped to her small processing plant out on the western outskirts of Chicago. There was a picture of her in the plant in the article wearing a hard hat and a sharp business suit. At that time, her food and snack product line is in all of the local Chicago grocery markets, restaurants are buying it and she's starting to diversify her offerings into other snack and food products, all with a Mexican spin."

"Great," the chief replied. "She's making progress, sounds legitimate."

"And then five years ago she takes the big leap," Paddy continued and held up an article. "She made the *Wall Street Journal.* Her company, now called Spectrum Universal, was distributing products throughout the Upper Midwest. It had an assessed worth of one hundred seventy-five million dollars based upon its growth. And then she did what the article writers thought was a very odd thing."

"Which was what?" the chief asked.

"She moved the business here," Mac stated, following along and then looked to Erickson. "Didn't you say that the Lazaro Cardenas Cartel was active in Chicago up until about five years ago and then seemingly disappeared?"

"I did now, didn't I," Erickson replied, thinking along the same lines as Mac.

"She moved the operation here along with the cartel," Mac speculated. "It was getting too hot in Chicago."

"But the cartel needs her trucks to get the product in and—"

"The money out," Mac pointed back at Erickson. "With

trouble in the Windy City, they beat the heat and set up shop up here in the sleepy Twin Cities."

"And now her company is worth an estimated eight hundred million," Paddy reported, flipping through another set of pages. "I mean, this is all out on the Internet and she's been on a buying spree. The business is diversified beyond the Mexican salsa, guacamole, cheese dip, Salsamole products. The company now owns high-end organic grocery stores they've opened here in the Twin Cities as well as in Chicago, Des Moines, Omaha and Kansas City. The company also owns two different restaurant chains and is continuing to further diversify outside of food into investment, real estate, and I think I saw a reference that they were thinking of getting into banking. Billionaire status is right around the corner."

Mac snorted a little laugh. She was diversifying her portfolio. He'd met Laura Peterson at an investors' dinner two weeks ago. That investment had nothing to do with the food industry.

"But still, why?" the chief pushed. "Why does she get involved in all of this?"

"Maybe the oldest reason known to man—romance?" Mac hypothesized. "The photos I've seen of Javier Alvarado suggest he's a good-looking dude, rich, maybe even mysterious or a bit of a bad boy. I met Laura Peterson a few weeks ago at an investors' dinner. Neil Kline is right. She is a very pretty lady."

"Really?" the chief asked.

"Yeah," Mac replied. "I had dinner with her at this table with other folks. She couldn't have been more pleasant to be with." He looked back over to Paddy. "The one article you cited talked about how she'd spent a lot of time in Mexico looking for avocados, right?"

"Yup, this one," Paddy replied, holding up the article. "But it's not romance, *it's family*."

"Come again?"

"This is where the resources and weight of the DEA and FBI helped," Paddy answered with a nod to Erickson. "Laura Peterson was born in Arizona. Her mother's name on the birth certificate was Anita Rose Mendes. The father on her birth certificate was listed as Hector Luis Alvarado."

"No shit?" Erickson asked in total wonder.

"No shit," Paddy answered. "She's the illegitimate daughter of Hector Alvarado, founder of the Lazaro-Cardenas Cartel. She is the half-sister of Javier Alvarado."

The room sat back in stunned silence. "She's all in on this then," Dick stated.

"She needed an investor. Laura made the calculation years ago that to get where she wanted to get business wise, she had to go along with, if not into the family business," Mac surmised.

"It all kind of fits," Erickson added. "She's in the business of Mexican food and grocery stores. The cartels are heavily into the agricultural businesses in Mexico," Erickson added. "They've muscled their way in, Lazaro Cardenas included."

"Laura wants to grow her business, needs capital and wants the best avocados she can get, along with other fruits and vegetables," Mac posited. "Hector and Javier need to get their product into the country and get the cash out and doing it this way, they hide it in a cloak of total legitimacy."

"It's a match made in heaven," Erickson agreed.

"That's right," Mac replied. "She took all that money and has run with it and I'm sure the cartel has made out just fine as well. Heck, until Sam Shead started poking around, nobody had any real idea that the cartel was even here. They'd been very low profile until now."

"But Mac, how do you *prove* that?" the chief answered. "I mean, you're taking a massive intuitive leap here on Laura Peterson. Hell, Javier could be her brother sure, but maybe she was just visiting with him when she was seen at that house. That's the only thing you have tying her to this whole thing."

"What the hell, Chief? Do you want to find the bastards who shot our boys or not!" Mac snapped.

"Damn right I do," the chief barked back. "But how? *How*? Mac, we arrest and convict on proof. How do you *prove* this tie-in? You don't have enough here for any sort of subpoena or search warrant on Laura Peterson. You're not getting a grand jury on this. The county or U.S. Attorney would laugh you out of their offices."

"You're putting the cart before the horse, Chief," Mac replied. "We just got onto this. Let's go out and get us some proof."

"But how?" Dick asked. "I get the chief's point. Kline doesn't know where the drugs are delivered to and he's told us they're not using the house in Rogers anymore since we'd gotten onto it. This Jockey Mike doesn't know. So how do you suggest we get the proof? They're going to be spooked by Kline being missing. They've already changed up money collection and distribution. They see us coming and they're preparing. Kline has told us about the operation, the players, but we still really don't have any *evidence*."

"Now *you're* fighting me?" Mac asked, perturbed.

"No, merely pointing out where we stand," Dick replied calmly. "You're all excited, thinking we've solved this thing when, in reality, we don't know dick, no pun intended. And you must be completely exhausted because you're snapping at everybody."

"When's the last time you slept, Mac?" the chief asked, concerned.

Mac exhaled and collapsed back into his chair and threw his head back, slowly breathing. "I don't know. Not since I got back to town, I guess."

"You need sleep," Captain Peters stated. "You're going to fry out."

"Yeah, even if it's only for a few hours," the chief added.

"Wait a minute," Paddy interrupted, looking at his notes. "We've been trying to identify The Avocado, but now, isn't this really all about the avocados?"

"What do you mean?" the chief asked.

"I mean the theory Mac is pushing is that the drugs come in with the avocados and then the money goes back to Mexico on the same trucks, right? Isn't that what Kline said?" Paddy asked.

Everyone nodded.

"Well, they can change how they distribute the drugs and collect the money, but they can't just change *where* the avocados go."

"Yeah," Mac answered, perking up and he could tell Paddy had something. "What are you thinking?"

"I'm thinking one of the other things I've found out this morning is that Spectrum Universal owns a processing plant up in Monticello, up northwest of the cities, another ten miles up I-94 from Rogers. The avocados have to be delivered somewhere, don't they? If you find the avocados—"

"You maybe find the drugs," Mac finished.

"Now that's a thought," the chief answered. "That's something we need to be looking into."

Mac looked up to Paddy with tired eyes. “Good one, cuz.”

“You’d have gotten there too,” Paddy answered. “But Lich and the chief are right, you’re dead on your feet.”

“Alright, Mac, you’re going to bed,” the chief ordered and then to Dick he said, “Let’s you and I see about getting some eyes on that processing plant.”

30

"GOOD NEWS AND BAD NEWS."

Mac went home, slept a hard four hours, showered and then was back at it, meeting up with Dick, Paddy and Erickson to set off for Monticello and the Spectrum Universal processing plant.

"I hated giving up those four hours. We should have had eyes on that plant right away," Mac grumbled from the backseat.

"It's like he doesn't think we know how to do our jobs, isn't it?" Paddy said to Dick with a bemused expression.

"I know, right?" Lich replied with a smirk. "It's like we're dumb or something." He turned and looked back to Mac. "Listen up, hotshot. We've had eyes on the place. The chief made a call up to his opposite number in Monticello. There has been casual observation on the plant for the last three hours courtesy of the Monticello Police Department, all so you could get some beauty rest."

"And?" Mac asked with mock annoyance.

Dick shook his head and looked to Erickson. "This guy."

"I'm waiting," Mac was getting snarky back now, with a grin.

"It's been quiet, only the odd single truck has stopped there," Paddy answered. "None of them plain white."

"Well, I guess good work then."

Monticello itself was a growing town that rested forty miles northwest of Minneapolis. The town was out in the middle of farm country, positioned between I-94 to its west and the Mississippi River to the east.

"I can't believe the population of this town is over thirteen thousand," Dick remarked. "We're so far out here."

"I think a lot of that growth happened before the housing bubble," Mac answered. "There was a lot of house building out here before 2008 when everyone thought the boom would never bust. People, families, wanted the big house with the big kitchen on a quarter-acre lot, but to afford it they had to move out—way out—to get it."

"If you worked in the cities, man, it would take you an hour, probably more than that to get to work in the morning."

"Probably more," Mac answered. "This married couple I know from law school live up here. He works in downtown Minneapolis and she works up in St. Cloud. He says his commute is an hour to ninety minutes from his garage to the parking ramp. Hers is like twenty minutes, traffic free, both ways."

"She got the better end of that deal," Paddy observed.

"Wives always do," Dick answered cynically.

Paddy hit the turn signal to take the exit for Monticello. He turned left at the top of the ramp, drove back over the interstate, then another half mile down the county highway before taking a left into an area of industrial operations. The processing plant was the third facility on the left.

Spectrum Universal was stenciled in block lettering along the top of what was the equivalent of a three-story building.

The loading bays for long-haul trucks were on the east end. Paddy drove them past the plant, went another block and executed a U-turn and came back west to do another quick drive by. There were six loading bays on the east end, one of which was currently occupied by a black semi with a black and red trailer that had images of red and green peppers adorning it.

"It's not just avocados," Dick mused.

"No, Peterson's food companies make a lot of different stuff," Mac answered. "She's very diversified and very successful."

"No real security," Erickson observed. "At least not that I can see."

Mac nodded. "That tells us something perhaps. That nothing is really going on right now. But maybe when the security does show—"

"Then something *will* be going on," Dick finished the thought.

Mac started looking to his left and the potential available surveillance options for watching the plant. There were some small businesses on the opposite side of the street: an aged tool and die shop, a fabricator, a floor tile store and a landscaping operation. None of them provided the privacy and cover they would need. Everyone else was scoping on the same thing.

"Maybe the roof of the tool and die place," Dick suggested.

"Too much profile," Erickson answered, a man familiar with surveillance. "Too easily seen," he added. "I don't know that we'd need to be this close."

"Let's look farther south then," Mac suggested.

Paddy drove to the end of the street, took a left and drove another quarter mile down the road to a sign for the Monte

Club, which indicated that the club was permanently closed.

"Let's give this a look," Dick said.

Paddy took a left onto the long driveway that wound its way up a gentle hill. The Monte Club appeared to have been a supper club and banquet facility at one time. Paddy stopped Mac's MKX at the front door. They all filed out of the truck and, ignoring the light misting rain, started walking around the property which was perched on top of the hill. Mac walked around the building, which was built in the shape of an octagon, to the north side. At the northwest corner he had a view overlooking the valley below to the north. He dropped his backpack from his shoulder, opened it up and took out a pair of binoculars.

"That's a good view of the plant," Paddy observed. "You can easily read the Spectrum Universal sign from here."

"Indeed," Mac mumbled, focusing in on the east end and loading bay. "Paddy, find out who we talk to about getting inside this place."

"I'm on it," his cousin replied, reaching for his cell phone and walking back around to the front.

"This should work," Dick suggested as he walked up with Erickson, the two of them having gone around the east side of the club. "The question, Mac, is what do they do when they realize you made a move on Kline? What happens then?"

Mac looked over to Dick with raised eyebrows. His partner had just made a very good point. "We have to make it look like we're still looking for Kline too. Put those two sharp guys from the Narcotics Unit, Martinez and Weed, on Kline's house. This time, tell them to make it just a little obvious so that those cartel assholes know we're looking for Kline too. And tell them to be very careful, guns close, watch their backs and have backup nearby."

"Copy that."

Felix pulled into a visitor's parking spot at Flying Cloud Airport. The airport, located southwest of the Twin Cities in the suburb of Eden Prairie, was a small commuter airfield used mostly for various kinds of Cessna, Cirrus, and Beechcraft planes as well as small corporate business jets. He made his way out to hangar number three. He sipped his bottle of water as he watched the plane taxi into the hangar. The pilot cut the engines and once they'd gone completely silent, the door opened and the steps folded down. White, followed by Helena, descended from the plane.

Helena's mother told her who her real father was when she was on her deathbed. "He knows about you, he's sent money for years but has respected my wishes that you not be part of the family business."

"What's the family business?"

"Cartel business."

Ten years later, a widow looking to start her own line of Mexican food items, she was traveling throughout Mexico trying to make relationships for the best vegetables and ingredients and was particularly interested in the Hass avocados growing in the Michoacán state. It just so happened that the best ones were growing on the farm controlled by her father. Back then it wasn't a big secret where Hector Alvarado lived. So she showed up at the front gate of her father's estate unannounced and asked to see him.

Hector himself went to the front gate and immediately

recognized her. "Helena!" he greeted excitedly, embracing her.

Initially shocked by the embrace, she was a bit shy but said, "I go by Laura, Mr. Alvarado."

"None of this mister stuff, I won't hear of it. You, child, can call me Papa, that's what my boys call me. And as for Laura, that's your American name, but your mother named you Helena after my mother so here, at my home, you are Helena!"

"Okay."

"So, my beautiful Helena, what brings you to me?"

"Avocados...Papa."

"Ahh, business. Always business," he beamed proudly.

Hector never had any daughters with his late wife. But discreetly he'd kept track of Helena over the years and knew of her furtive business ventures in Chicago. Finally, meeting his daughter and seeing what a lovely and beautiful woman she was, he was only too eager to help.

At the same time, Felix was in Chicago on Javier's orders trying to make headway in establishing a foothold in the Upper Midwest of the United States. There was always risk in transporting their product into the United States and then properly processing and distributing it once it got there. They needed to find a solution to that problem and suddenly here was Helena looking to pick the avocados out of their fields.

Hector and Javier listened to what Helena had in mind and the two of them saw a business opportunity that helped them all. "We can get you all the avocados you need, my child," Hector said eagerly. "But, there is also a way for you to help us."

"How?"

"Javier can explain it."

Helena, eager to grow her business, caught up in the excitement of reconnecting with a long-lost part of her family, and intoxicated by the grandiose wealth and power of her father, agreed. At first, she had little to no involvement in the drug side of the business. She bought the trucks with Hector's money and registered them to her company. She saw that the avocados were delivered and then she didn't see the trucks after that and that was the way Hector wanted it. He had always been happy that she became part of the business, but he didn't want her to risk getting too involved. It was important to him that she maintain a certain distance from the dirtiness of their operation. However, four years after meeting her father, he unexpectedly died of a heart attack and Javier took over and unlike his father, he was not so concerned about using his sister to his advantage when the opportunity presented itself. As it turned out, she didn't mind dirtiness.

Helena wanted to expand her business. Javier wanted to legitimize more of his assets.

"Have you ever laundered money?" Javier asked.

She needed more capital so she agreed. And that's how it started. The more money she and the drug operation made, the more the two operations became intertwined with one another, such that when the drug operation moved from Chicago to the Twin Cities she needed to move her base of operations. The same would be true now.

"How was the trip?" Felix asked once inside the office.

"Fine," White replied as he leaned against the desk. "Our friend down in Kansas City has a good line on a potential farm outside of town on the Kansas side for processing. There was a small Mexican restaurant chain that recently went out of business down there. We can scoop up all four places pretty cheaply and get them up and running."

"With Salsamole," Helena added enthusiastically. "We'll rebrand them the same as our places here. I'm thinking I'll open some places in Des Moines as well and we'll start franchising them out."

"You're okay with the move then?" Felix asked Helena.

"In a business sense I can make it work, especially moving the processing. There is a plant south of Kansas City that approached me a year or so ago about working together. I politely said no at the time, but I re-established business relations yesterday and we'll work that out," she replied. "As far as living and running my company down there, well—" A look of consternation swept over her face. "We're going to need to talk about that more. Like I said, if we need to move the Salsamole processing down here, we can do that. But moving my corporate HQ? Javier and I are going to have some more discussions about that. I love the Twin Cities. I don't want to leave."

"It may not be safe," Felix suggested.

"And if all of a sudden I, for no real explicable reason, move my entire operation to Kansas City five years after I moved it here from Chicago, you don't think people might raise their eyebrows at that and start asking questions? Especially with that stunt you pulled at the 280 Grille. You know, the police could be smarter than you give them credit for. This Mac McRyan White mentioned on the plane? I met him a few weeks ago at a dinner and read up on him after. Behind the aw-shucks personality and the rugged good looks is a wicked-smart cop. He was involved in the investigation before and now that you've done what you've done, killing people who are *his* friends, you know he's going to be coming after you. I don't want to give him the chance to add one plus one."

"I'm sure we can talk about this some more," White counseled. "Javier is concerned..."

Helena steamrolled him. "I could make a claim that the tax situation is better in Missouri or Kansas perhaps, but that does not outweigh the many business advantages of the Twin Cities from a human capital, infrastructural and quality of life standpoint. Land is cheap down there. It's cheap for a reason."

"Again, Javier feels..."

"I know how Javier feels," Helena replied with a wan smile. "I will explain to him how I feel. But look, obviously I get that you need to move what you do and the trucks need to keep moving. So you have to move the base of operations to keep the product flowing and take care of the money and I will do whatever I can to help, you know that. And I'm not saying I'll never move down there, but I'm not going to make a move so suddenly without thinking through all of the other business ins and outs of it."

"Okay," White replied, conceding the argument for the time being. It wasn't his call anyway. She and Javier would have to work it out. He turned to Felix. "Another thing Helena and I discussed, and I think she makes a good point, is that we need to pull the plug on the fronts and pay the employees through their last day."

"All of them?"

"Yes," Helena answered. "You have a man at each one of those places that is your man for the operation, correct?"

"Yes," Felix answered.

"Yank them out of those places and tell them you'll be in touch but the stores are closed. Just walk away."

"I'll take care of it," Felix answered. "Anything else?"

"Neil Kline. He's a problem you need to take care of."

"I think we need to wait a little longer on that," White

added. “That needs to be the last thing we address on our way out of town. I fear if we do it right now, we’re walking into a trap. The police are watching him and watching him quite closely.”

“I don’t care,” Helena replied sharply. “You two are paid to deal with that kind of problem. Kline was there the night Javier and I were there, the night that ex-cop was there. He’s seen my face and he’s seen Javier’s more than once. I can’t believe we still have him running around out there. You need to take care of that and like right now.”

~

Paddy found the leasing agency for the Monte Club and then the owner. By early afternoon they were inside and out of the light rain. Once in Mac went immediately over to the floor-to-ceiling windows of the northwest corner. Their view of the processing plant was unobstructed. “What do you make for distance?” Mac asked Dick, who had a scope on it.

“This is telling me five-hundred and twenty yards to the loading dock sign,” Dick replied, and then dropped the glasses from his eyes. “That looks about right to me.”

“In other words, the distance of a good par five,” Mac replied agreeably and then turned to the group that now included not only Paddy and Erickson, but two of Erickson’s fellow DEA agents as well as Armstrong and Schmidt. “We’ll operate from here. Have the cars and SUVs ready to roll if need be.”

“Any idea when they might show?”

“Assuming they still come,” Dick muttered.

“I think they will,” Mac replied optimistically.

“Why?”

“Because they shot our guys. They did that for a reason.

I'm thinking the reason is there is a shipment coming in that they were looking to protect. We'll have to be patient and see if I'm right and if Paddy is right and this is the place where the avocados and other vegetables come. So everybody might as well settle in."

Mac's phone buzzed in his pocket. He took one look at it and breathed a sigh of relief. "Thank God."

"What is it?" Dick asked.

"A text from the chief. Riles. He's awake. He's going to make it."

"What about Rock?"

"He's coming around too."

"Finally. Finally, some good, good news."

"We need to go see them."

Mac and Dick left the group behind to set up. It took them about forty minutes to get back into downtown Minneapolis and Hennepin County Medical Center. They stopped at Rock's room first to find his wife Shirley and son Kelvin.

"He was awake briefly, but the doctors are keeping him sedated for the time being," Shirley reported, who was also a nurse. "There is a lot of pain from the wound to the abdomen and then the surgery, of course. He'll rest more comfortably this way."

They moved to Riles' room next where they were greeted outside of his room by his wife who, while a wreck from the last three days, looked to be breathing a little easier. Mac went to Jackie Riley and gave her a big hug.

"He's really weak, but go on in," she said. "He's been asking for you two."

Mac and Dick softly made their way into Riles' hospital room. The big man enveloped the entire hospital bed, tubes running out of him, the various monitors quietly humming and lightly beeping. Mac went to the left side of the bed and Dick to the right. Mac lightly clasped Riles' right wrist and his eyes fluttered open. He didn't move his head but eyed Mac and then shifted his eyes left to see Dick. He almost imperceptibly nodded and looked back to Mac and his eyes focused on Mac's belt. "What are you wearing?" Riles asked with a raspy voice.

Mac looked down and his shield was clipped to his belt just to the right of his gun. He looked back to Riles. "Someone came after my boys."

"Have you guys made any..." Riles took a ragged breath. "...any progress?"

"We think so," Dick responded quietly.

"How close?" Riles rasped as he looked back to Mac.

"We're working it hard," Mac replied. "We may have a line on them, a decent one."

"Let's just say Mac has..." Dick struggled for the right term. "Well, let's say he's gone to the limit and then some on this one."

"Good." Riles took a breath and it almost looked like to Mac he was summoning up some energy.

"What is it?" Mac asked.

"At the 280," Riles croaked out, "we..." He was struggling to breathe.

"It's okay, Riles. It can wait."

"No," he replied. "No...it can't. We were...set up."

"Yeah, you were," Mac replied, looking over to Dick, who was listening intently on the other side. "What are you thinking?"

"One shooter." Riles eyes closed again and he took a long breath. "One shooter said to...Fisher... 'Sorry Kurt.'"

Mac glanced quickly to Lich and then back down to Riles. "Are you telling me he said it as if he knew Fisher?

That he was telling him, *sorry Kurt, but you're no longer useful to us*?"

Riles nodded his head, took a deep breath and his eyes closed. "Fisher was dirty," he whispered. "He was dirty."

Dick was already reaching for his phone and walking away from the two of them. "Chief, I got something we need to get into right now."

Mac turned his attention back to Riles, who was breathing slowly. Summoning the energy to talk about Fisher had exhausted him. Their good friend might have been out of the woods, but he was going to have a long, *long* recovery in front of him. With his eyes still closed he whispered, "Mac?" Riles reached out his right hand.

"Yeah," Mac replied, leaning down, getting closer and clasping the hand. "I'm still here."

Pat's eyes opened again. "These guys go down," he croaked out, squeezing Mac's hand as hard as he could muster. "For Double Frank, Ortega, Shead, for everyone... these guys go down."

White was slumped in his desk chair sleeping when he was snapped awake by his phone. It was five minutes after midnight and Felix was calling. "Yeah, I'm here. What is it?"

"Have you heard from Neil Kline at all?" Felix asked.

"Neil?" White was rubbing his eyes, "No, why would I? You know the rules, no business on the phone. A rule you're violating."

"I know," Felix answered, not caring. "We've been carefully watching his house for the last three hours and there has been nothing."

"What does *carefully* and *nothing* mean?"

"Carefully means we're avoiding the two-man police team that seems to be watching for him."

"And nothing means?"

"No Neil. No sign of his Tahoe. The house is dark, has been since we started watching."

"What about his little driver, that Jockey Mike character. Have you seen him?"

"No," Felix answered. "His piece of shit car is parked in front of the house though."

"That probably means the two of them are out," White answered, now in the kitchen grabbing a bottle of water out of the refrigerator.

"Probably," Felix answered uncertainly. "But the cops watching him is a bit of a worry."

"Maybe," White replied. "Of course, if they're after him, maybe that tells us they're not..."

"After us."

Captain Peters arrived with four Internal Affairs detectives.

The building landlord slipped the key in the deadbolt and opened the door to the apartment. Peters followed the Internal Affairs detectives into Kurt Fisher's small apartment.

It took ten minutes of searching. There was a small panel in the clothes closet in the bedroom, down low behind three shoe boxes. Inside were eight white envelopes. Inside the envelopes were stacks of one-hundred-dollar bills.

"Five thousand in most of the envelopes, although the two stacked on the top had ten grand and twelve grand in them," the Internal Affairs detective reported. "It's certainly a good indicator he was on the take. We'll keep looking for more."

Peters nodded. "Be discreet," he stated as he pulled out his phone and called Chief Flanagan. "Good news and bad news."

"What's the good news?"

"It looks like Fisher was the rat," Peters replied and explained what had been found.

"What's the bad news?"

"Fisher was the rat. We can't learn anything from him."

"That's true," the chief replied, "but I think there is a silver lining here. Now these guys aren't getting any intel on what we're doing."

It was approaching one in the morning, now Monday morning. Mac was slumped in the metal folding chair, his arms folded across his chest, his shoeless feet crossed, his binoculars resting on the floor to his left. To his right sat Neil Kline. Mac wanted him onsite and with a pair of binoculars if the trucks and others showed. Six others were sacked out behind them on the floor in sleeping bags. Empty pizza boxes and fast food bags littered the long banquet table they'd set up.

"Man, this is boring," Kline remarked, leaning forward in his chair, elbows on his knees, a bottle of water in his hand.

"It's not like television."

"I know," Kline replied. "You know, the only show that I ever thought got it right was *The Wire*. At least my side of the game."

Mac smiled and nodded. "*Shiiiiiittt.*"

"Ahh yeah, you watched *The Wire*," Kline smiled, nodding. "I should have figured."

"What cop didn't? What drug dealer didn't?" Mac replied, turning to Kline. "Best. Show. Ever. End of discussion. It's not even close."

"For sure," Neil replied with a small smile. "For sure."

Mac was always up for a conversation about *The Wire*. "Who was your favorite character?"

"Proposition Joe."

"Really?" Mac replied, mildly surprised. "I'd have pegged you for Stringer Bell or maybe White Mike."

"White Mike, that's funny," Neil replied with a snort, thinking to the one of the few white drug dealers the show portrayed in its five-season run. "As for Russell 'Stringer' Bell, he was always trying to be someone else, trying to take all the money and get out of the game to become some sort of condo developer. But the truly respectable guy to me was Prop Joe. Joe knew who he was and didn't try to be anyone else. Joe was just Joe, always offering up a deal."

"Until time ran out on him," Mac replied. "When Stringer was killed at the end of Season Three, that was a shock, but when you thought about it, it was inevitable, it had to happen. Now when Prop Joe got knocked off, that was just kind of sad. I didn't necessarily see that one coming."

"So which character was your favorite?" Kline asked.

"Omar."

"No way! Omar? Seriously? Omar?"

"Surprised?"

"Duh. I'd have pegged you for sure as being a McNulty, Bunk or Lester fan. You know, the detectives. I mean, shit, you could be McNulty."

"McNulty was a great cop who was a total mess," Mac replied. "I'm not a mess. I've got my shit together."

"Oh, do you?"

"Yeah, I do," Mac replied seriously, but then got back to the discussion of the characters. "But don't get me wrong, I loved those depictions of the detectives, they were spot on—but Omar? What a character. Think about it. A gay chain-smoking black man with a sawed-off shot-gun and trench coat robbing drug dealers blind. Are you kidding me? He feared no one and smart? He was one smart dude. Any scene involving Omar was to be savored." Mac went into Omar's character. *"Don't get it twisted, I do some dirt too, but I ain't never put my gun on nobody who wasn't in the game."*

"A man must have a code," Neil quoted Bunk's reply.

"Oh, no doubt," Mac replied, quoting Omar back and the two of them had a brief chuckle.

Kline looked back to the processing plant, looked down at the floor and shook his head. "These guys you're after, they have no code. They just kill and they don't care. For my own sake, I hope they show up here."

"Me too."

"Alright, I guess it's our turn," Armstrong said with a yawn as he and Bonnie Schmidt came over. Mac was someone who could stay up for long stretches of time, but at two in the morning, having gone almost nonstop for three days with maybe four hours of sleep, he was ready to lay his head in the corner.

He fell to sleep immediately. It lasted only a few hours.

"Mac, Mac, Mac! Wake up."

"Yeah, yeah..." Mac burst up to see Dick rousting him awake. "What is it?"

"We might have a problem."

"What's that?" Mac asked as he rubbed his eyes.

"You know the list of businesses that Kline gave you, the fronts? The ones we've started watching to see who comes and goes?"

"Yeah, what about them?"

"They're all closed."

31

"MY NAME IS NOT MY NAME."

Mac and Dick wanted to see the situation for themselves and drove back into St. Paul. They avoided Kline's shop on Rice Street, but stopped at two of the others that Kline gave them, another auto repair shop and a donut shop. There was a sign on the front door of the donut shop, *Business Closed.* At the auto repair shop on Arcade Street they stopped at, two men who had worked there were loitering around, confused as to their suddenly changed employment status. In Linked-In parlance, they were seeking a new opportunity.

Dick approached one of them. "When did they close?"

"I guess today," the man named Arnie answered, appearing dressed for work in his stained light blue auto repair shirt and tattered navy blue pants.

"Did you have any warning?"

"No, nothing man," Arnie replied, confused. "We just show here today and boom, sign on the door."

"How was business?" Mac asked. "Slow?"

Arnie shook his head. "We were plenty busy every day. There's been at least five people who rolled by planning to drop off their cars. I guess they have to go somewhere else and so will I."

They left Arnie to commiserate with his fellow technicians now out of work and made a quick run by three other fronts, finding similar scenes: a couple of employees hanging around, confused, a sign on the doors and the operations shut down. After they drove by the last store, a furniture repair shop, Mac drove to a diner a few blocks away.

"What do you make of this?" Dick asked after coffee was delivered. "Did we spook them with taking Kline?"

Mac slowly stirred some half-and-half into his coffee, deep in thought. He took a slow, careful sip and then sat back. "Did we spook them by taking Kline? They don't necessarily know we did that. Fisher was their mole and they killed him, taking care of that loose end."

"Unless they have two moles."

"Then we're screwed," Mac replied with a weary smile. "I'm not even going to consider that one at this point."

"Still, to up and close these places this fast with no warning, with the employees having no sense it was coming. Something is definitely up."

"True, but it might have already been in the works," Mac answered calmly. "Like Kline said, they weren't running money up to Rogers anymore. This White told him that they were changing up the operation. This could all be part of that change up."

"As important as Neil Kline supposedly is, don't you think they might have clued him in on that?"

"Not with us watching him. Kline told us that. They weren't telling him anything so he didn't know. They wanted him to sit still hoping we'd be so focused on him, we didn't pursue anything else."

"That's a fair point."

"Also, remember Neil described the operation as a—"

"Siloed operation, yeah, yeah," Dick answered with a disgusted wave. "Still, you know what this means."

Mac nodded. "They're not just rearranging the deck chairs. They're making a *big* change up."

"At best. At worst, they're leaving town all together," Dick moaned and sat back into the booth, bitter at the thought of their prey slipping away again. "What do we do? How do we find these guys? We can't let them slink away on us."

Mac folded his arms, sat back and closed his eyes to think. Dicky Boy's concerns were far from unfounded. It was legitimate to ask if they'd spooked the cartel by taking Kline. Again, how would they know? Were they looking for Kline, couldn't find him and thus concluded he was talking to the police and so that caused them to shut everything down? Again, how would they know? They'd cut off their own information source by killing Fisher. Did they have another source on the inside feeding them information, either intentionally or inadvertently and thus knew that Kline was talking? It was a possibility he couldn't discount, although they'd kept any information about Kline to a very tight and limited circle of people. While not dismissing the possibility entirely, he just didn't buy it.

"So why the shutdown?" he muttered, leaning forward to the table and staring down into his coffee cup. If he assumed that they didn't know about Kline, what could be the explanation? An organization like the Lazaro Cardenas Cartel, while not intimidated by the police, would nevertheless respect the ability of state and federal law enforcement to investigate, pressure, and disrupt, if not flat out destroy their operation once aware of its existence. Upon further reflection, *that* was what Mac thought was going on here. When in doubt, go with the most logical answer. "I'm thinking they shut it down because it's getting too hot. They decided it was time to cut and run."

"They're moving it altogether?"

Mac nodded. "That would be my guess. I'm thinking that they did the 280 to give themselves the time and space to make the move. The sudden closing of all the fronts fits with that approach. And now they're probably cleaning up any loose ends and taking care of any last business and then they're gone."

"We were too late, I guess," Dick replied. "Or too open and obvious in what we were doing. Hell, if you're right by the time we were engaging in your little ruse on Kline, they'd already decided what they were doing. They're probably as good as gone."

"Maybe, maybe not," Mac replied, not yet ready to give up.

"What are you thinking?"

Mac took a drink of coffee and leaned forward. "Let's just assume for the moment they don't know we've taken Kline. Kline was important to their operation here, correct?"

"It sure seemed like it."

"So if you were moving your operation, might you want him to move with you if you still valued him?"

"I suppose, but of course you've made that rather difficult, haven't you?"

"He doesn't have his phone any longer, *but we do*," Mac answered. "We're monitoring it and it's been quiet. We're watching his house and it doesn't appear that anyone has come to knock on the door looking for him, right?"

"No, Weed and Martinez would have seen that."

"Right. So if they're not looking to keep him, use him and so forth, what's the flipside of that?"

"He's a liability."

"A loose end who knows much more than you'd want someone to know. He can identify Javier Alvarado and Laura Peterson. He knows it's the Lazaro Cardenas Cartel. He can identify this Mr. White and the killer Felix. I bet you the corner boys or these guys Kline hired to work these repair shops don't know they're working for the cartel, or even if they suspect they're with a cartel or something like it, they don't know which one."

"Probably true."

"Yet Kline does know this, so..."

"You might want to take care of him like you took care of Orr. If you're fleeing town, why leave someone behind who could tube you?"

"Right," Mac replied. "We still have Weed and Martinez on Kline's house, right?"

"Yes."

"Pull them off."

"Wait? You *don't* want to watch the house?"

"No, I do, but with new people. I had those two watching so as to be seen, so if the cartel was also monitoring Neil they would see we were too."

"So that if Neil was missing, they wouldn't think we had Neil."

"Right," Mac answered. "Because if we're looking and they're looking, then they might assume Neil is what?"

"Hiding."

"Exactly, my friend. So now let's pull Weed and Martinez off and have them make it kind of obvious. I want it to look like we've lost some interest. Then let's get two new teams on that with vans conducting a looser, more distant surveillance."

"On the theory that?"

"The cartel might still be trying to find him and may get

more aggressive in their efforts," Mac answered. "Maybe as a backup plan to that processing plant, we get on them that way."

"What do you want to do with Weed and Martinez?"

Mac told him.

"Okay, that makes sense and that's a possible third way to get onto them," Dick replied with a smirk. "I'll take care of that. What are you and I doing?"

"We're going to have a good and hearty breakfast and then we're going back up to Monticello. That's still our best bet."

~

"No sign?" Mr. White asked as he held the door open.

"No," Felix replied as he came in the back door to White's house from his long night of sitting on Neil Kline's house. "No sign of him anywhere."

The two of them repaired to White's office, which was now cluttered with cardboard boxes, the packing up of the office nearly complete.

"Are the police still watching Neil's house?"

Felix shook his head. "They had a unit watching the house, but they pulled off a couple of hours ago."

White sat down in his office chair while Felix cautiously inched back a curtain to check the street. "You're thinking they pulled off Kline's house because why?"

"They lost interest or..."

"They have him," White finished. "One thing about that, though."

"Which is?"

"If they did have him, Neil would ask for his lawyer. I haven't gotten that call."

"Call and check with our lawyer."

Mr. White did as Felix asked, calling the downtown lawyer they used for Neil. There had been no call from Neil or from the police. It was all quiet.

"Are the police sitting on Neil's repair shop?"

Felix shook his head. "They pulled off there too a couple of hours ago."

White felt Felix's unease. The question was whether the unease was of Neil being out of pocket or having to call Javier or Helena and inform them of that. They may have waited too long to address the issue.

"You know Neil is not dumb. He gets hauled in by the police. We take out Orr. He pretty much knows we shot up the 280. We take him off money collection. We tell him to stay in the repair shop and keep his head low. We change up big parts of the operation. He might perceive it as if we're easing him out and now we close all the shops, including his. So what does Neil think?"

"That we'll want to take him out."

"Right, so he goes into hiding," White replied. "If I'm in his shoes, that's what I would do. I mean, if you started sensing Javier was unhappy with you and suddenly viewed you as a liability, what would you do?"

"He would never do that."

White waved dismissively. "I know, I know, you're family. But if he did or if you sensed it, what would you do?"

"I'd get myself somewhere safe so I could think about... what to do, where to go, who I could trust. He was telling Orr to run. He just might be doing the same."

"Right," White answered. "After tonight's delivery we're done here. We'll process everything at the farm, a place Neil knows nothing about, get it packaged, have our people make deliveries and take payment and in the meantime, by

Wednesday afternoon you and I are in Kansas City looking for places to live."

"And Neil? What if he decides to go to the police? What if he's already gone to the police?"

"What can he really give them?"

"Our names."

"Which are not our names, after all. In Chicago, I was Mr. Black. Here I'm Mr. White and when we go to Kansas City I'll be Mr. Gray. My name is not my name. And around here you're Felix Calderon. In Chicago, you were Felix—"

"Cardenas and in Kansas City, I'll become Felix something else."

"Right," Mr. White answered. "In the meantime, today, we keep looking for Neil and if he comes out of hiding..."

"Boom."

32

"I MIGHT HAVE TAKEN A MOMENT TO MEASURE THAT ONE UP."

With the crew still up watching the processing plant, Mac and Lich went about the process of solidifying support if and when it was needed.

It started with a meeting with Flanagan and Captain Peters. Flanagan placed another call up to the chief in Monticello with whom he'd been chatting for the last twenty-four hours since a focus of the investigation was now his jurisdiction. That led to an early afternoon meeting back up in Monticello with Flanagan, the Monticello chief and the Wright and Sherburne County sheriffs. Both sheriffs were needed since Monticello rested on the south side of the Mississippi River.

"If these trucks show up, the ones we're looking for, they might well have drugs on them," Mac explained.

"To be honest," Dick added, "we're really hoping they do."

"Agreed," Mac nodded in assent. "But if they do, we don't believe they'll be unloading the drugs at this processing plant. It will be somewhere else and it could be anywhere on either side of the river, which is why we've called both you sheriffs in. We could be in Wright or Sherburne counties."

"It might not be either," Sherburne County Sheriff Bobick replied with a wry smile. "But all us counties around here watch each other's backs. I can make a call or two and tell folks we could have some interesting action the next few nights."

"I appreciate it, Sheriff," Mac answered.

"And you think these guys have something to do with the shooting at the 280?" Wright County Sheriff Hammer asked.

"Yes," Dick answered.

"And you think these guys are part of a Mexican drug cartel?" Sheriff Bobick inquired with scorn in his voice.

"We do," Mac replied. "And if there are drugs and we do track the trucks to another place, things could get dicey. If they were willing to do the 280, they will not go down quietly. You should know that."

Sheriff Bobick waved Mac off. "We're in no matter what, and if it involves what happened at the 280, then we're really in. You call, we deliver."

After the meetings with the Monticello chief and county sheriffs, Mac and Dick made their way back to their perch at the Monte Club.

"Anything?" Mac asked Bonnie Schmidt upon their return, which included a stop to pick up a box of fresh sandwiches and a Styrofoam cooler of assorted beverages.

"The odd truck coming and going," she replied as she dropped the binoculars from her eyes while sitting cross-legged on the floor. "But the trucks have all been singular and none of them all white. There's been no extra security. We've seen nothing unusual that would raise any eyebrows."

"Given they pulled out of everything in St. Paul, do you

think these guys will ever show?" Detective Armstrong asked.

"I don't know, Tommy," Mac replied. "If they do, it'll be soon. Otherwise, they've flown the coop."

Felix sat in the backseat of the Range Rover a block down from Neil's house. His two men manned the front. It was nearing eight thirty in the evening and night was rolling in. *Where the hell was he?* Felix kept wondering. The more he thought about it, the more he thought White was right. Neil went into hiding.

He checked his watch and then his phone beeped. He reached for the phone and checked the screen for the update. Neil Kline would have to wait.

"Let's go," Felix ordered and his man started up the truck. With his phone he selected another number. "Gear up."

"They're moving out," Shawn McRyan reported into the radio from his perch in the back of the black surveillance panel van. "Black Range Rover proceeding south. They'll come by you in two blocks. Two guys in the front seat, another in the back."

"Copy," Vice Unit Detective Louis Ruiz answered and looked to his right.

"There they are," Ruiz's partner, Janice Dooley said, spotting them through the gap between two houses.

"Give them a block...okay...and go," Ruiz suggested and his partner dropped their car into gear. "Shawn, are you coming up behind?" Ruiz asked as they turned onto the street and eyed the Range Rover a block plus ahead, signaling to take a right turn.

"We're turning around right now."

"Let's see where these guys head off to," Ruiz muttered.

~

"Car pulling in," Martinez reported.

"That's her?" Weed replied.

~

Shawn McRyan was riding shotgun in the surveillance van peering attentively ahead. They were rotating the tail with Ruiz and now an unmarked State Patrol unit that was looped in. The Range Rover was traveling west on Interstate 694 approaching the junction where 694 from the east and 494 from the south interchanged and weaved in Maple Grove. The Range Rover veered to the right, taking the two lanes heading northwest toward St. Cloud.

Shawn reached for the radio. "Mac?"

"Mac here."

"We're on 94 now, just passing Weaver Lake Road in Maple Grove. I'd say there is a decent chance we're coming your way.

~

"Interesting," Mac mused, now at the floor to ceiling windows with his binoculars up to his eyes, focusing in on the loading bay area of the warehouse. It felt like something was brewing and it was coming their way. And for once, they seemed to have some pieces in place.

He looked over to Dick and said, "Let's put Monticello, Wright and Sherburne Counties on alert that we might be making a call."

~

"Ruiz, back off just a bit now," Shawn McRyan counseled from the passenger seat into the radio. "The traffic is lightening and we have an idea of where they might be going."

"Copy," was the quick reply.

Ninety seconds later the Range Rover took the expected exit. Ruiz was getting ready to signal when he looked up to the top of the exit ramp.

~

"Hold here on the green," Felix ordered.

"Boss?" his driver asked, confused.

Felix was looking back to see if anyone exited behind them.

"Boss, it's going to go yellow."

"Go."

~

"Shawn, we're skipping the exit," Ruiz reported.

"Why?"

"He's just sitting at the top with a green light. It's possible he's looking back."

"Copy."

Shawn was another half mile back of Ruiz in the van. As they approached the exit, he could see the stoplight was still green. They slowed a bit and they could see the Range Rover at the top. Just as they were reaching the bottom of the exit ramp, the Range Rover took the left turn to go back over the bridge.

"Okay, we're taking the exit," Shawn reported and then called for Mac and explained what they'd just experienced. "I think we're clean, but he's definitely checking his six. You'll want to keep an eye out for a black Range Rover."

Mac put the night vision binoculars to his eyes and focused on the processing plant. Kline was to Mac's right. Dick manned a scope located another window down with Erickson from the DEA. The Monticello police chief was to Mac's left with a portable radio in his right hand. They had four vehicles in the back, all unmarked and the Wright County sheriff had his men, including his Emergency Response Unit staged farther away.

"The Range Rover is turning left toward the plant, Mac," Shawn reported. "We're backing off and we're going to double back to the Kwik Trip station to wait."

And there it was. The Range Rover motored down the avenue, signaled and turned left into the loading dock area for the processing plant.

"Neil, tell me what you see," Mac ordered.

Neil put the binoculars to his eyes and peered at the plant.

"That's Felix and those are two of his main guys. I recognize the both of them. Tito on the right and Jorge on the left."

"Mac, I have two more vehicles coming," Erickson reported.

Mac looked back to the street and two more vehicles approached, an Escalade and a dual cab Chevy Silverado. Both of those vehicles parked next to the Range Rover. Seven more men in total piled out. After a brief huddle, the men spread out and stood post. Two walked the perimeter looking around.

"Is it me, or do they seem awfully paranoid?" Dick mused lightly.

"It's not you," Mac replied and then looked to Neil. "The other men, do you recognize them?" Mac handed the night vision binoculars back.

Neil spent a few minutes scanning the area and finally nodded. "I think the ones talking to Felix right now are the two guys Jockey Mike and I picked up at the airport that I told you about. It's hard to tell for sure at night, but shaved heads, thick necks—they sure look like them. The others I don't. Like I said, sometimes they bring in extra help from California, the CA-57s."

"So gang guys then?" the Monticello chief asked.

"They're a little more than gang guys, I'd say," Mac remarked. "They move around a lot like soldiers or professional security."

"The CA-57s would have guys who engaged in if not military training, at least some basic training on how to shoot, track people, surround them and whatnot," Erickson stated. "These guys carry themselves as if they've had at least some of that."

"How armed will they be?" the Monticello chief asked.

"Only heavily," Erickson answered with a little wry smile. "Those guys absolutely won't fuck around. They'll have firepower within reach."

"Mac!" Shawn's voice bellowed out from the radio.

"Go, Shawn."

"I have three great big all-white semi-tractor trailers rolling by me right now, coming your way."

"Here they come," Dick called out excitedly. "This is it."

The three semi-tractor trailers slowly pulled into the loading dock area and backed in one by one. The trailers sealed to the black rubber bumper around the loading dock door. From their distant perch there was no way to see what was being unloaded, although the tops of the trailers were not opened. Meanwhile Felix's men were in something of a rectangular formation around the trucks. Their view was focused on the immediate area around the processing plant.

"They don't seem to have any night vision equipment," Mac observed.

"No, they don't," Dick agreed. "Just using the naked eye."

The men on security post didn't seem to be looking up the hill to the south and the abandoned club in the grove of thick trees. The other men stood patiently at their posts, scanning the area. Interestingly they all wore a light coat of some kind, but when one of the men pivoted, Mac could make out a bulge in the small of the man's back where his weapon was stored. Nothing needed to be said, but everyone in the room knew the men watching post around the trucks would not hesitate to throw down. They worked for the drug cartel, that was part of the job description.

Mac turned to the group. "Let's get geared up." While Mac continued to watch everyone else pulled on their vests, checked their weapons and got themselves ready.

It was approaching midnight when Mac spotted one of the drivers coming out a door and jumping up into the cab of his truck. Soon the other two drivers followed and the men standing security moved toward their own vehicles.

Mac kept his eyes on Felix, who jumped into the back seat of the Range Rover. The rest of the security got into the other trucks they'd arrived in. They set up a convoy with Felix's Range Rover in the lead, followed by the semis and then the other two trucks pulling up the rear.

"Okay, we're moving here," Mac reported. "Let's go."

Mac hopped into a Suburban with Dick, Wright County Sheriff Hammer and Erickson with Hammer driving. The convoy turned south onto County Road 25 and drove right by the long winding entrance up to the Monte Club. Shawn was the first tail, pulling past the club entrance as Mac's group made their way down.

"Let Shawn take the lead at first," Mac stated from his perch in the passenger seat. He then looked back to Erickson and Lich. "This is the hard part. We don't know where they're going or what we're going to find."

"Leave that to me," Hammer answered confidently, his hand draped casually over the wheel. "These are my roads."

The convoy weaved its way west through the Wright County countryside, out in farm country. Little cover and low light prevented them from following that closely, but the flat land, the multi-vehicle size of the convoy and the light emanating from it let Mac and Company keep a distant yet watchful eye on them.

"Have everyone fall back except us," Mac suggested ten minutes into the drive.

~

Felix raised his radio. "Juan, anyone following?"

"No. There is one set of lights trailing well back of us. They look like normal car or truck lights."

Felix's driver knowingly took the left turn off Country Road 37.

"Keep alert."

~

Ahead, the lights of the distant convoy started veering right. Mac looked to the GPS display in the dashboard.

"Country Road 37 turns back slightly northwest there," the Monticello chief reported.

"Does it then take a hard left?" Erickson asked.

They could see ahead that the convoy was indeed making a left turn.

"That's Bishop. It's a short dirt road."

"That leads to where?" Mac asked.

"Another dirt road. 60th Street."

~

"This is the turn ahead, right, boss?" Felix's driver asked.

"Yes, but pull past and stop. The drivers know where to go from here."

~

Sheriff Hammer approached the end of the dirt road and the right turn onto 60th Street. Mac was focused to the west and the convoy in the distance, still able to make out the small rectangular yellow lights along the top of the trailers for the three semis. Mac kept running through his head that Felix was acting very cautious. There was the extremely heavy security presence and there was that stop at the top of the exit ramp coming into St. Michael. To Mac, Felix was giving off the vibe of paranoia.

"What do you think?" the chief asked, a hundred yards from the turn.

To their right was a soybean field, short enough that he could see well into the distance to the right, but tall enough that they themselves could not be seen. He could see the convoy to the right and it looked to be making a course change again as there was a slowing and the semis almost looked stopped.

"Stop short of the end of the road and kill the headlights."

Hammer pulled to a stop. Mac climbed out of the Suburban, but with the night vision binoculars to his eyes. Hammer joined him with his own set of binoculars.

"They're turning left, Sheriff."

"Yes, that's Colbert Avenue, I believe," Hammer replied. "That road there is a dead-end, Mac. Goes down a piece and ends in some woods as I recall."

"What else is back there?"

"I'm not sure. We'll need to look at the map."

~

"You see anything, boss?" Tito asked.

Felix looked back down the road they'd traveled. He then looked up into the sky and neither saw nor heard anything. He took one last long look back down the road and finally shook his head and breathed a little easier. "No, it's clear. Let's go get this unloaded and then get out of here."

Jorge got behind the wheel of the Range Rover and took them down the long, straight and level dirt road that then angled to the left into what looked like a tunnel that had formed under the canopy of tall trees. Once they emerged from under the canopy they drove into a clearing that housed a large aluminum pole barn and a small, two-story white clapboard farmhouse. The first semi was already inside the barn while the other two waited their turn to drive inside and be unloaded.

~

Mac had Sheriff Hammer and Monticello Chief Baker order the Emergency Response Team, additional officers and deputies and Erickson's fellow DEA agents to gather at the end of Bishop Road. In the meantime, to get a quick lay of the land, Mac sent Shawn and his partner up ahead to do a drive-by of where the semis had turned onto Colbert Road. It took them just under ten minutes to loop back.

"What did you see?" Mac asked.

"We slowed some as we went by," Shawn answered, looking down at the map on the hood of Sheriff Hammer's Suburban. "I was kind of surprised they didn't leave anyone at the end of the road as a sentry. But since they didn't, we drove on by and then looped back and gave it another pass. As we slowed I really tried to get a look back into that grove of trees. I couldn't make anything at all definitive out, but you could see some light filtering out from back in those woods so there is something going on back in there."

"What about the condition of the road?" Mac asked.

"Looked pretty smooth, cousin," Shawn answered with a nod. "It's dirt, but it looked flat. You'd need it to be if you're taking those big rigs back there."

Mac reported those findings back to Chief Baker and Sheriff Hammer.

"The sheriff is right," Chief Baker stated. "That road

dead-ends back there, at least according to our maps here." Mac had pulled up Google maps on his computer and it seemed to verify that as well. He was also interested in the grove of trees. In the middle of that grove looked to be a large barn. That was probably the light source Shawn spoke of.

"Pole barn," Sheriff Hammer added, "big old metal kind." He took a closer look at the satellite image, zooming in closer. "That looks like a newer barn at the time these satellite images were taken. The roof is plain silver metal, but it has that new kind of shine to it."

"Not there for fifteen or twenty years?" Mac asked.

"I don't think so. It's newer. Look at the cement apron around it and tell me what you see," the sheriff prompted.

Mac took another look and nodded. "It's bright in color, clean."

"Right," the sheriff replied. "That's a new cement apron. That's a new structure."

"Is it normal that the cement apron would be that much larger than the barn itself?" Mac asked. "Not that I spend a lot of time on farms, but from the few times I have been and seen places like this, I don't really recall this much cement."

The sheriff took another look and nodded. "It is a bit odd."

"Why might you do that?" Mac asked with a leading tone.

"Perhaps because it's not just an apron. It's also a..." The sheriff smiled. "It's also a cover, perhaps a roof over something."

"I was hoping you'd say that," Mac replied.

"It might be nothing too," the sheriff cautioned, "but I don't see that setup terribly often out here and when I have—"

"That's at least one of the reasons why."

"Correct."

Based on the Google maps image, the dirt road known as Colbert Road, was straight and then perhaps fifty yards short of the woods, turned to the left at something of a forty-five-degree angle and led into the thick grove of trees. Once the road emerged out of the trees, it led to one end of the barn. Out of the other end the road continued and looped back creating something of a circular driveway.

"What are our options?" Dick asked.

There was quiet as everyone contemplated the map, the resources they had and the opposition they thought they were up against.

"What if we take them on the road once they leave?" Dick suggested. "Box them in?"

"That assumes you know what route they're going to take," Mac replied. "I'd assume they'd go back the way they just came, but there is no guarantee. Whereas right now we have them corralled in one location with as best I can tell, only one way out."

"If we're looking at taking them where they are, then there are really two options as I see it," Sheriff Hammer surmised. "We wait at the end of Colbert and block them in or we go charging up that road. I don't really like either option, to be honest."

"Me neither," Chief Baker replied and then looked to Mac. "What do you think?"

Mac paused for a moment and exhaled. "I think no matter what we do, they're not going to just raise their hands and give up. They're going to throw down so you all better understand that part of it. The only question then is, where tactically do we want that to happen?" He leaned down on the hood and rested his chin on his steepled hands and studied the map, focusing on the dirt road leading back to the grove of trees. "You know, there is a third option of the two Sheriff Hammer suggested. How long do you figure it'll take to unload those trucks?"

Felix took the cigar from his mouth and checked his watch. 2:40 a.m. The last of the panels were being power drilled back on the top of the third long-haul truck. The other two rested outside the barn idling, waiting to depart back to Mexico.

The whole process took nearly two hours. Inside the barn the drugs were unloaded from the truck. In the first truck was the heroin. The second truck held cocaine, and in the third, the half loads of meth and marijuana. The drugs were offloaded, put on the small conveyor belt that led to the processing plant underneath the pole barn where it would be processed and made ready for sale. It would then be distributed not only to the Twin Cities, but throughout the Upper Midwest through their crews in Chicago, Milwaukee, Des Moines, Fargo, Omaha and Kansas City. From there further distribution would be made out into the suburbs and rural areas. It was this kind of facility that would have to be built down in Kansas City.

At the same time the delivery was being unloaded the sealed and bound bundles of cash were placed in the same compartments. Since they were moving their base of operations from the Twin Cities, the money load was bigger than usual. It didn't all fit in the compartments on top of the trailers. As a result, six large pallets were loaded inside the last trailer. Each pallet included multiple stacks of cardboard boxes filled with cash.

"They never search when we go *into* Mexico," one of the drivers said to Felix. "Only sometimes when we come out."

Felix looked to his two CA-57 friends, Sylvester and Juan, who'd been keeping an eye on the close perimeter around the barn.

"It's quiet," Juan reported, his rifle hoisted over his shoulder.

"Let's just get moving," Felix replied more anxiously then normal. He wanted to get on the road.

"We're good in like two minutes," the driver answered. "The trucks are running. We're just finishing securing it all."

Felix got into the back of his Range Rover as the trucks began lining up. As the first truck began to pull forward he called White. "We're pulling out now."

"Everything loaded?"

"All compartments are full, plus six big pallets."

"Six? Wow!" White responded gleefully. "That's huge."

"It is."

"Good," White responded. "Helena's plane is at the airport, fueled and ready to take off at 6:00 a.m. We will be in Kansas City by 8:00 and away from here."

~

Mac was lying flat on the ground twenty feet into the end of a grove of trees to the southeast of the barn, perhaps fifty to sixty yards away from a grouping of men huddling at the front of the long-haul trucks. He, along with his cousin Shawn who was ten feet to his left, had been in position for a half hour, observing. In the interim two of Erickson's men from the DEA had taken the same approach from the southeast and positioned themselves farther to their right where the woods were a bit denser. As

Mac glanced farther to his right, he could just make out the movement of two more of Erickson's men approaching. This would make six of them positioned to the south and southeast of the barn in something of a crescent moon formation.

"They're getting ready to leave," Mac whispered into the radio. "Come down the road now. Let's pin them in."

"Copy," Sheriff Hammer answered.

The Emergency Response Team's armored truck led the way down the road and stopped right at the point where the road turned to the southeast at a forty-five-degree angle. Their main grouping moved into formation there. The sheriff had called in additional backup that was set back as another layer of defense at the end of Colbert that could move forward when called.

"Mac, we're set."

"Copy," Mac replied. A minute later the third long-haul driver got up into his cab. The first truck revved the engine and started its slow creep forward. "They're moving out."

"Copy," Hammer answered back.

The three semi-tractor trailers slowly started moving forward with the three SUVs falling in behind the long trucks.

Mac had anticipated that the smaller trucks would lead out. He suddenly worried about what the semi-tractors would do. "Here they come," Mac reported. "The semis are leading it out, not the SUVs. They might try to ram through when they see you."

"*Copy that*, Mac," Hammer replied appreciatively.

~

Ramon tried to stifle a yawn as he emerged from the canopy

of trees and began to accelerate a little more as he pulled forward.

"Light 'em up!" Hammer ordered.

The ERT truck, the one Suburban to its left and the three to the right hit their headlights, spotlights and light bars all at once. There were twenty men with cover and weapons drawn.

"We got cops! We got a lot of cops! *What do I do?*" Ramon screamed into the radio.

"Boss, we got cops!" Jorge, the driver exclaimed.

"*What?*" White yelled back into the phone. "The police?"

"Ram them! *Ram them now!*" Felix roared, pulling his own gun out.

The first semi charged ahead at the police.

The police opened fire and Felix and his men saw the first semi's front end suddenly drop and the truck stopped in place. Then the front end of the second semi dropped the same way. They'd taken the tires out. They were backed up and couldn't move laterally.

"Get out of the vehicles with your hands up!" a voice boomed over a speaker. "Get out of the vehicles now! *Now!*"

"We're trapped!" Jorge reported.

"*Go back! Go back!*" Felix ordered and then to White he screamed, "Get Helena and get the hell out of here!"

~

Mac and the others had moved forward to the edge of the tree line.

"*Here they come!*" Mac yelled as the last SUV in the convoy came roaring back their direction. Mac opened fire on the first SUV at the front, taking out the tires and engine as did Shawn and the two DEA men, stopping the first SUV in its tracks.

The men inside were not going without a fight as the doors on the opposite side of the SUV opened.

~

"They're behind us too!" Jorge screamed. "They just hammered Sylvester and Juan's truck! They're pinned down!"

"Go to the right! Go to the right! Go around them!" Felix yelled.

Jorge veered to the right.

~

"Mac! Here comes the Range Rover!" Shawn yelled.

The DEA men with the M4s pinned down the men from the Escalade. Mac quickly rolled to his left to take cover behind another large tree, leaned to the right and fired at the Range Rover as it careened behind and past the disabled Cadillac. Shawn took out the tires on the front and Mac fired higher.

~

Glass shattered, spraying everyone inside.

"Auugghhh!" Felix moaned.

"Boss!" Tito yelled back as Felix slumped over, hit high up in his left chest. "*Boss!*"

Jorge yanked hard right on the wheel, which forced the SUV away from the gunfire and hard forward, crashing into the side of the pole barn.

~

Shawn and Mac moved to their left, maintaining cover along the edge of the trees. As Mac reloaded he quickly glanced right to see the Silverado trying to get around the immobilized Escalade, taking fire from the DEA men.

Mac glanced back left to the pole barn. "Shit!" Three men came running out of the barn. They all had assault rifles and they were coming right at him.

"*Shawn!* Get down! Get *down!*" Mac yelled as he dove behind a tree as the men from the barn opened fire, bullets pelting the trees, mostly to his left toward Shawn.

Mac had good cover behind the big base of the tree. He looked left and saw Shawn down low, pinned and vulnerable behind a much smaller tree. There was another thicker tree farther back into the woods if he could get to it. Mac dropped to a knee and quickly peered around the right side of his tree and zoned in on the man nearest to him with an assault rifle and fired. And kept firing.

The man went down, hit in the head. It had the desired effect. The other two men suddenly pivoted in Mac's direction. Mac popped up and move to his right for a better angle on the second man and quickly fired off four more rounds. One hit the second man in the leg, sending him to the ground.

"Shawn, go! *Go! Go!*"

Mac glanced quickly left to see Shawn scrambling back to the better cover.

There was still the other man and then another two came running out of the barn.

Now Mac was the target and suddenly he was out of room to move.

"Boss! *Boss!*" Tito yelled.

Felix was slumped over and groaned, his whole left side searing in pain.

"We... we have to get out of here, boss! We have to get out of here!" Tito screamed as he

opened the second door on the passenger side. He reached under Felix's arms and dragged him out of the Range Rover while Jorge scrambled across the center console and dove out the open front passenger door. He pushed himself up and helped Tito. "Come on, boss," Tito grunted as he dragged Felix out of the Range Rover.

"We can't shoot our way out of here. We need wheels," Jorge exclaimed.

"Out back behind the barn is a truck. I know where the keys are," Tito ordered, lifting Felix up and over his shoulder.

Mac was totally defensive, caught behind a tree and he could feel the three shooters closing in. With his back pressed up against the tree he quickly glanced to his left to the north and could tell the cavalry was caught up in gunfire back that direction with the Silverado and the last semi that had backed up into the woods choking off the approach of his support.

His tree was getting pelted by bullets, debris from the tree raining down on him. Mac couldn't hold the position. He was a sitting duck. The three men firing on him knew they were going down. But before they did, they wanted to get themselves a cop.

Twenty feet farther into the woods there were two larger trees that had blown down. The trunks were massive. If he could get there he'd have cover.

He glanced back to the right and could see Shawn, who'd now found deeper cover and was slamming in a new magazine and gestured to Mac that he was moving to his left. Shawn took a step left and unleashed, drawing all the shooters' attention.

"*Mac, go!* Go!" Shawn screamed as he fired away.

Mac took off at a full sprint, leaped and dove over the two downed tree trunks, landing hard on his left shoulder. "*Fuck*," he groaned as he felt his left shoulder pop out of its socket.

He pushed himself up with his right hand and peered over the top log. One of the men from the barn was down. The other two had now pivoted toward Shawn. Mac had one good arm. He raised his right arm and focused on the man to the left and fired.

The man turned toward him, but Mac didn't stop. He just kept shooting.

The man went down.

There was one more man.

Then there was a cascade of fire from Mac's right. Two DEA men mowed down the last man with their M4s.

Mac fell to the ground.

"Mac! *Mac!* Are you hit?" Shawn cried out as he approached.

"Nah," Mac replied with a grimace, sitting on the ground, his left knee bent up, his hands clasped around the knee and pulling it to his chest.

"What are you doing?" Shawn asked, confused.

"Trying to pop my left shoulder back in," Mac replied. "I did this one other time and a buddy had me do this and..." There was an audible pop and the arm was back in the socket. "Ahh..." Mac breathed heavy and lay back against the fallen tree trunks. "Fuck, that hurt."

"Listen," Shawn reported calmly, looking back over to the barn. "I think the guys in the Range Rover, the one that Felix was in, are still on the loose."

"Where?" Mac growled, pushing himself up.

~

Tito held up Felix against the backside of the barn. His boss's whole left side of his body was blood-soaked and he could see two clear wounds to the shoulder that were oozing. Jorge came running out the door. "I've got the keys to that van they use to bring the workers out here."

Tito looked to Felix. "Can you walk, boss?"

Felix nodded weakly. "Let's go."

"You get him to the van," Jorge said to Tito. "I'll cover us."

"Okay boss, take this gun," Tito said, putting it in Felix's good hand. "I've got mine. Let's go."

~

Mac ignored the throbbing of his left shoulder and sprinted

along the tree line, focused on the area south of the barn. Shawn was twenty feet behind him doing the same. Just south of the barn there was another dense grouping of shorter trees, scrub bushes and buck thorn perhaps fifty feet wide. There was a rough narrow path on either side. Mac looked to Shawn and silently waved with his left hand for Shawn to take the right path.

Mac took the left.

Jorge looked back to his right. Tito and Felix were limping toward the van that was parked along the edge of the trees. There was a rough path back through the woods that led to a narrow dirt road that ran off the back of the farm property. It was the road they used to bring the workers in to operate the processing facility.

If they could just get there they could slip away. Then he caught movement to his left.

The first shot hit him in the left arm. He never knew where the second shot hit him.

Mac glanced quickly right and through the brush could see the man down and Shawn slowly approaching him. He quickly pivoted back left and coming into view were two more men. One of them was wounded, being carried along by the bigger man.

Mac planted his feet.

Tito looked back upon hearing the gunfire. "Jorge!"

"Keep...moving," Felix grunted, struggling along. They were twenty feet from the truck.

Someone whistled.

Tito spun to his left.

Mac dropped the first man with two shots.

The second man, Felix, slowly turned and tried to raise the gun in his right hand.

Mac fired twice more, sending Felix careening backward into the rear of the panel van.

With his gun still focused on the killer, Mac cautiously approached, watching Felix slowly slump down to the ground.

Felix was spitting blood out of his mouth as he tried to breathe, riddled with wounds. Mac thought for just a brief instant that he could call for a paramedic. Maybe Felix could be saved and they could interrogate him and learn something about the cartel, about White, about Laura Peterson, about their future plans with their organization. The DEA could gain needed intel on the flow of drugs throughout the country. The man was a potential fountain of vital information.

Then, just as quickly he thought of Ortega, Riles, Rock, Double Frank, Cruz, Shead and the two Minneapolis cops. What proof was there that Felix was the shooter at the 280? What proof did they have that Felix shot Rafael Cruz or murdered Sam Shead? All they had was Neil Kline's statement that if it happened, Felix would have done it.

That wasn't enough.

The DEA and everyone else would just have to find another way.

"This one is for Tommy," Mac whispered as he pulled the trigger, putting one last bullet between Felix's eyes.

Shawn approached from the right, gun in his right hand now hanging loosely to the side. "I got the other goon back there."

Mac nodded and looked back down at Felix.

"Looks like you took care of him," Shawn said evenly.

Mac turned to his right to take the measure of his cousin, who was absolutely flatlined. "A hell of a night, cuz. How are you doin'? You okay?" He knew that Shawn had fired his gun only one other time and certainly not in anything like this.

Shawn shrugged. "That was pretty intense, I guess."

"You *guess*?" Mac snorted a laugh at his cousin's understated reply. "That would be one way to describe it." He was impressed with his younger cousin's cool under fire. His days in a patrol uniform were going to be over.

"*Fuck!*" Erickson exclaimed loudly, smiling broadly. "You won't fucking believe it!" the DEA senior agent yelled with Dick in tow, approaching Mac and Shawn as they loitered around the dead body of Felix. They were coming from the pole barn. "There is a huge, and I mean *huge* room underneath the barn. There must be fifteen workers down there. You can't believe the mass of drugs. I've never seen that much shit in all my life. It's going to be some kind of record and we haven't even gotten to the money in the trucks yet."

"This is the mysterious Felix, I take it," Dick inquired, standing over the dead man with his hands on his hips.

"It is," Mac answered, holstering his Sig.

"I see he met the appropriate demise."

"He did."

"Nice shot there right between the eyes."

Mac glanced to his partner and whispered under his breath, "I might have taken a moment to measure that one up."

"I should hope so," Dick answered. "Your buddy Tommy would have approved. I guarantee Rock and Riles do."

Mac's phone was buzzing in his pocket. He reached inside and pulled it out. "Weed, whatdaya got? Hold on. Say that again? Seriously? And this is where? Okay, stay on it. We're coming."

"What?" Dick asked.

"The night's not done yet," Mac replied, waving for them all to follow. "We gotta hustle."

33

"I ALWAYS LIKE A GOOD GAME OF CHICKEN."

"Felix! *Felix!*" White hollered frantically into the phone. All White could hear was gunfire and then a groan. "Felix! Are you there, Felix? Felix, *answer!*"

Felix didn't answer. He could hear scrambling and then what he thought was Tito's voice yelling "*Boss! Boss!*" and then the phone went dead.

White went to the windows around his house, expecting the police to roll up on him any second, but all was quiet on the street. He reached for his phone. Helena answered on the fourth ring in a sleepy voice, "Hello?"

"Get up now, Helena!" White ordered. "The police took the farm. Felix is down and I don't know who else. If the police are on to the farm, they're going to be on you and me very, very soon."

"What do we do?"

White thought for a moment, running his hand through his thinning hair, triaging the situation. "Okay. I'm going to come and get you. In the meantime, get your plane ready to fly out earlier than we'd scheduled."

"That takes time."

"It takes more every minute you wait. Call now!"

"Where to?"

"Same flight plan to Kansas City. Lee's Summit, the little municipal airport. Then call Javier. Have him get us a plane down to Morelia."

"There's extradition from Mexico!"

"I know!" White barked in reply. "One problem at a time. Extradition takes time if we're actually arrested down there. Right now, we just need to get out of the country. After that we can figure it out. Get packed. I'm coming now!"

White had already packed his clothes so he grabbed one of his suitcases and his computer bag. He opened the safe and grabbed another duffel bag and filled it with cash. The pilots might need to be instructed and motivated to do some things they didn't want to do. He checked out the windows one more time and to his continuing surprise didn't see anyone outside. From the house he made the trek south as rapidly as he dared, going just above the posted speed limit through downtown St. Paul and then south on Interstate 35E to the Highway 110 Exit. Within twenty minutes of his call to Helena he was turning left and pulling up the long driveway to her massive home on the west side of Sunfish Lake. Helena emerged from the house and hurriedly moved to the car.

"Is the plane going to be ready?"

"The pilots are up. They're making their way to the airport. They asked why we were all of a sudden moving up the flight."

"What did you tell them?"

"My aunt was dying and I was trying to get down there before she passed. It was all I could come up with."

"That'll work for now. Did you call Javier?"

"Yes. He said it would take too long to get his jet up

there. He's making other arrangements for us," Helena replied anxiously. "You're sure they have Felix?"

White nodded. "I don't dare call him and he hasn't called me and I don't have that phone now anyway, I threw it out the window as I was driving on 35E. Now, about the plane?"

"They're filing the flight plan for Kansas City right now. Once we get down there Javier is trying to arrange to have another plane waiting for us."

"We need to leave."

~

Weed semi-reclined back in the driver's seat, raising his cup of lukewarm coffee to his lips. Martinez sat to his right, slumped down in the passenger seat of the van, a baseball cap pulled down low, his rhythmic breathing and occasional snoring suggesting that the narcotics detective was carefully surveilling the inside of his eyelids. From their position up on the hill, they could look down to the massive home and yard below that rested on the west shore of Sunfish Lake. Other than a dim light in what he thought was the kitchen, the house of Laura Peterson was dark.

"What time is it?" Martinez asked, stirring himself awake with a snoring snort.

"2:45 a.m.," Weed replied with a chuckle, shifting in his seat. "I kind of need to piss."

"Apparently, so does this Helena Peterson," Martinez replied. "We have lights on upstairs."

"And now down too," Weed added.

"Rich woman, big money, running a company, maybe a drug cartel as well. She probably has lots of stress. Stress complicates sleeping."

"That's quite the clinical diagnosis, Doctor."

The two of them watched as the house came to life with more lights and with their binoculars they could tell that Peterson was flitting around the house. Ten minutes into the activity they caught a glimpse of her in the living room pacing around, and it looked like she was talking on her phone, gesturing repeatedly and frantically. She hung up, disappeared from their view for a few minutes and then she came into the living room and then into what was possibly the kitchen.

"Now she has a suitcase," Weed reported.

"We have a car coming up the driveway," Martinez added. "It's a Cadillac sedan, a CTS I think, black or dark in color at least."

Both detectives were now out of the van, standing in front of it, as close to the edge of the bluff as they dared, focusing in on Peterson's house.

"Older white guy, thinning hair," Martinez noted, adjusting his glasses. "I think that is this Mr. White guy Lich and McRyan are looking for."

"I better make the call."

"Make it while we're driving. They're getting into the car."

~

"Where are they now?" Mac asked.

"They're on 494 in Bloomington, driving west."

"To where?"

"I don't know," Dick replied. "I have no idea. Weed and Martinez are just following."

"Hang on," Shawn reported calmly as he turned hard left onto Highway 55 in Buffalo, now ten miles south of the farm. He had a flashing light and the state highway patrol was aware they were coming hard east.

"Where could they be off to?" Mac asked. "It's the middle of the night."

"Can they just pull them over?" Shawn suggested.

"Nah, they're in a surveillance van. No flashers." Mac answered. "But you're right, let's not take any more chances." Mac looked back to Paddy. "Let's call on the State Patrol or a LEO along 494 and pull them over."

"I'm on it."

~

"Copy that," Weed replied. "Have them call my number. I'll guide them in."

"They're taking the exit for Eden Prairie Center," Martinez noted. "And they're going left. Better get on them."

"Got it," Weed answered, accelerating down the ramp, seeing the light turn yellow. "Shit."

The light went red.

"What do you think?"

"I think you better run it," Martinez exclaimed.

Weed ran it hard, a good three seconds after it changed turning hard left, the backend fishing tailing slightly.

"They're right ahead," Martinez exclaimed, pointing ahead as flashing lights suddenly appeared behind them.

"Are you kidding me? Are you fucking kidding me?" Weed screamed as he pulled over. He immediately jumped out of the van, holding his badge up high as he walked toward the patrol unit.

"Hold it right there!" the patrol officer yelled, up out of his car, right hand on the butt of his gun.

"I'm a St. Paul cop," Weed yelled. "We're tailing a

suspect." He looked back toward the van and could no longer see the taillights. "My partner is in the van. You need to let us keep going."

"Hold on," the Eden Prairie cop replied, holding his position but listening to his shoulder radio and looking past Weed at the van and then his shoulders slumped. "Sorry, you ran the red..."

"Worry about that later, just follow. We're looking for a dark Cadillac CTS." Weed answered and then yelled back to Martinez, "Where did they go?"

~

"What!" Dick exclaimed into the cell phone. He was in total disbelief.

"What happened?" Mac asked.

"Weed and Martinez lost Peterson in Eden Prairie, in the area around the mall. They got pulled over for running a red light. They lost eyes on Peterson and they think White."

Mac just shook his head.

They'd reached the entrance ramp for south Interstate 494. With his lights flashing and siren blaring, Shawn merged onto the interstate and took the center lane and put the gas pedal to the floor and had the department issue Suburban over one hundred.

"They're looking everywhere around Eden Prairie Center," Dick reported. "They had eyes on the Cadillac, but then they were pulled over. Dispatch made the call to stop. The Eden Prairie patrol officer got the call on the Cadillac thirty seconds later, but by then..."

"They'd lost sight," Mac replied, noticing they were passing the Crosstown exit. Highway 5 into Eden Prairie was another mile down the road.

"Weed says they now have three Eden Prairie patrol units searching the streets with two more on the way. Troopers are coming," Dick reported. "The area will be flooded with police soon."

"How long had they lost sight of the Cadillac before they started searching?" Mac asked.

"Weed said he thought less than two minutes. But that's a massive mall, shopping, dining and entertainment area with winding streets in every direction."

"So why go that way anyway?" Shawn asked. "Aren't they making a run for it?"

"The mall certainly isn't open that early in the morning," Paddy answered. "Are they meeting someone?"

"That could be," Dick posited. "And then getting into a different vehicle?"

"Does that really compute?" Shawn asked as he slowed taking the Highway 5 exit west. The exit for Eden Prairie Center was a half-mile ahead. "I mean if they're skipping town, why go *that* way? There is no good route out of town that way unless you're going to take Highway 169 south but that goes to Mankato and that just doesn't make sense. Unless there's something that way I'm not thinking of."

"Dick, put them on speaker," Mac suddenly requested.

Dick did as Mac asked.

"Weed, it's Mac. Were Peterson or White carrying anything when they left the house?"

There was silence on the other end of the phone for a moment, then Martinez spoke, "Yeah, Peterson brought a big shoulder bag out."

"Like a duffel bag or suitcase or was it just a purse?"

"No, I remember it. She had a lady's shoulder bag on one arm and she...wheeled a bag out, a suitcase. They tossed them both in the trunk."

Shawn pulled up to the top of the exit, blew through the red light and turned left on Prairie Center Drive.

Mac looked over to Paddy. "In all that research on Peterson, do you recall anything about a plane at all? Like a corporate jet or anything? I mean, her company is big enough, right?"

Paddy thought for a moment and then nodded. "I recall a picture of her standing next to a corporate jet. The articles talked about her flying down to Mexico."

"Shawn, take that right up there. That's Flying Cloud Drive."

Dick got it immediately. "You think?"

"Yeah, get everybody heading to Flying Cloud Airport."

With Helena's pass card they got through the security gate and out onto the driveway along the perimeter of the airfield. The two of them could see Hangar Three, the door open and the lights on inside. The jet was at the door, the door open and the steps were down.

White pulled up to the hangar and popped the trunk. He grabbed his bag and hers. They were hurrying. "Helena, slow down a bit," he counseled. "We don't want to raise too much suspicion. Your aunt is dying. Just look sad and tell them we need to leave immediately."

The two of them eased their gait and turned the corner into the hangar. As they approached the plane, the pilot stuck his head out the door. "I'm sorry to hear about your aunt."

"Thank you. When can we take off?" Helena asked.

"As soon as we're secured."

"Straight or right, Mac?" Shawn asked as he approached the airfield. A long line of flashing lights was coming up a mile behind them, everyone heading to Flying Cloud Airport. "Uh...take a right," Mac exclaimed and Shawn turned right onto Pioneer Trail, drove a quarter mile and turned hard left into a parking lot for the small commuter airfield.

"Run the gate," Mac ordered.

Shawn blew through the drop arm for the gate and turned left toward a series of hangars. As they drove along the road in front of the hangars, they were all either closed or dark.

"Mac, over on the east side," Paddy pointed. "There are lights on in that hangar, see?"

"There's a plane taxiing," Dick yelled, pointing across the airfield. "It's taxiing west."

"Shawn!" Mac exclaimed.

"Hang on."

Helena was buckled into her seat. White sat opposite of her on the right side as the plane turned left out of the hangar and then made a familiar right turn to make the long run to the other end of the runway for takeoff.

He relaxed just slightly in his seat and let out a sigh of relief. Then out of the corner of his eye he caught the flashing light, watching it as it blew through the gate and then cruised rapidly along the road in front of the hangars on the north side of the field.

White looked to his left. "Helena, we have company."

She unbuckled her seat and rushed to his window and

she too saw the flashing lights and then more coming up Flying Cloud Drive.

"We need to get off the ground fast," Helena yelled up to the pilot. "I'll make it well worth your time. Step on it."

White took a gun out of his duffel bag and moved forward to the cockpit. He pointed the gun at the pilot. "Get this bird off the ground. *NOW!*"

~

"The plane is taxiing to the end of the runway," Dick exclaimed into his radio that had now been looped in with the State Patrol and Eden Prairie police.

"If she gets turned around," Paddy yelled, "it can go. She's getting ready to turn."

"We gotta catch it," Dick yelled.

"I don't think we can," Paddy wailed.

"Or we could..." Mac was about to suggest.

"I gotcha, cuz," Shawn replied, thinking the same thing as Mac. He turned hard to his right, driving through the grass infield.

"*Good call!*" Mac roared as Shawn plowed through the infield and up onto the main runway, then turning left.

~

The plane turned to the right for the runway and the pilot revved up the engines for takeoff and the plane started accelerating forward.

"Is this guy crazy?" the pilot exclaimed.

~

"Oh shit, here he comes," Paddy bellowed.

Shawn put the accelerator down, closing the gap. "I always liked a good game of chicken."

"And I think he just blinked!" Mac yelled.

"Go! Go! Go!" White yelled as the pilot eased off the engine.

"I can't do it!" the pilot growled in reply. "I don't care what you pay me or what you do to me. No chance!"

The plane came to a stop halfway down the runway. Shawn braked hard twenty yards short of the nose of the plane. As Mac got out of the passenger seat he looked back to see the cavalry coming, Weed and Martinez in the police van and too many squad cars to count.

The whir of the engines ceased as Paddy, Shawn and Dick all had weapons focused on the cockpit. Mac moved to his right as the door opened and the steps were let down. "Hands up!" Mac yelled at the pilot, who did as he was ordered and made his way down the steps and onto the tarmac. His co-pilot did the same. Four Eden Prairie officers were quickly out of their vehicles and took the two pilots into custody.

"The man, White, has a gun," the pilot reported as he was being cuffed.

Mac looked back to Dick, Paddy and Shawn. They were all still in their Kevlar vests. Shawn was the first one up the steps. He quickly peeked around the corner into the plane's cabin. "Hand's up! Both of you, now! Up where I can see them! I won't ask again. *Now!*" Shawn stepped up into the cabin, his gun still up, directed forward. Paddy followed him up and then into the cabin.

Dick went in next, followed by Mac, who found White and Laura Peterson now sitting in their seats. Shawn was cuffing White while Paddy did the same to Peterson, with Dick standing guard.

Mac holstered his gun and took three steps forward and took the seat that faced Laura Peterson while Dick sat down across from White. Paddy and Shawn were behind them now, standing in the aisle.

"Well, if it isn't the mysterious Avocado," Mac needled Laura Peterson.

"I have no idea what you're talking about."

Mac laughed as he rubbed his face and sat back in the seat. "Laura, I can't tell you how disappointed I am to find *you* here. Why? Why'd you do it?"

"Do what?"

"Really? I mean...really?" Mac sighed tiredly. "You're done, Laura. You're just...*done*. You will be going to prison and for a long damn time. I have three of your trucks, your avocado trucks, filled with drugs. First, they stopped at your processing plant in Monticello and then out to a farmhouse several miles southwest of town. We have coke, heroin, meth, marijuana. I mean, it's probably some kind of record bust I'm sure. I have the drivers. I have the processing facility outside of Monticello. I have millions and millions of dollars. Your buddy Felix, he's dead. Not to mention his two bodyguards and a few others out at that farm. So I have all that and I know that you both are responsible for the deaths of at least Luther Ellis, Sam Shead, Terrence Orr, Rafael Cruz, Tommy Ortega, Frank Franklin and I'm sure the list goes on."

"Helena, don't say a word. They have nothing," White muttered.

Dick flew out of his seat and punched White in the mouth, knocking the lawyer's head back into the seat. As White's head recoiled off his seat, Dick whaled on him again.

Mac moved over and grabbed White by his shirt collar. "My new best friend, Neil Kline, is going to nail your ass, you worthless piece of shit."

~

With an ice pack wrapped around his left shoulder, Mac slumped in the square, uncomfortable corner chair, fitfully dozing, the rhythmic hum of the medical monitors lightly chirping in the background.

"Did you get 'em?"

Mac's eyes slowly rose open to see Rock's tired gaze focused on him. He pushed himself up and stepped to the side of the bed, rubbing his eyes. "It's good to see you awake, my friend."

"It's good to be awake," Rock replied with a raspy voice. "How's Riles?"

"Getting better. Lich, the chief, a bunch of others are down in his room," Mac answered. "Can I get you anything? You want some water?"

Rock nodded, held his head up slightly. Mac held the Styrofoam cup and directed the straw for him. Rock laid his head back. "Now, I asked a question. Did you get them?"

"Yeah, we did, buddy."

"No," Rock asked a little more forcefully, his eyes narrowed and focused. "Did *you* get him? The one who killed Ortega and Double Frank? The one responsible for Riles and me?"

Mac nodded. "Oh yeah, he's gone, I smoked him myself. They're all gone. On their way to hell as we speak."

"Good." Rock nodded in satisfaction. "Good, man. So tell me how it all went down."

Mac gave a little smile. "Well, let me tell ya, last night was one hell of a night."

34

"I KNOW WHAT IT IS TO LOSE A DAD."

Monday morning.

Mac left the hospital and Rock and Riles to return to the chaos that was Chief Flanagan's office and the St. Paul Department of Public Safety. There was much work to be done. The local media had learned of Laura Peterson's arrest and were now swarming the building for the noon press conference that would include Chief Flanagan, his counterpart Chief Jurgenson in Minneapolis, as well as the mayors of the two cities, the governor, and Erickson from the DEA.

Neil Kline was put into protective custody by the DEA. His entrance into the Witness Protection Program would come as soon as the prosecutions were completed. The U.S. Attorney's Office and Ramsey, Hennepin and Wright County Attorney's offices would be coordinating the overall prosecution with the U.S. Attorney taking the lead due to the involvement of the Lazaro Cardenas drug cartel. While the local operation for Lazaro Cardenas had been decimated, undoubtedly there were other elements operating in the

United States and the FBI, DEA and Homeland Security were all interested in learning more. Javier Alvarado was now the focus of interest for the federal agencies. With President Thomson in the White House and the cartel having blown up his hometown, the White House would be looking to help and apply pressure on the Mexican government in any way possible.

White was not talking, at least yet. The FBI determined his name was actually Bernard Bruce, originally from Bloomington, Indiana. He'd been a lawyer in Indianapolis for a number of years before he drifted away and went to work for the cartel. How exactly that had happened, they did not yet know. Bernard Bruce was not talking and was simply speaking with his lawyer.

The same was the case with Helena Peterson. She too had brought in her lawyers and was refusing to talk, again for now. The FBI, Homeland Security and the U.S. Attorney's Office were swarming her company now and were just getting started on pulling back the layers of Spectrum Universal and its operations and finances.

The U.S. Attorney, Malcolm Garrity, was an attorney on the political rise and eager to make a name for himself. He also was a St. Paulite and something of a McRyan family friend, having graduated high school with Mac's sister Kate. Malcolm was relishing the case that had suddenly fallen into his lap. "Don't worry, Mac. From what I've seen this morning and what you've just told me, these two are toast. And as much as I would love to do it, I doubt we'll ever get anywhere near a trial. But look, we've got another problem."

"What's that?"

"Mike Willows, the driver for this Kline. I'm not sure we can get Witness Protection for him. At the same time, putting him back on the streets—"

Mac held up his hands and smiled. "I think I got that covered."

"You...have...that covered," Garrity replied, confused. "How?"

"Just let me worry about that. I just need you to protect him for another couple of days until I can get in touch with someone and make some arrangements."

The chief wanted Mac for the press conference.

"No. No, no, no," Mac replied emphatically. "Keep my name out of it."

"I'm not sure that's possible, Mac," Chief Flanagan answered. "People are going to want the story on this. Your involvement cannot be hidden."

"Sure, it can. This case was the result of the inspired work of Richard Lich, Paddy McRyan, Shawn McRyan, Bonnie Schmidt, Tommy Armstrong, Weidenbacher, Martinez, Pat Riley, Bobby Rockford, Tommy Ortega, Frank Franklin, Agent Erickson, the folks up in Monticello and Wright and Sherburne Counties, the Minnesota Bureau of Criminal Apprehension, as well as assistance from other agencies and professionals."

"And you're what? Other agencies and professionals?" the chief asked wryly.

"Exactly," Mac answered. "I was never here."

~

A new break in the case arrived later Wednesday when Felix's apartment was discovered, shortly followed by White's house. At White's house was a treasure trove of records regarding the front operations for the cartel. Ultimately twelve different businesses were raided, along with several local drug crews in St. Paul and Minneapolis.

"This will make a definite dent in street activity," Dick mused. "A lot of guys are going to get yanked off the street for a stretch here."

Mac was nonplussed. "Maybe, but there always seems to be more people willing to jump into that line of work. Nature abhors a vacuum."

"That all may be true," Garrity answered. "But all of this plus Kline buries White, or Bruce or whatever we're calling him now. And it nails the coffin shut on Peterson."

Felix's apartment contained little in the way of business records but it did contain one item of interest. "Look at this," Mac said, holding up a set of boat keys he'd found in a drawer.

They found the boat in a slip down in a harbor off the Mississippi River southeast of St. Paul in Hastings. The boat was an Eastern 35 Cabin Cruiser. In a storage compartment underneath Mac and Dick found two items of great interest: weights and three canvas body bags.

"These guys sure were sadistically prepared," Dick remarked. "This explains Sam, Mac. Same fabric as they found on his body," Dick said as he rubbed the canvas fabric with his gloved fingers. "Throw weights like those in the bag and let the body drop to the bottom."

"Yeah, it's as if they did this...more than once," Mac replied after a moment's thought and made his way back up top. He put the boat's key in the ignition not to start the boat, but to fire up the electronics and, specifically, the boat's GPS chart plotter. "So how do we get into GPS history?" he muttered to himself as he worked the touchscreen.

"What are you looking for?" Lich asked.

Mac worked through the screen and in a minute found what he was looking for. The map appeared on the screen with numerous red lines taking the boat north from the marina up the Mississippi River to a familiar location. "Well, would you look at that!"

"Look at what?" Dick wasn't following Mac's train of thought yet.

Mac turned to Dick. "JuJu, Kline, Jockey Mike, and a few others said bodies would just what? Disappear, right?"

"Yeah, so?"

"They have to go somewhere. They dumped Sam in the river, right?" Mac asked and then pointed at the plot lines on the screen of the GPS plotting chart. "I don't think that was their maiden voyage in that regard. It sure looks like they took a lot of trips to Baldwin Lake and the areas around Grey Cloud Island and I don't see a lot of fishing gear on this boat."

Dick got it now and slowly shook his head. "It's a graveyard out there, isn't it?"

"Could be."

"I better call Washington County. We're going to need some divers."

By the following Sunday morning eight bodies had been recovered, all weighed down in body bags. One of the bodies had been identified as Luther Ellis. The search was ongoing.

~

With Sally overseas, he'd done what he could to keep busy and occupy his mind; visiting family, other friends and taking care of final details on the investigation. Yet in the quiet hours at home Mac could feel the sadness of it all overtaking him. A person of faith but not always a reliable attender of church, he'd made a trek over to see Father John at the Cathedral of St. Paul. Father John had baptized him, given him his first communion and helped him through his father's death. The two of them sat in the pews of the grand cathedral and just spent some time talking.

The funeral for Ortega was on Friday. Officers from all over the state of Minnesota, as well as a small contingent from Denver, arrived for the service and provided a miles-long motorcade to the cemetery.

Sally made it back for the funeral. He was thankful she was there to lean on, especially as he looked two pews ahead to Jenny Ortega, Tommy's widow, holding the hand of her son Robby, nine years old and now without his father. Mac couldn't help but think back to when his own father was killed. At the time Mac was a senior in high school, so quite a few years older than Robby, but he knew what the boy was feeling, contemplating his future years without his father and wondering how he would make it.

After the funeral, as was tradition, all police officers current and retired made their way to McRyan's Pub. At the pub Mac sat with Sally and watched Jenny and Robby accept the condolences of everyone. Jenny had a good job, a management position with her company, so she and her son would be stable. There would also be death benefits from the police pension so financially they would be okay but, with Robby and another baby on the way, it would be a long haul for them. In that moment, Mac decided he needed and wanted to do something that would help with the Ortegas' road ahead. He told Sally what he had in mind.

"Go ask her if it's okay," Sally said, squeezing his hand. "I couldn't support it more."

"Come with me," Mac asked and the two of them got up from their table.

"Jenny, can I talk to you in private for a minute?" Mac asked. "Sally will sit with Robby."

"Hi Robby, I'm Sally." The boy smiled. Sally was a pretty lady and no young boy would mind the attention.

Mac pulled Jenny into the back hallway, away from the crowd. "Jenny, Tommy was...is one of my best friends. It was so good to reconnect with him here. I just wish..." His voice trailed off.

"He was excited about that too, Mac. You know life gets so busy, we move and we lose touch with our friends. But even when we were out in Denver he spoke of you often, especially when he spoke of home, of growing up. And we were both proud of you, all that you'd accomplished. You two didn't see each other for a long time, but the bond between you two was obvious and strong."

"And that's why I want to do something for you and Robby and that baby you're carrying. I hope you'll let me do this."

"What?"

"I want to pay for college. For both."

"Mac..." Jenny's lip started to tremble.

"Wherever they want to go, wherever they get accepted, college or university, public or private, trade school, culinary school. Whatever either of them wants to do, when that day comes I'll take care of it, everything. I'm going to set up funds for them and..."

"Mac, you don't have to—"

Mac sighed. "Jenny, I know what it is to lose a dad." Mac looked back to Sally and Robby, who were talking. "I was older than him when it happened to me, but I know the challenges you and Robby are going to face." He looked back to Jenny, her eyes filled with tears. "Let's make college not be one of them. I can do this. I want to do this. I need to do this. Let me take that off your plate."

"Thank you, Mac. Thank you."

"So I can go?" the U.S. Marshall standing post outside the dingy motel door asked Mac hopefully, early on Saturday morning.

"Yeah, he's my responsibility now."

Mac knocked and went inside the small motel room. "Come on, Mike, grab your stuff and let's go."

"Hey, wait. You're that cop that Neil was dealing with, right?"

Mac nodded. "That's right."

"Where are we going?"

"To the bus station. You're on your way to Louisville."

"What's in Louisville?"

"Do you still want to work with horses? I seem to recall you really wanted that kind of work. I can't think of a place with more horses than Kentucky."

Jockey Mike gave Mac a long look. Mac could literally see the wheels turning in the little man's head. He might have been physically and emotionally beaten down, but dumb Jockey Mike wasn't. He'd pieced it all together. "It wasn't some rival drug crew that kidnapped me that night. That was you?"

Mac shrugged. "I have no idea what you're talking about."

"Right," Jockey Mike replied as he took one look around the dingy motel room and said, "So how long does it take to get to Louisville?"

"Twelve or thirteen hours, give or take."

"And who am I going to work for?"

Mac chuckled mischievously. "Oh, I think you'll recognize him."

On Saturday night Nikki Fireball hosted a private party and benefit to honor Sam Shead, Tommy Ortega, Double Frank and Rafael Cruz at Fireball. Dick had declared it was to be treated as an Irish Wake. "We're drinking and telling stories. It's the way all of those guys would have wanted it."

Nikki was the ultimate host, providing endless food and drinks. BTG, Heavy G, DeNasty, Roux, Leslie and the whole crew were in attendance, manning their posts. BTG and Heavy G worked the doors and made sure only invitees got in. DeNasty was in rare form, giving every cop in the joint endless amounts of good-natured grief.

The President and Judge Dixon had given Sally the rest of the week off. Her presence allowed Mac to completely cut loose and he didn't hold back, regaling anyone who'd listen of his high school football and baseball exploits with Tommy Ortega. Mac must have said, "We were state football champs!" a hundred times. "McRyan to Ortega, touchdown!"

"I haven't seen him be this big a puddle in a long, *long* time," Dick said, throwing his arm around Sally. "Your hubby's an absolute wonderful emotional mess."

"He sure is," Sally replied, laughing. "And I think he needed it."

"He did, but I think after tonight he's going to crash," Dick counseled quietly. "And all that's gone down here is going to hit him and hit him hard. I know you're busy politicking and all but you need to keep an eye on him."

"I will."

A little after midnight, Jockey Mike stepped down off the bus steps and out onto the sidewalk. He looked to his left and saw a man in blue jeans, denim jacket and a straw cowboy hat holding a sign that said *Willows*.

"You must be him," the blue-jeaned man said. "Come on." The driver led Jockey Mike to a well-worn Chevy Silverado. "You can throw your bag in the back."

The drive took forty-five minutes out into the gentle countryside east of Louisville. Eventually, the headlights illuminated a long white horse fence along the left side of the road and then the driver hit the left turn signal, slowed and turned in under a wrought iron arch that read *Swinton Boone Farms*.

The truck made its way up the long drive and then turned to the left toward a long barn or what Jockey Mike quickly recognized as a paddock and a little smile crept across his face. Then he saw who was waiting for him by another pick-up truck and he suddenly froze.

"Ha!" the driver guffawed. "He said you'd react that way when you saw him."

"W...we...well," Jockey Mike stuttered.

"You have nothing to fear here," the driver replied with a big grin and a big pat on the shoulder. "You're going to love it here. I do."

The man who'd interrogated and scared the living daylights out of him in that dingy cinder block basement room was standing all casual-like in tan cowboy boots, blue jeans, a white long-sleeved collared shirt and a baseball cap. He approached the truck with a big smile while the driver powered down the window. "Jockey Mike. I'm Tony Swinton. Swinton Boone Farms is my place and as I recall, you like horses."

It took a little over a week but with the discovery of the treasure trove of documents at White's office, the FBI forensic accountants working their way through the books of Spectrum Universal, along with the bodies being recovered in Baldwin Lake, White and Peterson caved.

Both tried to pin a lot on Felix, but Malcolm Garrity wasn't buying it and told them both so in a conference room with mountains of documents around him.

"What do you want?" Laura Peterson finally asked.

"What I want from the two of you is everything there is about your operation, about Spectrum Universal, and most importantly, everything there is about Javier Alvarado," Garrity answered. "He was the boss. Him, I want. If you want the best deal you can possibly get, you give me everything you have on him, including where to find him."

Mac stayed in the cities through the following week. With White and Peterson talking the case was slowly winding down. The night before he was leaving for D.C. there was a knock on the front door of his house. He opened the door to find Chief Flanagan. Mac invited him in and the two of them repaired to the basement and Mac's bar for a drink.

"White and Peterson have cut their deals. They've given the DEA and FBI a ton of information. Alvarado is on the run and the Mexican Federales are giving chase. Latest word was that Javier escaped up into the hills and mountains of Michoacán state and is constantly on the move. Erickson from the DEA told me they missed him by maybe a half hour the other night in the town of Arteaga."

"Good to know," Mac answered. "But Chief, Erickson called and told me that too." He took a drink of his bourbon. "Why are you *really* here?"

Flanagan sighed. "I lost a lot of good men, Mac. Ortega, Cruz, Franklin. I lost Fisher, who was a rat, but he was a detective. Riles and Rock are all banged up but good. I'm not sure when or if they can come back and if they can, in what capacity. My roster is what you would call depleted. I'm wondering..."

"No, Chief," Mac replied, beating him to the question. "I can't come back. I just can't. Not right now."

"I didn't think you could," Flanagan replied, nodding, "But I had to ask. I mean, if you and Sally ever do come back, do you think you would come back to work for us?"

Mac nodded. "Sally has said she wants four years in D.C. working at the White House. So, I have two more to go. If, after that we decide to come back here to St. Paul, I'd consider returning under the right circumstances."

"Any idea what those circumstances would be?"

Mac shrugged. "Why don't we cross that bridge if and when we come to it? A lot can happen in two years."

"In the meantime, we're short-handed."

Mac shook his head in disagreement. "You're not as shorthanded as you think. You still have Lich and despite his somewhat checkered history, he's a damn good mentor for young detectives. From what I can see, in his own idiosyncratic way, he's bringing Paddy along nicely. And I know Shawn McRyan has expressed interest in getting out of uniform. He was steady under fire, he didn't rattle even a little bit. You need to get a cool head like that into plainclothes."

Flanagan nodded but then asked drolly, "Any people who aren't named McRyan impress you?"

"Weed and Martinez did a nice job. I bet they could transition out of the Narcotics Unit and clean up and get into Homicide and do the job. Bonnie Schmidt and Armstrong are solid competent cops who can close a case. Carson, once his leg and mind get right, will be fine with some seasoning. And as for Rock and Riles, those two boys will be back in time."

"I don't know, Mac..."

"Chief, they don't know how to do anything else. All they know how to be is cops. It's who they are and who they always will be. It's their identity. I mean, Shamus already went down and told them the Pub is totally staffed, no openings, so they'll just have to go on being cops. They'll be back. In the meantime, make some promotions, move some personnel around and you'll be fine."

"Okay," Flanagan replied and then changed gears. "Jenny Ortega told me about what you're doing for her, for Robby and the baby-to-be."

"I really wish she wouldn't have said anything," Mac answered. "I don't want any recognition or anything for that."

"I'm glad she did. The secret is safe with me, but I'm glad *I* know about it and I'm grateful for you doing it."

"It seemed right," Mac replied. He was leaned over, hands on the bar, looking down to the floor.

"How are you doing, son?" the chief asked.

"I never thought I'd say this, Chief," Mac answered, looking up, his eyes watering, "But I can't wait to get to D.C. Even if Sally's not there, I need to not be here for a while."

EPILOGUE

The owner of Ray's Auto Care in Portland, Maine took his customer inside his shop and to his man working the service counter. "George, this guy needs a new set of tires, this kind." The owner handed him a slip. "Can you go place the order for them?"

"I'm on it," George Easton, formerly Neil Kline, responded. "If I order today we should have them by noon tomorrow. We can get them mounted and probably have everything ready by the end of the day. Will that work?"

"I was hoping to get this all done before Christmas, so that should work," the customer answered to Ray and George. "We're supposed to have some big snow coming Christmas Eve, Ray. It'll be a white Christmas for sure."

Neil went into the back office and to the computer to place the tire order. A small flat-screen television sat on a stand in the corner and was tuned to CNN with a *Breaking News* chyron.

"*Mexican government officials are confirming that the head of the Lazaro Cardenas Cartel, Javier Alvarado, is among six who are dead from a shootout between members of the cartel and Mexican authorities.*

Alvarado was killed when the Mexican Federales cornered him and a group of his men in the town of Petacalco, just south of the town that is the namesake of the cartel, Lazaro Cardenas. As you can see from the footage, the shootout took place in the harbor on a pier. It appears that Alvarado was attempting to escape Mexico by boat.

Alvarado has been the focus of intense search in Mexico. The Mexican government has been under significant pressure from United States authorities, including the White House, to find Alvarado. Both countries sought Alvarado related to a string of drug-related killings that included the murders of six police officers in Minnesota back in August of this year."

Javier Alvarado was dead. White and Laura Helena Peterson were both in prison and were unlikely to ever get out.

Neil sat back in his chair behind his desk and breathed a slight sigh of relief. While at times he wondered if he truly deserved it, he had a new start, a new name, a decent-paying job, a clean apartment, all in a quiet city far away from the world of drugs where he could try to lead a decent life.

For him, it would indeed be a merry Christmas.

ABOUT THE AUTHOR

Roger Stelljes is the New York Times and USA Today best-selling author of the McRyan Mystery Series and the FBI Agent Tori Hunter Mystery Series. His books have been downloaded and enjoyed by millions worldwide. He has been the recipient of numerous awards including: The Midwest Book Awards – Genre Fiction, a Merit Award Winner for Commercial Fiction (MIPA), as well as a Minnesota Book Awards Nominee.

Never miss a new release again, join the new release list at www.RogerStelljes.com

ALSO BY ROGER STELLJES

MCRYAN MYSTERY SERIES

First Case - Murder Alley

The St. Paul Conspiracy

Deadly Stillwater

Electing To Murder

Fatally Bound

Blood Silence

Next Girl On The List

Fireball

The Tangled Web We Weave

Short Stories

Stakeout - A Case From The Dick Files

Boxsets

First Deadly Conspiracy - Books 1-3

Mysteries Thrillers and Killers - Books 4-6

FBI AGENT TORI HUNTER

Silenced Girls

To receive new release alerts join the list at

www.RogerStelljes.com